GHOUL AS A CUCUMBER

GRIMDALE GRAVEYARD MYSTERIES, BOOK 3

STEFFANIE HOLMES

Copyright © 2023 by Steffanie Holmes

All rights reserved.

No part of this book may be reproduced in any form or by any electronic or mechanical means, including information storage and retrieval systems, without written permission from the author, except for the use of brief quotations in a book review.

Cover Design: Rebecca Frank

ISBN: 978-1-991099-26-6

 Created with Vellum

GHOUL AS A CUCUMBER

You discover that the three hot AF ghosts who haunt your manor house are madly in love with you. What do you do?

a. Run away screaming.
b. Call a priest for an immediate exorcism.
c. Get a little kooky and spooky with all three of them…together…

I'm Bree Mortimer, and I chose option c.

That's right – me and my three ghosts are a thing now. I'm officially a #ghostslut and I'm okay with it.

And now that I've discovered I possess resurrection magic, I might just be able to bring them back to life again.

That is if the dark priests of the Order of the Noble Death would stop raising serial killers from the dead to come after me. And if I can keep my parents and my ex-bully from discovering the truth about my ghostly powers.

Oh, and I should probably figure out why it's impossible to admit that I have feelings for them. I want to jump their bones every second of the day, but when I try to say those three little words, I get seriously spooked.

How can you fall in love with someone when they're already dead?

Bree and her ghostly men are back for another spooky adventure in *Ghoul As a Cucumber*, book 3 of this darkly humorous cosy fantasy series by bestselling author Steffanie Holmes. If you love a sarcastic heroine, hot, possessive and slightly unhinged ghostly men, a mystery to solve, and a little kooky, spooky lovin' to set your coffin a rockin', then quit ghouling around and start reading!

JOIN THE NEWSLETTER FOR UPDATES

Want a free bonus scene from Bree's school dance and Bree's playlist? Grab a free copy of *Cabinet of Curiosities* – a Steffanie Holmes compendium of short stories and bonus scenes – when you sign up for updates with the Steffanie Holmes newsletter.

http://www.steffanieholmes.com/newsletter

Every week in my newsletter I talk about the true-life hauntings, strange happenings, crumbling ruins, and creepy facts that inspire my stories. You'll also get newsletter-exclusive bonus scenes and updates. I love to talk to my readers, so come join us for some spooky fun :)

Go and catch a falling star,
Get with child a mandrake root,
Tell me where all past years are,
Or who cleft the devil's foot,
Teach me to hear mermaids singing,
Or to keep off envy's stinging,
And find
What wind
Serves to advance an honest mind.

—John Dunne

PROLOGUE
22 YEARS AGO

Here I am again.

She stares up at the battle-weary facade of Grimwood Manor. The windows are grimy and in need of a good scrub. There is a small ecosystem growing in the gutter. The face of a savage Roman warrior glares at her through the turret window.

She switches her pink suitcase to the other hand and rings the bell.

The magic tugs at her chest, the silver threads spinning through the air around her as Grimwood's ghosts make themselves known. She remembers when she first came into her power, how she could see only a few of them, only the most tormented spirits. They used to frighten her. But over the years, as more have appeared to her, she has learned to block them out, the way we disregard cars zooming past on the motorway outside our window when we're trying to sleep.

But here, at Grimwood, they are harder to ignore...

The door is flung open by a handsome man in his late twenties, his face at once both new and achingly familiar. His light brown hair is dotted with dabs of multi-coloured paint, and he wears paint-splattered overalls. She winces as the brush in his hands drips red paint onto the porch.

"Welcome." He smiles at her – a friendly smile, tinged with gratefulness and a little bit of panic. She'd panic too, if she were him. His home is old, and huge, and crumbling away at the edges. He needs her. "Come on in. Welcome to the Grimwood Manor B&B. I'll take your bag for you."

"Not a problem. I can manage." She grips the handle tightly, and he doesn't fight her on it. He steps aside so she can sweep past him into the large entrance hall. Inside, their money problems are less obvious.

The walls are adorned with gilded portraits, and two wing-back chairs sit in front of an ornate stone fireplace, which is blazing despite the warm spring day. Tourist pamphlets are neatly arranged on an end table next to a vase of flowers. Everything has been polished for her visit.

But she doesn't have to see the cracks to know they are there.

"I'm Mike." He takes a deep bow, which is rather endearing given that the top of his head is splattered with purple and gold paint. "I apologise for my appearance – I'm in the middle of painting a mural and it's rather run away from me. My wife Sylvie was supposed to answer the door but she's got cake batter all over her hands. We're so happy you're here. You're our very first guest. Oh, and this little munchkin is my Bree-bug."

He scoops a toddler off the floor from where she was playing with a set of colored blocks. She has a little splatter of gold paint behind her ear.

The lights flicker.

"Mike, darling!" A woman's voice calls from deep in the house. It's forcibly chipper, the edges tinged with panic. "Could you come here a second? The oven has done that *thing* again."

"Coming, my love." Mike flashes her a knowing grin. "Sorry about the lights – the old wiring in the house wreaks havoc with the appliances. But don't worry, we've had it checked out and it's perfectly safe. They can't find a single fault. The lights just flicker sometimes and the oven tries to eat itself. If you'll excuse me, I must put on my Superman cape and save the day once more. If you could keep an eye on Bree for a moment, I'll be back in two shakes of a lamb's tail to show you to your room."

He dashes off. Bree stares after her father with a serious expression on her face, before returning to diligently building her tower.

The pink woman sets down her suitcase and kneels beside the child. Movement on the staircase diverts her attention for a moment, but it's only the ghost of the Roman centurion. He unsheaths his sword, waving the tip menacingly at her. She nods at him.

"I'm not here to hurt her," she says to the ghost. "I'm here to see if she is one of us."

The centurion steps back, nodding sagely.

The woman kneels down beside the child and picks up a block. "You're very good at this," she says. "Perhaps your destiny is to become an architect."

Bree's head swirls around to look at the centurion. His face softens as she peers at him with her wide honey-brown eyes. He grins at her.

Her face crumples and she knocks over her tower with a chubby fist.

The woman smiles. "Or perhaps, a demolition expert."

She kneels on the playmat, tucks her legs underneath her, and hands the yellow block to the child, who turns it over in her hands before picking up a blue block and fitting them together.

"That's a lovely colour combination," says the woman. "Listen, we don't have much time before your father gets back. I just need to check something."

She reaches out and grabs the silver cord spiralling from the child's stomach. Bree's face twists, and she drops the blocks and waves her tiny fists in the air. Behind her, the centurion takes a menacing step forward.

The silver cord hums between her fingers, and she tugs gently until it stretches enough for her to glimpse the shimmering light that runs through it.

"Ah yes. It was as I thought. It does often skip a generation or two."

The woman drops the cord and folds her fingers back in her lap. Bree bangs two blocks together and cracks up laughing. The Roman warrior returns to his post on the steps and frowns at her.

"You've been given a remarkable gift, Bree Mortimer," the woman whispers, stroking the child's tufts of light brown hair. "But there are some who will have you believe it is a curse. When the time is right, I will come for you. I will teach you what you need to know – that is my promise. But others will come, as well, with fear and malice in their hearts. You must choose your own path."

Bree doesn't respond, which does not surprise the woman. She is not such a fool as to expect a child to understand the monumental power that hums in her veins. She is here only to observe, to ensure that Bree will be safe at Grimwood until it is time.

"Is everything okay?"

The woman whirls around to see Mike Mortimer leaning in the doorway, his face and upper torso now covered in black soot. But Mike can't see her.

He peers down at his daughter on the playmat, and at the woman's abandoned pink travel case still sitting by the fire.

"Bree-bug, did you see where the Pink Woman went?"

I

EDWARD

Brianna's scream rends my soul.

And not in a metaphorical, poetic way.

In a painfully corporeal, "my heart is being torn from my chest and eaten by carrion birds," way.

Brianna is behind me, with Ambrose, and every metaphorical bone in my ghostly body longs to turn to her, to drag her far away from this horror and comfort her with the myriad of sensual skills I have yet to share with her.

But if Brianna is behind me, she is safe, for now.

Unlike Pax.

His body jerks as the Ripper drives the knife through his chest. Pax tries to grip the blade with his big, stupid hands like the fool he is, but they slide away, slick with blood. The Roman's head lolls to the side, his eyes finding mine.

I'll never admit it to him, but the artist in me has always been drawn to Pax's eyes. They're an icy, expressive blue, usually sparkling with some kind of Roman mischief. But now they swim with pain.

Pax in pain? The idea that such a brutish creative can *feel* undoes me completely. If the Ripper can fell the mighty Pax

Drusus Maximus, then what hope do the rest of us have to stand against him?

"Friend..." Pax rasps, his words rattling. He stretches out a hand to me. "Go. Protect Bree...you must..."

His words are drowned as blood spurts from his lips.

No. This cannot be.

Pax's eyes roll to the heavens, and a serene expression appears on his features. Bile rises in my throat, a somewhat novel sensation since I don't have a throat or a stomach to produce bile. But I'm close enough to Brianna that she can give me these old, Living sensations.

And the sensation I feel now, as I watch my friend dying, is *shame.*

Pax is giving his life now, with happiness, because he believes it will save us. He came to this cemetery to die by his own hand. He thought his sacrifice was the way to protect Brianna.

His is true nobility, not like my tainted bloodline of cowards and selfish pricks.

Pax thinks this because I told him so. I made him believe that he is the cause of all our misery, that he is worth more to us dead than alive.

How could I do this to him?

To Bree?

Is this what he looked like the day he died on the battle-field? The mighty oak felled?

No.

No.

All the bullshit I've been wallowing in ever since Pax became a former ghost seems so utterly pointless when my friend is bleeding out in front of me. Pax, who might drive me to thrust my head into the liquor cabinet with his incessant...*Paxness*, but who is more loyal a friend than anyone I knew when I was alive.

And when that monster is done with the Roman, he'll turn on Brianna. I might be able to hide her for a while, but he will find my weaknesses. Everyone always does. He will get past me and Ambrose and he will rip into Brianna's body with that horrid knife of his and I can do nothing to stop him because I am a godforsaken *ghost*—

An idea comes to me then. A desperate, doomed-to-fail idea, but I am nothing if not attracted to the forlorn and hopeless.

"You won't hurt him!" I yell as I hurl myself at the monster.

"Edward, no!" Bree cries, her voice breaking with pain. I don't know why she's so upset. Unlike Pax, the monster can't do anything to me.

I'm already dead. And after all the wretched things I've done, I should stay this way.

The Ripper turns toward me as I come for him. His eyes are twin red windows into hell itself. He throws back his head and laughs and laughs, and the pure evil of that laugh makes my knees buckle as I grab his cloak with both hands.

It's only because of Brianna's powers that I manage to keep hold of him. My face is inches from his. This close, I can *smell* the putrid, rotting scent of his breath. My skin burns from the heat of the red steam that leaks from his eyes. His thin, inhuman lips twist into a grin and everything about him is so *utterly* wrong that I briefly forget what I was about to do.

"You think that you can hurt me, spectre?" he roars, his body trembling with a full belly chortle. "I am no longer on your side of the Veil, and I have no master to control me. I am flesh and blood once more."

"Good," I growl.

I surge forward.

I fall *into* his skin.

Inside him.

"Edward, what are you doing?"

Brianna's cry reaches my ears, but it's muffled by the screams that assail me as I slip inside the Ripper. After all those times I have accidentally slipped a little too deep inside Brianna (although never in the way I most wish to), and dwelt within her memories, I had hoped this ghostly possession might work.

But I never expected it to feel so...horrid.

I gasp at the rudeness, the wrongness, of it. I am within the creature, my ghostly body slipping through his veins and organs, occupying every atom that is already filled with his being. I am squeezed on all sides, hemmed in with the pain of being part of something physical and Living that does not belong to me.

And the memories...

I see and feel and smell all those brutal crimes the Ripper committed over a century ago, and all those he has committed for Father Bryne since...as if I am the one who wielded the blade. The Ripper's victims scream as one as he tears – as I tear – into their flesh. Polly Nichols, Annie Chapman, the beguiling Mary Kelly, and Vera...

The pain is *exquisite*. Compared to this, walking through a wall or falling into the sofa feels like an annoying itch. Squeezing myself inside the Ripper reminds me of lying, broken and bloody and bitterly cold, in the garden for three days while my friends partied inside.

It reminds me of my father abandoning me, my friends betraying me.

But pain has always been my muse. I can sculpt agony to my will, make it beautiful as well as harrowing. And so, I slip deeper into the Ripper's skin, allowing the memories of his horrific deeds to wash over me, to make me strong.

"What..." the Ripper gasps as I reach to the very edges of his psyche. "What is this? What are you doing? *Get out of me!*"

"Edward, where did you go?" Brianna cries to me. "I can't see you. Edward!"

My fingers are inside the monster's now. I feel myself gripping Pax as the last of his life drains from his body. I feel my fingers closing around the hilt of my beloved knife. I feel pain like Guy Fawkes has lit a hundred fuses inside me.

You must endure, Edward.

I have dwelt on for hundreds of years after my pathetic demise with only a Roman oaf and a Victorian golden retriever for company. I know a thing or two about *enduring*.

I push through the pain and focus on the hand holding the knife. I peel one finger from the blade. The monster's will wars with my own. I blink, and through the haze of the Ripper's memories, I see *her*.

My Brianna.

My strength.

"Edward?" Brianna asks. She steps out from behind the grave, those huge champagne eyes of hers wide with concern and hope and terror and...and *love*. After we hurt her tonight, I didn't think I'd ever be so blessed to feel her love, but it's there, written on her features, even if she cannot speak it.

And it is enough for me. She has always been enough for me.

I tear two more of the Ripper's fingers from the hilt of his blade.

Ambrose clings to Brianna, his perfect jaw square as he watches without seeing. He can put together what is happening from the sounds and smells and his own keen intelligence. He places his body in front of Brianna, as if he can somehow fend off the monster if I don't succeed.

Ah, Ambrose, always the Panglossian one.

"Take the knife, Ambrose. I can't hold him for long." My body trembles as the monster fights for control. His thoughts and memories race through my mind, and I gasp as I'm once more sent reeling from the present moment into some grim and ghastly memory.

A darkened street, the cobbles wet with rain. A woman in a ratty dress, her lips purple from the cold as she swallows the sweet wine I've given her. My hunger for her, for her blood, her screams, tugs in my belly.

And then, another memory. This time, I'm standing near the back of a crowd that has gathered around a body. I relish their gleeful dissection of my every stab and slash. Large black boxes snap bright lights, while people gossip about the poor unfortunate woman while they crowd around to get a closer look at her injuries. A man in a faded greatcoat tries in vain to push the crowd back, his face haunted. I think he may be a police detective, similar to Hayes and Wilson who have investigated the murders in Grimdale, judging by the way those around him defer to him and call him, 'Guv.' I am intrigued by him. I want to watch him suffer as he tries in vain to catch me—

"Edward, hold him a little longer."

Brianna's voice tears me back to the present. She has flung herself into the monster's path and is trying to tear the knife from his hand. The Ripper tries to push me out of his body so he can deal with her, but I feel her fingers grip his arm, *my* arm. She gives me strength.

I peel back the final finger and—

CLANG.

The knife drops on the concrete path.

Brianna and the monster both lunge for it, but I'm able to hold him back and she gets to it first. She grips the handle, flips the blade, and plunges it into the monster's chest.

Ow.

Owowowowow.

OWIE.

That smarts something awful.

I topple out of the Ripper just as he grabs Bree, his hands snaking toward her neck. My ghostly heart leaps into my throat, but she ducks under him and drives the knife deeper, twisting the handle until the Ripper's mouth falls open into a horrible scream.

"You don't know what you're doing," he howls, his words piercing the stillness of the night, loud enough to wake the dead. "I am not flesh and blood. I am..."

But he sounds confused. Unsure.

"Your master may be gone," Brianna places both her hands on the blade's handle and drives it home, "but you're still bound by the spell that brought you back from the dead. If you are flesh and blood, then you can die like the rest of us."

The monster's eyes widen, red smoke billowing from the sockets. He tosses his head back and, with a final, inhuman wail, he disintegrates.

Where he had been only moments ago with his deadly blade, there is only ash.

Bree drops the knife and falls to Pax's side.

Pax.

I pull my broken, pain-soaked body together and float over to them. Brianna has his hand in hers, stroking his sausage fingers and sobbing. I press my hand to Pax's heart. He doesn't move or react as my fingers slip into his skin.

Pax's body doesn't make mine tingle the way Living things do when I touch them.

For he is no longer Living.

2

BREE

"Pax." I fall to my knees. Father Bryne's cross falls from my pocket and clatters on the ground beside the Ripper's discarded blade. I think I see red mist curling from it, but I'm not paying attention. Not when Pax is...when he...

"Can you hear me, Pax?" I cup my warrior's face, trying to lift him, wishing, hoping...

...but the moment my fingers touch his skin, I know that he's gone.

No.

No.

Please, no.

It can't be. I can't imagine being without Pax. He had everything he ever wanted. He had life again. I could touch him and hold him and kiss him. He was real. He's always been real to me.

How can he be gone?

Tears stream down my cheeks. They drop onto his tunic, mingling with the blood still seeping from his wound.

It's not right. Pax's blood should be inside him, not staining Grimdale's graveyard dirt.

So much blood...

"Brianna."

Edward looks up at me from where he has his hand pressed against Pax's heart. His eyes swim with shame and regret. What Edward just did is perhaps the bravest and stupidest thing he's ever done, and there's so much I want to say to him but not now, not when Pax is...

I can see Edward's dark eyes turning bleak with desolation. And I know then with a certainty that drives the air from my lungs that this isn't just Edward's morose poet side coming out to play. He is on the other side of death, and he can feel Pax's heart, can *feel* that it has stopped beating...

Please, please. I don't know who I'm begging. If one of Pax's ancient gods is even listening right now, maybe they'll hear my prayer. *I'd give anything to have him back again.*

I look down at my warrior, my beautiful brave Pax. And I see Edward's cord burning bright, winding from his chest all around us and back through the cemetery. But Pax's cord is unspooling, the blue light fading to nothing as it winds out of his body at high speed, whipping through the air and snapping free of its owner.

I don't know how I know what to do. I can't explain it. Perhaps it's because I finally have a name for what I am – a Lazarus – but I feel a surge of power as I reach down and grab the cord just as the very end unspools from Pax's body. With my other hand, I pull apart his lips and stuff the end of the cord inside.

It doesn't work. The cord wants to slip back out, like a piece of spaghetti sliding off a fork. I sob as I try to shut Pax's lips, but his chin is all slack and weird-feeling and I can't do it I can't I can't and he's gone...

Desperate, not knowing what else to do, I lean down and place my lips on his.

Pax's lips are warm, but they're still, lifeless – nothing like kissing my warrior should feel. The cord hums between us. It jerks against my lips, trying to break us apart, but I'm not ready to let go.

Tears fall thick and fast, but I don't break the kiss. *Pax, I'm so sorry. You had everything you wanted...except the one thing I couldn't give you, those three words that I'm too afraid to say because of exactly this...because if I love you and you leave me I will fall apart completely. But if you'd just come back to me, I will say them now, because they're true. I love you, and I have loved you for longer than you know, and I'm a big, foolish scaredy-cat but I am* your *scaredy-cat...*

Pax's lips open.

And before I can hope, and pray, and think, he is kissing me. My Pax is kissing me, his lips raw with a desire that tears me open and spills my unspoken words against his tongue. His lips burn bright and warm and *alive* as he devours me, pushing my lips wider so his tongue can wrap around mine.

We dance with the silver cord that slides down his throat. All that matters to me now is that cord moving between our lips as it winds itself back inside Pax, and the fact that I will never *not* be able to resist this man, not when he is alive and mine and kissing me with the fervour of his battle lust.

"Pax?" I try to speak, but the words are crushed away by the force of his kiss.

My eyes fly open, and they meet two sparkling blue orbs, pale as the sky on a perfect New Zealand summer's day. A hand grasps the back of my neck, thick fingers tangling in my hair, pulling me closer.

Pax. You're alive. *Alive!*

He kisses like he doesn't want to breathe air unless I'm breathing it, too. He clings to me as if I'm the only thing tethering him to the world. And maybe I am. The cord slithers between us, making my teeth sing as it hurtles down his throat, winding tight inside him once more, where it should be.

Somehow, I manage to extract myself from Pax's kiss. I sit back on my knees and stare at him, at his beautiful, Living eyes. Pax grips the side of my face, his thumb grazing my cheek, and the look he gives me is pure adoration.

"That's two debts you now owe her for your life, Roman." Edward, of course, must break the moment.

I'm too giddy with joy to care. Besides, we all owe Edward our own debt right now.

And Pax. And Ambrose. Every one of my ghosts has saved my skin tonight.

"Pax is okay?" Ambrose asks. He leans over Edward, his hand passing through Edward's shoulder. Edward, oddly, doesn't seem to mind.

"I am not okay! I am lying down when I should be stabbing. We have a monster to vanquish." Pax gropes around for his sword, but Ambrose uses the tip of his cane to hit it out of reach.

"Aren't you hurt?" Blood still leaks slowly from the wound in his chest. The edges of it glow with the faintest traces of red mist, but that fades away before my eyes.

"It's merely a flesh wound." Pax grunts as he sits up. "Where's the monster? He has a hot date with the pointy end of my sword…"

Pax's words dissolve into a wince as he clutches his stomach. I try to push him back down, but have you ever tried to make a Roman warrior do something he doesn't want to do? Instead, I slip my arm around Pax as he staggers to his feet. He leans heavily on me – so heavily in fact, that I topple over and bang my elbow on the marble step of Edward's mausoleum. Tears of pain spring in my eyes, but I'll take any kind of pain if it means Pax is still alive.

Pax braces himself on one of Edward's garish cherubs and hoists himself to his impressive height. His face is beet red with the effort. "Fetch my sword," he demands. "I am naked without my sword."

"You wandered around the house in that flimsy tunic of yours for hundreds of years," Edward drawls. "We've seen it all. You're not naked, and you won't be slaying any monsters in your condition."

My prince leans against another cherub, frowning as the glass shard in his backside rubs against the angel's lute. He looks even paler than usual. He did just crawl *inside* Jack the Ripper.

I can't even imagine what that does to a ghost, let alone sensitive, poetic Edward.

I tuck the Ripper's knife and Bryne's cross into my pocket. I don't know if the Ripper is gone forever or not, but those two objects are clearly magical and might come in handy.

Pax is upright now, and his wound seems to have mostly closed over. I blink, trying to reassure myself that he is still here, and real, and alive. Then I move to Edward.

My prince jerks his head away as I reach for him, his lips drawing thin. I press my hand against his cheek, feeling the hum of his ghostly presence against my palm. Edward relents, his long lashes tangling together as his eyelids flutter.

"Did he hurt you?" I ask, dreading the answer.

"You should not ask me this. I'm not the one with the hole punched through my chest."

"Not all scars are on the outside, Edward. What you must've seen in that monster's memories..." Fresh tears sting my eyes as Edward shudders beneath my touch. "Are you okay?"

"Please, Brianna," he whispers, drawing his lips across my hand. "I am fine. Save your pity for someone who deserves it."

"You deserve so much more than my pity. You saved Pax," I whisper. "You saved all of us."

"I did, didn't I?" A faint smile tugs on the corner of his lips, but it is tinged with sadness. His eyes flutter open, and those dark orbs study me with that burning intensity of his that always makes me feel naked and *seen*.

Edward has always *seen* me. He's always been able to sweep aside the lies I tell myself and find the truth, even when I don't want to face it. After all, we're both runners. We both ran away and hid instead of facing our problems.

But how often have I done the same to him? It's too easy to forget that beneath all that pomp and arrogance is a heart that sees beauty in all the darkest places. Edward's in a dark place now, and he has been for a long time.

I don't know how to pull him out. But I have to try.

I cup both hands on his cheeks. His ghostly skin tingles beneath my touch. His collar falls open, revealing the tiny, round bruise on his neck that's been there ever since he died, and he has no idea how he got it. His silver cord spirals between us, filling the air with his burnt sugar and opium scent. I meet his gaze and dare him to see me, to see that I won't lie to him the way I sometimes lie to myself. "I swear to you, that as soon as we are certain that we sent Jack the Ripper back to...wherever in hell he came from, we will find a way to bring you back to life. That's my promise to you."

"Don't make promises you cannot keep."

"I mean it. I have a name for what I am. I have the magic that brought Pax back *twice*. All we have to do is find your unfinished business and—"

"I am beyond even your magic, Brianna." Edward's eyes flicker with despair. "Do you not think I have already turned my considerable intellect to figuring out what infernal task tethers me to this purgatory? I was a spoiled prince who had everything

I ever wanted in my life, and I squandered it all. I wanted for nothing. I have no unfinished business. That is my punishment, and it is a torture that I deserve."

Tears leak down my cheeks. "Is that how you feel? Is being my friend a torture to you?"

"You are the only thing that has ever had meaning to me." Edward's lips brush the top of my head, making my brain shimmer. "I wish you could see what I see when I look at you."

I laugh hollowly, thinking of everything that's happened tonight. I've hurt every person in the world I care about – so much so that Pax thought he'd be better off dead than in my life – there's a dead priest on my floor, and I just had to stab Jack the Ripper. "And what's that? A hurricane wearing the face of a girl and destroying everything in her path?"

"No, Brianna. You are a rare and lovely flower – you make the world more beautiful just by existing. Centuries ago, I wrote poetry about love, even though I had never truly been in love. I felt as though when I looked at artwork, heard stirring music, or read something beautiful, I could reach out and touch the edges of it. Anything that could cure this wretched longing in my heart must be the most remarkable magic.

"So I wrote about the only thing, I – the most spoiled prince in all the lands – have never been able to possess; a love that endures. I didn't realize then that I had written my poetry about you. Sometimes it feels as though I dreamed you into existence, but that is far too exquisite a gift from the gods for the likes for me."

I try to speak, but my voice catches. How can he say these things? About me? After everything he's endured, after the way I've hurt him over and over? How can he feel this way?

Edward's eyes blaze, and I find myself drowning in the depth of his feelings for me, flailing about for something to hold me above the surface. He blinks, and he places his hands over mine. His ghostly fingers dig into me, and his touch that is not quite touch pulls my hands from his face.

"Brianna." He sounds serious and so, so, sad. "There's something I must tell you. But when I tell you, you will hate me and—"

"You literally crawled inside a monster's skin to save us tonight. Nothing you say to me can make you hate me."

Edward's face crumples. "Usually, I enjoy gambling away my fortune on impossible bets, but alas, that is a wager you will lose."

"I think we should get back to the house," Ambrose says behind us. "We have to figure out what to do about Father Bryne, and Pax is struggling, and—"

"Pax is fine!" Pax growls. I look over and see that he has found his sword and is waving it aggressively at a spindly bush. "Get back, foul demon!"

Ambrose runs over and tries to get Pax to stop waving the sword around.

Edward's eyes flick to Ambrose, and then back to me. He strokes his finger down my cheek. "Never mind. I am being silly. What I have to tell you is nothing of importance. It can wait."

THE FOUR OF us stagger back to the house. With every step, Pax's body grows stronger. He's no longer disoriented and lunging at shrubberies. By the time we reach the front door, he seems more like himself. Almost as if I didn't just watch him die.

But I did. And I won't forget it. I don't think I'll ever stop feeling this sheer, terrifying panic at the idea of him never being in my life again.

And Edward…I glance over at my prince, who trails behind us, his features haunted. My stomach churns with unease. What did he wish to tell me before? He says it's not important, but I'm not an idiot – I can tell it might be the most important thing Edward has ever done. But he needs to tell me on his own time, when he's comfortable. I don't want to push him even deeper into this depression that's come over him.

Besides, Ambrose is right – we do have a little priest problem that needs sorting.

Pax skips through the open front door and comes to a stop over Father Bryne's prone body. He bends over and shakes his ass in the priest's slack face. The loud tear of a fart rips through the silent manor.

"Take that, for by Bacchus' hairy testicles, I am alive!" Pax cries at the priest. "Your puny Ripper couldn't hurt Pax Drusus Maximus or his friends or his beautiful not-girlfriend!"

Edward makes a face. "What was *in* those cocktails? You smell like you were pulled into hell alongside the Ripper."

Ah, how quickly Edward pulls that arrogant mask over himself to hide what's going on inside.

They start bickering, but I tune them out. There's a dead priest on the rug. Unlike his monster, he hasn't disappeared.

He's real. A real dead body. A real murder victim *on my rug*.

Ambrose moves beside me, his hand finding mine, his ghostly fingers comforting. "I am sorry about this," he says sadly. "I would turn myself in to the authorities if I could…"

"It's okay. You saved us all, too." All three of my ghosts have been incredibly brave tonight, and after I said such horrible things to them…

My stomach churns with shame.

"And I will never apologise for that," Ambrose says with a savage finality that makes my knees weak. I turn to him then, studying the tense set of his perfect features, the way his brow is furrowed in concentration. "I know it was a happenstance that placed that gun in my hand and sent the bullet flying true, but I need you to know that I would lay down my life to protect yours, Bree. We all would."

Tears prick in my eyes. "I know you would. And I'm sorry for—"

"Hush, there's nothing to apologise for." Ambrose runs the tip of his finger along the inside of my wrist. "How will we rid ourselves of the troublesome priest?"

"Just because I helped save Pax's life doesn't mean you can all start quoting that playwright willy-nilly," Edward huffs. "I still have *some* standards."

I rub my eyes. I'm so fucking tired. It must be after three in the morning now. And I still have to figure out what to do with Father Bryne. I can't leave him here – I'm pretty sure B&B guests leave bad reviews if they discover a murdered priest in the entranceway.

I could call the police and say...what? Pax and I were the only ones home, the only Living humans who could have shot that gun. Father Bryne had been staying with us for weeks, letting people in the community get to know him as a kindly man of God. Wilson won't believe I mistook him for an intruder. And Pax doesn't exactly have records like a birth certificate or a passport. That's going to make him more suspicious than his penchant for stabbing.

If they discover Father Bryne's body, one or both of us is going down for his murder. And I'm so exhausted that it almost sounds like a relief.

Ambrose must be thinking the same thing. "Perhaps you could bring the priest back to life, as you did to Pax? It's not ideal, I admit, but you cannot be accused of murder if no murder took place."

The idea of pressing my lips to the priest makes bile rise in my throat, but Ambrose has a point.

However, when I bend over to inspect Father Bryne's body, I realize that's no longer an option. I can't see any trace of a silver cord. I pull out the priest's cross from my pocket, but it's no longer leaking the red mist. Once again, I have no idea how I know this, but I sense that Father Bryne can no longer be brought back the way I brought Pax back. And I can't see his ghost nearby, so he has no unfinished business.

Good. I surprise myself with the ferocity of the thought. Father Bryne was a murderer. He brought Jack the Ripper back to life...or a semblance of life...to kill Lazarii like me and Vera. He sent his monster after *Pax*. The world is better off without him.

But the ring of red spreading across the rug is a problem.

Edward floats over, his eyes dropping to the body before returning to meet my gaze. His mask of princely arrogance is firmly back in place, leaving no trace of the vulnerability back in the graveyard. "As much as I'd like to take you to your boudoir right now and ravish you with all of my ghostly tricks, what are we going to do about the good father?"

"I don't know..." I say honestly. "He can't stay here, but gosh darn it, with all my travelling I never had the time to take a class in body disposal. I don't suppose you have any ideas?"

Edward shakes his head sadly. "My father always had the palace guard deal with the mess after he got a little enthusiastic with the beheading blade. I don't suppose you're suddenly flush with cash so you can hire that shirtless Spartan fellow to kick him into a demonic abyss?"

It took a second for my sleep-deprived brain to catch on to what he was talking about. "That's Leonidas from the movie *300*. He doesn't exist. Well, he did exist, thousands of years ago, but he doesn't now, and I haven't seen his ghost around. Besides, we don't need a burly, Spartan king when we have Pax."

"Yes, I am here to serve Bree." Pax takes a deep bow, then starts rolling up Father Bryne in the rug. "I know what we should do with him. He was a Roman, like me! So we give him a Roman funeral. It's the only right and proper thing to do to honour the gods and wipe away Ambrose's guilt for being the one who killed him."

"He's a Roman *Catholic*, Pax. It's not quite the same thing."

"I don't know this Catholic – is it a province we conquered?" Pax's face lit up. "I love conquering new provinces. It means we get more takeaway options back in Rome."

"If Pax is going to get rid of old monster-britches' corpse for us, I say we humour him," Edward says.

I'm barely listening. My gaze is distracted by something I see out the front window. A figure is walking up the driveway toward the front door. A very *familiar* figure wearing an incredible purple-edged toga.

No.

Not now.

Of course now. Because that's how my life works. It all goes to shit at once.

Pax hoists Father Bryne's rolled-up body onto his shoulders. "Yes! We shall give him a proper send-off."

"And just what exactly does that involve?" Ambrose asks tentatively.

The figure steps around the zodiac mosaic, and the moonlight captures her features and the determined look on her face. Raw panic courses through me, especially since Pax is now blocking the doorway with Father Bryne's body rolled up in the carpet. *His rosary is sticking out the end.*

But if she's here, maybe...

Maybe I can dare to hope...

Maybe it's time I truly let her in, let her see all of me.

"First, we must have a loud funeral procession through the

streets of the village," Pax declares. "We bang drums so that everyone comes out. Then we take him to the graveyard and light an enormous fire and throw his corpse upon it, and collect the remains and place them inside an urn. Then we will host a mighty feast in his honour, with the finest wine and prostitutes we can afford. I will go next door and ask Maggie if she can bring along enough scones for the whole village—"

"As much as I personally would like a Roman funeral when I die, especially one with scones, I don't think a procession and a feast will help us keep this a secret." I wave at the figure as she steps onto the porch. "But maybe Dani will help us."

"Bree? What are you doing awake?" Dani steps onto the porch. This close, I see her eyes are ringed in red. She looks as tired and wrung out as I feel.

"I…" I run my fingers through my tangled hair, aware of how awful things were between us when I left her, and that despite that, she's *here*. "I've had quite an eventful night, and I'll tell you all about it if you want. But why are you here? I thought you'd never speak to me again."

"Alice and I have been cleaning up the mess at the party and dealing with the museum security and she said to me…" Dani rubs her eyes. "It doesn't matter. I'm glad you're awake. I was going to sit in the cemetery a while, get my head together, but when I saw the lights on I got worried that something might have happened."

A wave of gratefulness washes over me that Dani wasn't a half hour earlier and ended up meeting the Ripper in the cemetery.

"You came to talk to me?" My voice cracks with hope.

"I guess so, yeah. I came to apologise. I was angry and I said some things I didn't mean and I—" Dani stops short, her eyes darting between my bloodstained yoga clothes and the rolled-up rug on Pax's shoulders. "Bree? What's going on?"

3

BREE

"Let me get this straight," Dani glares at the rug Pax insists on holding over his shoulder after I gave her a two-minute run-down of what happened after I got home from the party. "You're a reincarnation of a dead saint and you want me to help you get *rid of the body* of a priest that your blind ghost boyfriend shot?"

"*Accidentally* shot," Ambrose says quickly.

"That's pretty much it, yes." I squeeze my eyes shut. "I don't *think* I'm a reincarnation of Lazarus. I think I'm...like a descendant? I have a gene or something that gives me his powers. And there are others out there like me, and this Order of the Noble Death is trying to eradicate us unless we join their ranks and Father Bryne resurrected Jack the Ripper to kill us all and I—"

"Yes, yes, I got all that." Dani holds up her hand. She's still staring at the carpet, and I haven't even got to what happened in the cemetery. "I'm stuck on the whole *murdered priest* bit."

Panic rises inside me at the word *murder*.

This is bad, so bad.

Dani could run to the police right now. She *should* go to the police. It's exactly what a sane, normal person would do if their

35

best friend told them that her ghost boyfriend accidentally shot a priest in her house.

I turn away from Dani and look out over the cemetery. The moonlight casts the tops of the highest monuments in long, elegant shadows that might appear creepy to some people. To me, they're as familiar as old friends.

"Remember that night we snuck that bottle of your mum's scrumpy?" I whisper, afraid to speak the memory aloud in case Dani thinks I'm trying to manipulate her. Maybe I am, I don't even know anymore. "It was a still, clear night, just like this one, and we sat on the steps of Edward's mausoleum and drank all the cider and ate those horrendous pie-and-mushy-pea flavoured crisps and pinkie swore that we'd have each other's backs no matter what and help to bury the bodies?"

"Of course." Dani comes to stand beside me. Her eyes flick over Grimdale graveyard, and a thin smile plays over her lips. "I remember you singing Sisters of Mercy lyrics at the top of your lungs, horribly off-key, and then you were trying to climb back through the fence and you threw up scrumpy all over your boots, remember?"

"I remember. I totally ruined my brand-new pair of boots." I wince. "Dani, I know I'm not your favourite person at the moment, but if that promise meant to you what it did to me, I need your help to get rid of this body."

"You live next to a graveyard. Can't you do your own gravedigging?"

"I meant *metaphorically*. I was hoping you had some chemicals that would, like, dissolve him."

Dani's face makes it clear what she thinks of my idea. "My job is to preserve the remains of my clients, not to speed things up. And you can forget about what you see in movies and read about in those mafia romance books of yours. Getting rid of a corpse is much harder than you think. Even if we had a vat of lye, which we don't, we'd have to heat it to three hundred degrees to get the job done, and it'll take several hours, and the smell would wake half the village. And you can't pretend he drowned in the duck pond, either—"

"Dani, please?" I clasp my hands together in a pleading motion. "Pax died tonight and I found out what I am and I know this is bad, but I'm afraid."

Dani leans against the doorframe, as if she needs the house to hold her upright. "Pax doesn't look dead."

"I...well, I brought him back." As quickly as I can, I explain to her the final part of the story, how the Ripper had stabbed Pax but I'd managed to push his silver cord back inside him, and now his wound has healed.

"I would love to help you, Bree. I *would*. I'd never turn you over to the police for killing that scumbag priest, not after he brought the Ripper to life and tried to hurt you. But if you can't pull this off, I'm not going down with you. I won't lose the job I love or Alice over this. So that means I can't help you, okay?"

"Okay." My shoulders slump. That's fair.

"What I *will* tell you," Dani says, that cautious smile once more playing at the corner of her mouth. "Is that old Ralph Sommersby was just interred at Grimdale. The grave is still freshly dug and he ordered an extra-large coffin so he could be buried with all his golfing trophies. If I wanted to get rid of a troublesome priest—"

"Argh! Not *him* again!" Edward wails.

"—I'd sneak in there late at night, say..." Dani glances at her phone screen. "...around 3:42 AM, and I'd have my Roman warrior dig up the grave, remove said golfing trophies, and toss the priest in on top."

"Really?"

Dani shrugs. "The last place anyone would think to look for

a body is in someone else's grave. As to what one might do with the trophies, you're on your own."

"Thank you, Dani."

"Yeah, yeah." Dani frowns at Pax's parcel. "And get rid of his stuff from his room, too. If anyone in the village asks, say that he got called away on urgent business for god. You won't be entirely lying. Now, get out of here before he stinks out the place."

"I resent that. My flatulence has a rich and varied bouquet." Pax hoists the carpet back onto his shoulder and pumps his fist in the air. "Back to the cemetery!"

4

BREE

And that's how I end up in Grimdale Cemetery at four AM, digging up poor Ralph Sommersby.

Technically, Pax is the one doing the digging. Edward is composing a poem for the occasion. Ambrose is calling out encouraging statements like, "Doing a great job, old chap!" and "That's it, put your back into it!" And I am leaning against a cherub, trying not to throw up.

"In shadows deep, 'neath moon's embrace, A clandestine task, we inter a face...less man. The earthy womb accepts its due, A secret kept, known to but a few—hey stop that, you careless oaf!" Edward yells. "You threw that clot of dirt right through me."

"Serves you right for not helping."

"Even if I were able to lift a spade, these hands were not made for manual labour." Edward holds up his hand, turning his long fingers in the moonlight. "In my day, graverobbing was the work of doctors. Perhaps the village physician will lend a hand if you can't stomach it yourself?"

"We're not robbing a grave," Ambrose points out patiently.

"Technically, we are placing something *into* a grave. We're grave-accessorizing."

I palm Father Bryne's cross as I stare down at Ralph Sommersby's final resting place, which he will soon be sharing with a rather righteous evil priest. Sommersby was a grumpy old man who hated everything except golf, but even so, I don't think he'd appreciate being stuck with Father Bryne for eternity.

I don't like this. We're disturbing a man's eternal rest.

But if I don't want to spend the rest of my life rotting in jail so I can make sure that Jack the Ripper doesn't hurt anyone else, it's the only thing we can do.

Even though Father Bryne was part of my world, where the rules don't always apply, he was still a formally living, breathing human who is now a meat Popsicle, thanks to me. And if I don't get him out of Grimwood Manor and remove the bloodstains from the flagstones, then the police will come after *me*.

And I will not rot in jail for killing an evil man.

THWUNK.

Pax's spade strikes something hard.

"I've found the coffin," he declares.

"Okay, good." My heart hammers in my chest. "I've got the crowbar—"

"I don't need no crows." Pax leans down and prises open the lid with his bare hands.

I don't look. I *can't*.

I listen to the smashing of various trophies being piled up beside the grave, followed by a thud and some awkward shuffling as Pax loads Father Bryne's body into Ralph's coffin, followed by the priest's small bag of possessions. He replaces the lid, leaps out of the hole, and starts shoveling the dirt back in.

"I can help with this part," I say.

"Oh, no, you don't." Pax runs his hand over his hair and streaks dirt down his cheek, which is already crusted with dried blood. "I will always bury the bodies for you."

"I sincerely hope this is a one-time occurrence," I say as I pick up the second shovel Mr. Pitts keeps on hand. "I should at least get my hands a little dirty."

In no time at all, we have all the dirt packed back into the hole. Pax gathers up the golfing trophies and stalks off in the direction of town to toss them into the duck pond while I trample down the dirt on the grave and wash and replace the shovels in Mr. Pitts' maintenance shed.

I glance at my watch. It's 5:42AM. This whole night has been one nightmare after another, at least twelve chapters worth of horror. I can barely keep my eyes open, and yet...I look at Edward and Ambrose as they watch me (well, Edward watches me, Ambrose whistles a tune and tries to smell the wildflowers growing around the Witches' Monument) and I feel a surge of something electrifying and terrifying.

All the awful things I said to them during our fight come flooding back, and I hate myself for being so petty and so afraid. I hurt them so deeply and yet they still came to my rescue; they laid everything they have on the line for me.

"I'm beat." Ambrose lifts his head from the evening primrose to wipe imaginary sweat from his brow. "This has been a day of excitement, but I think all I want to do is listen to Bree take her bubble bath and then curl up in bed."

"No, Ambrose," Edward pipes up, his voice taking on that bleak, wretched tone that breaks my heart. "You will do no such thing. Brianna made it clear that she doesn't wish for us to be in her life anymore. We have lost her, and our efforts tonight will not change her mind. We have kept her safe, but we must respect her wishes."

"No." Ambrose's eyes widen. "It's not true. It can't be true."

"That is what Brianna asked." Edward's eyes flick to me. "Isn't it?"

"Bree, tell him that it isn't true! Tell him that we had a silly fight, and you said things you didn't mean. Tell him...tell him that despite everything, you want us in your life?"

I step toward them both, my breath catching in my throat.

What *do* I want?

On the one hand, I've had a tantalising taste of a normal life outside Grimdale – travel and food and sex and fun without any ghosts bothering me about turning the TV channel or trying to sniff my food.

But on the other hand, what's the point of being normal when it was like wearing a coat that didn't fit? What good is a life on the road without Dani's wry humour, or Pax's fierce protectiveness, or Edward's terrible poetry, or Ambrose's boyish enthusiasm? Sure, we may be up to our ears in murders and chaos and mayhem, but I'm still the happiest I've been in my whole life.

Why was I so desperate to run away from this life? From them?

Maybe...now that there's a name for what I am, I can stop being so afraid to be myself.

Maybe I'm ready to stop running.

I hold out both my hands. "Please," I say, because I know what I'm asking. They were willing to give up on me, on us, because that's what *I* wanted. They're always the ones sacrificing for me. This time, I want to be the one who sacrifices. "I want you to take me home. To *our* home."

5

BREE

Once more, I drag my body over the threshold of Grimdale. This time, I have two ghosts at my side. A rush of warmth circles me knowing that I'm safe with them, that no amount of fucking up I can do will make them give up on me. Ambrose practically skips in the direction of my bedroom, but Edward morosely drags his feet. If he had chains, he'd be rattling them right now.

I am so tired that I need an industrial forklift to hold my eyes open. My yoga clothes are crusted in blood and grave dirt. I must smell like a dream.

But I don't care. I figured out something important tonight.

I know who I am.

I'm not afraid of my power anymore, not when it can save the people I care about.

And...I know what I want.

I want *them.*

Edward, Pax, and Ambrose.

I know it's messed up and crazy. I shouldn't want three men at once, especially when two of them are ghosts. I shouldn't dream of three men out of time and all the filthy, delicious

43

things they can do to my body. I shouldn't chase this warm, aching need that clenches my heart.

But I'm tired of lying to myself.

I want them more than I want to be normal.

We pass through the foyer. There's a dark stain on the flagstones where Father Bryne died, but I can't even think about cleaning it right now. Ozzy is still hanging from the chandelier above, emitting adorable squeaky snores.

I'm a little jealous of the fuzzy wee dude. I'm in desperate need of that bubble bath I mentioned. But one look at that dark bloodstain on the tiles where Father Bryne died brings all of this horrid night back, and I know I won't sleep.

The party. The fight. Running away from the ghosts. Discovering Pax missing. Father Bryne attacking us. Pax in the cemetery. The monster. Pax dying. Edward jumping into the monster to save us. Me, twisting the Ripper's knife in his chest until I sensed his life slip away…

Pax *dying*.

The all-too-familiar fear clenches in my chest. I turn toward the front door just as Pax runs through it, very much alive, his yoga clothes dark with blood and dirt and clinging to his muscled body in all the right places.

"Bree, what's wrong?" Ambrose's fingers brush my arm. "You're trembling. You have nothing to fear. The monster is gone and we're rid of Father Bryne. Nothing can hurt you inside these walls."

"That's just it," I murmur. "I came so close to losing you all tonight. I need…I need…"

Edward's eyes darken. He turns away. "I should go."

"Don't." I leap after him and place my hand in his, my fingers falling through him a little, sending that now-familiar tingle along my arm. "Please, stay with us."

Edward's eyes burn into mine. "I don't deserve you, Brianna. Everything that occurred tonight is because of me."

"That's not true. You saved Pax. You saved me. This is all *my* fault. I was so upset after the party and I—"

"No." Edward jerks his hand away. "I will not allow you to blame yourself. If you knew the wretched things I have done, you would not wish to forgive me so easily. I am the one who told Pax you were better off without him."

I wince. I can't help it. It's an awful thing to say. Edward turns away, his shoulders sagging as he hides his face from mine. I can't hate him when he already hates himself enough for all of us.

Pax glares at Edward. "The prince is right, Bree. You should not have brought me back. I am the cause of all your pain. I must do the only thing I can do to protect you from myself. You must give me my sword so I can finish this."

"Pax, no..." Tears stream down my cheeks. I *hate* this. I hate that Pax believes he has to leave me to protect me, and that Edward is so broken that he's determined to push us all away. I grab Edward's shoulder, and this time, I'm so angry and hurt and desperate that my fingers grip him, and I spin him around so he's facing me. Shock registers on his face, but it's replaced in a moment by misery.

"I don't know what's going on with you, but it ends here. Tonight. You think that what you've done is so evil that you cannot be forgiven. But I am telling you there is nothing you can do to me, or any of us, that will make us hate you. Right?"

I turn to the others. Ambrose nods vigorously. Pax folds his arms and gives the kind of nod that indicates he'll happily prove his point with violence.

I struggle to get the next words out through my tears. "I'm not your father, Edward. I won't ever put conditions on my feelings for you. You can't push me away with your bullshit, so stop trying. I will fight for you, always, even when you no longer wish to fight for yourself. Father Bryne may have been part of a secret society of priests who want to kill me, but he did teach me one thing – forgiveness is powerful. You can decide not to hold your sins against yourself. So, is there something you need to say to Pax?"

Edward looks away, his shoulders trembling beneath my fingers.

I wait.

Pax drums his fingers on the hilt of his sword.

It's a long time before Edward clears his throat.

"Listen, Roman. I spoke to you with anger in my heart. I didn't mean the things I said. I am bereft that I hurt you, and made you want to hurt yourself—"

"Excuse me?" Pax says with a grin, his hand cupped over his ear. "I didn't quite hear you."

"I'm sorry!" Edward yells. "Must I prostrate before you before you accept my apology? Do you wish me to write it into a poem? I am happy to oblige."

Before anyone can stop him, Edward steps into the middle of the room, his feet planted wide and arms held expressively in what we've come to regard with trepidation as his oratory stance, and he recites,

"Upon this hallowed eve, I humbly bow,
Before thy valor, Roman, I doth vow,
A tale of grievous wrongs, I must confess,
And beg for mercy in my dire distress.
With quivering voice, my tale I shall unfold,
Of deeds unkind, in folly days of old,
In fevered fury, blinded by my pride,
I struck thee down, thy noble form defied..."
Pax covers his ears. "Make it stop."

Edward drops to one knee, one hand outstretched toward Pax, the other held over his heart.

"If fate permits, thy clemency bestow,

And heal the heart that throbs with guilt and woe—"

I collapse into giggles even as tears stream down my cheeks. I laugh so hard that I can't breathe. My stomach burns and I have to gasp for air. Edward looks affronted, and his haughty expression only makes me laugh more.

Pax rushes over and picks me up off the floor. "You are forgiven," he tells Edward, "provided you never again speak such a ridiculous poem. You have broken Bree."

"I'm okay." I rest my head against Pax's chest, right above where the Ripper's blade pierced his flesh. His heart thuds in my ear, strong and regular and blissfully alive. I reach up and stroke his cheek, relishing the warmth of his flesh and the rough stubble on his jaw. "I just realized how much I...I need the three of you. And that I don't want to be alone right now."

"I will take up my post once more." Pax starts to set me down. "I will make certain that no man or beast enters your room—"

"Come to bed with me," I whisper as I cling to him. "I need to feel you inside me. I need to know that you are truly alive."

Pax's face collapses in confusion. "I am not good for you. I am the one who messes up your life."

"That's not true. I mean, yes, it is true. All three of you are a complication I didn't ask for and sometimes, like at the party, it gets to be too much." I swallow. "But when I almost lost you tonight, I realized that you're a complication I don't want to live without. Ever. I can't imagine the world without you in it. *All* of you."

I beckon Edward and Ambrose over. Edward looks unsure, but he touches Ambrose's arm and guides him closer, until the three of them surround me. I touch Ambrose's smooth cheek, wishing more than anything that he could feel as warm and solid as Pax. "That's why I've been so hesitant about figuring out your unfinished business. I am terrified that I'll do something wrong and lose you forever. But I have a name for what I am now. I'm ready to try. I'm ready to stop running from my fear."

"That's wonderful, but I don't believe we will ever figure out my unfinished business," Ambrose says brightly. "I am content to simply be your ghost, if you'll have me."

Edward shifts. "Brianna, I must—"

I shake my head at him. I've already spoken to him about his own unfinished business. "I have some ideas about yours, Ambrose. I don't think things are quite as hopeless as you believe, but it can wait until tomorrow. For now..."

"Bubble bath." Pax scoops me up again and lurches toward my room. I wrap my arms around his neck and cling to him as he carries me into the bathroom. I press my ear against his chest, listening to his heart beating through his torn leather armour. I'll never get sick of feeling the reassuring *thud-thud-thud* of the organ pushing blood through his body.

He's alive. Because of me.

Because I'm a Lazarus.

Whatever that is.

But there's time enough to figure that out. When I'm not so tired. When I'm not being held by a miraculous Roman warrior while he prepares to run me a bubble bath.

Pax shifts me to one hand while he leans over and turns on the taps. He manages to pop the lid on my favourite raspberry bubble bath one-handed and pours far too much in, then tests the water to make sure it's piping hot, just the way I like it. I call out to Ambrose and Edward to join us.

"The Victorian and I have something to discuss," Edward

calls back. "We will await your pleasure when you finish your bath."

Weird, but okay. "You promise?"

"I promise, Brianna."

"Okay, because I—hey!"

Pax drops me into the tub, clothes and all. I gasp as I sink into the hot water and the growing piles of pink bubbles rise up to swallow me. I gulp in a mouthful of water before I manage to scramble above the surface.

"Pax, part of the joy of having a bubble bath is being able to climb in oneself, slowly." I swipe my matted hair from my eyes.

Pax lowers his eyes. "I am sorry. At the bathhouse, we would run from the changing rooms and dive right in. Because the walk from the changing rooms without a tunic is so cold, it makes your verpa shrivel. Better to get in the hot water quickly before the ladies think you have no verpa at all."

"The Roman version of ripping off the Band-Aid, I got you. But for future reference, I can get into my own bubble bath." I try to tug my top off, but the workout fabric clings to my wet skin. "I could use a little help with this, though."

I raise my hands over my head. Pax obliges me, his huge hands sliding around my middle as he tugs off the top and tosses it aside. He helps me roll the leggings and my underwear over my hips. Father Bryne's and Pax's blood darkens the pink water.

Pax grips the side of the tub, his icicle eyes blown out as he cups water in his huge hand and tips it over my head. His hands are so big that it's like sitting under a waterfall. I run my hands through my hair as he pours the water over me, getting out all the tangles and muck of this horrible night.

He watches my every movement. My skin tingles under his gaze, and despite the weariness soaking every bone in my body, I feel myself come alive for him.

"Get in," I say.

Pax shakes his head.

"You're a Roman. Bathing is practically your national pastime. Get in."

Pax frowns. "But you like to bathe on your own. You said as much to Ambrose. You want to be by yourself to read your filthy romance novels and—"

"I don't need a smutty romance novel when I have the real heroes right here with me. Pax Drusus Maximus, you get in this tub *right now.*"

He lets out a dramatic sigh, puffs out his bottom lip, and stands. As I watch, mesmerised by the power and grace of his body made for war, he strips off the blood-soaked yoga top and skintight leggings. His dick – sorry, verpa – is already half hard, a bead of pre-cum on the huge, purple tip.

A shiver of pure lust runs through my body at the memory of what having that verpa inside me feels like.

Pax steps over the edge of the tub. Water cascades over the rim as he settles down opposite me, his legs tangled in mine, his back bent against the taps. It must be uncomfortable with his large frame, but he doesn't say a word.

Giggling, giddy with happiness and horniness, I pluck a handful of pink bubbles and place them on top of his head. "There, now you look pretty."

Pax's face breaks out in one of his wide, dangerous grins. "You used to try and dress me up all the time when you were a little girl. You made me a crown of daisies, but it wouldn't stay on my head."

"I remember. You were always willing to play tea parties with me. And to be the beast in my silly princess games." My favourite game as a little girl was pretending to be a rogue princess who secretly trained as a swordmaster. I'd sneak out of the 'castle' (my bedroom), and Ambrose and I would meet in a tavern on the road before stabbing the beastly monster Pax to rescue Edward, the hopeless prince trapped in the tower Dad made for me out of cardboard boxes.

"I swore an oath to Jupiter to protect you, to make you happy always. If this means I must be fake-slain by you in pretend battle so you can save Edward the useless prince, then I will die with honour by your sword. Even though you'd barely be able to stab an elephant with your lousy sword skills."

"I've heard stabbing an elephant is notoriously difficult. What with the giant creature trying to stomp on you or choke you with its trunk."

"You heard wrong." Pax grins wickedly. "First cut is easy. Second cut, not so easy."

"Please don't stab any elephants."

"If you wish it, I swear by Mars' musk-scented man-nuts that all elephants are safe from my blade." Pax inclines his head, his fingers clasping the tiny coin he wears around his neck, the coin his soldiers placed in his mouth to pay the ferryman for his ticket across the river Styx.

A lump forms in my throat. This man has been here for me my whole life. All he knew from his own life was death and bloodshed, yet he sat with me for hours pretending to have picnics with my teddy bears. He would come running whenever I fell over, and once attempted to beat up a gravestone after I tripped over it and skinned my knees. He may be stabby, but he's also so sweet, and he never asks for anything in return. He never asks anything of me except that I am happy...

...and now that I'm not a little girl any longer...

Pax twists his arm around to find the sponge I keep on the little table beside the bath. "You have dirt on your face," he says. "I will wipe it away."

"No," I swipe the sponge from his hand. "Let me."

"But..." he frowns.

"Tonight, it's my job to look after you."

Pax's eyes narrow. "That is...it is not..."

"This is happening, Pax."

"Very well." He crosses his arms and squeezes his eyes shut.

I stare at the sponge in my hand and the hunched figure of a Roman warrior, the perfectly sculpted contours of his body rigid with tension, and I realize that this is uncharted territory for Pax. He's never had anyone to *look after him* before. As a soldier, he was a cog in a war machine. As a ghost, he's been literally invisible until I came along. As my friend, he's always been about *my* needs, and *my* happiness, but when have I ever asked him about *his* needs?

I run the sponge over his body, scrubbing the graveyard dirt from his skin. As the warm water sluices over him, his muscles slacken a little. He stops squeezing his eyes shut and gazes up at me, those blue irises as deep and unfathomable as the sky.

"This feels..." he searches for a word. "Nice."

His voice has gone all gravelly, and it *does* things to me. It's like a punch straight to my throbbing clit.

I dunk the sponge in the water and move it over his shoulders, his arms, his chest. Pax's body is a map of his career — scars crisscross his chest from battles fought long ago. A small white scar over his heart is all that remains of tonight's battle.

I run my fingers over the scar. Pax sucks in a breath.

"Does it hurt?" I whisper.

"Pain is part of living," is his reply. He doesn't sound resigned, but reverent, as if it has been his afterlife's wish to feel pain again.

I lay my lips against the wound and kiss it. His skin is so warm. He trembles a little beneath the kiss.

I don't understand what I did tonight and why Pax is alive again, but he is, and it's a miracle, and I *did* that.

Tonight, for the first time, I realize that what I've always considered a curse is really a gift, as it brought these three remarkable men into my life, and even made one of them *real*. And maybe I don't have to feel like a freak because of that.

"Turn around," I command. "I want to scrub your back."

"I cannot resist you when you order me around," Pax murmurs.

A tsunami sweeps across the bathroom as Pax whirls around and kneels in the tub, allowing me to scrub his back. I wipe away the dirt and blood to reveal those glistening muscles that do absolutely *nothing* to slow my heart rate or make me sleepy.

"Pax, I..."

"No more of this." Pax makes a growling sound low in his throat. He leans back and his thick arm goes around my middle, dragging me around his torso to press my back into his chest. Under the water, his verpa is no longer half-hard. He is fully erect, pressing against my thigh so hard that it hurts a little.

I swallow. I almost forgot how big he is.

Almost.

"Now it is my turn to look after you," he growls against my ear.

I am utterly unable to protest. Not when he's holding me like this, with all that thick, hot Roman muscle pressing down on me. Not with that needy growl in his voice. Pax does have needs, and one of those needs is to serve...

...and I'm more than willing to be his general if it means...

While his arm continues to hold me in place, Pax slides his other hand down between us, finding my clit. I gasp as he attacks it. Pax doesn't do gentle or soft, but I don't need that from him. I want the warrior, the slayer of men, the protector.

His fingers move in harsh circles while he lays tantalising kisses along my neck, over my collarbone. "Scream for me," he whispers. "Make all the gods hear you and know that I am yours."

"Is that a command, Pax Drusus Maximus?" I manage to choke out.

"No." He lifts the fingers of his other hand to my chin, wrenching my head around to face him over my shoulder. "A prayer."

Pax's lips crush mine, and those fingers of his work me beneath the hot, scented water, and I am gone, gone, gone. The orgasm breaks me open, spilling me for him so that he has no choice but to swallow my pleasure and make it his own. I jerk against the side of the tub, sending another tsunami across the bathroom.

As the wave of my pleasure subsides, I slump against the edge of the tub. But Pax is not done with me. Oh, no. He places his arm around me again, gripping me firmly as he lines himself up.

He bucks his hips forward to push inside me. I grit my teeth as the head of his cock pushes in, stretching me. The water seems to heat another ten degrees. Pax kisses the side of my neck, sending a delicious shiver through me, as he pushes in another inch.

Oh. *Oh.*

It's all I can do to grip the side of the bath and hold on. Pax grunts as he pushes in another inch, his kisses fluttering against my neck as he waits for my body to adjust before thrusting again.

By Pax's gods, this is such exquisite agony. This is exactly what I need – to feel *alive.*

Pax's teeth dig into my shoulder when he finally pushes his entire length inside me. I'm so full of him that I can hardly breathe. I relax against him, letting him hold me, letting him have control. I know that I'm safe in his arms.

"You are an enchantment," Pax's gravelly voice rasps against my ear, his stubble grazing my skin. "Men have burned empires for less than this."

"What about you?" I manage to choke out.

"If you asked it of me, I would burn the world for you. I would lay down my life for yours."

"I know." Tears prick at the corners of my eyes. "Please, don't ever try to do that again."

"I promise. It is my honour to live for you as I would die for you. You are my goddess, my *beloved*."

And with that, he draws his hips back and thrusts.

No more talking. The ability to speak is driven out of me by the force of his thrusts. Pax ravages my body like it's a city he has been ordered to destroy. He trembles against my body as his hips piston against me in that perfect rhythm that has me soaring. Water splashes over the bath. Pink bubbles float around my face.

Pax's hips buck against me, driving me against his splayed fingers as he holds me in my kneeling position, making sure that he's not pile-driving me into the side of the bath.

Even in the midst of his own ecstasy, he looks after me.

That's who he is, my warrior with the soft heart. His hard muscles hot and tight against mine, his body taut with need of me as he drives me right to the edge, putting his hand between my legs to punish my clit because he won't allow himself release until I come again.

So I don't hold back. I can't give him the words he is so desperate to hear, but I can give him this. I come apart on his fingers, split open by his monstrous cock.

A French guy I met in a bar in Queenstown told me in a quintessentially French attempt at flirting that in his language, an orgasm is called *la petit mort*, or "a little death." I told him that sounded completely fake and made him pay for two more drinks before going home with an Australian skier who didn't take himself as seriously.

Well, the joke's on me, because I died a little in Pax's arms, and a little piece of my soul breaks away and binds itself to him.

Pax finally allows himself his release, and his muscles tense as he nearly tosses me across the room. But he manages to catch me before collapsing against me, his cheek resting on my back, stubble scraping my skin. I manage to pull myself around and wrap my arms around him. I look down and burst out laughing when I see the tiny puddle of water left in the bathtub.

Pax notices too, and he beams. "Now you know how to bathe like a Roman."

6

AMBROSE

I hover over the corner of the bed and listen to Pax and Bree in the bathroom. From the sounds of Bree's happy squeals, they're having fun. I wish I were having fun with them, but Edward insists that we stay out here. He says he wants to talk to me, but he hasn't uttered a word.

Finally, I can't stand it anymore. I stand and move toward the bathroom. "If you don't need me, I'll be taking a bubble bath—"

"Ambrose," Edward says my name like a prayer. "Wait."

"Do you have something new to teach me?" I can barely control my excitement. Edward has been instrumental in showing me the finer details of pleasing a woman, and I believe I've made some progress in the area, especially for a ghost. "Some new and wondrous way to make Bree scream?"

"No." There's a hint of a smile in Edward's voice. "I mean, yes, always. You have so much to learn, and you're such an obliging student. Tonight perhaps we will cover the five senses...however, that's not what I wish to ask you."

"What then?"

"If you were a human, would you still..." Edward's breath rushes out. "Would you still be my friend?"

"I don't understand."

"If you and Pax were...were both alive, and the two of you could be with Brianna in the way that only three humans can be, then surely it would be easier if I were gone from Grimwood?"

"Grimwood is your home, Edward, as much as it is ours and Bree's. None of us would wish you to leave it."

He takes my hand and squeezes it. As ghosts, we've always been able to touch each other – his ghostly skin feels cold and clammy, a symptom, no doubt, of the troublesome evening we've had. "You say that, but I cannot help but think that a spectral prince, no matter how handsome and charming he might be, will only hinder you and Brianna and Pax from living your fullest lives. You will be forever acquiescing to the needs of the dead, instead of enjoying the pleasures of the Living. What if you and Brianna wanted to travel? I couldn't come with you, but nor would I wish to keep you here against your will."

Edward must see a flicker of unease pass over my face, because I can feel him flinch.

I rush to reassure him. "You don't know that. With the moldavite stones, we may be able to take you with us—"

"But that's just it. I would always be a burden to you."

"This is a silly conversation." I drop his hand. "What does it matter when the situation you describe will never happen. Neither you nor I know what our unfinished business is. If we have not been able to solve this for ourselves in several centuries, then what hope does Bree have? For all that she wishes things to be different, I am perfectly content to remain in this house forever, knowing that I have a piece of her love. You should learn the same contentment."

"So you can watch Pax and Brianna doing *that,*" he spits the word, just as Bree's moans echo from the bathroom, "and not be wracked with envy that you cannot join in?"

"I *could* join in if I weren't out here having a fruitless conversation with a sad poet prince."

"It's not the same," he mutters angrily. "It's not the same if we cannot have her heart or her soul or her body. It's not the same when he has a body and we don't."

I shrug. "I am happy for them both."

"Argh, why must you be so *nice?*" Edward clutches his head, his fingers tearing through his unruly dark hair. "You're supposed to hate me. Why can't you hate me?"

"Edward, you are my dearest friend. Remember the day I appeared at this house, a newly minted ghost, and you took me under your wing? You explained ghost mojo. You helped me avoid being skewered by Pax when he decided to practice stabbing Druids. You showed me your trick with the liquor cabinet for the days when I did not feel like my cheerful self. You wrote me that dreadful poem for my birthday – a travesty of literature, but I appreciated the attempt. I could never *hate* you."

"Some friend I am," Edward murmurs. "Ambrose, if you had any idea of what I've done to you… Pax gave me his forgiveness tonight, and it is extraordinary and wonderful, and it made me realize that there's something I need your forgiveness for. But I am not worthy to ask for it, not after I—"

But then, he stops talking, because Bree and Pax enter the room. And I can tell from the sharp intake of breath and the lack of clothing rustling, that they are both naked.

7

BREE

Edward is speaking, urgently and ardently, but he stops as soon as I step into my bedroom. His dark eyes burst with flame-filled light at the edges as he sees me naked, carrying the handful of moldavite stones I had in my pocket. The corner of his mouth quirks up into his signature smirk.

"Thou art a dream," breathes Edward, taking a step toward me as if he is dragged by invisible hands. "A living sculpture, a vision of loveliness that surpasses all my earthly description—"

"Good, you're back to your old self," I say with a smile as I squeeze Pax's hand. "Don't describe me. There are many more things I'd like you to do with that tongue of yours."

The air in the room shifts. Edward's eyes roam down my body, and he wets his bottom lip in an expression I can only describe as hungry. Ambrose remains still, listening, his face open, rapturous. A dark, wanton heat sinks into my stomach.

"I almost lost you tonight," I say, my voice catching on the words. "I...I know I said terrible things to you, and that we have a lot of stuff to work out, and we don't even know if Jack the Ripper is gone for good. But for the next little while, I don't

61

want to think about any of that. I don't want us to be compli-cated. I just want to be...us."

Ambrose inclines his head. "I'd love nothing more," he says formally, as if I were inviting him to tea instead of an orgy.

"I promised that I would show Ambrose another way to please a lady." Edward's Adam's apple bobs in his throat. "Roman, will you indulge my whims, since you are the one who can touch her as we cannot?"

Edward and Pax regard each other, and something long unspoken passes between them. I know they're both searching for their place in this new hierarchy of ghost and Living, both used to being the alpha males of their own domains. But Pax shrugs and leans in to kiss the top of my head.

"Not for long," I promise Edward. "I swear to you, I will free you and Ambrose, too."

"How much it would please me, were that true," Edward says as he closes the space between us. He raises his hand to my face, and I try not to think about how I can see my bed through his translucent form. His fingers graze my cheek, warm and tingling against my skin. The touch of a ghost who almost but can't quite grasp me.

He tries to anyway, cupping my cheek and tugging, drawing me forward so that our lips meet.

Unlike Pax, who is all blood and enthusiasm, Edward's kiss is measured, languid, probing, as if we have all the time in the world and he intends to use it to map every inch of my skin with his mouth.

Gods, how I want that.

For a few glorious moments, I forget that he is a ghost. He feels so real, his lips searing hot against mine. The way he makes me feel – that's more real than anything. This needy ache drops through my body, right into my toes.

But then, his fingers curl into my hair. They accidentally slip through my skull. The heat of it *burns*, and I experience a flash of memory from inside Edward's head – his father, the king, red-faced and yelling at him in front of a room filled with courtiers. The ache in my belly becomes a churning sickness, a gnawing, twisting shame.

Edward pulls back. He fixes his too-perfect features into a mask of mirth. I wonder what he saw in my memories.

"I am sorry," he says, his lips the perfect poet's pout. "I cannot even kiss you without taking more from you than I have to give. I don't deserve this. I don't deserve you."

"You will always be enough for me, just as you are." I reach for him, but he steps away.

"I cannot. Not tonight."

"Edward, please..." I'm not even ashamed of the need in my voice. "I love kissing you. You feel amazing. I don't care about the memories..."

He shakes his head. "Brianna, do you trust me?"

"Always." The word falls unbidden from my lips.

Edward seems startled by my answer.

"Very well. Then you have nothing to be sad about. We will still have our revels. I am nothing if not the Prince of Debauchery. Come with me." His fingers slip through mine as he leads me to the chaise lounge beneath the large bay windows in my bedroom. "First, put down the moldavite stones. We will require them nearby."

I place the handful of stones down on the sofa.

"Now place your feet here, facing the arm."

I do as he instructs. I'm facing the opposite wall of the room. Edward and Pax are behind me, so I can't see them. Ambrose stands near the other end of the chaise. He shrugs off his black frock coat and undoes the tie that pulls his dark hair off his face. It spills free, and my fingers dig into the arm of the sofa as I think about running my hands through it. It doesn't quite feel like real hair, but it's something. Pax has his cut for battle and doesn't have much hair to speak of.

Ambrose tosses his frock coat on the bed. "What next, Edward?" He has a rapt expression on his face, like a schoolboy the first time he sees a pair of breasts.

Warm, ghostly fingers trail down my back, drawing patterns along my spine. *Edward.* I let out my breath slowly, my body poised with anticipation at what's next.

The fingers splay out across my back.

"Bend over," Edward says in that commanding drawl of his.

I bend, draping my arms over the end of the chair. My ass is high in the air, and a wet ache pools between my legs. A thrill runs through my veins at the thought of the intimate view I'm giving Pax and Edward.

Edward's fingers stroke down my legs, first one, then the other, leaving trails of fire across my skin. He pushes on my ankles. "Wider. The Roman needs room for his enormous hips."

Obediently, I shift my hips wider, aware of the cool air in the room kissing my clit and how desperately that bundle of nerves wants to be touched.

"Good. I like it when you obey me so readily." Edward sounds satisfied. His voice is steady, authoritative. I can't see his face, but I sense that this is where he is comfortable. When he kisses me, he gives me his memories, and that's too vulnerable for him right now, especially when he's already been flayed raw by what's happened tonight. But being the puppet master of our tryst is a role he's confident to play.

"Roman, take that tie from around the curtain and bind her hands. Bind them tightly to the other end of the chaise."

Pax, who is well used to taking commands, leaps into action. He comes around the side of the chaise, where I can see him, and unwinds the curtain tie. It's a thick, golden rope with a decorative tassel on each end, and I swallow down my apprehension as he approaches me with it between his huge hands.

I've never been tied up before. It's not something I'm interested in. I think that I'm so used to running away my whole life that the idea of being incapacitated in any way makes me freak out. I prefer to have one foot out the door, ready to bolt.

But I trust Edward. So we're doing this.

I hiss out a breath and try not to flinch as Pax wraps the curtain tie around my wrists, tying some complicated Roman knot I could never escape even if I wanted to. He wraps the other end around the curved arm of the chaise, pulling me forward so that my arms rest on the cushions, but I'm stretched out across the chaise with my ass high. I have to stand on my tiptoes to hold the position.

It's a stretch, but it feels so good.

Do I like this?

I think I like this.

What feels amazing are their eyes on me. Pax steps back, his icy eyes wide with awe. I can't see Edward, but my skin burns from his gaze, and I want nothing more than his hands or lips on me *right the fuck now*. I try to move toward him, but then the cord bites and I remember I'm tied up.

I can't move.

Why do I like this?

Why is my pussy throbbing with need?

This is so *deliciously* cruel.

I feel something land on my back. The moldavite stones. Edward instructs Pax to line them up along my spine. They feel strange, a little heavy, but at least with them close, the ghosts can touch me and I can touch them.

"Did you know that this chaise lounge has been in the house since I owned it?" I see Edward's hand out of the corner of my eye. He runs his fingers over the inlaid wood. "It used to be in the master suite. I have laid many a countess over the arm of this sofa, just the way you are now. And yet, none of them have looked as beautiful as you, or meant so much to me. Pax, tie her ankles next."

Pax leaps forward to fulfil Edward's demands. His rough fingers tug my ankles wider, tying them to the feet of the sofa. He makes quick work of the knots. I test the restraints. I won't be escaping any time soon.

"Ambrose." Edward's voice is thick with need. "You can touch her now. I want you to see how beautiful our Brianna is tied up like this, like a present waiting to be unwrapped."

Our Brianna.

I like the sound of that.

I like it almost as much as the way my whole body ripples and tightens from just the movement of air across my bare skin. There is something so raw about this, and yet so safe. They make me feel safe.

Ambrose bites his lip as he steps forward. He reaches out a ghostly hand. His fingers dance across my back, and that now familiar ghostly tingle shoots heat straight between my legs.

He moves his hands over me, his face turning rapturous as he explores my naked skin. He slides his fingers first along the curve of my ass, then back over my shoulders and down, down, to cup my breasts. He grazes the sharp points of my nipples, and I gasp, straining against the restraints for...what?

For whatever they will give me.

I moan in protest as Ambrose moves his hands away, dancing trails down my arms, over the inside of my elbows, to my bound wrists. He stops.

"You said that you'd show me another way to please a woman? But Bree is tied up? How can this be pleasing?" His voice rises.

"Love and sex and death and agony," Edward intones.

"These are the worlds a poet inhabits. They are more linked than we might believe. If we bring our greatest fears into the boudoir and confront them while in the safety of a lover's embrace, we might find that we have nothing so much to be afraid of anymore. And Brianna's greatest fear is what will happen if she can no longer run away. How do you feel, Brianna?"

"Good," I say, my voice coming out husky. "Strange. Nervous, but in a good way."

Ambrose looks unsure. His fingers pass through the cord. "Is she truly restrained?" he asks, his voice catching. "She can't escape and run away?"

"I got a Centurion Scouts badge for my Roman knotwork," Pax declares happily. "She won't be slipping out."

"Good," Edward says. "Now, for the final touch. See that scarf draped over the back of that chair? I want you to wrap it around her head, covering her eyes and her ears."

"Edward..." I start to warn as the fear plunges into my chest. But it's too late, Pax is pulling it over my eyes. I blink in the gloom. I can still see a few snatches of light from the wall sconces and the moonlight out the window, but I can no longer see them.

"Now, Roman, I need you to come with me," Edward says. I can just make out his words with the scarf over my ears. "We require some supplies from the kitchen, and obviously I can't be expected to carry them myself."

Ah, yes, there's that old Edward.

He lowers his voice as he explains his plan to Pax, but they're too quiet for me to hear their plans. Next thing I know, Pax plants a kiss on the top of my head and promises they'll be right back.

Wait, what? They'll be right back?

This is not happening.

"Wait?" I call out.

But they didn't answer. Those absolute bastards. They just left me here, tied to the chaise, my pussy aching for them. I jerk my arms, but it's no good; I'm trussed up tight, although one of the moldavite stones rolls off my back.

"Edward, I am going to kill you!" I yell.

"You can't kill that which is already dead," he cheekily calls back.

"Bree, are you okay?" Ambrose's muffled voice breaks through.

Am I okay? I don't know anymore. I trust them, I *trust* them, but the urge to run, to be free, rises inside me, and...

I feel something cold jerking on my restraints, and then a flash of one of Ambrose's memories – I'm sitting beside a roaring fireplace at an inn in Germany, eating a hearty stew while snow falls outside. I'm thinking about the ruins of a medieval castle I visited that day, how the tower stairs were worn smooth beneath my stick from centuries of feet moving up and down. Contentment settles in my belly, but there's something else there, too. A loneliness, a wish that I could share this joy with another...

As quickly as the memory appears, it fades, but the contentment remains. And so do the cold, frantic fingers tangling with the cord.

"Ambrose, what are you doing?"

"I'm trying to untie you, but my fingers aren't able to grasp this knot."

"No, don't untie me."

His fingers still. "You like what Edward has done to you?"

"I think so. We'll see. But I trust him to set me free if I don't." I try to think of a way to explain. "You know when you have a train ticket to somewhere exciting, and your journey isn't for a few days but it's all you can think about?"

"I know this feeling well."

"That's exactly how I feel right now. Except that instead of a train, I have you and Edward and Pax…"

"I suppose that is a train, in a manner of speaking…"

"Ambrose Hulme," I exclaim. "Did you just make a filthy joke?"

"Perhaps," he says with a smile in his voice. Ambrose's fingers caress the curve of my ass, and my eyes roll back in my head and I'm not thinking about anything except how good he feels.

I hear some noise in the background that must be the guys returning from the kitchen. Someone replaces the moldavite stone.

I go still, my body tensing as I wait for whatever Edward has planned.

No one says a word for several long, agonising moments. My thighs ache and my clit hums impatiently because Edward is making me wait—

What is that?

Something cold and wet runs across my shoulders and down my spine. It should feel icky, like being kissed by a lizard, but it's so lovely against my hot, sensitive skin that I let out a gasp.

It's ice. Edward has ice.

The ice cube roams all over my back, between the stones. I squirm beneath the onslaught of the cold, but there's nowhere for me to go. I have to take it. Not being able to move forces me to focus on the sensation, and I can feel myself slipping under Edward's spell as the hairs on my skin stand on end…

Now, a second cube has joined the first, but this one is slid underneath me and rubbed against my hard nipples. I grit my teeth because it's so intense, I want to scream. It's painful, so painful having that cold cube against my sensitive nipples, but at the same time, my clit is throbbing with pleasure.

And then, something hot lands on my back.

I jerk. The heat leaves my skin a moment later, leaving only a sensitive spot that has all my nerves alight. But then it happens again, and again – little pinpricks of searing pain that are quickly cooled by another ice cube. I jerk and strain against my restraints, but I don't really want to be free. Not anymore.

Through the scarf covering my eyes, I can see a flickering light moving at the edge of my vision. That's how I realize that they're dripping wax from a candle onto my skin.

My breathing picks up. *This is so fucking intense.* My skin is *alive* and super sensitive – I can feel every shift in the air as they move around me. I'm a bundle of raw nerves and desperate want, and they're playing with me, driving me closer to orgasm without even touching my anguished clit.

Drip, drip, drip.

I lose myself in the sensation as whoever it is (Pax, I'm assuming) presses the ice cubes against my nipples. They don't even hurt anymore, or maybe I'm so far beyond the pain. From somewhere behind me, I hear Edward murmur, "That's it, just like that. Now, we shall try something else. Something for Ambrose."

The ice is removed, leaving me tense and panting. Something cool is spread along my back and over my ass cheeks. I can't describe the sensation except to say that it feels like I'm a piece of bread being slathered with chocolate spread, and I am *here* for it. I can even *smell* chocolate.

"Taste her, Ambrose," Edward's voice commands. Even though he's muffled by the scarf, he's near my head. "See how her skin becomes the most exquisite dessert."

Someone leans over me, and then a tongue is licking away whatever Edward spread there. Chocolate sauce, I realize.

Edward's drizzled me with chocolate sauce like I'm an ice cream sundae.

Ambrose doesn't just lick the lines of sauce, he *devours*. He sucks on my sensitive skin, getting every last morsel as he works his way down my back. As a ghost, I know he can't taste everything, but it doesn't seem to matter to him.

He reaches my lower back, and his tongue follows the trail Edward laid…over the curve of my ass. Ambrose is licking and sucking and nibbling my ass cheeks.

This is…it's so filthy. It's so *intense*.

I love it.

I'm not analysing the situation. My brain has completely shut off, and I simply exist, floating in this cocoon of wild sensations. Every touch sears through my body, making me ripple and tighten like I'm a jelly.

The ice, the fire, the ghostly fingers joined by Pax's real ones, it all blurs together until my pussy is screaming for release, until my stomach is a hard coil of nerves and wanting, until someone bites my ass and I cry out with pleasure.

Something cool and hard presses against my lips.

"A drink, m'lady?" Edward asks as someone – I presume Pax – tilts a wine bottle against my lips. "Ordinarily, I would serve only the finest French Champagne with a meal, but since my infamous wine cellar was drunk dry by my ungrateful friends, you will have to make do with this £4.99 Sainsbury's pisswater. Pax will pour for you."

I can't make words form, so I tilt my head back and allow Edward to pour a little of the cheap bubbles down my throat. As I swallow, I feel the splash against my skin as he sloshes some into the small of my back.

"Taste her now," I hear Edward prodding Ambrose.

Tingling, ghostly lips caress my skin, sucking up every

morsel of the Champagne as it pools into the little crevice made by my arched back and then...

...and then lips touch my clit.

"Argh!" I jerk in the restraints. After so much anticipation, the touch of those warm, ghostly lips against my most intimate parts is far, far too much.

I think I might come right now, just from that one gentle kiss.

But I don't. It's like I'm floating on the edge of an orgasm, and they won't let me fall. Bastards.

I think it must be Ambrose. Yes, that is Ambrose lovingly, tenderly stroking me, drawing out the most inhuman sounds from my throat as he drives me closer and closer to that cliff edge without allowing me to go over.

My body can't take it. I squirm and buck, but I can't escape, and that makes it even more intense. Edward is saying something but I can't hear – it's as if he's calling from some great distance away.

I think I have an orgasm, but I actually can't be sure. It's as if I truly have fallen over the edge of a cliff, only instead of falling, I'm *flying*. My heart thrums in my ears and blood rushes into my head and I'm being buffeted on all sides by wild winds, but instead of wind, it's emotion. It comes in waves, and each is a mini orgasm that threatens to send me falling back to earth, but I'm held and lifted and carried away...

Woah...woahhhhh...

White spots dance in front of my eyes, and slowly, slowly, I'm pulled back to earth. But it's not over. Edward wouldn't allow that. No, now someone else is between my legs, rough hands gripping my ass as he buries his face into my pussy. Pax. He hungrily takes my clit in his mouth, sucking all the juices that he helped to create.

While Pax is doing that, I feel something else touch my lips.

It's light and soft and makes my mouth tingle with warmth. It takes me a moment to realize it's a ghost cock.

"Be a good girl. Take your prince in your mouth," Edward orders.

I'm too far gone to call him out for being an arrogant ass and calling me 'good girl.'

Pax is still between my legs, eating me out with a ferocity that makes my legs quake. I can feel another orgasm growing like a distant wave inside me, cresting as it nears the shore.

I open my lips, and Edward slides himself inside.

He tastes amazing. He tastes the way he's always smelled to me – like burnt sugar and summer blossoms, with a kiss of opium. Because he's still a ghost, I can't quite grip him with my lips, but I do my best.

I take Edward deeper, sucking hard and using my tongue to swirl around his tip. I try to give him as much sensation as I can, knowing that as a ghost I might not be able to make him come.

"What should I do?" Ambrose asks.

"She quite likes you playing with her breasts, and her clit," Edward says. "And I think you enjoy it, too."

"Oh, yes."

And then Ambrose's hands are on my breasts, thumbs lovingly stroking over my tortured nipples. On any other day, the sensation would be too soft for me, but after the way Edward built me up with the ice and the wax and the food, each swipe of Ambrose's warm, ghost fingers nearly has me tearing free of my restraints.

Edward strokes my head, which is something I've always hated guys doing, when they push your head onto their cock like they think they're in some porn film. But when he does it, it doesn't feel controlling. It gives me a little depraved thrill. Or maybe that thrill comes from the fact that I have one ghost's cock in my mouth while another is playing with my nipples and a Roman warrior has his face buried between my legs?

Yeah, that could be it.

Between my legs, Pax sucks my clit into his mouth, and the wave crests and the ocean roars in my ears as I come apart again for him. I surface from the waves just as he asks Edward what he should do next.

"You may untie her ankles, Roman. No, not with your sword…"

I take pride in the way his voice trembles a little and his fingers tighten in my hair as my lips work his shaft.

The cords around my feet snap away. Rough fingers grab my ankles, yanking my legs wider apart.

"Yes, like that. Now, put that blade down before you put someone's eye out," Edward instructs. "I think you know what to do now."

Rough hands grab my ass cheeks, driving my hips into the sofa. I scream around Edward's cock as Pax enters me with a powerful thrust.

This is it, this is how I die, tied to a chaise lounge sucking ghost cock while a Roman centurion splits me open.

What a way to go.

Pax plows me into the sofa, so hard that the frame creaks and groans. With every thrust he goes deeper, stretching me and touching places that I don't think have ever had cock before. All I can do is float in a haze of pleasure and take it, like a fucking *good girl.*

All through this pounding, Edward and Ambrose don't let up. Ambrose rolls my nipple around on his tongue while his fingers tease my clit. Ghost fingers are made for giving orgasms, the way they hum and tingle against human flesh.

And Edward…he fills my mouth as much as he's able. He tastes like caramel burnt sugar, and I just want to eat him all up. He's not like a Living guy, who might be sweaty or smelly. He's perfect.

As Pax pounds into me, the prince leans in close and manages to lift the scarf to whisper in my ear.

"How much have you wanted this, Brianna? How much have you wished that your prince could be whole and Living again so he could fulfill all your wildest, darkest desires?"

"I...I..." I can't get the words out because my body clenches and I'm dragged into yet another orgasm.

I lose count of the number of orgasms I have before Pax and Edward explode inside me. I don't remember being untied, but the next time I recall, I'm being tucked into bed, my back pressed against a snuggly Roman warrior, while two ghosts curl protectively around us, making my skin tingle wherever they touch.

Something has changed tonight. I can't explain it, but the nervous energy that's always plagued me – that sense that I need to move, run, get away – is gone, and it's replaced by a warmth that stretches right from the crown of my head to the tips of my toes.

And I wonder, I wonder if maybe I'm falling for them. If maybe I've already fallen, and the ocean of their love for me is about to pull me under, where everything is dark and I cannot escape...

8

BREE

I'm pulled from sleep by a presence, a sense that I'm not alone, that the air around me has shifted. I open one eye. A lone figure hovers over the end of the bed. The sheets beneath him do not dent and I cannot feel warmth from his body. The sunlight streaming through the open curtains shines through his body, creating dappled rainbows on the duvet where the light bends around the prism of his ghostly limbs. He does not look at me, and from the slump of his shoulders, I suspect he's been there a while.

Edward runs his fingers through his unruly dark curls as he stares pensively out the window at the cemetery. The spires of his monstrous gothic mausoleum pierce the grey sky. Another beautiful English summer's day, by the looks of it.

"Where are the others?" I ask, sitting up.

He whirls around, his eyes dark and serious as he watches me rearrange the pillows behind my head.

"I sent them away," he says gravely. "I have something to show you, but I cannot bear them to be here when I do it."

"Edward, what is it?" I take in the gravity of his features, the somber notes in his voice. My throat closes over.

77

This is it. This is the thing that's been weighing on him for weeks.

He stands abruptly. Once more, I'm taken in by the aristocratic loveliness of him, the noble set of his shoulders and the way his tall, toned body oozes power and elegance. And the way he wears his sadness as a mask.

"You must come with me. I will need you to...to remove something from its hiding place."

I cast one forlorn look at the inviting comfort of my bed, then throw off the covers. I step into a pair of boy-cut jeans and a shirt with tiny bones all over it, and shove my feet into my fluffy black cat slippers. I am not ready for morose Edward first thing in the morning, especially not after last night. I need an IV of coffee, stat.

I take Edward's hand. His fingers slip through mine a little, and I see his face shift as one of my memories passes to him – another new power of mine that seems to have developed since I returned to Grimdale. I get a flicker of something, too – another opium-fuelled party, and a golden-haired countess tied to the couch the way I was last night, screaming in ecstasy. Heat creeps along my cheeks.

"Where are we going?" I ask as Edward leads me to the door.

"To the attic." His voice wavers on the words. "To the scene of my greatest failing."

The attic?

Is this something to do with Father Bryne? Edward found me in the attic last night and told me that Pax was missing, and as we came down the stairs, Father Bryne attacked us. But Edward wouldn't even go in the attic, not while Ozzy was there. So why is he leading me there for the second time in two days?

Confused, I follow Edward out of my room. We step over the dark patch in the entrance hall. I really have to clean that up today and get a new rug to cover it. Edward leads me up the stairs, but I drag my feet, pausing halfway up to admire the family photographs hanging there. It's been a long time since I really stopped and looked at them – pictures of me playing with a red bucket at the beach, Dad and all his brothers sitting on the hood of a vintage car, my great grandmother in her favourite pink outfit...

"Look, Ozzy's still here! Hi, Ozzy!" I wave to the furry ghost hanging by his feet from the chandelier. He opens one lazy wing and winks at me before clamping it tight around his fuzzy body.

"Brianna, are you trying to delay the bitter truth of the tale I must impart?" Edward shrinks away from the bat. "For it is with a heavy heart that these verses I must compose. In hopes the pain of my candour may impose—"

"Sorry. I wasn't trying to dwardle. I'm just remembering last night." I shudder, but I allow him to continue leading me up the stairs. "How close I came to losing you all."

"Within that foul vessel, a tempest brewed, and my foul soul he did darkly subdue. But none so filled me with woe and dread, as the horrors I have witnessed where the attic's shadows spread." Edward gestures to the still-open attic stairs with a flourish. "After you, m'lady."

Anything to make you stop rhyming. I start up the steps, expecting Edward to pinch my bum on the way, but he doesn't. *This really is serious.*

I flick on the attic light. Edward yelps as Ozzy flies over our heads and perches on one of the low beams, folding his wings and regarding us with those huge eyes of his. Edward glares at him. "This is a private matter."

The ghost bat raises one wing in what can only be described as a threatening manner.

Edward grimaces. "Fine. I suppose this is your home."

The bat lowers its wing. Edward visibly relaxes. I can't help but wonder what the tiny, fuzzy, dearly departed bat had done to my three ghosts to make them so terrified of him.

Edward crosses the room, his face a picture of misery. "Boxes and trunks, their contents veiled in gloom, Like ancient phantoms waiting in this room..."

"Edward, just tell me why we're up here, and then we can leave." I swipe a cobweb off my shoulder. I am *desperate* for coffee.

"Very well. Here it is. You must lift the lid."

Edward gestures to the old piano that's been up in the attic since I could remember. Dad had it valued once and apparently it would fetch a decent amount of money, but he couldn't find a contractor who could get it out of the attic. So here it remains.

Even more curious now, I grip the top of the piano and heave. It's heavier than I expect, but I manage to lift it, raising a cloud of dust that makes my throat itch.

"It's inside, in the corner at the back."

I fumble around inside, grazing my fingers on the strings and mechanisms. I brush something that feels like leather. I tug it free and drop the lid with a *THUD*.

Behind me, Edward makes a squeaking noise and Ozzy flutters down to peer at the object over my shoulder.

"It's a book?" I dust off the leather-bound volume and tug on the leather thong. No, it's not a book, but some kind of journal – handwritten pages tied together in a leather case. And the handwriting is strange – the lines are too perfectly neat, the tails of the letters g and y not hanging below the line as they should...

"It was a book, once," Edward says sadly. "This is Ambrose's manuscript. He hid it here to keep it secure after the fire at the publisher burned the remaining copies."

Of course. Ambrose used a writing frame placed over the

page to write his stories. This is why the tails of the letters don't hang beneath the line, and some of the letters overlap.

But how...how is this here?

"You found this when you were hiding up here a few days ago?" I stare at the heavy piano. Edward must have been terribly upset to stick his head through the thick wood of the piano. That would have smarted for a ghost.

Edward sighs. "No."

"I don't understand."

"Then I shall explain. It had been a particularly hot summer in 1878, and Pax had decided to forgo his tunic and armour and wander about naked. I was hiding up here to preserve my vision, when I heard a noise on the stairs. Ambrose came up here and hid it in the piano. It was just before he left for his Russia trip."

It takes a moment for Edward's words to sink in. "You mean, you saw Ambrose hide this when he was *alive?*"

Edward nods miserably.

"You knew this manuscript was here all this time?" I stare down at the neat rows of letters in my hands, my stomach twisting in knots. "If this is Ambrose's unfinished business, he could have crossed over earlier if only you'd told him about it."

Edward nods again.

"Oh, *Edward.*"

"I didn't want him to leave," he says quietly. "I never had a real friend before. Well, I suppose I have Pax, but our friendship is..."

"I get it," I smile. Pax and Edward have always been at odds with each other, friends due to circumstances rather than a genuine desire for each other's company. Their affection for each other is genuine – otherwise, Edward would not have dived inside the Ripper to save Pax's life – but Grimwood Manor has been shaken to the foundation by their disagreements over the years. But Edward and Ambrose are different. Edward sees Ambrose as a kind of corruptible younger brother whom he can school in the wicked ways of the world, and Ambrose is endearingly oblivious to Edward's more annoying traits. "I don't like that you lied about this, but I can't say I'm sad that Ambrose wasn't able to cross over. And now…"

As I stare down at the manuscript, a fissure of pure joy rockets through my weary veins. *This is the key, I know it is.*

This is what I need to bring Ambrose back from the dead.

"Oh Edward, thank you, thank you for finding this." I throw my arms around him, forgetting in my joy that he's a ghost. My hands settle on him for a moment, but then he jerks away before I can fall through him.

Edward trembles with horror as he backs away from me. "You cannot *thank* me. I don't deserve thanks. I never should have kept it secret. I wish there were some way I could make it up to him."

I look up, into the dark, fathomless eyes of my dark prince. "Perhaps you can. How long did you say Ambrose and Pax would be out?"

"They were not to return until nightfall, lest they should be forced to listen to my morose rhymes."

"Excellent." I tuck the manuscript safely under my arm and reach out to Edward. "Come with me, I have a plan. But we're going to need some help—"

9

BREE

"Bree? Edward? Are you here? Pax and I have exhausted our mandated banishment activities. Is it okay if we come in?"

Ambrose's cheery voice calls through the empty house. I set down the manuscript. After washing the Father Bryne's sheets, calling the charity to apologise for his abrupt departure, cancelling the rest of his booking on our B&B website, and doing all the things with Edward today, I sat down to read a few chapters. I'm in awe at Ambrose's brilliance. He could make even the most mundane travelling narrative an adventure. You felt as if you were right there alongside him. I couldn't wait to discuss it with him.

But first...

Beside me, Edward goes even paler, if that's even possible. I reach across and squeeze his hand, my fingers slipping a little into his. His features soften. I hope if he's seeing a memory of mine, that it's a happy one.

"How many views do we have now?" Edward whispers.

I check my phone. "Over twenty thousand. I can't believe it. Are you ready for this?"

"No, but today is not about me."

"We're in the guest sitting room," I call out and I head toward the hallway, Edward dragging his feet behind me. I'm dragging my feet too, if I'm being honest. We've been on the go all day while the other two have been out, except for a brief moment at lunch time when Ambrose's ghost mojo ran out and he popped back home for twenty minutes to recharge (that's a thing we discovered – hanging around me can mean the ghosts can go a little further from Grimdale for a longer on their own). I have to hope it's been worth it.

In the entrance hall, Pax holds the door open for Ambrose, who floats right through the darkened patch of dried blood on the flagstones. I really *should* clean that up, but I've been a little distracted today. I'm still so tired, and it's not as if we have any new guests arriving. It can wait for this.

"We went to the Roman Museum," Ambrose explains, waving his hands around with enthusiasm. "Alice was there working on her exhibit. Pax apologised for smashing the glass case and helped them to repair it. And then Alice let him arrange his bones."

"She did?"

Pax nods. "It was fun. I am a very handsome skeleton. Alice said so. She told me all sorts of things she knows about Ancient Rome. She thinks Romans are very cool. Those are her exact words. I am very cool! The gods will smile upon her."

"I'm glad you both had a good day." I grab Ambrose's hand. His fingers tingle against mine. "Come with me. Edward and I have something to show you."

I lead Ambrose into the guest lounge. Edward's eyes meet mine, and I can see the battle raging inside him. The corner of his mouth turns up into a sad, knowing smile.

"Hello, friends," he says in that false dramatic voice of his, the one that's used to hosting elaborate opium parties. "Brianna and I have something we wish to share with you. When it is over, you will commence gutting me with rusty pitchforks. I assure you that I will not run away or attempt to bargain my Afterlife for your mercy—"

"This sounds fun," Pax cracks his knuckles.

"Edward, is everything okay?" Ambrose asks, his voice full of genuine care. Edward blanches, his eyes pleading with me to take over.

I stare at the object on the table, and at Edward's sorrowful eyes, and I find that I don't have it in me to be angry at him anymore. He did what he did because he's broken and imperfect, and because for the first time in his life, he had a real friend and he wanted to hang on to that. I can't blame him.

But I'm not the one he needs to apologise to, and I don't know what Ambrose is going to do when he finds out...

"Sit down," I say to Ambrose, and I can't help it. It's already nearly dinnertime and I'm running on three hours of sleep and my emotions are fucking *frayed*. I start crying. "I have to tell you something."

"Errr..." Ambrose turns around and feels behind him, not quite certain where the sofa is. He settles for hovering an inch above the cushions. "It's okay, Bree. I am ready for whatever you need to tell me."

"Do I need to stab someone?" Pax asks hopefully.

"No," I laugh even as more tears roll down my cheeks. "This is happy news."

"But why are you crying?" Ambrose's voice trembles.

How did he notice? I thought I'd been hiding my tears so well. But of course he noticed. He's Ambrose. He pays attention to every little detail. He cherishes every piece of me.

"Not all tears are sad." I hold my phone up to my face. I have to blink several times to make out the words. "I'm going to play a video for you."

"Okay."

I suck in a deep breath and hit the play button. The video starts on the screen – it's from the Grimdale Cemetery account, and it's of me, standing in front of Grimdale's iron gates. Edward is behind the camera, directing me with all the passion of a pageant mother, but luckily, he hasn't come through in the recording.

Ambrose leans in to listen.

"Few people have heard of history's greatest traveller," Bree on the screen says. "But I'm going to change that. I'm Bree Mortimer, and it's part of my job as a guide here at the Grimdale Cemetery to unearth the stories that matter from our past. And today I want to show you one of my favourite graves."

The camera follows me as I move through the cemetery, walking along Poet's Way, past the ornately decorated graves of London's elite, before stopping at the unassuming grave wedged between a poet and an infamous courtesan. Edward did an amazing job. It took us a few tries because the phone kept slipping through his fingers, but I added two more pieces of moldavite to my pocket and that helped him hold the phone steady.

"This is the grave of Ambrose Hulme, who died at the age of twenty-five." On-screen, I gesture to the grave. Ambrose sucks in a breath. He turns his head to listen better. "From a young age, Ambrose had a love for adventure, and he always wanted to see and experience the world beyond England's green and pleasant land. He joined the Navy to fulfil his dream, but was blinded by illness before his ship made it all the way to the Americas, and was sent home as an invalid. Blind people during Ambrose's time were objects of pity, who were considered to be a drain on the poor tax unless they could be employed in 'useful toil' at jobs considered appropriate for the blind – usually piano tuning, or basket- and rug-weaving. But that wasn't the life Ambrose Hulme wanted."

Ambrose's long eyelids tangle together as he blinks. His mouth hangs open a little, but he doesn't speak. The video continues playing.

"The loss of his eyesight could not tame Ambrose's thirst for adventure. He was determined to see the world, but when it became clear that the lot of a blind person would not make that easy, he decided he would eschew what society thought best for him and put his dreams first. He worked and saved his money until he could bargain passage on a schooner, and he took off to tour Europe, Asia, and Africa on foot. With very little money and even less sight, he navigated through the world, walking on ancient sites, eating strange and delicious foods, and meeting many wonderful people who were all enchanted by this quietly courageous man on a mission to explore the world.

"Between his trips, Ambrose lived as an eccentric house-guest with the Van Wimple family at Grimwood Manor, which you can see just up the hill." On the screen, I point in the direction of the house, and Edward shakily turns the camera to film it. "He spent his days at Grimwood writing his travel memoir. Braille hadn't been invented yet, so Ambrose carefully formed his letters using pen and ink and a frame around his letters for a guide, like this..."

The video cuts to shots of Mina writing using a stiff card-board frame with a string across it to define the lines of the page. Of course, I roped Mina, and Quoth into working on this project with me. They were only too happy to help, especially when Edward explained, through me, what it could mean for Ambrose.

Beside me, Ambrose has gone very stiff.

On-screen, I continue. "Ambrose's memoirs were published in 1879. They were initially a hit, but later, the novelty of a blind traveller wore off and critics began to discredit his eloquent words by claiming a blind man couldn't possibly write with his authority and imagination. Ambrose Hulme's work faded into obscurity, and his book went out of print."

Quoth had added a fade-to-black transition and some sad music that made Ambrose smile.

"Despite this, Ambrose's yen for travel and adventure never wavered. He took his meagre book royalties and used those to fund passage to Russia, where he sought to find a passage across Siberia, only to be met with the Tsar's soldiers. They did not believe he was a blind man who wished to see the world, and had him executed as a British spy. And there ended the life of one of the most remarkable explorers of the nineteenth century. With an active mind and a curious, energetic spirit, Ambrose had broken a record for the furthest one man had travelled around the globe on foot, and he is also one of the very first people who travelled for the sheer joy of it. I think..." On the screen, my voice wavers. "I think if he were alive today, he'd be the life of every party, and a wonderful friend."

Ambrose sits rigid, his hands folded neatly in his lap, everything about him taut. His eyes water. He doesn't try to blink away the tears as they pour down his cheeks.

"Join my channel for more videos about life and death at the Grimdale graveyard." I wave at the screen. "And please spread the word about Ambrose Hulme and Grimdale Cemetery tours."

The video loops and starts playing again. I pause it. I don't say anything.

"Bree...what is this?" Ambrose turns toward me, his cheeks streaked with tears.

"It's a video we filmed for the Grimdale Cemetery Instagram," I say. "It's about you."

"I hear that, but...but when did you do this?"

"Today." I lean forward and pick up the leather-bound

journal from the table. "Edward helped me write the script, and Mina and Quoth helped to film and edit it. They're all much more artistic than me. I'm thinking of hiring them to do the Grimdale history project full-time."

The faintest glow shimmers around Ambrose. His silver cord twitches, jerking toward the object I hold in my hands.

"But why? The project was supposed to be about the most famous and remarkable graves at Grimdale—"

"Why? Because you're *remarkable*, Ambrose. You are wonderful, and no one ever appreciated you in your first life. So many of us spend our lives wishing for a second chance. But even though you were ripped off because people couldn't see past your blindness as a novelty to appreciate you as a person, you never have wished to do it over. You have always been content with what is. Well, today, you get your second chance. Edward and I...we want everyone in the whole world to hear your story. And it's working, better than we could ever have imagined."

"Bree, something's happening to me."

Ambrose holds his stomach, where the silver cord stretches and unfurls, coiling between us. Silver light pours from his eyes, from his open lips. The tears on his cheeks turn to rivers of silver, and I don't think I've seen anything more beautiful.

I follow his silver cord until it plunges into my own chest, and I grit my teeth as it pulls taut. The pain shoots through my body, but this time, I'm ready for it. A familiar fear rattles in my heart, that I don't know what I'm doing, that I will accidentally send Ambrose away instead of bringing him to me. But I hold strong.

I know who I am now.

"Ambrose, we have so much to tell you." I look over at Edward, who smiles broadly – not his self-satisfied smirk, but a real, genuine smile. We have had the best day. "We put this video up this morning, and it's already gone viral. It's had over twenty-five thousand views. Hundreds of people have commented on it. Mr. Pitts says that the phone's been ringing off the hook with people booking cemetery tours. Someone's asking about a documentary. And that's not all…" I grit my teeth through the pain as I raise my phone to click through a button to another site. "Mina helped me to set up this page. It's for people to take pre-orders of your book. We've already sold eighty-two copies…"

"What book?" Ambrose's eyes darken. "I don't have a book."

"You do. A memoir about your adventures."

Ambrose's body shimmers with light. He looks a little queasy. "But the only copy of my manuscript burned in the fire."

I drop the leather-bound volume in his lap. Ambrose yelps in surprise and the book falls through him and lands on the sofa with a *plop*. I should feel at least a little guilty, but the silver cord wraps tighter and tighter, and now I feel only him – his love for me stretching across the void that separates us.

"That's your book," Edward says stiffly. "I found it hidden in the piano in the attic. You put it away there for safekeeping and forgot about it. I saw you do it before you left for your Russia trip."

"You saw me hide my book?" Ambrose's eyes widen as he leaps away from the book as if it might bite him. "When I was alive?"

"Yes, and I should have told you about it, but I didn't." Edward stares at his shoes. "It was wrong of me. I realized then that if you had the book, your unfinished business would be complete and you'd cross over and leave me all alone with Pax again. And the Roman might be cool—"

"I am cool!" Pax calls out.

"He isn't...that is..." Edward coughs. "He and I have a different kind of friendship. I did not want to lose you."

Ambrose swallows. His whole body glows with light. "I understand. I don't want to lose you, either."

"No, you don't understand. I should have said something sooner, on the very day that Brianna made Pax Living! I should have said something earlier than that. I should have given you the choice—"

"You have nothing to be sorry for," Ambrose says.

"I have *everything* to be sorry for," Edward rages. "At first I was afraid of losing you, but then, I was jealous. Pax got to touch Brianna. He got to be with her in all the ways that I have hungered for her since she returned to us. All I have longed for in these years of exile between the living and the dead is the kind of love that would make a true poet of me. And now I have that love but I...I cannot touch it. I cannot make it real. All the relationships I had in my life were because people wanted something from me. My friends cared for me only because I kept the party going and the absinthe flowing freely. My string of adoring countesses were enamoured of my wicked tongue and the things it could do to them, but they never knew my heart as Brianna knows it, as you and Pax know it. I had everything in life, and yet I still managed to squander it all. So what could I possibly wish for so hard in death that it tethers me to this place for eternity? There is no answer to that question, for the truth is that I am not a ghost because I have unfinished business, but as the ultimate punishment for my sins."

Ambrose reaches for his friend. "Oh, Edward, no—"

Edward backs away and continues talking. "Do not feel sorry for me. I have accepted the truth of it now. But when I found the book, I knew it meant that Brianna could bring you back, too, and I didn't want to be the only one left as a remnant. I didn't think I was strong enough to endure the torture of it. And so I kept it hidden. But now I know that I can endure anything if I can have but a taste of Brianna's love. And so, I want you to have what I can never have. I was not a good friend to either of you. For that, I apologise. To make it up to you, I shall write an epic poem immortalizing my distress—"

"No!" Edward, Ambrose and I yell in unison.

The room fades from my vision as the silver light spools around me. The tightening in my chest becomes unbearable, and I gasp for breath. But I keep holding on, keep winding tight the silver thread that tethers Ambrose to me and to the Living world. The light welcomes him inside, envelopes him in my magic, and his life runs through my fingers, decades of unlived time still waiting for him...

"Thank you, my friend." Ambrose's eyes fill with starlight tears. "Thank you for this gift. Thank you for not telling me before, where on my darkest days I may have chosen to leave this place forever, and I would never have met Bree, and I wouldn't have this moment, right now, with you. Thank you... thank...heavens, but I do feel strange...and has it got bright in here all of a sudden..."

Ambrose reaches for Edward, his limbs encircled in the silver light. As he moves, the light moves with him, tugging at—

"I..." Edward looks away. His shoulders shudder, and I see that he's struggling to hold in his emotions. But when he turns back to Ambrose, he's wearing that typical Edward grin. "Why, Ambrose, silver is an excellent colour on you."

Pax laughs. I can't smile because Ambrose's cord is tugging so hard that I gasp for breath.

Ambrose leans down gingerly, brushing his fingers over the book.

"Bree..." His eyes flutter shut, his long lashes. "I can feel the book. *Truly* feel it. I must be dreaming. This can't be real. But I'm a ghost. I don't dream."

"This is real." I smile as the cord squeezes tighter, until I am drowning in light. I bite down my fear. *I know what I am now.* "And soon, you'll be real, too."

"I..." Ambrose bows his head as his fingers reach for the cord. "I feel strange."

I step in close, the way I had with Pax. And I plant my lips to his. This time, when I feel the cord wrapping around us, I don't try and fight it. I'm still terrified that I'll do something wrong and I'll lose Ambrose forever, but his lips on mine are loving and trusting.

The light shimmers and glows, until Grimwood and Edward and Pax disappear completely, until nothing exists but me and Ambrose and the tugging on my heart as the cord winds and winds and winds and...

And then a hard, warm body is pressed against mine, and the lips that devour me are sweet, and soft, and *real*.

"Bree?" Ambrose's eyes fill with wonder.

"Ambrose."

He's even more beautiful in real life. His hair is strings of glimmering starlight, and his azure eyes dance with mischief. But it's his scent that captures me – that fresh, zesty, sunshine scent of a Mediterranean adventure making me dizzy with the reality of him.

Ambrose raises his hand to his cheek, his fingers touching his no-longer see-through skin. He moves to my cheek, using his thumb to rub along the length of my jaw. He wets his finger on my lips, and his face breaks out into the most exquisite smile.

"I'm alive," he breathes.

"And Living looks damn good on you."

My heart swells.

I did it.

I did it and Ambrose is here with me, *alive.* He's not the only one who gets a second chance.

The cord that stretches from his chest is no longer completely silver, but it glows with a bright blue sheen, the way Pax's does. I wonder if blue light means someone who has had resurrection magic worked on them.

Ambrose's hand slips around my neck, and he pulls me into another sunshine kiss. When we come up for air, he continues to hold me against him. I press my head to his chest and listen to the *thud-thud-thud* of his heart.

"You feel...I feel..." he breathes. "Amazing. This is just amazing."

I pull back a little, looking at him all over, touching the beautiful soft fabric of his frock coat. "What do you want to do first?"

"Can I kiss you some more?" He looks like an excited puppy.

I laugh. "That's exactly what Pax did. But after the kissing?"

"I want to..." Ambrose's eyes light up. "Get on an aeroplane! No, eat an ice cream. No, swim in the ocean. No, pet Moon—"

"Meow!"

Moon leaps from a shadowed corner and darts from the room.

I laugh. "One thing at a time. As much as I'd love to go on an adventure with you, I have to stay in Grimdale and house-sit. I wouldn't feel right leaving until we know for sure that Jack the Ripper is definitely gone. And we'll have to wait for Moon to sit still long enough for pats. But the ice cream thing we can definitely sort out."

"I'm alive!" Ambrose takes my hands and dances me in a giddy circle, not even caring when he crashes into an end table and sends my mother's collection of Peter Rabbit figurines tumbling across the rug. The blue light in his silver cord pulses joyfully. "I'm alive and we're going to have ice cream—"

He's interrupted by the heavy thud of the front door.

"Who's that?" Edward snaps. "It better not be Ozzy deciding to learn the drums."

"SQUEAK!"

BANG-BANG-BANG.

"I swear, bat," Edward waves his fist in the air, "if I had corporeal limbs and magical powers, I'd curse you to forever be forced to hang out with actors, and that you will often walk into a room where everyone is laughing, but no one will tell you why. Oh, and may you forever sign up for annoying moving picture subscription services that are impossible to cancel—"

His empty threats cease as a familiar voice echoes through the house.

"Yooohooo, Bree darling. We're ho-ome!"

IO

BREE

"Mum?"

I close my eyes. This can't be happening. Not now. Not when I have a missing B&B guest and I *still* haven't mopped up the bloodstain on the floor.

And Ambrose...

I glance over at him. He's frozen in place, his joy at becoming human turning to terror. He reaches out with a shaking hand to me. "Your parents," he whispers.

I stagger back, accidentally crushing Benjamin Bunny beneath my boot.

"I get to meet Bree's parents!" Pax jumps up and down, causing all the furniture to shake.

Oh no, oh no no no no no...

Panic sinks in as I realize that my parents are home and I have two recently Alived ghosts who have no idea how to act in the modern world, let alone in front of my *parents*. At least Ambrose has perfect, if somewhat old-fashioned, manners. But Pax...

"No, wait—"

But there's no stopping my excitable Roman, who skips out the door, leather sandals slapping against his feet.

Edward looks at me with something like pity. "You probably should stop him before he challenges your father to an arm-wrestling match."

"Thanks for that, Captain Obvious."

I race after Pax, but then I hear a crash behind me, followed by a sad, "Oops, drat and botherations. I hope that wasn't Sylvie's favourite figurine." Great. I forgot that Ambrose can't exactly walk through objects he can't see anymore. I race back, grab his arm, and yank him after me while he frantically swings his stick around his ankles in an attempt to quickly build a map of his surroundings.

I'm too late. Before I've reached the landing, I can hear Pax's voice booming through the entrance hall.

"Mike! Sylvie! I am Pax, Bree's boyfriend. I see the gods have blessed your journey. Did you march for many days? Did you visit Rome? Did you happen to hear anything about soldiers being back paid for their duties—"

"Mum, Dad!" I yell, hoping to cut Pax off. I race down the stairs, dragging Ambrose behind me. "You're home. *Why* are you home?"

Mum and Dad exchange a look. They're still standing in the doorway, with Pax's bulk blocking their entry to the house. Mum's wearing long shorts and a white t-shirt with 'I HEART PARIS' on it, and a travel pillow is still nestled around her neck. Dad's wearing his favourite Who concert t-shirt and an expression of utter bewilderment, his hand clutched against his chest in that way he does now with his Parkinson's.

"Why, Bree-bug, we're so happy to see you, too," Dad says cheerfully.

"I didn't mean it like that. I just didn't expect you home for a few more weeks." (*After* I'd figured out my life and made sure

Jack the Ripper wasn't going to return for a murderous rampage.)

"Oh, well, with all the murders and mayhem in Grimdale, we wanted to make sure that you were all right," Mum gushes as she surges forward and plops her suitcase down right on top of the bloodstain. "Besides, we had to get your father back in time for the Giant Vegetable Festival. They had to move the date up a few weeks because the raspberry harvest came early this year."

"The *what?*"

I'm trying to process this.

"The Grimdale Giant Vegetable Festival, of course," Dad says with a grin. "It's the whole reason you've been watering the cucumbers in the greenhouse."

Cucumbers? Greenhouse? Do we even have a greenhouse?

Dad sees my vacant expression. "Bree-bug, you *have* been watering my cucumbers, haven't you? I told your mother to make sure you knew they needed a daily watering of no less than two litres of water and a regular feeding of fertiliser—"

"Oh, er..." Behind Dad's back, Mum makes a desperate face at me, the kind of face that says, 'I was so distracted with making sure I packed the right shoes that I forgot to tell you about the cucumbers. Please save me from your father's wrath.'

So I wrap my arms around Dad and squeeze.

"I'm so happy you're home," I whisper, burying my face in his shoulder. For a moment, I forget about dead priests and monsters and ghosts and cucumbers. All my worry and hurt and love rush back to me as I breathe in Dad's familiar, woodsy scent. I haven't hugged my daddy in five long years, and he smells exactly the same.

When he lifts his arms and hugs me back, he feels the same, too. A little older, a little thinner, but still the same man who kissed my skinned knees and helped with my science fair projects and participated in every silly Grimdale event. He's still my daddy. This disease hasn't taken everything from him.

"I missed you, Bree-bug," Dad whispers into my hair.

"I missed you, too." I swallow, trying not to cry. I didn't realise until this moment how much I've missed him.

Mum throws her arms around us both. Her scent mingles with Dad's – spicy and fruity, enhanced with an unfamiliar Italian perfume. Her silver bangles clatter on her wrist, and her no-nonsense expression softens as she kisses the top of my head.

"It's good to see you haven't burned the place down," she says as she pulls back. My mother has never been much for sentimentality when she has a to-do list running through her head. "Now, tell me, are they still making steak and kidney pie at the Goat? Because after all this foreign food what I'm craving for dinner is a good old-fashioned British meat pie."

"Oh, yes. Could we have meat pies?" Pax flexes his muscles. "According to the moving picture box, meat is good for my muscles."

"I haven't tasted a meat pie in a hundred-and-forty years," Ambrose says excitedly from the top of the stairs.

"At least you've actually tasted one," Edward scoffs. "When I was alive, it was all truffled pheasant and hare stuffed with manchet and comfits."

"We will go to the pub," Pax booms. "I will carry Ambrose so he doesn't trip over anything. And we will feast long into the night while Sylvie and Mike regale us with tales of their adventures and the enemies they've slain."

"I'm sorry?" Mum frowns at Pax before her gaze shifts to Ambrose. "Who are you again?"

Oh gods, here we go. I clear my throat, silently begging the two ex-ghosts to behave. "This is Pax. And that fellow on the stairs is Ambrose."

"How do you do?" Ambrose gives a small bow. He grips the balustrade with white knuckles and looks a little petrified. "I would come and shake your hand, but I dropped my stick and I've quite forgotten where the armchair is and I don't want to break any more figurines..."

"Wait, what figurines are broken?" Mum turns her gaze to me.

"Oh, ah, none of them. Don't worry. Ambrose is blind and he's a little unsure on his feet right now," I say. "Come inside and I'll find his stick for him and—"

"Yes, but what is he and this unwashed giant doing here?" Mum's nostrils flare. "Ambrose is dressed in a rather natty frock coat. Are you three going to a party? Which one is your date? Is the other one Dani's date? Oh, I knew we should have called first, but your father wanted to surprise you. Don't let your old folks get in your way."

"We're both Bree's dates," Pax says proudly. "We're her boyfriends."

Mum turns to me with a sharp look. "Both of them? You don't think that's a bit...greedy?"

"No, we're...I mean, they're..." I search for the words. Sometimes it's hard to keep up with Mum. "They're not my boyfriends. They're just friends of mine, from my travels. Yes, friends I met overseas. They're in Grimdale for a bit so we've been hanging out, and they've been staying in the unused guest rooms. That's it. Just friends."

Pax's face falls. I think Mum is too busy admiring Ambrose's coat to notice.

"And I'm Edward, your Prince of the Realm, your Lord and Master." Edward supplies in his insouciant tone as he floats down the staircase.

"What did you say, Bree-bug?" Dad looks confused.

Of course, my pockets are full of moldavite so they can hear Edward. This just keeps getting better.

"I was wondering if you're sick of pasta yet?" I add hastily. "Because I was thinking of heating some up. For dinner. That way you wouldn't have to go out."

Dad makes a face. "Please, no more pasta. After Italy, I feel as though my arteries are made of tagliatelle."

"And we don't need you to go to any bother for us," Mum waves her hand. "We might nip out for dinner and get an early night. Although we would love to get to know your not-boyfriends. We've just been visiting Innsbruck in Austria. Very dull, too much sausage and recycling, not enough sexy Italian men for my liking."

Edward extends his hand in front of Mum's face, knuckles facing up. "I will allow you to kneel and kiss my ring."

"Did you um...do any fishing?" I add quickly, when Mum makes a puzzled face. "I heard that the fishing is very good in Innsbruck."

"In...Austria?" Dad looks confused. "It's landlocked. Are you alright, darling?"

"Don't fuss, Mike," Mum scolds. "Bree's still reeling from all the murders. Why else would she have all these boys staying in the house and look like she hasn't brushed her hair for days?"

Why indeed.

"Hey, where's the rug?" Dad frowns as he lifts Mum's suitcase. "I traded that rug with Albert for a handmade birdbath ten years ago. Did you move it? And what's this stain on the flagstones?"

"Oh, um, it's raspberry daiquiri mix," I say quickly. "Dani and I had a party that got a little raucous."

"I hope you weren't too loud," Mum admonishes me. "We have to think of our guest. Father Bryne probably doesn't enjoy your death rocker music."

"It's heavy metal, Mum, and Father Bryne left early. He was called away on an important church matter. I've tidied up his room." *And hopefully removed any evidence that a blind ghost accidentally shot him in the foyer.* "I'll get the stone professionally cleaned as soon as I—"

"Don't worry about it," Dad says with a smile. "I kind of like it. It makes the room look like something interesting happened here."

You have no idea.

"Mike, don't be ridiculous. Our guests don't want to see a huge red stain the moment they walk in the door. It looks like one of the Grimdale murders happened right here." Mum furrows her brow. "We'll get that cleaned up this week. Now, Pax, was it? If you're keen to make yourself useful, I have several suitcases that need bringing inside. And Ambrose, you can come down from the staircase and help Mike make us all a cup of tea. You may be blind but you have two working arms. Brianna, you'd better fetch him his stick, and you'd better not be rolling your eyes behind my back..."

II

BREE

I'm tugged from sleep by Entwhistle batting my eyelid and a desperate, all-consuming need for coffee. I glance at my phone – 10:14 – a thoroughly respectable time to be getting up. I drag myself out of bed (alone this time. Edward moped off to his boudoir and I managed to convince Pax and Ambrose to share one of the other guest rooms to keep up the story I told Mum about them being friends I met on my travels who we were putting up for a bit. Ambrose looked so gutted when we went our separate ways, but I'm not quite ready for my parents to find out what I get up to with my seventeenth-century ghost prince and two ex-spirits.), and follow a delicious, familiar scent toward the kitchen.

Down the hallway, a door opens. Pax stomps out, dressed in dark grey jeans and a black t-shirt that tugs at his huge chest and shoulder muscles. He drags Ambrose behind him, who is forced to wear the same outfit he's been wearing for the last hundred and fifty years because in all of yesterday's excitement Edward and I forgot to buy him some clothes. Poor Ambrose is trying to use his walking stick as a cane to dodge around the various pieces of junk shop furniture my father has painted in bright colours, but Pax is too excited to slow down for him. With the wondrous scent permeating the whole house, I don't blame him.

I fall in step behind them as we make our way to the kitchen. Mum stands over the stove, flipping bacon and sausages in the pan. Beside her, Dad butters toast. I still can't believe they're here, in the flesh.

"I've been craving a Full English," Dad says as he sets down a bowl. Baked beans slosh over the sides. "In Norway, it was nothing but herring for breakfast, lunch, and dinner. I've been dying for some beans and hash browns and black pudding."

"I am starving." Pax circles the table, heaping food onto his plate.

I collect a plate for Ambrose. "What do you want? There's bacon, hash browns, baked beans, fried tomato, black pudding..."

"Yes."

"And what about a—"

"*Yes*," he says with vehemence.

I grin as I fill his plate and coffee cup and direct him to a chair between Pax and my dad. It takes Ambrose a couple of attempts to remember how to use a knife and fork, but Mum and Dad are too busy whispering to themselves to notice. I fill my own plate, pour a huge mug of life-giving coffee, and sit down next to them, expecting Mum to start rattling off a list of jobs our strange guests can help us with around the place, but their heads are still bent together, their whispers tense.

"Mom? Dad?"

My stomach sinks as my parents turn to me, guilty expressions on their faces. This is *exactly* the way they looked when they video-called to tell me about Dad's Parkinson's diagnosis.

I drop my fork. "What? What is it now?"

"Nothing!" Mom says brightly. "Have more beans—"

"Mum, something's wrong."

"We shouldn't discuss it with guests at the table."

"I think Bree's boyfriends can handle it, Sylv," Dad says.

"They're not my boyfriends," I say quickly.

"We should just tell her, Sylv," Dad winces. "Bree deserves to know."

They exchange another long, meaningful look.

"Tell me what?" I snap.

Mum leans back in her chair, gripping her coffee cup so tight that her knuckles are white. "Honey, we have some news. Your father and I have decided to sell Grimwood Manor."

12

BREE

At first, the words make no sense. It's as if my mother has suddenly started speaking Basque or ancient Akkadian. I roll the syllables over on my tongue, trying to discern their meaning.

But all too soon, reality hits me. And I'd do anything to have those few blissful moments of ignorance back.

Beside me, Ambrose goes rigid. "Would you really get rid of Grimwood?"

"It's a funny joke, right?" Pax grabs his belly. "You pretend that you want to get rid of the old house, but actually you are going to let a camera crew from a moving picture story come in to give the place a makeover. Hahaha, so funny. You are real jokers."

But Pax isn't laughing with his eyes. He looks at me with such forlorn hope, as though I have the power to will my parents to change their minds.

"But...but why?" Raw panic swells into my chest.

"I didn't expect you to be upset." Mum reaches across the table to grab my hand, but I jerk it away.

"It's just a lot of house for us, Bree-bug," Dad says. "Something's always breaking or falling off, the lights are flickering worse than ever, no matter how many hours we spend cleaning, there's still dust everywhere, and the guests are becoming more demanding. Present company excepted."

"The lights are fine." I glare at Edward, who has the gumption to look suitably chastised.

"It's not just the lights." Mum rolls her eyes at the ceiling as she takes another sip of coffee. "Running the B&B is hard work, and we're not getting any younger. We'd like to do other things with our lives instead of being tied to Grimdale all year round. And with your father's Parkinson's, it's going to be harder for him to do the jobs that need to be done to keep this old house standing."

"I could help," I say. "That's what I've been doing all summer. I've been doing perfectly fine on my own."

"We're not going to ask you to give up your life and move back to Grimdale permanently." Mum's losing patience with the conversation. She and Dad have already made this decision and she needs me to get on board. I can practically see her to-do list scrolling behind her eyes. *Item 1. Tell Bree about house sale. Item 2. Cook more bacon since the enormous guy in the black t-shirt has eaten it all. Item 3. Get rid of mysterious stain on the foyer flagstones...*

"So that's it? You're just going to sell our *home*? But it's been in your family for generations. Your grandmother left it to you. Isn't that stomping on her legacy, giving up on your sacred duty—"

"It's just a house," Mum snaps. "Grandmother Elsie trusted me to do what was best for my family. She even left instructions in the will for certain protocols she wished to follow if a sale went through."

"It's *not* just a house." Tears prick in the corners of my eyes. "I grew up here. All my memories are here."

My whole life with the ghosts is *here*. And there's the little matter of Jack the Ripper and the Order of the Noble Death coming after us. I have to make sure he can't come back, but how can I do that if we have to move?

What if I can't figure out how to bring Edward back? What if we leave Grimdale for good? What if we go somewhere that he can't follow?

I glance over at Edward. Dark storms brew in his eyes as he has the same thought. Pax drums his fingers on the table, his expression miserable because he can't stab this problem away. Ambrose is barely paying attention. He's focused on his first Living breakfast in a hundred and fifty years. His fork hovers uncertainly over his plate, but I can't find the energy to move my limbs to help him.

"We didn't realize you felt this way about Grimwood, Bree-bug," Dad reaches across and squeezes Mum's hand. "You wanted nothing more than to get away from the house and this town, and you haven't been back here in five years. We thought you'd be—"

"Oh my gods!" Ambrose cries.

"What?" I whirl around. His fork is hanging out of his mouth, and his eyes are glazed over.

"You terrified me!" Mum clutches her chest.

"I spilt my tea," Dad reaches for a cloth to mop his shirt.

"Sorry." Ambrose grins sheepishly as he stabs another breakfast sausage. "This food is simply *divine*."

I push my chair out. "I have to go."

"Bree-bug, don't be like that. Let's talk about this." Dad peers at me with huge eyes. He plasters this silly expression on his face, the kind of face he'd make for me as a kid that never failed to cheer me up.

It won't work this time.

I spin around and stomp out to the garden.

"WHY ARE YOU FOLLOWING ME?" I growl at one spirit and two ex-ghosts as I trudge through Grimwood's overgrown vegetable gardens. The rows of raised beds butt up right on the edge of the Grimdale Wood. Over the years, the wilds have crept in to claim them. Vines twist around the beds, cracking the stone planters and snaking through the jungle of weeds and foxgloves that have taken up residence. Roots poke through the cobbled paths, creating an uneven surface that's making life rather difficult for Ambrose. He frowns as he pokes at the ground with his stick. Pax slips Ambrose's arm through his elbow and leads him toward me, Edward floating at the rear with a sullen expression on his too-pretty features.

"Because you're upset," Ambrose says.

"Because you haven't had an orgasm in at least twelve hours," Edward adds.

"Because you need to tell me who I should stab to make it better." Pax folds his arms over his barrel chest.

"No stabbing," I say automatically.

It's too much. It's all too much. I thought that after Father Bryne's confession and that one word – Lazarus – that things would be better. I have a name for what I am. But the name means nothing when my powers still make no sense, and when Pax nearly died, and I don't know if the Ripper can come back from where I sent him. And now I'm going to lose Grimwood, just when I came to see it as home...

I sink into a bed choked with foxgloves and peer up at the house. To most people, Grimwood is a scary, cold, creepy manor. To me, this is one place where I've always felt safe. Even when I was on the other side of the world, Grimwood and her ghosts called to me, tethering me to my past, my family, my secrets.

All my life I've told myself a story about why I left, a story I've repeated so many times that I've started to believe it. I left Grimdale because I wanted a chance to be normal.

And that's part of the truth, but it's never been the whole truth. I left to keep my home *safe*. Safe from me and my strange powers. Safe from me hurting the people I love, the way I hurt the ghosts so much that they left me.

If my parents sell it, I won't have a home anymore.

The thought is scarier than facing down a resurrected Victorian serial killer.

"I know it's upsetting, but there is always a positive way to look at things. We're not tied to the house anymore," Ambrose says helpfully. "Home can be wherever you rest your head. Wherever you want to go, we will make a new home with you."

"Speak for yourself," Edward mutters.

Ordinarily, Ambrose's suggestion would resonate with my vagabond soul. I glance to my right, across to the cemetery, where only two nights ago I had stabbed Jack the Ripper and buried Father Bryne's body in another man's grave. I think of Vera, and Penny Hatterly, and I know that I cannot run fast enough or far enough to stop the Order of the Noble Death from finding me.

But Ambrose is still stuck on the idea. He paces through the garden, his stick swinging wildly in front of him, getting tangled in the weeds. "With enough moldavite, we can take Edward anywhere with us, couldn't we? We could go to Egypt, or the Wild West, or this Bali place you were telling me about. We could have cocktails on the beach and...hey, what's this?"

His walking cane clangs against something metal. I glance

over and am nearly blinded by the sun reflecting off a flat surface. Is that...glass?

I stumble over and clear away some of the weeds to reveal several panes of dirty glass in a metal frame. The rest of the structure is completely buried beneath weeds and vines. "This must be the glasshouse Dad was talking about, where he's growing his cucumbers. I can't believe he's got anything to grow out here."

I try to shove open the door, but its too choked with weeds. Pax picks me up and plonks me down to one side, which the angry feminist inside me would object to if it weren't kind of hot watching him attack the weeds.

Edward turns his head to the side and smiles as he watches Pax tear out the thick weeds with his bare hands. "He may be annoying, but he is a glorious specimen."

"Yes, yes he is."

Pax makes short work of the weeds and yanks the greenhouse door open. Edward, Ambrose and I follow him inside. I'm surprised to see that the interior is relatively tidy. Dad must have cleaned it out before he started his giant vegetable experiment. A few weeds have crept through underneath, but the majority of the space is filled by two raised beds of cucumber plants.

The first bed has cucumbers of a normal size, although without me knowing they were here, the cucumbers have grown too large to taste good. Many have been pecked at by birds or insects.

But in the centre of the greenhouse is a remarkable sight – one enormous cucumber easily the size (and roughly the shape) of a basset hound.

It's magnificent. It's the largest cucumber I've ever seen, and that includes the one Pax carries around in his tunic...

Ahem, never mind.

But it's also in bad shape. The skin has started to wrinkle, and the leaves of the plant have shrivelled up and turned brown.

My mouth goes dry.

Dad must have worked so hard at this, and I let it die. How am I going to tell him—

Hang on, what's that?

I step up to the sizable fruit and place my hand on the surface. A faint silver thread dances across the shrivelled skin. It looks similar to the silver threads that come from the ghosts and from people, although it's a lot fainter.

My fingers tangle around the thread. I can barely feel it, but I close my eyes and concentrate. I close my fingers around the cord, and I give it a little tug.

"Brianna, what are you doing?" Edward asks mildly.

I can't explain it, but something inside me shifts as I hold that cord. A warmth that spreads from my chest down my arms and into my fingers. I'm tingly all over, as if I've just walked through a ghost.

"By Apollo's avaricious apples, it's *swelling*," Pax cries.

Stop it, Bree. Stop thinking filthy thoughts.

My eyes fly open. I can't believe it. The cucumber really *is* swelling. The skin smooths out and the brown spots fade. My fingers that hold the cord sizzle with energy, and the silver cord glows brighter, almost as bright as Edward's.

By the time I remove my hand, the cucumber looks as good as new.

"That's intriguing," Edward drawls.

Yes, it is.

I stare at my hand, unable to believe that once again, I brought back to life something dead. But how can that be? The cucumber doesn't have unfinished business.

"This cucumber would feed an entire legion!" Pax claps his

hands. "Let's take it inside. Bake-Off last week had an excellent recipe for cucumber frittata I want to try—"

I throw myself in front of it before Pax can cut into it with the knife he's no doubt concealed on his person. "No one is touching this cucumber. It goes from this greenhouse to the judging tent and that's final."

My life may be falling apart, but dammit, my dad *will* win the Grimdale Giant Vegetable Festival.

13

BREE

"Mr. Pitts, I'm terribly sorry, but I'm going to have to cancel my tours today. My parents have returned from their travels, and they've decided they're going to..." I can't bear to say the words. "...sell Grimwood, and they need me to help them prepare the house for the agent."

Mr. Pitts frowns. "Selling Grimwood? That's a terrible shame."

"Yeah." I have to look away so he doesn't see the tears brimming in my eyes. "It is."

"I do wish you'd told me sooner. Thanks to that Ambrose Hulme video you posted, I've got two busloads of tourists down from London and a school group and I hate to cancel on them this late. I suppose I can do the tours, but I was hoping to make a start on stabilising the Witches' Monument. It's starting to list to the side, and if we don't get on that, I'll have Health and Safety on my ass. And I've just discovered that there are loose flagstones in the Poet Prince's mausoleum which will need seeing to—"

"Not to worry." I step aside and gesture at Ambrose, who gives a deep bow. "This is my...um...my friend. His name is Ambrose too, isn't that a wild coincidence? Anyway, he's a local history buff and he's taken the tour several times. He'll have no problem leading the groups for me. And look, he even dressed for the occasion."

Mr. Pitts eyes widen as he takes in Ambrose's Victorian frock coat and pocket watch chain.

"Greetings, old chap." Ambrose switches his cane to his left hand and offers his right to Mr. Pitts.

"Er, yes, hello, Ambrose. You're the spitting image of...no, never mind. Thank you for filling in for Bree." Mr. Pitts shakes his hand, looking quizzically at me. I know he's trying to think of a nice way to ask Ambrose if he'll be able to navigate the cemetery on his own when he's blind. It's a testament to Mr. Pitts' character that he chooses not to ask this question at all.

"I appreciate the opportunity," Ambrose says. "The cemetery is very close to my heart. I know my way around these old paths, and I've even researched a few new stories I can use to delight our visitors."

"Wonderful. Okay, if you come with me to the ticket office, I'll show you where we keep the maps and brochures."

Mr. Pitts is going to trust us.

I give Ambrose a hug. "You're going to do wonderfully," I say. I watch him walk off with Mr. Pitts, chattering happily about his favourite graves, and I see Mr. Pitts already being utterly drawn in by Ambrose's charm. Satisfied that my tours are in good hands, I head back to the hole in the fence and slip through, taking the overgrown path back to Grimwood.

I reach the top of the hill and turn back toward the cemetery just as the first busload of tourists arrive. Ambrose greets them cheerfully, handing out brochures and making sure everyone purchases their tickets. Apparently, Mr. Pitts isn't the only one to notice his resemblance to the now internet-famous adventurer Ambrose Hulme, and several university-aged girls clamour to take selfies with him. A mother asks him about his clothing, and he starts to explain all the features. He shows the delighted children his pocket watch before leading them merrily off along Poet's Way.

He's going to do brilliantly.

Which is good, because what I told Mr. Pitts about my parents needing me was a fib. Mum and Dad have to clean the house top-to-bottom because it's going to be full of guests over the Grimdale Giant Vegetable Festival, so they don't want me cramping their style.

But as much as I love my job, I need to get serious about finding out more about the Order of the Noble Death – and answer the question of whether or not I've banished Jack the Ripper for good. And for that, I need the help of a mortuary expert and a vampire-slaying amateur sleuth.

"WELCOME TO NEVERMORE BOOKSHOP," Mina smiles as we enter the main room of the store. I'm told the bookshop used to be gloomy and dusty, but it certainly isn't that any longer. Every surface that isn't covered in books houses lamps of all shapes, sizes and styles, and fairy lights and LED strips outline the shelves. Mina and her guys have transformed the shop because Mina needs the lights to find her way around.

"Hi, Mina and Oscar. It's Bree, Pax, and Ambrose, and Edward is floating behind us," I say as I step inside. I learned that it's really helpful to announce yourself and any companions when you meet a blind person. Mina recognises my voice, but it's useful for her to know who else is with me, especially if she and I want to gossip about the guys, because it's only fair that she knows if they're there or not. "Sorry that we're late. We missed our first bus because *someone* got distracted smelling the flowers in Maggie's garden."

"Have you ever sniffed a freesia before?" Ambrose says. "I'd forgotten how absolutely delightful they are, like fresh strawberries."

"I can't say that I have, but bring me a bunch next time and we'll go to town." Mina finishes sticking Braille pricing labels on a stack of books, pushes her chair back, and grabs hold of Oscar's harness. "Heathcliff! It's your turn to man the desk. Try not to murder any customers while I'm gone."

"I make no promises." Mina's six-foot-four, smouldering beast of a grumpy lover – the villainous Heathcliff from *Wuthering Heights* (yes, really. It's a whole story) – stalks out of the back office and lowers himself into her vacated chair. Quoth flies from his perch on the antique chandelier and lands on Mina's shoulder as she and Oscar lead us upstairs.

We climb up two floors to the small flat where Mina, Heathcliff, Morrie, and Quoth live. It's filled with even more lamps and tons of silly LED signs that say things like 'What Would Moriarty Do?' and 'You Had Me At Morally Grey.'

"I've been redecorating," Mina says with a grin. "Heathcliff hates the signs, which is why I keep putting them up. Morrie commissioned a sign maker to create a giant portrait of himself, and he's going to hang it over Heathcliff's bed."

"Remind me not to be in Argleton when Heathcliff discovers it," I say with a smile.

Dani emerges out of the tiny flat kitchen with a platter of cheeses and stacks of cream doughnuts from the bakery on the corner. "All ready for our epic brainstorming session," she says. "Mina, do you want anything to drink? Morrie left you a bottle of wine on the counter."

My heart thuds. I haven't seen Dani since the night of the burying. She hasn't answered my texts. I don't know where we stand, but she's setting out nibbles and pouring drinks like nothing is wrong.

"Is it a Bordeaux?" Edward perks up. He and Mina's other lover Morrie (short for Moriarty. As in, James Moriarty, the villain from Sherlock Holmes.) share a taste for expensive alcohol.

"It's red. And you can't drink it anyway." Dani takes a giant bite of cream donut, getting a little on the end of her nose. "Hey, it's kind of fun being able to hear Edward now."

"Fun for whom?" Edward mutters as he moves to the window that overlooks Butcher Street. "You should all be grateful that I'm still a spectre with no earthly body, for my revenge list is long and my repertoire for torture extensive."

"Let's get onto this. I don't have much time before some bloke comes in and asks Heathcliff to recommend a book he can read on the train to make girls want to sleep with him, and Heathcliff's head explodes." Mina settles herself into one of the chairs beside the fire. "Bree, did you bring Vera's box? Quoth, can you unroll the murder board?"

A black cat leaps out of the way as I dump out the contents of my inheritance on the coffee table. Quoth soars up to a perch above the fireplace, inserts his beak through a small circle, and tugs down a large screen. Pinned to the screen are fabric swatches, red ribbons, and a photograph of two skeletons kissing on top of a wedding cake.

"Are you in the middle of another case?" I ask. "One possibly involving an overburdened wedding planner offing her difficult brides?"

"Oh, don't mind that, I forgot that Heathcliff is using the board for wedding planning. You can shuffle his stuff to the side." Mina waves her hand. "I'm praying to all the goddesses who will listen that my wedding day will be murder-free."

I spread out the objects from Vera's box on the table, and explain again what I saw and felt when we slayed Jack the Ripper. Dani writes a timeline on the murder board and pins up a picture she doodled of Father Bryne and his strange, spiky cross. I'm beyond touched at how into this she is.

"At least Father Bryne has given us something new – I have a name for what I am, and I know that there are more Lazarii out there. But before we go looking for them, our most pressing issue is to make sure that Jack the Ripper isn't going to come back. I believe that Father Bryne overheard us talking about Penny and sent the Ripper after her. I don't want anyone else to get hurt. So how do we use this strange assortment of objects to do that?"

Mina rolls the small velvet bag between her fingers. "This is filled with herbs, right? My friend Jo is a medical examiner. I can get her to analyse the contents in her lab and give us a list of exactly what's inside. I assume it's a spell of some kind, so if you know the ingredients of the spell, you can look up the exact recipe online and find out what it does."

"That's a good idea. Maybe it's a protection spell or...or...I don't know." I throw up my hands. "I can't believe we're even talking about *spells*."

"In Rome, you'd pay two obels for a spell-in-a-bag with a lovely golden cord like that," Pax says wistfully. "That's a top-tier curse, that is. I could never afford a nice curse-in-a-bag. I had to make do with tying a curse stone to the tip of my sword, and they always fell off."

"Surely the sword severing one's head is curse enough?" Edward asks with his trademark sardonic smile.

"You'd think so, but—ARGH."

Pax yelps as Quoth lands on the table, black feathers flying everywhere. The raven picks through the images and pulls one out – a man in a dark cloak has his hand in the air, and from his fingers come strings that tug on the limbs of another man, who is naked and dancing wildly across the page, his bare feet crushing a pile of skulls. Curls of smoke pour from the naked man's eyes and fingertips. Quoth taps his beak on the image, and I see that the cloaked man is wearing a cross around his neck that looks exactly like Father Bryne's.

I think she was trying to use these pictures to show you some of the creatures that might come after you and your powers, Quoth says inside my head.

"I hope not." I stare at the large pile of monsters littering the desk.

I think this image depicts a member of the Order, and one of their summoned servants, like the Ripper.

Mina speaks what Quoth said out loud, since only she and I can hear him in his raven form.

"I think Quoth's right," Dani says. "We never noticed before, but that man in the black robes looks like Father Bryne. The cross is the same. And Bryne controlled the Ripper, but Bree doesn't control Pax and Ambrose like that. I looked this up before and the internet says it's a revenant – a resurrected soul who is corrupted and controlled by another. And there's some writing beside the skulls, see? Maybe that tells us how to defeat him."

"Oh, excellent," I sigh. "Good thing we're all experts in Latin—"

"It says, 'A revenant is a foul and abominable creation, where the restless spirit of the deceased, once subjected to these dreadful incantations, may rise from the grave to fulfil such foul tasks as their master sets forth." Pax jabs a finger at the writing. "Or that could be a U, in which case it gives a recipe for a very delicious fish stew."

I lean forward. "Does it say anything else?"

Pax shakes his head.

"We don't need any more Latin when we have the internet." Dani taps away on her phone. "I came across revenants in my research, remember?"

"It's like a demon?"

"Not quite. A revenant is more like a zombie. It's someone who has died and been brought back to life again by a sorcerer or dark priest."

"So, Pax and Ambrose?" I bristle at the idea of being referred to as a 'sorcerer.'

"No. Revenants don't have souls. They operate on base instincts, which is why the Ripper was going around killing in the exact manner he used in his life. Their sorcerer controls them, and gifts them with unholy powers, whatever that means. Although, the revenant must stay near their sorcerer to be called on when they're needed."

"That makes sense," I say. "Both Father Bryne and the Ripper talked about having a connection, and the Order would want undead servants they can control."

Everything Dani says feels instinctively correct to me, as though it's knowledge I already possess but have somehow forgotten until this moment. I think about the sensation I had in the graveyard when I shoved the knife into the Ripper, and again when I pushed Pax's silver cord back through his lips. I knew *exactly* what to do, even though this is all completely new and utterly terrifying to me.

Dani continues. "When you sever the link to their sorcerer, the revenant loses the magic that protects them. They become completely mortal, and can then be killed by the same method as any other human."

Like with a knife through the heart.

"So the Ripper is gone for good?" Relief floods my veins.

"I'm not so sure." Dani's eyes flick over her phone screen. "Revenants are driven by a desire to relive the things they enjoyed in life. If their will is particularly strong, they may be able to return where 'the Veil is weak' without a master, to fulfil their life's purpose. And Jack the Ripper has only killed two victims."

"Three." I count them off. "Vera, Penny, and Pax. Just because I brought him back doesn't mean he didn't—"

—die.

I can't say the word. I don't even want to *think* it.

"Okay, so three victims," Mina says carefully. "Canonically, Jack the Ripper killed five women, although experts debate this heavily. There are as many as two hundred additional deaths that might be attributed to his blade. Don't ask me how I know this; when you're an amateur sleuth and you're dating literature's greatest criminal mastermind, you listen to a lot of true crime podcasts."

"Remind me not to get on your bad side," Edward says dryly.

"Hey, I heard him that time!" Mina says happily. "Edward, the only way you'll get on my bad side is if you come into the bookshop and ask me to match a book to your outfit."

I swallow hard, the panic rising so fast that I don't even register Mina's joke. "So the Ripper *could* come back without Father Bryne's help."

"According to the internet, which we all know is never wrong, he could." Dani frowns. "We don't know what they mean by this 'weak Veil' thing. A wedding?"

"It's a poetical metaphor," Edward says. "It's the shroud that separates the world of the dead from the world of the living."

"Thank you, Edward," Dani says, looking at a spot somewhere past Edward's right shoulder. "That was actually helpful. And maybe if the Veil is weak, it means that things can squeeze through."

"But we don't know where the Veil is weak," Ambrose says. "Maybe it's miles away from here. We can research it."

"And we should see if there are ways to protect against revenants," Mina says excitedly. She reaches down beside her chair and picks up a stack of dusty tomes, which she drops on the table. "These are all our fancy occult books, including at least one that is actually magical. Maybe there's something in there that can help ward off the Ripper or at least help Bree figure out how to control her Lazarus powers. Dani, I'll take over internet-sleuthing, since I can use my screen reader."

"Done."

Dani and I grab books and start flicking through them, although I have no idea what I'm looking for. Ambrose hovers behind Mina, listening with one of her earbuds as she scrolls through occult websites. Pax feeds Quoth berries, giggling as the bird eats them off the ends of his fingers. Edward stares out the window and sighs dramatically.

Dani plonks down on the sofa beside me, a heavy book spread across her lap. She engrosses herself in the book, not even looking at me, and I can't stand it anymore.

I swallow. "Dani, I..."

"Look at this guy!" Dani taps the page where a creature of shadow and smoke slithers across the ground like a serpent.

Curled horns grow out of its head, and it carries a whip made of fire. "It's called a Soul-Eater. Isn't that delightful?"

"*Dani.*"

"I know." Dani holds out her hand without even looking up from her book, and curls her pinkie finger around mine. "We have each others backs, and we bury the bodies."

"We bury the bodies." I wrap my pinkie around hers and we squeeze. My heart has never felt so full knowing that my best friend is back in my corner, even after I asked her to do an unspeakable thing.

"Hey," Dani turns to me with a big smile that makes my heart soar. "You know who'd be really good at researching this stuff? Alice."

My elation turns to alarm.

"What's that look for? Alice loves spooky old stuff. That's why she studied archaeology."

"True, but if I want Alice's help, I'd have to explain that I can commune with ghosts and that Vera was killed by Jack the Ripper and the guy who tore up her birthday party is really a Roman warrior back from the dead, and he helped her arrange *his own bones* for display."

"I think she'd believe you."

"Dani, *no.*" Raw panic surges through me. I've only just started to trust Alice again after all the shit that went down in high school. "I accept that Alice is not the same mean girl from high school. She's cool, and I'm happy that you two found each other. But I'm not ready to trust her with this secret. We'll figure this out ourselves."

"Okay." Dani nods. "That's fair. It's your story to tell. But you know, there's a simple solution here that you haven't considered. Do you need these dusty old books when you happen to have three bonafide witches in your life who could teach you how to use magic?"

Of course, the three witches.

Dani's right, they'd be a more direct source of knowledge. But do I really trust Agnes, Lottie, and Mary to help me learn about magic? They're just as likely to force me to spend all my time transmuting doughnuts for them to sniff. "We don't even know for a fact that they *are* real witches. Most of the women hanged for witchcraft were just ordinary civilians who fell foul of their neighbours and were the victims of horrible medieval smear campaigns—"

"Last week Lottie told you that she hexed a pig farmer who wouldn't give her a cup of flour so that whenever he went to the market to sell his meat, all that would come out of his mouth was oinking sounds. They're *witches.*" Dani grins. "You should ask them. What harm can they do?"

I shudder. *What harm can it do?*

Why does that sound like a warning?

14

BREE

The next day, I find the witches hanging around the village green. A man and woman were having a romantic picnic beside the duck pond, so Mary is busy sniffing their Scotch eggs while Agnes and Lottie heckled the man's kissing technique, which truth be told, *could* use a bit of work.

I hide in the foliage nearby and wave at them. "Pssst, over here."

Of course, the couple look up from their canoodling and see me just as I'm waving in their direction with leaves all through my hair. My cheeks flush with heat, and I press my mobile phone to my ear and yell, "No, still no signal here in the bushes. I'll try a little closer to the scout hall."

Right, Bree, good save. They don't think you're at all strange.

I hurry along the tree line. As soon as the couple turn back to feeding each other Scotch eggs, I start waving again. "Agnes, Lottie, Mary, over here…"

Finally, Mary notices me. She floats away from the picnic, hands on her hips. "What is it, Bree? I'm a little busy at the moment. Oooh, are those cucumber sandwiches…"

She whirls around and starts floating back again.

"Please, come back!"

"Hey lady, can I help you?" The bad-kisser looks like he's ready to call the police.

"Don't mind me," I fake-laugh, pulling twigs out of my hair as my heart hammers against my chest. "I'm just...er, looking for my lost puppy. Have you seen her? She's a white Pomeranian. Please come back little Ghostie, please?"

Finally, the three witches seem to get the idea. Mary sighs dramatically, Lottie pulls her head out of the picnic basket, and Agnes stops trying to yell into the woman's ear that she can do better. The three ghosts follow me deeper into the trees. I take a seat on a fallen log, hoping that we're far enough from the walking trail that no one will overhear me.

"I hope you have a very good reason for taking me away from the picnic," Mary says, rubbing her stomach. "And it better involve cupcakes."

I whip out the white bakery package I'd been hiding behind my back. "Your favourite – Maggie's red velvet with the butterscotch icing."

I open the lid and Lottie and Mary bury their heads inside, inhaling deeply. But Agnes narrows her eyes at me. "What do you want?"

"Excuse me?"

"You've never been nice to us or brought us cupcakes for no reason before. You want something."

"I'm always nice to you!"

Agnes narrows her eyes. I gulp. Agnes has what I refer to as Big Scary Horror Movie Ghost Who Will Tear Your Soul Out Through Your Nostril energy.

"Okay, okay, you got me. The cupcakes are a bribe."

"I'm amenable to bribes." Mary dives for the box, but I snap the lid shut.

"Hey!"

"Here's the thing." I set the box on the log next to me and wring my hands. "I've managed to bring both Pax and Ambrose back to life, and I even did it to Pax *twice*. I have a name for what I am now – a Lazarus. I know that I have resurrection magic, and I...I see things. I see silver cords stretching from people – both the Living and ghosts. They wind and tangle through the air around me, but I only see them sometimes. But I don't really know what I'm doing with the cords or how to control my powers, and that makes me afraid. I don't want to be afraid of this power. I want to learn how to control it. Will you...teach me how to use my magic?"

The three witches stare back at me,

"How *dare* you ask such a thing?" Mary snaps, her eyes glazing over.

"We were *killed* because people accused us of being witches," Lottie huffs, her hands on her hips. "And all we're trying to do is enjoy our afterlife when you have to come around here using the 'w' word and putting us off our picnic."

"Millions of innocent women were killed because people like you spread misinformation about witches. And you call yourself a feminist," Agnes sniffs.

I really wish I hadn't taught her that word.

My stomach twists. "I'm sorry. I didn't mean to—"

The three witches look at each other.

They burst out laughing.

Sigh. Witches.

"You should have seen your face!" Lottie gasps between giggles.

"You were redder than a red velvet cake," Mary chortles.

"I can't believe you fell for that," Agnes scolds. "That's hardly the kind of gumption we want in a new coven member."

I blink. "So you *are* witches?"

"Of course we're witches." Agnes waves her hand. "You couldn't be a woman in our day and not know a little magic. Otherwise life was thoroughly boring. Now, stand up and hand over those cupcakes. If we're going to teach a complete magical neophyte like you, we need fortification."

"So you'll help me?"

"Of course we will!" Lottie claps her hands.

"For a price," Agnes folds her arms.

"I brought you cupcakes!"

"That will do...for a start."

I sigh. *So close.* "What do you want? Another feast? My parents are home, so it will be difficult to arrange, but I suppose we could have a picnic."

"We want to be alive again," Agnes says.

"Like Pax and Ambrose," Lottie adds.

"I don't want to just sniff food anymore," Mary sighs, rubbing her belly. "I want to *taste* it."

"I want to find out if men have improved their lovemaking since I was a Living lass." Lottie's eyelashes flutter. "Although judging by that guy at the picnic back there, I'm not missing much..."

"Okay, yes, fine. I'll do what I can. You have to understand that to bring you back, I need to know your unfinished business. And right now, helping Edward and protecting this town from Jack the Ripper are my priorities. But if I can resurrect Edward, then I promise that I will attempt to help you discover your unfinished business and become Living again."

The three witches look at each other. Mary squeals with delight. Lottie leans forward and hugs me, which sends a warm tingle through my body.

"We have an accord." Agnes cracks her knuckles. "Now, let's make you a magic user worthy of burning at the stake."

15

BREE

"The first thing you need to know about magic is that it's in everything and everyone," says Lottie.

"Kind of how Lottie was when she was Living—OW, don't pinch my arm." Agnes glares at Lottie.

"Then don't derail our lesson. Now, as I was saying, magic is in everything—"

"—all witches do is slosh the magic around." Mary sweeps her arms through the air. "Like stirring the marshmallows into a hot chocolate...gosh, I can't wait until we're Living again and I can try a real hot chocolate..."

My very first magic lesson is off to a roaring start.

We're standing near the ancient altar where I found Pax's body. The archaeologists have finished with the site and replaced the dirt, but the grass hasn't grown back yet, so there's a bare patch that I try not to stare at while the witches bicker.

I lean back against the crumbling altar stones as the witches raise their arms and start walking in a circle around me, inspecting me as they waggle their fingers, kick out their legs, and chant strange words.

"I can see her aura," Lottie intones in a deep voice. "She's absolutely bursting with a kind of magic I've never seen."

"Surely you noticed this before?" I can't help but mutter. "Since you're all such magical geniuses."

"You disguised it well behind your generally gloomy disposition," Agnes growls. "Now, will you be quiet and let us concentrate?"

I sat back as they continued their reels, circling and chanting and humming and jerking their bodies spasmodically. I expected to see something odd, like silver light rising from them or wood sprites appearing to weave daisy crowns into their hair. I check over my body for any strange sensations, but all I feel is mildly foolish.

The witches dance faster and faster until they all fall over in the dirt.

"What did that achieve?" I ask as they pick themselves up. "Can I do magic on command now?"

"Heavens no." Agnes grinds her hips. "But it has loosened up these old arthritic joints."

"You can't have arthritis. You're a ghost!"

"Not according to *your* ghost rules, missy."

"Ailments, disabilities, and personality flaws don't get magically 'solved' when you die," explains Lottie. "That's why your friend Ambrose is still blind. Those things are part of us, they leave an imprint on our soul."

"Is that what ghosts are? Souls floating around without bodies?"

"It's actually interesting that you ask." Mary lifts her head from where she was sniffing a toadstool. "Pythagoras holds that the soul is of divine origin and therefore exists both before and after death, but Epicurus—"

"Are you here to debate the philosophy of death, or are we going to do some magic?" Agnes barks.

I leap off the altar and hold out my hands. "Go on then. Show me what to do."

"What do you want to do? Because if you plan on turning the Roman into a toad, then I must protest," Lottie licks her lips. "A man with that juicy a cucumber will be wasted as an amphibian."

"How do you know the word amphibian?"

"We watched it on a David Attenborough documentary through the Kingson's front window. That's also how Mary knows about souls. But you want to know about your magic and how to control it. You'd better begin by telling us exactly what you've experienced."

I explain to them all the times I've used my resurrection magic over the last few weeks. Agnes asks me to describe the silver threads I see as I look around, and she looks unamused when I tell her that I can't see any, not even theirs.

"I only see them sometimes," I say. "Such as right before the Ripper killed Pax, or when Arthur crossed over, or—"

"That's because you haven't figured out how to channel magic. You can only tap into your power when you're highly stressed or desperate," Lottie explains. "If an axe murderer or a witchfinder burst through the woods right now, you'd probably be able to knock him out with a single thought."

"Is that just the way my magic works?"

"No. You can learn to summon it at will. But you need to be able to focus even when there's not something terrible at stake."

"Let us begin." Agnes raises her arms again and says in a warbling, croaking voice, "Clear your mind."

"How do I do that?"

Agnes makes a face as if I'm a complete no-hoper. "You just...do. You think of nothing."

"How do I think of nothing?"

"I find it helps to have a place I go to in my mind, or an object to focus on." Mary closes her eyes and raises her hands, palms facing the sky. "It has to be something that gives you pleasant or neutral feelings. Not something scary or ugly. I think about a plate filled with delicious pastries. I think about that and whenever a distracting thought comes, I toss it away and continue to gaze at my pastries."

"I think about my husband's prick," Lottie adds helpfully. "Since it was nonexistent."

"Okay, I'll try it." I stand up tall and raise my hands, palms up, copying Mary. "I'm not thinking about Lottie's husband, though. Do I call on a goddess or something?"

"You can. It might help. Thinking of an entity helps some witches to focus. Equally, a nice beach or a delicious steak and kidney pie may do the job. It's up to the individual witch."

Ooooo-okay.

I do as they say. I close my eyes, and as I hold my hands out so my palms feel the warmth of the sun, I imagine all of my current problems flittering around me – they become little fire-flies dancing inside my head.

One by one, I wink them all out.

My parents selling the house. Wink. Edward's lack of corpo-real form. Wink. Pax's inability to stop thinking about stabbing for five minutes. Wink. When I wink out the last problem, my mind is dark and blank. But almost immediately, I can feel the worries and questions creeping back.

I need to fill it with something so I don't get distracted. Something *pleasant.* I want to think about the guys, but they're too close to all my issues right now. I need to go further back in time.

I pick a memory at random, one that always makes me smile. It's me and my dad in his workshop, painting the sides of a soap box racer he made me for the annual Grimdale Soap Box

Derby. He's got his old CD player (CDs! So cute) playing a Who album, and we've both singing along with 'My Generation' and 'Boris the Spider' while we paint.

Nothing much happens. It's just nice to hang out. I like the satisfying slap of the paintbrush against the wood, and my dad's warbling voice, completely off-key.

I open my eyes.

The world has changed.

The woods are overlaid by a lattice of silver cords. They wrap around trees and thread along the walking trails. A sparrow takes off from a nearby branch, her silver cord trailing behind her. There are even faint traces of silver running through the dirt, where each earthworm makes its path.

"I see them," I whisper. "The silver cords."

"That's a relief," Agnes mutters. "We almost didn't think you had it in you."

"Speak for yourself," Mary says. "I always knew Bree was one of us."

"What do I do now?" I ask, watching a mouse dragging his silver cord in circles around the base of a tree.

"Start small." Lottie points to a tiny plant that I'd stood on when I walked into the clearing. "Let the magic flow through you. Remember, it lives in everything – you're not creating something new, you're just moving things around. Your power wants to be used. It calls to you. You only have to listen."

I'm not sure any of that actually makes sense, but the silver cords stretching out of my chest hum with agreement. *Okay, we're doing this.*

I kneel down in front of the plant. It's completely dead, the stalk broken, the leaves hanging limply. A faint silver cord falls from the severed stalk, the end curling through the air as the cord fades...and fades...

I reach down and pinch the end of the cord before it can

disappear completely. I grasp it between my thumb and forefinger. It leaps and jerks in my hand, desperate to do...whatever it's supposed to do.

I connect the cord to the end of the stem, in a similar way to when I shoved Pax's cord back into his mouth. I look to the witches, silently asking if I have to kiss the plant, too. The cord wavers as I lose my grip on my magic, and I retreat back into my head, back to that lovely day with my dad painting the soap box racer.

And I know what to do.

I don't know how, and I can't exactly explain it, but as I dip my brush into the red paint, I kind of dip my fingers into the cord and the stem, and I *paint* them together with my mind. It's as if I'm making it so that cord and stem are no longer two separate things – one a dead plant, the other a random piece of magic I don't understand – but have become one again.

In the memory, Dad says, "That looks perfect, Bree-bug."

"Well, will you look at that," Agnes whistles through her crooked ghost teeth.

I stare down at the plant. The stem is no longer snapped but whole. The leaves unfurl, green and bright and tilting toward the dappled sunlight. The entire plant shimmers with silver light as the silver cord wraps tight around it and sinks back into its flesh.

"I did it!" I stand back, staring at the plant in awe. "I can't believe I did it."

"We never doubted you," Lottie says with a grin. "That was amazing."

Mary throws her arm around my shoulders, sending a warm tingle down my spine. "We'll make a witch of you yet, Bree Mortimer."

"Hmmmph. There's more to being a witch than bringing some poxy shrubbery back to life," Agnes grumbles. "I hope you're prepared for hours of chanting, memorising the properties of different herbs, and learning the precise recipe for mixing a potion without blowing your own eyebrows off. And, of course, you're not a *proper* witch until we've initiated you into our coven with a full moon, skyclad ritual."

"A what—"

"Oooh, that's my favourite ceremony," Lottie claps her hands in excitement. "We haven't had a proper skyclad dance in at least two hundred years. You'll love it, Bree. We all get stark naked and rub ourselves with—"

"Hang on, you never said anything about naked dancing!"

What have I got myself into?

16
PAX

Bree didn't want Edward and I along for her first magic lesson with the witches, and Ambrose had already left to take over her shift at the cemetery by the time Bree rose from her slumber.

Mike and Sylvie went out for the day – they're delivering small, ugly votive offerings they picked up on their travels called 'keyrings' and 'fridge magnets' that say things like 'My friend went to Italy and didn't take me.' When Sylvie showed them to me, I said that I'd gladly help her deliver them to her enemies, but she gave me an odd look and said that these were for her friends in the village. And I asked if they would still be her friends after receiving such cursed gifts, and she left in a huff.

I will never get used to the customs of Bree's people.

I spend the morning practising sword drills in the back yard. Edward spends it in his boudoir, practising his poetry and glaring at me out the window.

Mike returns home around lunchtime and heads off in the direction of the greenhouse. He walks differently now, with a little shuffle in his steps, and he wears a strange headdress made of straw on his head, probably something he must wear when giving his ritual offerings to Ceres for a bountiful harvest. I wave my sword at him and ask if he'd like to spar with me. He ducks beneath my blade, saying he needs to see if there's anything salvageable from his cucumbers.

He bounds back through the garden, his face aglow. "Bree was kidding about forgetting my cucumber! It looks amazing. She must have been watering it just right for it to grow so huge. I think I'm in for a real shot at winning first place at the Giant Vegetable Festival."

"Praise Ceres!" I exclaim, because Mike is happy, and that makes me happy, even though I don't understand why you would grow a giant cucumber that no one was allowed to eat.

Mike meets my eyes, and then he scans the sword, his brow furrowing. "So Pax, do you…do medieval re-enactment?"

I don't understand the question, but I can tell from the way he's looking at my sword that he's asking about it. "I stab things," I say helpfully, giving him a demonstration of some of my most valiant moves from the battlefield. "I can teach you, if you like. I've been teaching Bree, although she isn't very good. She keeps being distracted."

"Ah, maybe some other time. I need to get the lunch on before Sylvie gets back. But thank you, Pax." He pats me on the shoulder. "It's good to know that Bree's had you looking out for her while we've been gone."

I wave as he goes back into the house. I just had a real conversation with Mike! And he didn't guess that I'm really a Roman centurion. I am very good at being a modern human person.

I can't wait to tell Bree.

"You did *what?*" Bree screeches. "You tried to give my dad a sword-fighting lesson?"

"I'm surprised Mike didn't take him up on it." Edward winces as he passes through the wall of Bree's bedroom. "He does enjoy useless hobbies."

I waggle the tip of my blade at him. "You won't say this is useless when I stick it up your—"

"Would anyone like a scone?" Ambrose bellows from the doorway, a tray piled high with date scones and little jars of cream and jam balanced in one hand, while he raps his cane with the other. "I ran into Mike and Sylvie on the driveway. They were heading to the pub for quiz night, but Mike left these on the kitchen counter for us."

"Oooh." I take two, generously slathering them with butter, jam, and cream. I turn around to offer one to Bree, but she's staring at her phone screen and biting her lip.

"Uh-oh," Bree says.

"Who needs stabbing?" My hand flies to my sword.

"No one." Bree holds up her hand. "I've just had a text from Mum. 'Hi darling, we're two rounds in and our team is winning! We should be home around ten. Just a reminder that we have a real estate agent coming to appraise the house in the morning, and then I need to prepare the house for our next round of guests, so your friends won't be able to stay over again. Sing out if you want me to bring anything home, Mum.'"

"What does that mean?"

"It means that you can't sleep in the spare room."

"Where will we go?" Ambrose's lip trembles.

"The answer is simple. We will sleep in Bree's bed." I slap my hand on the iron bedhead. *This means she has to tell her parents that we're her boyfriends. Today is a good day!*

"You can't do that," she says, her voice sharp.

"But where will we go?" Ambrose's voice rises with panic. "I don't have any money for an inn, and I don't want to leave Grimdale. You and I haven't even...that is, we haven't..."

"He's trying to say that the two of you haven't had any rumpy-pumpy," Edward pipes up. "There has been a distinct lack of amorous congress, an absence of wick-dipping, a want of a bit of crumpet, a deficiency of debauchery, a shortage of shagging. The pink fortress has yet to be conquered, the beast with two backs has bolted from the stables, and all the trout in the peculiar river have swam away—"

"We get the idea, thank you, Edward. And that's not it at all. I swear." Bree's cheeks glow red as she clutches her phone. She squeezes Ambrose's hand. "I'm sorry. I know...I know that you've only just become a human, and I want nothing more than to share tonight with you. But I can't exactly tell Mum that the two of you have nowhere else to go. That's not how I endear her to you, especially since this has probably come about because Dad saw Pax training with his sword."

"What's wrong with training? I would dishonour myself before your father by *not* training. I wouldn't want to duel him and accidentally take an eye out."

"Pax, you're not duelling my father." Bree folds her arms. "You didn't challenge him to a duel, did you?"

I hang my head.

"Pax!"

"We've always lived here," I frown. "I don't want to leave, not even for a night. I have to stay nearby to watch over you. What if the Ripper comes back?"

"The witches don't think that he will. They say that the Veil is the invisible barrier between the living world and the dead world, and that it's perfectly thick and girthy around here. Lottie's words, not mine. Besides, I've been training all day." Bree flexes her fingers. "I've brought at least ten flowers back from the dead. I think I can take him."

She can't be serious?

"You *need* my sword." I thrust it out in front of her, like an offering. Bree *needs* me. She *must* need me. Because without her, I have no purpose.

"Pax, you're so much more than your sword. And you don't know my mother. This is a test. That's why she waited until 8PM at night to tell me you two can't stay. She wants to make sure that you're not sponging off me, and probably also that you're not insane, sword-wielding maniacs who will smash up the place the moment you're asked to leave." Bree buries her face in her hands. "I'll talk to her, I swear. But please, just for tonight, I need the two of you to sleep somewhere else."

"Fine. I shall take the guest room on the far end of the—"

"No! You can't." Bree's eyes are wild. "Mum has spent all afternoon cleaning those rooms for the real estate agent and the new guests. If a bed is so much as creased, she's going to know you slept there."

"We could sleep in my bedroom," Ambrose offers.

Bree shakes her head. "Pax's shoulders won't fit through the secret door."

"Then where are we supposed to go?" Ambrose asks.

I know of only one place. "The attic."

"We have to go back to the attic?"

"I can't ask you to do that." Bree holds up her phone. "I'll call Dani. Or Mina. Someone will be able to take you in—"

"No, I'm not leaving you in this house with only Edward to protect you. The attic it is."

Bree kisses me on the cheek. "I guess...you'd better head up to bed then. Mum says that they'll be home in an hour or so." She stands on her tiptoes and leans in to brush her lips against mine. I can't help myself – I wrap my arms around her and hug her tight against me, as if I could crush her bones to my bones, make us one. My lips force hers open so that our tongues can dance, and when she pulls back, her eyes shine with lust and regret.

"I don't like this any more than you do, but it will only be temporary. I promise. I'll talk to Mum." Bree kisses my cheek. Her lips leave a warm impression against my skin that I hope never, ever fades. "And Pax, please be quiet up there. If there are a few random noises, my parents will assume they're from mice, but mice don't sound the same as a seven-foot-tall Roman warrior stomping around the attic, okay?"

"Okay."

I can be quiet when I need to be. I got my Stealth badge at Centurion Scouts, too.

Bree turns to Ambrose, pulling his body against hers for a lingering kiss. "I promise, we will have our – how did Edward so eloquently put it – amorous congress very soon."

"Goodnight, then!" Edward calls in his smug voice. I glare at him when I realise that, as a ghost, he gets to stay in Bree's bedroom.

"Edward, perhaps you don't want to make Pax angry, as he has once threatened to push a straw through your nostril and drink all your bone marrow."

Edward gulps. "Right, yes. Well, then, sleep well, Roman. Don't let the, er, bedbugs bite."

Ambrose stops at a small cupboard in the hallway to collect an armload of blankets. He holds onto my arm as we trudge up the staircase. At the top, I yank open the door to the attic staircase so hard that the handle cracks the wood panelling.

"I think we're supposed to be *quiet*," Ambrose says as I stomp up the stairs.

"I *am* being quiet." I shove the attic hatch open. It clatters against the floor. I haul myself up and turn to help Ambrose. He cries in surprise as I lift him under the elbows and haul him into the attic, dropping him on the floorboards and sending up a cloud of dust.

"Er, thank you kindly, Pax." Ambrose brushes dust off his frock coat. "But I'm fine and dandy to climb up here on my own. I'm blind, not an invalid."

"Sorry. I'm a little on edge." I flick on the light and look around. "We haven't been up here since—"

"I know," Ambrose says dejectedly. "Only now that we're human, it's worse, as our bodies have human needs. I don't recall there being a bed up here. Or a latrine."

"In Rome, if we didn't have a house with pipes, we'd throw our business out a window into the street."

"Yes, that was the custom in London, too, even if one's home *did* have pipes," Ambrose says wistfully. "There was even an unofficial points system. I once got a perfect score for hitting the king's footman in the face. A complete fluke, you understand. But I relieved myself after dinner, so a bed is the most pressing matter—"

"A soldier is used to sleeping anywhere he lays his head," I say as I lean up against the piano. Ow. It wasn't exactly comfortable compared to the linen sheets and memory foam mattress I'd been sleeping on since I arrived in the Land of the Living.

"Well, I'm most pleased for you." Ambrose unfolds the stack of blankets he's brought upstairs into what looks like a surprisingly comfortable bed. I debate asking if he'll let me snuggle up with him, but realize it's pointless. I won't sleep tonight, not while I'm here in the attic with...

...Ozzy.

He's up here somewhere, I know he is...

There. Hanging from that rafter, pretending to be asleep but watching us out of one half-closed beady eye.

I suppress a shudder.

I watch Ambrose doze off, my eyes never leaving the little furry Druid-butt, poised for the moment he decides to strike. Opposite the piano is a small, grimy window that looks down onto Grimwood Crescent. The porch light flickers on, and I hear voices raised with laughter as Sylvie and Mike arrive home. Then the light flickers off and I'm plunged into darkness once more, the only sound Ambrose's laboured breathing, the only light the pale moon reflecting in Ozzy's beady eyes.

I think about Edward, sound asleep in Bree's bed, or perhaps not even sound asleep but busy with amorous congress, oblivious to our toils because he's still a ghost—

Something horrible hits me.

"Psst, Ambrose."

"Pax?"

"Are you awake?"

"I am now. What is the matter?"

"If the real estate agent is coming, then we don't have much time."

"Time for..."

"Time to figure out Edward's unfinished business."

"What does that have to do with the real estate agent?"

"If Mike and Sylvie sell Grimwood Manor, we'll all have to leave. And then we can't go poking around into Edward's business, especially since he won't be able to leave with us."

Ambrose sits up. The moonlight casts his face in long shadows. "You're right. There's a very good chance that Edward's unfinished business has to do with this house. But if Mike and

Sylvie sell, we won't be able to solve it without access to the house *or* Edward. He'll be stuck as a ghost forever."

"And we don't want that?"

"No," Ambrose says firmly. "We don't want that."

"But think how annoying he will be as a human."

"Bree wants him," Ambrose says simply.

He's right. If Bree wants Edward, then I will do anything in my power to give her what she wants. Even if I do sometimes secretly wish I could braid his muscles into a long cord and play jump rope with it.

"Perhaps we can solve this before the sale. You've known Edward the longest – you have no ideas?" Ambrose sits up, folding his feet under himself and wrapping the blanket around his shoulders. I settle back against the piano and wrap my hands around my knees.

"I have already exhausted my ideas." I unsheath my sword and turn it under the beam of moonlight, admiring the way that the pale light throws rainbow prisms against the steel surface. "All the years when it was just the two of us, when he mocked my sandals, and claimed that English cooking is better than Italian cuisine, I have thought nothing more of solving his unfinished business so we could get a little peace. The number of times I've pushed him out of windows just to see if that made the gods realise they'd made a mistake keeping him as a ghost, but I could never come to an answer."

Ambrose's mouth makes a grim line. "Edward's business is the most difficult of all. With me and you, we both had things in our lives that were important to us – I had to tell my story, and you had to know your men respected you enough to give you a proper burial. But nothing was important to Edward except for drinking and *amorous congress* and his terrible poetry, and I can't think how any of those things could be unfinished business, since he literally finished every bottle—"

A small, dark shape drops from the ceiling in front of my eyes. I shriek and dive for the safety of Ambrose's blankets, sending a stack of boxes crashing to the floor.

"Pax, we're supposed to be quiet," Ambrose hisses. He tries to disentangle me from his bed, but I burrow deeper. *It really is quite warm and cosy under here.*

"It's Ozzy. He tried to attack me."

"Oh." Ambrose shudders against me. "What's he doing now?"

I peel back the edge of the blanket and look. "Nothing. He's just standing on the piano, staring at us."

"Oh." Ambrose slowly lowers the blanket. His chin quivers. "Hello, Ozzy. We're sorry for bothering you. We'll only be here a night, and I promise Pax won't make any more annoying sounds—"

"Sssssh." I clamp my hand over Ambrose's mouth, my eyes fixed on Ozzy.

The fuzzy little devil is moving *now*. He jumps up and down. He grabs his throat with his own hands. He makes a face with his tongue poking out and topples backwards off the edge of the piano. I lunge for him, but he rights himself mid-fall and floats to the floor, holding his ass.

Right in the spot where a glass shard stuck out of Edward.

"I think...I think that Ozzy is trying to tell us something."

I lean forward.

Ozzy starts his dance again, his wings spread out as he hops from one foot to the other, waving his tiny fingers around. He kind of looks as though he's pushing an invisible person. Then he jabs his wingtip at the window, where Grimdale Cemetery slumbers beneath the pale moon, while his other hand wraps around his neck so that his eyes bug out.

He's choking himself.

No. He's being choked.

And then he falls off the piano again.

And again.

I'm a warrior – I recognise an attack, even if it's been badly acted by a furry little woe wizard.

"I think Ozzy is telling us that he saw Edward's death," I say as I lift up Ambrose's blankets and snuggle down inside. "Edward didn't just drunkenly fall out the window. He was *pushed*."

17

AMBROSE

"We have to tell Bree." Pax thumps his fist on the floor, rattling the beams.

That's exactly what I'm thinking.

The real, corporeal human heart I now possess is racing. This is *big*. Monumental. In all the centuries the three of us have been together in this house, we have never had a clue about Edward's unfinished business. But we'd never thought to ask Ozzy before.

"Thank you." I hold out my hand toward where I think Ozzy is. A moment later, my skin tingles where two little clawed ghost feet hop across my hand. How strange to be on the other side once again and feel a ghost!

"What are you doing?" Pax demands. "Why are you being friendly with that fuzzy demon?"

I reach out with a finger and gently, warily, stroke the top of Ozzy's head. He leans into me, nuzzling my hand with his. His face goes a little bit of the way inside my skin, and he makes a contented little squeak.

He feels warm and tingly and soft and...quite nice, actually.

Ozzy's body vibrates and he lets out another little squeak.

His head falls deeper into my hand and suddenly, I feel ashamed of how we treated him. If Ozzy saw Edward's death, then he's been in this house at least that long, up here in the attic, all by himself.

When we all moved up to the attic, Edward tried to shoo him away, and of *course* Ozzy reacted violently to protect the only part of the house that was his. I feel a pang of regret that we'd spent so many years being terrified and cowering in fear of him when really, all he wanted was for us to be his friends, too.

"Thank you, Ozzy," I say, scratching him under his ghosty chin.

"I cannot believe you're making friends with that servant of Hades."

"He helped us save Bree from Father Bryne," I say. "And now he's given us this information about Edward. I think that Ozzy is trying to bury the hatchet."

"I'll show him how to bury a hatchet—"

"Ssssssh."

"But this is good news?" Pax scrunches up his face. "We go downstairs immediately to show Bree what Ozzy told us, and then we can ask Edward and—"

"It is good news," I whisper, desperately trying to get him to stop talking in that booming voice of his. "But I can hear Mike and Sylvie in their bedroom. They're right below us. If we go downstairs, we'll wake them up and they'll know Bree is keeping us here. We have to wait until they leave to get their morning coffee."

"Hmmmph." Pax considers this. "Yes, perhaps you are right. We rest before we go into battle for Edward's mortality."

He grabs the corner of my blanket and yanks, taking most of it with him as he rolls over. A burly arm drapes across my chest. The weight of it is ecstatic for this newly minted Living ex-ghost. But it is also significant. I wonder if it will collapse my lungs.

I try to wriggle free, but Pax has a tight grip on me. "I suggest you don't wriggle about and wake me while I am visiting the land of Somnia," he murmurs as he snuggles his muscled chest against my back. "The last man who did that had his neck broken."

Ah. Note taken.

A few minutes later, Pax's snoring echoes through the attic.

Something brushes my shoulder. I jerk away. Ozzy makes a disgruntled squeak. I open my other arm and the little ghost bat crawls in beside me, folding his wings over his face, and goes straight to sleep.

"Ambrose? Pax?"

"Stay away from me, foul Druid!" Beside me, Pax jerks awake, arms flailing as he tries to toss off the blankets to scare away his invisible foe.

"It's just me, Pax. I came up to tell you that Mum and Dad have left to see if Maggie knows how to make a proper cup of Italian coffee, so you can come downstairs." Bree takes my hand and threads it through her arm. "I'm making drop scones. That is, if you want to get out of your cosy snuggle pile."

"I want drop scones!" Pax scrambles to untangle himself from the blankets. Bree pulls me free before he can take my head off.

"I also would appreciate some drop scones." I crick my head to the side. "And a neck massage."

"You are becoming more like Edward every day. Seriously,

you two are adorable, and I wish you could snuggle in my bed. But at least I've sorted out the issue for the moment so you won't have to sleep in the attic again." I hear Bree tapping on her phone with her free hand. "You're both going to stay with Mina in the bookshop."

"No. That's too far from the house," Pax frowns. "I won't be able to protect you."

"I don't want to be away from you, either," I say.

Especially not now, when I have just become a Living man again, and my body feels strange and ill-fitting except when I'm beside her.

"It's just until after all the guests for the Giant Vegetable Festival leave, and I can figure out how to tell my parents about us and…" Bree swallows. "I'll come and stay with you sometimes, I promise. And Mina will make it fun. Just don't annoy Heathcliff or let Morrie pull you into one of his schemes and you'll be fine."

"You'd better tell Mina that she needs to make room for one more," I say, as a little furry body burrows his way out from the collar of my coat.

"Oh, Ozzy, you're adorable." Bree pats him on the head, which he seems to like because his little ghost body vibrates, and he makes a low humming noise. "I don't think Ozzy will be able to come with you. The moldavite only works with me, and I don't know how powerful it is on non-human ghosts."

"I wasn't talking about Ozzy."

He squeaks in protest and I reach up and pat his head affectionately. Behind me, I hear Pax groan.

"Then who were you talking about?"

"We're going to solve Edward's unfinished business," I announce.

"I admire your enthusiasm, Ambrose, and we're definitely going to work on it. But I don't expect us to figure out Edward's unfinished business quickly. We have no clues and—"

"We do have a clue!" Ozzy squeaks in protest as Pax picks him off my shoulder. "Show Bree what you showed us."

"Squeak!"

"Show her! Don't make me fulfil my threat to tickle your kneecaps with your—"

"Squeeeeeeeak!"

I can't see what Ozzy's doing, but I can hear his little demon wings flapping and a loud *THONK* as he throws himself off the piano again. A few moments later, Bree whispers, "Is he saying what I think he's saying?"

"He doesn't say anything except squeaks."

"Yes, thank you, Pax. I mean, is Ozzy trying to tell me that Edward was murdered?"

"I think so."

I hear another *THONK* as Ozzy demonstrates again.

"I wonder if there's a way to confirm this...Ozzy, come here." I feel Bree lean forward. "I saw a memory of yours once. If you let me touch you, can you show me again?"

"Squeak."

"Thank you. You're so kind."

Everything goes silent for a few moments. Then Bree lets out a huge sob. Pax and I both reach for her, but she pushes us gently away.

"It's okay. I'm fine. I saw what Ozzy saw that night from his perch on the chandelier in the hallway. Edward *was* arguing with someone in his room – I couldn't see his face. And then there was a struggle, and Edward yells 'I'll get it!' or 'I'll get you!' and then a sickening crash as the glass broke. The expression on his face was..." Bree shudders. "Horrible."

"But we know it's true – someone pushed Edward."

"Yes. I think that he held him by the neck. Edward has a small bruise on his collarbone. I've noticed it before but never said anything about it. You know how sensitive he is about his looks." Bree squeezes my hand. "While I was in Ozzy's head, I *also* saw that the three of you stormed into Ozzy's attic home seven years ago, took over his favourite sleeping spots, threw out his rat corpse collection, and then Edward called him a 'plague-carrier' and threatened to drown him in the gutter."

"Yes...er, we're sorry about that, Ozzy," Pax says sullenly.

"Yes, we're most sorry."

"So to get you back, he..." Bree collapses in giggles. "Oh, Ozzy, that's genius."

I wince. "He'd better not be showing you that incident with the grandfather clock."

"Or the time with the peacock feather," Pax roars. "That wasn't playing fair!"

"Pax, I've never seen your face so red." Bree must scoop Ozzy up, because he squeaks with happiness. "Ozzy is a *genius* and he's officially part of our team. Hell, maybe once we bring Edward back, we can figure out his unfinished business next."

"Squeak!"

"It sounds like Ozzy would like that," I say.

"I don't see why I should help that spawn of Hades," Pax growls.

"Because I want you to," Bree says. "But first, we have to figure out what to do about this new information about Edward."

"I believe that Edward's unfinished business is to figure out who murdered him." I rub my hands together gleefully. I love a good mystery. "So it's simple – we solve the murder, and you can use your resurrection powers to bring him back."

"You want us to solve a four-hundred-year-old mystery that's eluded even the most illustrious royal scholars?" Bree leans over and squeezes my hand. "Fine. Okay. Let's go find Edward. He can tell us all about which of his friends disliked him enough to shove him out a window."

"I don't think we should tell him," I say. "I think we should make it a surprise."

"Oh, I love surprises," Pax claps his hands. "I once put the head of a Celtic king into a clay pot and gave the pot to his mother. It was a big surprise!"

Bree laughs despite herself. "That's not quite the surprise Ambrose has planned. But shouldn't we tell him?"

"What if we get it wrong? I don't want to get Edward's hopes up if we chase a dead end. He's convinced himself it's impossible, but we know it's not." I squeeze her hand back. She feels so amazing, so *real*. "Nothing is impossible with you, Bree."

When Bree speaks to me, her voice is soft. "Ambrose, why do you want to do this for him? After he kept the secret of your book..."

"Because..." I shrug. "I think it will be more fun."

And it's true. I love being alive, and I can't wait to share all these remarkable feelings and sensations with my dear friend Edward. How can I possibly hate him for hiding that book from me? If he'd given it to me years ago, I would have crossed over and never have met Bree. I wouldn't be alive now.

Edward hates himself for what he did to me, but truly, he saved me.

"This plan is excellent," Pax says. "Legionnaire-level stuff, worthy of great Caesar himself. There is but one problem. How do we find out who might have wanted to kill Edward if we can't ask him? I suspect everyone who ever met him wanted to kill him, and that is a very long list."

"Well, it can only be people who were at Grimwood Manor that night," Bree says. "So that narrows down our suspects. I bet one of the history books has a guest list, although I wouldn't know the first thing about how to narrow it down."

"I bet we can figure it out. We don't need to ask Edward a

thing – Pax and I have been listening to him harp on about these so-called friends of his for years. We know everything there is to know about them."

Pax snorts. "You mean you listen when Edward talks?"

"Fine. *I* know everything about them. And Mina and Quoth could help, too. I think that between us, we can put together a list of suspects and start crossing them off."

Bree laughs and throws her arms around me. "Okay, Ambrose. We're going to do this. You're officially in charge of our Make Edward Human Again campaign."

I lean my head against her shoulder, revelling in the warmth of her arms around me, so solid and trusting. My stomach rumbles, a novel sensation that I remember indicates that I'm starving. I turn to Bree. "Did you say something about drop scones?"

18

BREE

"No. no, no, no. This won't do at all. We'll need to change out *all* this furniture for the staging."

Gwen, the real estate agent who's stepped into Annabel's shoes now that we put her behind bars for fraud, glares around the purple guest room, hands on hips.

"Why?"

The word slips from my mouth before I can stop it. Mum glares at me, but I don't take it back. There's nothing wrong with this room. It's one of our most popular guest rooms. Dad painted the walls a vibrant purple to match the purple and gold drapery Mum made. There's a heavy old four-poster bed and some old antique furniture we picked out at jumble sales, and Dad painted a mural on the wall behind the bed with a bunch of gold dancing flamingos.

Why would Gwen want to change it?

Gwen makes a face. "This room is too...kooky. With all these dark colours and this heavy wooden furniture, I feel like I'm on the set of the Addams Family. Today's buyers are looking for modern, light, airy. They don't want a lot of clutter everywhere. Trust me, all this..." she frowns as she gestures to a grinning monkey lamp my dad found on the side of the road, "...*personality* may work for the B&B guests, but buyers don't want to see it. We need to give them a blank canvas where they can imagine their own life."

I don't want them to imagine their own life. I want them to get out of ours.

"What do you propose?" Mum's taking notes on a little clipboard while Dad pats the monkey lamp lovingly on his fuzzy head.

"We'll paint all the bedrooms in a nice cream, something with a hint of warmth to it. I've got some furniture you can use for staging. You have that old outbuilding down the back of the garden? Put all this..." Gwen glares at the monkey lamp again, "...*flair* into it. I'll keep the prospective buyers away from the outbuilding – I can tell them there are spiders. Buyers hate spiders almost as much as they hate flamingo murals."

"We have to take out all the furniture?" I remember the day they purchased the bed frame, and Dad rigged a makeshift pulley system so we could winch it over the balcony since it wouldn't fit up the staircase. "How do you suggest we do that? Take the roof off and helicopter it out?"

"Bree, hush." Mum looks forlornly at her drapes. "The curtains, too?"

"Yes, definitely. And this *has* to go." She gestures to the mural.

"No," I say.

"I'm sorry, Bree, but this isn't about what you like anymore." Gwen puts on a voice that suggests she's had this conversation with a million other clients' stubborn daughters before. "These manor houses are notoriously difficult to sell. There aren't many buyers with the cash to take on the upkeep of an old property. If your parents want a hope in hell of getting a good price for this old pile, they're going to need to make some drastic decor changes. And that definitely includes any murals."

"But..." I glance at Mum for help. She's biting her lip. She doesn't want the mural painted over, either.

Pax's head appears around the door. "Is there a problem? I heard voices raised, which usually precedes an evisceration..."

"Pax?" Mum and Dad exchange a look. Dad's brow furrows, and I know he's thinking about Pax waving a sword around in the garden. I think Mum is, too, because her lips pull into a little smile and she grabs him by the hand and drags him into the room.

"Welcome, Pax, I didn't know you were coming over. Come in, come in. Gwen, this is Pax, Bree's boyfriend—"

"Not my boyfriend." If I claim Pax in front of my parents, then I'd be as good as rejecting the other two. Mum and Dad are pretty cool, but I don't think they're quite cool enough to accept me with three guys.

That's the reason why that word still makes my skin go cold and clammy, not because I don't want to have boyfriends.

Not at all.

"If you must know, yes there is a problem," Gwen huffs. "I'm trying to get the best results from this sale for the Mortimers, and your girlfriend is being very difficult."

"I'm *not* his girlfriend."

"Bree *can* be rather difficult." Pax's eyes bore into me as he strides across the room toward Gwen. "Stubborn, too."

"Exactly. She doesn't want to print over this rather dated and ghastly mural, which is going to turn off buyers—"

"But if Bree wants to keep the fresco, then the fresco stays."

"Young man, that's hardly your decision—"

"*The fresco stays.*" Pax cracks his knuckles.

Gwen gulps.

A dreadful silence descends upon the room, broken only by Pax's knuckles cracking, one by one.

I know I should run in and get Pax away, but I'm so touched that he's here to fight for me over a silly mural that I can't quite force my body to move.

Mum manages to regain her composure first. She places her arms over Gwen's shoulders and directs her toward the door. "Gwen, I'm sorry about this. Mike, could you take her into the kitchen and get her a cup of tea? Pax, sweetheart, could I speak to my daughter for a moment?"

Pax steps back. I nod, and he ducks out of the room. Mike leads a trembling Gwen to the kitchen, and I can hear him talking excitedly about the bay window in the snug and the Aga stove, trying to distract her from the large Roman warrior who is rather fond of frescoes.

Mum flops down on the purple bed. She pats the duvet meaningfully. I hesitate for a moment before slumping down beside her.

"Bree, honey." Mum sucks in a breath through her teeth. "I know it's hard to think about all these changes, but we have to listen to what Gwen says. She's the expert, and if we have to do a little sprucing up to get the best price for Grimwood, then that's what we have to do."

"But she's sucking the soul out of this place. Why does she have to throw out all our furniture and paint over the fresco...er, mural?" I kick the blanket box. A mistake. It's made out of mahogany, and now my toe is throbbing. "You and Dad picked every piece of furniture in this house. Your heart and soul are in this place. Why are you so ready to slap up some paint and destroy it all?"

Mum turns to me, and beneath her sharp expression, I can see tears brimming at the edges of her eyes. My anger flicks off instantly, like a tap turning off. I lean into her and wrap my arms around her.

"I'm not ready. Not even a little bit," Mum says stiffly. She won't let the tears fall. That's not who she is. "But what's the difference if we change things now? Gwen's right. Whoever buys this place is likely to paint over it themselves. That mural is hardly a work of art. Your dad copied it from a picture in a magazine because it was a cheap way of covering up the bad plaster job he did."

I stare at the wall. "I didn't know that."

Mum pulls away. This is too much emotion for her.

"Honestly, I'm surprised you're so attached to this house, since you fled it the first moment you could." Mum's words are matter-of-fact, but she's not looking at me, and I can still see those tears gathered at the corners of her eyes. "You haven't been back to visit in five years, and you only came back this time because we begged you."

The air flees my lungs. I feel like I've been punched.

Mum has never, *ever* mentioned the fact that I haven't come back since I left. She asked me home for Christmas and my birthday every year, but she accepted my excuses with her usual matter-of-factness and moved on to something else.

It's not that I didn't miss them. I had some horrible lonely nights in the New Zealand bush or in my tiny hostel bed in Vietnam when I closed my eyes, clicked my heels together three times and whispered 'there's no place like home,' because I wanted to be back in Grimdale so badly.

But I couldn't come back.

The idea of returning to Grimdale made me break out in a cold sweat.

I thought that was because I needed so desperately to feel as though I was normal, that going back would be like admitting that I'd failed at my life's dream of travelling the world. But the deep, dark truth I've carried with me is that I couldn't bear to return to a house empty of ghosts.

I sent my friends away, and I hated myself for it. I still do. Those two miserable years when I lived in the house without them were the worst years of my life. I didn't even know if they'd crossed over or not. I thought I'd lost them forever because I'd been so wrapped up in myself that I didn't appreciate what was right in front of me.

And because of that, I hurt my mum.

I hurt Pax, Ambrose, and Edward.

I missed out on all these years with my parents.

Running away really doesn't solve your problems. Who would've thought?

I stare at my hands. I hate myself today.

Mum sighs. "I didn't mean to snap at you, darling. I know you had difficult teen years. I completely understand why you had to leave, and your father and I are so proud of you for going off on your own and making such a success of yourself."

I don't know if I'd call five years of working in grungy pubs and being groped by pimply, Kerouac-worshipping tour managers who smell faintly of cheese 'making a success of myself,' but sure.

Mum clears her throat and continues. "We're proud of you… but we've missed you, too. Your dad especially. I know you're mad at us for keeping his illness a secret all those months, but we thought it was for the best. We didn't want you to worry while you were off having your adventures. We didn't want to stand in your way of going after what you've always wanted."

But what if what I always wanted is a lie?

"I'm sorry too, Mum." The words tumble out of me, as if they've been sitting on the tip of my tongue waiting to dive out. "I'm sorry that I made you feel like I ran away from you. That's not it at all. Grimwood was such a wonderful place to grow up. It was a haven from Kelly and Leanne and all of that.

But then...it wasn't anymore, and I didn't know how to deal with that. I was lost, and I needed to find myself. I thought I'd find myself in Greece or New Zealand, but I was wrong. I never meant to hurt you and Dad. I've missed you so much while I've been away, but the longer I was gone, the easier it became not to come back. And now I *am* back and everything's changing. And I don't mean to make it more difficult for you. I know that you have to do this. I just...I guess I just thought Grimwood would always be here. That you and Dad would always—"

Mum's face collapses. She gathers me into her arms. Unlike Dad, Mum's never been a big hugger, so this is kind of a shock. She presses me tight against her, crushing my cheek into her breast, "Oh, honey. Is that what this is about? Your father and I aren't going anywhere soon."

You don't know that. No one knows.

I've had a lifetime of ghosts yelling at me about the unfairness of death to back that up.

I swipe at my tears. "Dad's personality is in every room of the house. I don't want him to be painted over and shoved out into the outbuilding, especially not when he won't be able to paint murals at your new place."

"You listen to me, Bree Mortimer. Your dad may have some shaky hands and some new pills he has to remember to take, but he's not on death's door. Parkinson's isn't terminal. Your dad will face this challenge the same way he has faced every challenge in his life – with a smile and a silly joke and a lot of creativity." She smiles down at me, but the smile is tinged with sadness. "He will fill his life with new hobbies like riding his bike and annoying me about things he's misplaced."

"Dad has a bike?"

"Oh, yes. It's lime green with a big basket and a fog horn."

"Of course." I can't help but smile.

"Your father will never think that he is less than or that he has been given a rotten lot, so don't you think that, either."

"I know," I sniff. "But…"

"You don't have to explain." She strokes my hair. "I know. I fucking know."

I snort. I don't think I've ever heard my mother swear.

"I don't want to paint over Dad's mural." I sniff. "I know…I know it's silly, and I know that the new owners will probably paint over it anyway, but I can't—"

"Okay." Mum pats my leg. "We'll do everything else Gwen says, but we won't paint over the mural. But I expect you – and Pax – to help me take apart this sodding bed and move it into the outbuilding. Deal?"

"Deal."

"Good." Mum pats my knee. "And darling?"

"Yes?"

"If I were you, I wouldn't keep pushing those boys of yours away."

"I'm not—"

"Pax and Ambrose may be a little…unconventional, but they care about you. And if you care about them, you need to make sure they know it. I think sometimes you talk yourself out of things because you've told yourself that they're not for you, or you're afraid of getting hurt. But take it from someone who has been happily married to a wonderful and infuriating man for twenty-seven years – love is always worth the risk."

"But I'm not in love—"

Mum pats my knee again as she gets up to leave. "Sure you aren't, darling. Sure you aren't. Cup of tea?"

19

BREE

"Bree, you won't believe it." Ambrose arrives home with a clatter. He tries to hang his hat on the coat rack but misses and hangs it on the antler of a taxidermy deer instead. It makes me smile to see it sitting there, so I don't move it.

"What?" I wrap my arms around him, burying my face into his greatcoat, breathing deep to glut myself on the scent of him.

"Mr. Pitts wants me to have a permanent job leading tours at the cemetery. A job! I've never had a job since I had to leave the Navy! This is wonderful. He's going to pay me, although he says I need a bank account to do that. He also says that you and I should work out a roster for who will do the tours."

"Ambrose, that's amazing." I hug him even tighter.

The world isn't designed for people with disabilities. I've heard Mina rant about lack of accessibility and workplace discrimination enough to know that. But compared to when Ambrose lived – when people like him were often sent to institutions for their whole lives – this is a big fucking deal.

Plus, it will be nice to have one of the ghosts earning money. My measly paycheck and savings are being rapidly diminished by the need to purchase men's clothing and Pax's insatiable appetite.

"It is, isn't it?" Ambrose wraps his arm around my shoulders. His other hand grips his stick as he alternates between rapping it and sweeping it on the floor. Ambrose's usual method of finding his way around involves rapping the ball of his stick against the ground and using the echoes to discern his surroundings, but Mina has been showing him how to sweep a cane in front of him to identify other obstacles, and he's figuring out a combination of what works for him.

"I gave a tour to a group from the Royal National Institute of Blind People in Liverpool. They came specifically because they saw your video about my grave." Ambrose leads me into the kitchen, where Dad has left out a fresh plate of scones, which he'd fed Gwen to help calm her down after her disastrous visit today. Ambrose sits in the chair while I add butter, jam, and clotted cream to both our scones. He takes a huge, happy bite and licks cream off his fingers. "They wanted to know all about Ambrose Hulme and his walking stick and how he read train timetables and how he wrote his memoirs and all kinds of questions. One lady told me that she was so inspired by Ambrose's story that she booked a trip to Disneyland. I don't know what that is but this lady has never been out of the country before and now she's going to Disneyland. Isn't that amazing?"

"It *is* amazing." My throat closes up a little from the pride swelling in my chest. "But I'm not surprised at all. You make me feel brave, as if anything I dream of is possible. I'm not surprised other people feel the same way. And Disneyland is a theme park – it's full of hideously expensive food and carnival rides but a hundred times cooler. Maybe we'll go someday."

He beams. There's a dot of cream on his nose. "I'd like that. Is Edward nearby?"

"He's up in his boudoir, composing an ode to Grimwood Manor that we can read upon its sale." I lean forward. "Why? Have you found something about his murder?"

"Not so far, but I've only just got started. On my lunch break, I walked into the village and interviewed as many ghosts as I could find, in case any of them happened to be nearby and see anything that night."

"And?"

Ambrose shakes his head sadly. "Both the squashed Navvy and the Poisoned Schoolteacher weren't ghosts at the time, and Lottie says she *did* attend Edward's soiree on that fateful night, but she was rather distracted by a viscount's fine cucumber and didn't see a thing."

"Ah, yes, that sounds like Lottie."

"But don't worry." Ambrose reaches for a second scone. "I've only just begun my investigations. I feel certain that we will solve this mystery."

I glance up at the ceiling, where I can just make out Edward's muffled voice as he recites his lines. A moment later, the lights flicker.

I truly hope you're right. Because I don't think Grimwood Manor can handle much more of Edward's ennui.

AFTER DINNER, Mina's boyfriend Morrie arrives in a bright red Mini to pick up Pax and Ambrose. I wave goodbye from the porch. Pax looks hopefully at Mum, but although she gives him a quick peck on the cheek, she doesn't invite him to stay.

Even though she's warming to the ex-ghosts, she isn't quite ready to have them stay over. We do have to start moving furniture and painting in the morning, so I suppose that's a factor, too.

However, Mum doesn't know that I still have a man *inside* the house.

I retreat back inside. Mum heads into the kitchen to boil the kettle for tea, and Dad is sprawled out on the sofa in the main living room in the east wing – where they live – watching the news. His eyes are closed and he's snoring gently, and Moon is collapsed in an adorable loaf on his chest, her yellow eyes following me as I cross the room.

Edward hovers in the corner, peering at the contents of the television cabinet with disgust. "This is filled with twisted cables and hundreds of these silver disc things. Not a bottle of fine French wine or absinthe in sight. How do your parents live in such squalid conditions?"

"Those silver disc things are DVDs," I whisper as I scoot close to Edward. I glance over my shoulder to make sure that Dad's still asleep. "That's what we used to use to store moving pictures before we got Netflix."

"Fascinating," Edward says in a tone that implies anything but. He flicks a DVD through his fingers, and it rolls across the rug. Entwhistle bounds after it and bats it under the sofa.

"Pax and Ambrose have left with Morrie," I whisper. "What shall we do with our evening?"

"I can think of a few things..." Edward whispers in my ear.

"We have to be quiet," I whisper back. "My parents—"

"I'm not the one who's going to scream."

"You talk a big game, Mr. Poet Prince, but when I wrap my lips around your—"

"Did you say something, Bree-bug?"

I whirl around, my cheeks reddening as Dad sits up and rubs his eyes. Moon topples off his stomach and darts behind the curtains.

I let out a huge fake yawn. "Just that I'm really tired. I think I'll go to bed."

Dad looks at his watch. "It's only seven-thirty!"

"I know, but it's been a..." I search for the right word. "... stressful day. Besides, you will probably want to start moving furniture early in the morning, and you know how grumpy I get if I don't have my model's twelve."

"Sure, honey." Dad's eyes search my face. "But I thought maybe we could hang out. If not tonight, then another night, okay? I want to hear about your travels, and about these interesting friends you've made."

"I'd love that..." *Just not when a royal prince is whispering filthy things in my ear, and his hand is roaming along the curve of my ass.* "Another night, okay?"

"Okay." Dad swings his feet off the sofa. Edward lets me go, but he doesn't quite move out of the way in time, and when Dad goes to hug me, he swings his arm through Edward's neck. Edward collapses on the floor, howling with pain, and it's all I can do to keep a straight face while Dad's hugging me.

"Goodnight, Dad."

"I love you, Bree-bug." Dad kisses my forehead.

"I used to think you were okay, for a commoner, but that was before you put your elbow through my neck." Edward rubs the bare skin inside his open collar as he gets to his feet. His dark hair falls back from his face, and I catch a glimpse of the mark on his neck – a pale bruise that's always been there. I hate thinking that's from someone holding him, pushing him out a window.

I follow Edward outside, swinging the door shut behind me.

The moment the lounge door closes, Edward's lips are on mine. *Yes,* my mind screams, and I forget that if my mum decides to walk by, all she'll see is my mouth open and my eyes closed as I snog thin air.

But Edward isn't invisible, isn't nothing. Everything about Edward is real to me – his hands cup my cheeks like I'm something precious he must handle carefully, his dark eyes boring down on me – not closed, never closed, because Edward likes to see everything. The press of his desire against my thigh, so hard that it feels impossible that this time a ghost and Living couldn't...

Edward lowers one hand to the small of my back and guides me backwards down the hall as his tongue lays claim to every recess of my mouth. My breath catches as my hands roam over his chest and back, tracing the tight cords of muscle. The pulsing heat of his ghostly aura radiates against my skin.

It's so much, he's so much, and yet I'll never have enough of him.

I can't believe that we get to be together, two people whose lives should never, ever have crossed, who come from different worlds and different times, and yet I get to kiss him and touch him and lo—

I pull myself back into the moment before I can think of the next word. I'm not ready to go there yet.

Edward's ghostly fingers cup my breast, his thumb circling my nipple until it hardens into a peak. I gasp against his mouth. He swallows my cry so that my father can't hear it.

We'd better take this to my room.

Somehow, we manage to make it down the stairs without tripping. One of the stern great-relatives I never met stares out at me from her photograph as we stumble past, and I swear I see out of the corner of my eye her wink at us. We crash through the door of my bedroom. Edward kicks the door shut behind him, and the whole wall reverberates as it slams behind him.

Now that we're alone and safe from my parents, Edward's eyes grow dark and determined. His fingers slide from my cheek around to the back of my head, tumbling through the strands, sometimes gripping me, sometimes moving *through* my hair.

It's a strange and wonderful thing, making out with a ghost. You don't know when the moldavite's power will slip for a moment, or when they're no longer strong enough to touch you.

His other fingers keep working my nipples, pinching and rolling first one, then the other, until I'm gasping and moving against him, desperate for more.

Edward drops his hands from my cheeks, and he does something that makes my heart pound with surprise. He drops to his knees in front of me, his fingers toying with the buttons on my fly.

"What are you doing?"

"What does it look like? I've never knelt for anyone before," he murmurs as his hands go around my thighs, and he actually manages to shove down my trousers and panties without my help. "But for you, for my muse, I will worship at your feet every day and every night, grateful for whatever favours you deign to grant me."

"Edward, that's not what this is. I'm not with you as a *favour*—"

Whatever I was about to say is cut off as his tongue finds my clit.

I throw my head back as Edward's tongue works in delicious little circles. His hands cup my ass, holding me in place and radiating a supernatural warmth that courses through my veins. And his tongue…it's magical. That's the only way I can describe what he's doing and how he's making pleasure coil from my belly out through my whole body.

Just when I think I can't take any more, he'll change what he's doing, flicking me with the tip of his tongue, then laving over that sensitive spot, before pounding it into submission, until I think that I cannot possibly survive this, but what a way to go.

Gods. Yes. *more.*

Please, so much more.

"I will never get my fill of the taste of you," he murmurs against me.

I whimper in response, because he is undoing me with every sinful stroke of his tongue.

Edward strokes one finger over my pussy as he licks, teasing my entrance, coating himself in my juices. I moan. Gods, I want him inside me so bad. I'll never have enough of this man.

My pulse leaps and dances as he worships me with his mouth. My body is made of liquid. I have no idea how I am still standing right now.

"Let go, Brianna," he murmurs, his fingers digging into my ass as he pulls me closer. "Let yourself come apart for me. You are never so beautiful as when you cry my name."

"Edward..."

He sucks my clit into his mouth, and I'm *gone.* I sob his name as the pleasure spirals through me, fracturing me to pieces. I lose myself, the world around me fading to black.

When I come to, I'm on the ground. Edward stands over me, his too-pretty mouth curved with concern.

"Your legs gave way. I tried to catch you." Edward's eyes are downcast. "But you fell through my arms."

"You *should* be sorry." I grip the edge of the bed and drag myself onto it. "It's your fault that my legs don't work right now. What did you do to me, prince?"

He laughs gently, crawling onto the bed to lie beside me. I kick my legs out of the trousers and panties, but I'm still wearing my hoodie. He dances his fingers over my thighs, sending delicious tingles down my legs.

"Tell me something beautiful," I say. I touch his cheek. I know that we can't go any further than this, and it's tearing me up inside. I want to be close to him. I want to crawl inside him and know him in all the ways a person can know another. But I can't. I can't have that piece of his body.

So I will have a piece of his heart instead.

"Something beautiful..." Edward's dark orbs bore into me. "I'm looking at her right now."

"No, something else. Go on, Poet Prince, wow me."

Edward rolls onto his stomach, his chin on one hand. His elbows hover an inch above the bed. He furrows his brow as he considers my question.

"Did your father ever tell you how they came to adopt Moon and Entwhistle?" he asks.

"He said that he found them in one of the outbuildings. They were only a couple of weeks old and their mother had died. He buried her and brought them inside to sit by the fire, and by the time he'd nursed them back to health he couldn't bear to give them up for adoption."

Edward nods. His dark eyes grow cloudy at the edges as he disappears into a memory. "After I died, Grimwood Manor was left empty for many years while various people fought over my estate. Pax and I lived here together, of course, but we were constantly at each other's throats. I was perhaps not the best afterlife companion in those days."

"Perhaps not." I smile.

"He spent his days patrolling the forest for Druids, while I preferred the more poetic pastimes of remaining indoors and wallowing in my own self-pity. I watched my family and so-called friends come and go as they took their pick of my fine furniture, hunted in vain for my secret wine cellar, and bickered over how to spend my fortune. My father showed up on one occasion – he wished the house to be knocked down and my things burned so that all traces of his heretic son would be erased entirely, but Hugh talked him out of it. Hugh suggested instead that my father release a commemorative book of my poetic works, to show the nation that he was a father in mourning, and he said, "I'll not spend a single moment mourning for that waste of air. As far as I'm concerned, he's no son of mine, and his blasphemous poems should be burned."

"Oh, Edward." I run my fingers along his spine, tracing the lines of his misery. I can't imagine how cruel it must be for your own father to despise you.

A dark curl falls over one eye as he shakes his head and continues. "One day, I was floating in my boudoir, lamenting my sad end, when I heard a sound. It was tiny, barely discernible. A faint meow.

"I tried to ignore it, but it grew louder and more wretched. I couldn't think. I floated around the house until I entered the ballroom, where the guest lounge is now, and saw a trembling heap of bedraggled fur sitting in the middle of the marble floor."

"A cat?"

He nods. "I have seen this cat before. It was a little black cat with white paws – a wretched, skinny thing that the gardener chased with a pitchfork and the cook swiped from the kitchen with the broomstick. Sometimes, she came near the house during our revels, but my friends had no time for such a sad, skinny little creature. They sometimes threw things or teased her or, without meaning to, would be overly friendly and pull her tail.

"And now, here she was, inside *my* house. I should have been incensed, but her cry rent my soul. When she cried, she sounded the way that I felt inside – miserable and alone and desperate for love.

"And as I stared down at her, I realised that I could see through her midnight fur to the marble inlays below. She was a ghost, too. She had died all alone somewhere and her spirit had come to my house, seeking...what? The same thing we all seek, I suppose. Safety, warmth, kindness." His voice cracks. "I never gave this creature a moment's consideration when I was alive. But then, as she stared up at me with her huge eyes and her little pink nose, I realised that we were the same. We had both lived alone and died alone. We'd never known love."

"Oh, Edward." Tears pricked the corners of my eyes.

"I knelt down beside her, careful not to put my knee through the floor. She was terribly frightened. I can't blame her, for she had never known kindness from humans. She darted away but then slowly, slowly, she came back to me. She sniffed me. And then she leapt into my arms. She curled into my shoulder, her head resting on me, and her body vibrated with these perfect little purrs.

"I carried her back to my boudoir, careful not to disturb her, and we lay down together. Her little body radiated warmth that even I could feel as a ghost. I looked down at her and I thought that I was lucky I didn't have a heart any longer, because it would surely break. She slept. And I slept. Or I drifted to a place where I was the kind of person that could be loved, that could be deserving of love, even if it was only the love of a tiny, perfect little cat. For the first time since I had become dead, and really, for the first time in a very long time, I was at peace."

His breath stutters. "I awoke sometime later as the cat crossed over. Light surrounded her, the way it did with Ambrose, and she passed through the Veil to the next realm."

Tears spill from my eyes to think of that tiny kitten's life, and I hope that wherever she is now, she's chasing balls of yarn and eating all the caviar in the universe.

I remember what Edward had said at Nevermore about the Veil being a poetical metaphor. But now we know it's an actual barrier.

Edward continues. "She lifted her little head and looked me in the eye as she left. She seemed to be saying, 'Thank you.' All her life, people had ignored her and mistreated her. No one had loved her. That was her unfinished business. She just wanted to experience love. And I..." he shakes his head. "Sometimes I feel like that – as if all I want in the world is to be held and loved. And so, when I was wandering around the garden feeling sorry for myself one day, and I found those two kittens and their poor, dead mother, I burned out the fuses in the house so that Mike had to go into the outbuildings for the generator, and he found them."

I close my eyes as Edward's words wash over me. I open them again, and he gazes down at me, that arrogant expression gone from his face, his eyes swimming with pain and impossible hope. He blinks, and his mask goes back up.

"I wish..." he sighs. "I wish that I could be inside you right now. I wish that I could fuck you until you loved me."

"That's not how it works," I say. "But there is something else we can do. Something even more intimate."

He perks up. "Whatever you wish."

"You *could* be inside me, in a way."

He looks confused. "That's precisely our problem. I cannot, and it's driving me mad."

"No, I mean, I could toss the moldavite away, and you could float inside me, the way you did with the Ripper..." I shake my head as I see his expression. "Forget it. It was a silly idea—"

"It's not silly at all." Edward's features turn solemn. "It would be an honour. But I may see things in your memories that you wish were kept hidden. Do you accept this? Because I'd like to try if you'll have me."

I take a deep breath. Will I have him? Inviting him inside means giving Edward my memories – *all* of them. Even the things that I am most ashamed of, like the true reason why I was afraid to return to Grimwood all these years.

Like the way I really feel about him and Pax and Ambrose.

But what he's given me tonight is more precious than an orgasm. He's given me a hidden piece of his soul, a piece he's never allowed anyone else to see. I want to give him the same gift.

I lay back against the pillows. Slowly, I remove the handful of moldavite stones from the pocket of my hoodie and toss them into the corner of the room. They clatter against the wainscotting before dropping to the floor. I beckon Edward.

"Come inside me."

Edward bites his lip. He touches the collar of his loose white shirt, tugging it to expose that small bruise again. The moonlight streams from the window behind him, touching his midnight hair and making him appear much older and wiser – no longer the Poet Prince, the Lord of Debauchery, but someone infinitely more complex and beautiful.

I hold out my hand. He touches my fingers. The tips graze, but then he loses his grip and slips into me, his hand reaching down through my arm. My skin burns where he's entered me, and the inside of my arm feels tight, like my skin is holding more than it did before. It's awkward, but not unpleasant.

"Does it hurt?" I ask.

"It's wonderful," he replies. Which isn't exactly an answer. But then I remember things I've read about Edward, that during some of his most sinful pastimes, he has enjoyed pain as part of his pleasure. It's part of being a poet – finding beauty in the darkness.

"Go deeper," I urge him.

Edward's lips purse. His brow furrows as he leans forward. His lips brush mine for a moment before his whole body sinks into me.

It's...strange. It feels wrong, but in the way that wrong things can sometimes be exactly what you need. All of me feels stretched and full. He's moving around, making himself comfortable, and I am so nervous about him being there but also...this is beautiful. He's inside me. He's in my veins and my heart and my bones.

He is me and I am him.

His thoughts and sensations crowd out mine until I'm no longer certain where I end and he begins.

A memory surges to the surface. It's wobbly, the edges blurred. As soon as I settle inside it, my head swims.

This is an opium memory, I realise. It doesn't belong to me. Edward is high as a kite and so now I am, too.

"What do you mean, you don't wish to marry?" A woman's shrill voice enters my skull. "I will make you a fine wife. I will never tie you down, if that is your concern. I just want us to continue like this forever. I love you, Eddie. I want to be your wife."

My body swells with emotions that don't belong to me. There's pity and there's also a surge of hope, that maybe this is it for me, maybe her love is what will set me free. But I am resolved. I know that she does not truly love me as I long to be loved. She loves the *idea* of me, but I will never live up to her lofty ideals. As soon as I disappoint her, she will fall just as hard and fast and deep for another.

"You will regret this. You will regret giving up your life for me," I tell her, and this voice is mine but not mine, the words come from me and yet I've never heard them before. "I am not worthy of your devotion, and I do not love you as you deserve to be loved. You must stay, and endure, and let your pain fuel your art. But know that wherever I am, you will always be a muse to me."

And so I tell her no, and I watch her pretty face distort with sadness, and then rage. She balls her pretty little fingers into fists and beats them against a pillow.

She rages. "If I can't have you, no one can!"

She bursts into tears and flees the room, but I don't watch her go. My vision swims and I reach for the wine bottle next to the bed, but it's empty. Damn, I need more. I stagger to my feet, and that's when a dark shadow lunges at me, and everything goes black...

...and when I open my eyes, Edward hovers above me, his dark eyes wide with concern.

"Are you well, Brianna? I was inside you, and then you left me."

"I fell too deep into one of your memories," I say. "You were high and it dragged me under. Thank you for pulling me out."

"I should never have agreed to this. I should have known that I could hurt you."

"No, Edward, it was beautiful. What was it like for you?"

His long eyelashes flutter, and his lips curl back into a rare, genuine smile. "I saw you, Brianna. I saw all of you. I was you, and it was the most beautiful experience of my afterlife. And it made me realise something."

My throat closes. I don't want to talk about what he might have seen. "What?"

"When I was in the Ripper, I might have got a clue that can help us."

That isn't what I expected at all. But I'll take it. I've had far too much vulnerability for tonight. I sit up. "What is it?"

"I saw the Ripper watching as one of his victim's bodies was discovered. There was a man in a greatcoat trying to control the crowd. He was of special interest to the Ripper, who enjoyed taunting him. It was part of the game for him. I think this man might have been a police officer, and he probably knows the Ripper better than anyone. What if we could get his help."

"But he'll be long dead by now...oh." Edward's suggestion registers. "If he's a ghost, we could talk to him. You're right."

I crawl out of bed and find Vera's book of serial killers. I flip to the four-page spread on Jack the Ripper and point to a lithograph of a figure in the bottom corner. "Is this the man you saw?"

"That's the fellow." Edward squints at the page. "Inspector Frederick Abberline."

"He was in charge of the Ripper case. He never caught the killer."

"In my visions, the Ripper enjoyed watching Abberline's failures being raked over in the gutter press as every clue the Ripper planted led him in a new direction." Edward's eyes bore into mine. "That sounds like enough to drive a man to…"

"…haunt a bitch."

"If Abberline is a ghost, then we could go and ask him about the Ripper," Edward says excitedly. "He might know something about how to make sure he's really dead or how the Order resurrected him."

"It's worth a shot." I grab my phone and start typing furiously. It's strange, I've spent my whole life trying to avoid ghosts, and now I'm planning to seek one out. "If I were the ghost of a detective, I'd be haunting the site of my most famous unsolved murder. Which means the Whitechapel district of London."

"Oh," Edward's face falls. "Then I suppose you'll be leaving me to travel to London with Pax and Ambrose. Probably Mina, too, and the bird. What a merry band of detectives you will make."

"Nonsense. You're coming too." I hold up a piece of moldavite. "We wouldn't dare go to London without our prince showing us all the sights."

Edward sniffs. "I didn't frequent areas of ill-repute such as Whitechapel."

"Don't be ridiculous, Edward. You were a notorious rake."

He gives a broad, sinister smile that melts my insides. "If

you insist, Brianna. From the moment my feet touch London soil once more, my nose for debauchery will hunt out every purveyor of sinful delights and den of iniquity in the fair city."

"I'll give you a den of iniquity right now," I grin as I lean in and cup his cheek, bringing my face down to kiss him.

"If my lady insists," Edward drawls as we fall back into the bed.

20

BREE

"That's it. You're getting the hang of it!"

I crawl out of bed and head to the window, drawn by my father's excited cries. I bolt up in bed, momentarily panicking when I don't see Pax at his usual spot standing guard at the window, before I remember that he had to stop doing that when he: 1. Realised that he needed to sleep now that he's Living, 2. He got kicked out of the house because of the sale and, 3. He can't exactly act like a savage Roman warrior now that my parents are home.

My parents. *Dad.*

I run to the window and gaze down. Dad stands astride his lime-green bicycle, shouting encouragement as Pax wobbles in a slow circle around and around the zodiac mosaic on another bike. On the edge of the lawn, as far as they can possibly get from the flailing limbs of a precarious centurion, are Mina and Oscar, Quoth in human form, and Ambrose.

And Dani.

She smiles shyly and waves. I wave back. I don't quite know where we stand after she helped us find a place to bury Father Bryne, but she's here and I am so happy she's here.

"What is this racket that wakes me from slumber?" Edward wafts through the wall and peers down his nose out the window. "Ah, the Roman is doing something absurd again. I should have known."

"Bree, look!" Pax cries as he circles the driveway, his bulk wobbling atop the bike. "I am riding a horseless chariot."

"His 'horseless carriage' is bright pink," Edward says.

"Is that a problem?" Pax glowers up at us. "I like pink. Pink is the colour of Mars, God of war. What do you say is wrong with pink? Why don't you come down here and say it to my face."

"There is nothing wrong with pink," Dad winks at me. "I'm surprised you're being so sexist, Bree-bug. Pink is a very manly colour, isn't it, Pax?"

"It sure is," Pax declares.

"Really, Bree," Dani says with a smile, realising that my dad must've heard Edward speak and assumed it was me. "I've never known you to discriminate against pink bikes. I think you'll have to hand in your intersectional feminist badge over this."

Okay, so I think Dani's forgiven me.

I glare at Edward. "See the trouble you cause?"

"How is this my fault? I tire of this nonsense," Edward sighs. "I'm returning to my room to work on my poems. Call me when something interesting happens."

I sit in the window and watch as Pax and Dad circle around the driveway. Pax rings the pink bell on his bicycle as if he's declaring time at a Roman orgy.

Quoth helps Mina and Ambrose navigate through the chaos. Dani follows, carrying an object under her arm. Reluctantly, I scramble into some clothes and head downstairs to join them.

"Look what Mina gave me!" Ambrose declares, holding up a

contraption that looks a bit like a cross between a typewriter and a loaf of bread. "She signed me up for the Royal National Institute of Blind People, and they sent me a resource pack so I can learn to read and write Braille. What a delightful invention!"

"That's wonderful. Good morning." I kiss his cheek. His skin flushes with colour. I will never get over how deeply joyful it makes me to see him alive, enjoying life.

"You missed a great night last night," Mina says cheerfully. "We stayed up late playing poker with Morrie and Heathcliff, and Ambrose wiped the floor with them. He also had his first ever takeaway curry."

"What did you think?"

Ambrose rubs his stomach gleefully. "It reminded me of my days hopping trains in India."

"And Ambrose told me about what you discovered from the bat," Mina leans in and whispers. "We've come up with a few ideas about who might have murdered Edward. It turns out that we had plenty of books about the infamous Poet Prince in the bookshop, and they contain details and firsthand accounts from all the guests at Grimwood on the night of Edward's murder. So Morrie and Quoth and Dani helped us to come up with a list."

"That's awesome," I beam at them all. "But now that you have a list, how are you going to ascertain who's the murderer?"

"We came up with an idea for that, too," Ambrose says. "We interrogate them. Or rather, you do."

Of course.

Bree the Ghost Whisperer saves the day again.

"Edward and I actually came up with a similar idea last night," I say. "He thinks that we should find Detective Abberline's ghost in London and see if he knows anything that can help us find or stop the Ripper."

"That's perfect," Mina says. "Our top suspect is haunting a hotel down in London. This means it's time for a road trip!"

"Bree?" Mum calls from the front door, her apron around her waist and her hands covered in batter. "Would you and your friends like some breakfast? I'm cooking a Full English."

"Tiny potato squares of deliciousness!" Pax cries in excitement, throwing his bike on the ground. "By Jupiter's dribbling dongle, I'm there."

Mina makes a face. "A delightful visual image he's conjured there, but I do love a platter of crunchy bacon, so count me in."

As the others follow Mum inside, Dani steps up to me. "I made you something," she says, holding out the bundle under her arm.

I take it from her, my heart a hard lump in my throat. I don't deserve Dani's friendship.

"Don't look until you get to London," she says with a shy smile. "It's a ghost-summoning kit. I got the idea from Mina's mother, who makes these vampire-slaying kits that are kind of adorable."

"I've heard those have caused all kinds of trouble?"

"I'm hoping that this kit will keep you *out* of trouble, but that's wistful thinking when Bree Mortimer is involved." Dani inclines her gaze up to the second-storey guest suite, where Edward is no doubt in the middle of a sonnet. "How's Edward dealing with being the only ghost you're banging?"

My cheeks flush with her. "Please don't say it like that."

"How do you want me to say it?" Dani's lips curl into her trademark sardonic smile. "You have to admit it, you're a total ghostslut."

"I think I liked it better when you hated me," I moan. "Edward's...well, he's taking it exactly the way you'd expect Edward to take it – bouts of maudlin whining mixed in with some pretty incredible ghost sex."

"It's adorable that Ambrose wants to do this for him."

"That's Ambrose all over." I glance up at the window again. Edward appears in the glass. He frowns down at us. "I just hope that our surly prince appreciates the effort we're going to for him."

"Well, his last friends pushed him out a window, so I say he should learn to be happy with what he's got." Dani holds out her arm, and we link elbows the way we always have as we head up the driveway toward the house, my new ghost-summoning kit tucked under my other arm. "Your dad's looking good. He looks happy."

"Yeah. Seeing him has been amazing. I've been so afraid of what his diagnosis might mean for him, but now that I'm here and I can see him, he's *exactly* the same as always. He's still my dad, and Parkinson's won't take him away from us."

"Exactly." Dani leans her head against my shoulder. She's taller than me, and it's so awkward that we start laughing. She swipes her dark hair behind her ear and asks, "So, have you thought any more about letting Alice in on the secret?"

"Dani—"

"I know that it must be weird, because she'd be finding out that everything she used to bully you about is true, but Alice really would be helpful. We could come to London with you, help with interrogating the ghosts, and maybe go to a show, find a fun cocktail bar, make it a girls' weekend."

Dani looks so hopeful. And the idea of going to London with her and Alice (and maybe Mina) and having a fun weekend with real flesh-and-blood friends, the way I always wished I could, makes my chest swell.

"Plus, I think she's starting to suspect something." Dani looks sheepish. "After that day she spent with Pax and Ambrose at the museum, she keeps asking me how he knows so much about Roman history and where he went to uni to be able to read Latin so fluently."

And that's exactly how she'll put herself in the path of the Ripper.

I shake my head. "Not yet. Not until we've got rid of the Ripper for good. He can't have any possibility of coming back. I don't want to put Alice in danger. You know that if we tell her, she'll throw herself into the middle of this; she can't help it. I've already seen enough people hurt because of my powers. I don't want to add your girlfriend and my ex-bully to the list."

"Okay. It's your secret and your decision, but I just want it on the record that I think she's going to figure it out eventually anyway, and she could help us *now*. But let's forget about it for right now, because it's urgent that we get to the pile of bacon your mother's prepared before Pax demolishes it all."

We run, laughing, toward the house. Jack the Ripper and the Order of the Noble Death seem so far away. With my best friend back in my life, what can possibly go wrong?

"I'm on a *train*," Ambrose gushes as he leaps dramatically over the gap between the platform and carriage, swinging his satchel over his shoulder. "I'm actually *standing on a train* that runs on electricity instead of a filthy old steam engine."

"You are, but it's not quite as exciting to everyone else, so if you can turn your enjoyment down a notch so we don't give some poor businessman a heart attack, that would be appreciated."

"And step aside so your prince may board," Edward says in his bored voice. "In my day, men like you would lay down in the dirt so I could step on your backs—ow! Hey, watch where you're putting those big hoofs, thou gibbering bull's-pizzle!"

Edward shakes his fist at the man in the business suit who just walked through him. Pax is over by the vending machines, his fist raised as if he assumes that the only way to get the treats out is to smash the glass. As quick as I can, I usher them all onto the carriage and find our reserved seats.

Ambrose settles himself into the seat by the window. "Please tell me everything that we see."

"I promise—"

"Look, *he's* bringing *his* horseless chariot," Pax frowns as a cyclist loads his bike onto the train. "You said that I wasn't allowed to bring mine."

"True, but that cyclist can probably ride down the road without punching the windows of passing cars."

"They called me a Spandex Jockey!" Pax roars, slamming his fist onto the flimsy table between our seats. "I don't know what that is, but it sounds like an insult. The last person who insulted me—"

"—I know, I know, you used their intestines to floss your teeth. You're sounding more like my dad after a day of road cycling every day."

I let Edward slide into the seat beside me so he can sit opposite Ambrose at the window. A woman gives me a filthy look as she passes by, since it looks as if I'm blocking the seat so others can't use it. I turn away so I can't see her. I reserved all of these seats, even the one Edward is sitting in.

Mina is desperate to get edits on her book finished, so she's decided not to come along. Dani had to pull out at the last minute because her mother's cider still exploded. The four of us are going to London on our own, although Mina said that Quoth may follow along in his raven form in case we get into trouble.

Who are we kidding – we're off to talk to a bunch of ghosts with two recently Re-Living men who are completely out of time. Of *course* we're going to get into trouble.

Father Bryne's cross sits at the bottom of my bag, along with the bag of herbs in Vera's box and a bunch of her random notes, in case they were protection spells or something. I've also got Dani's ghost-summoning kit and a brochure for Jack the Ripper tours.

"I wonder how long my ghost mojo will hold out," Edward

says in his bored voice, as if he doesn't care at all and is not as excited about this trip as the rest of us. He peers out the window, unimpressed by the dick-themed graffiti art adorning the concrete walls of the station's tunnel.

I lift the handful of moldavite stones from my pocket and show him. "I'm gripping these as hard as I can."

Ambrose presses his foot against mine under the table. I press back. Edward doesn't know that we're counting on the moldavite to run out, so Edward's ghost mojo sends him home before we find our first ghost from his past. As far as Edward knows, we're only in London to find Inspector Abberline.

The journey to London is about what I expect, with Ambrose demanding a running commentary of the fluffiness factor of every sheep we pass (and this is the English country-side – there are a *lot* of sheep), Edward reciting a terrible pastoral poem he'd composed, and Pax loudly challenging fellow passengers to an arm wrestling match. One guy dressed in army fatigues takes him up on the offer and Pax puts his arm through the table. After that many of the passengers alight for the food car.

I can't stop smiling and laughing with them. I remember that a couple of months ago, I made the same journey in the opposite direction, alone and worried about my dad and nervous about what...or who...I'd find in the house.

We reach the city and take a cab to the cheap hotel I got for the night to drop our bags. There aren't enough seats for Edward, so he hovers up front with the driver, who shudders as he takes a corner too fast and accidentally sends my prince sailing into him.

"Bloody London weather," the driver curses.

"What did you call me?" Edward snaps. "I'll have you flogged for your impertinence."

"Did you say something, love?" The driver turns to face me as we pull up behind a red London bus.

"Oh, yes, I er, asked if all cab drivers are required to have insurance?"

At the hotel, we're too early to check in, which is actually a blessing, since we don't want Edward to accidentally meet the ghost who might be upstairs. The hotel stores our luggage behind the desk. We figure the best chance of catching Abberline will be later in the evening, but I'm happy to kill some time being a tourist, especially when...

"I can't believe I'm back in London!" Ambrose bounces on his heels with joy. "Can we visit the Crystal Palace? We could take tea at Holland House, or peruse the racy pamphlets on sale at the booksellers on Wych Street..."

"Why don't you simply ask to stand in the middle of Hyde Park with your arms outstretched and let the pigeons roost on you?" Edward scoffs. "I have no stomach for these entertainments."

"Well, that's fine, because nothing Ambrose suggested actually exists anymore. Is there anything you want to see, Edward?" I ask sweetly.

"I should like to see the palace where I grew up."

"Is that where the whale lives?" Pax asks hopefully.

"Not a whale, he's the *Prince of Wales*, Pax, and he's actually the king now and—"

"I didn't know whales had a monarchy," Pax says. "I always assumed they'd be Republicans, like Cicero."

We take a meandering route to the palace by taking the tube first to Camden so I can buy a new pair of boots, and then to Kew Gardens so Ambrose can wander amongst the botanical specimens and sniff interesting and delicious things. At the palace, Edward regales us with tales of his exploits from the days before his father banished him from court.

After I finally convince the Beefeater guards that Pax is an eccentric Italian tourist and not attempting to overthrow the monarchy, we take the tube to Whitechapel. I glance at my phone and see that we're right on time. The evening tours are beginning.

As we walk up the steps, we're greeted by a salt-and-pepper-haired gentleman wearing a Victorian greatcoat and waving a lantern madly about. "Do you care to peer into the dark and depraved mind of the most notorious serial killer of all time?" he calls to us. "Delve into the psyche of this rich gentleman who came to Whitechapel to indulge his gruesome tastes."

"No, no, no," a voice grumps over his shoulder. "That's *all wrong*. The papers made up the story of him being a gentleman. We actually believed he was a—"

"Er, no thank you." I rush past the Ripperologist, searching for the complainer, and almost immediately bump into a woman whose breasts are spilling out of a corset.

She holds up a sign and calls out in a terrible east London accent, "Walk with a modern prostitute of Whitechapel while we uncover the secrets of the women of the night who were cruelly snuffed out by the Ripper."

"That's all wrong, too. I *never* said that the victims were prostitutes. Just because they happened to be on the streets at night didn't mean they were ladies of ill repute—"

I spin around. Finally, I see him. Inspector Abberline looks just like all the drawings of him in Vera's book. He wears a faded great coat and matching trousers, and his misery hangs from his face like a shroud. I can see right through his broad chest to the corsetted woman merrily leading a large group of tourists down a side alley.

"That's not how it happened at all!" Abberline yells at another Ripper tour leader, who is busy telling his group about the grisly letters the Ripper sent to the press, complete with organs removed from the victims. "I hope that you all have women brutally murdered in *your* back yard and then everyone spends the rest of eternity making cheesy souvenirs about your greatest foible!"

That's the guy. He seems like a fun sort of fellow.

I square my shoulders and march across the square. The ghost sees me coming and leaps out of my way, but instead of walking through the spot he previously occupied, as he expects, I come to a stop in front of him and look him directly in the eye.

"Excuse me," I say as I approach him. "Inspector Abberline?"

"I—" The ghost stops. "You can see me?"

"Yes. My name is Bree Mortimer, and I can see ghosts. I want to—"

"Good." Abberline whips a little pad from his pocket and taps the nub of a pencil against it. "Then perhaps you can straighten these cretins out on a few crucial points. Firstly, with Catherine Eddows' body, there were no grape stalks found nearby, so no reason to assume that—"

"Um, here's the thing. I'm not really here to help you with the Ripper tours. I—"

"Next, with Polly Nichols, a newspaper reported that there was only a little blood found near the scene, but that doesn't mean the Ripper moved her body to Bucks Row, simply that the layers of her clothing had soaked up the blood—"

"Listen, Inspector Abberline, this is all very interesting, but I—"

"Is that girl crazy or something?" I overhear an American tourist whisper to her husband as their tour group passes. "She's talkin' to thin air."

"Maybe she's one of the Ripperologists?" her friend whispers. "They're a strange bunch."

"—and as for the absurd idea that the Freemasons were involved, I'm friends with a couple of Masons and they are absolute stand-up chaps—" Abberline clearly has a lot to get off his chest. I'm guessing they don't treat him too well on these tours – the man who failed to catch the Ripper.

"Actually, can we move over here for a sec..." When he doesn't seem to hear me, I hiss at Edward, who steps forward.

"My dear friend, you may not know me, but I am your prince. At least, I would've been if I were alive. I would love to write a poetic ode to your valiant struggle to bring this villain to justice, but right now, my Brianna needs you to listen to her."

"Listen? Why should I listen?" Abberline tosses his ghost pad on the ground in disgust. It disappears the moment it touches the cobbles and appears back in his pocket. "All I do is listen! Day in, day out, for over a hundred years I've stood in this square and heard about the killer I didn't catch. And as for *you*," he pokes Edward in the chest. "What's the bloody monarchy done for me, eh?"

Edward steps back, his sardonic grin wobbling into an expression of actual terror. In his ghost form, Abberline could actually hurt him. I notice an outline of a revolver in his pocket.

I start to step in between them, but Edward rallies, his eyes burning with passion. He flies at Abberline and grabs his collar. "Now, you listen to me, Detective Abberline, you may have a completely legitimate bone to pick with this crowd of Ripperologists making their coin off your name, but we are *here*. And I have something you don't have."

"Oh, yeah, what's that?" Abberline snaps back, but his eyes flicker with fear.

"An inflated sense of my own importance." Edward gestures to Pax. "And a savage warrior who has the power to churn your spleen into a lovely ball of mozzarella cheese if you don't cooperate."

Pax cracks his knuckles gleefully.

Go, Edward!

"Fine, fine," Abberline grumbles, waving his arm as he floats across the square. "Let's talk at the pub. But I ain't paying."

WE SQUEEZE into a booth at the old pub on the corner. Inspector Abberline makes me order him a pint of dark ale so he can sniff it.

"You know," Abberline settles back into the booth, his ass hovering over the seat, "everyone thinks the Ten Bells is the pub the Ripper frequented, but Polly Nichols and Annie Chapman more often than not drank in this very establishment. Kate Eddowes would often be at the piano, entertaining the place with a rousing song or a murder ballad. She had a beautiful voice."

He bends down and sticks his nose into the neck of his glass.

"Ah," Edward snaps his fingers. "Let me show you a trick. If you want to get the sensation of being mildly inebriated, then all you have to do is—"

I hold up a hand. "Before the two of you get drunk on ghost fumes and blow all the bulbs in this place, we're going to have our talk."

"Ah, yes." Abberline takes a long sniff of his beer. "What does a girl who can speak to ghosts want with me?"

"The thing is..." I take a deep breath. "Jack the Ripper is after me."

I expect Abberline to react in some way. But all he does is

sigh and fiddle with his policeman's pad. "So those fanatical bastards brought him back again?"

"Wait, what do you mean, *again?*"

"You know of this monster?" Ambrose leans forward eagerly.

"Just a minute." Abberline leans over and sniffs his drink before continuing. "I have information you want. If I give you answers, what do I get in return?"

I blink. Is he *shitting* me? "What do you mean?"

Abberline's face breaks into a terrifying, genuine smile. "I'll tell you everything you want to know...for a fee."

"You're a man of the law. And a ghost. What kind of fee can you possibly accept?" I growl. "Fine. I promise that you can come back to our room with us, and I'll order all your favourite dishes from UberEats so you can sniff them—"

"That's not what I'm after." Abberline shoots back. "You're going to bring me back to life."

I reel away, shocked.

How does he know?

Pax leans across the table, his fist menacingly close to Abberline's face. "How do you know of Bree's power? Are you working for the monster?"

"Please, I recognise a Roman warrior dressed in modern garb when I see one." Abberline pinches his nose. "Even as a ghost, your breath reeks."

"I'm *not* the vicious and bloodthirsty Roman centurion Pax Drusus Maximus." Pax doesn't move his fist as he struggles to remember the cover story I have drilled into his head. "I'm...a humble Italian tourist here to sample Britain's fine cuisine."

"You're a bloody Roman, sandals and all." Abberline turns to me. "And if I'm not mistaken, the gentleman sitting opposite me is from my own time. I'm right, aren't I? You brought them back from the dead. You're like *him.*"

"Like who? Father Bryne?"

"Pay up and I'll tell you."

I sigh. "It doesn't work like that. To make the resurrection magic work, we have to complete your unfinished business. Your unfinished business is identifying Jack the Ripper, one of the greatest unsolved murder mysteries of human history—"

"Oh, I know who the Ripper is," Abberline says. "I've seen him around, with his top hat and his airs and graces, the last time he was raised. He admitted his crimes to me over a pint once. It's Lord Fitzwilliam."

"So if you know who he is, then how come you haven't crossed over?"

"Because I haven't *stopped* him, have I?" Abberline pounds the table with his fist. Because he's sitting across from me and I've got moldavite in my pocket, his fist actually connects, sending his pint glass flying over my shoulder to hit the guy behind me in the head. The unsuspecting punter whirls around to give me a piece of his mind, but then sees Pax glaring at him and thinks better of it.

Abberline stares at his fist in wonder, then peers at me with wide eyes. "You *are* like him?"

Who's 'him'?

But I don't ask. Instead, I glare back at the inspector. "We're not talking about me. What about your unfinished business?"

"That was my job, to bring the Ripper to justice. But I never got to him and he disappeared before I could catch him, and then Lord Fitzy went and died of syphilis, which should have been the end of it, only he keeps being dragged out of hell to murder more innocent women, and I'm next to useless to stop him in this body, aren't I?"

"Okay, okay!" I hold up my hands in surrender before he can toss our bowl of chips over the poor guy's head. "I promise, you help us, and once we're rid of the Ripper forever, I will use my powers to bring you back to life. But, only if you acknowledge that I don't know what the fuck I'm doing, and I could accidentally trap you in some other dimension or reincarnate you as a penguin, okay?"

"I don't know what any of those words mean."

"Right, quantum physics wasn't discovered when you were alive, I forgot." I hold out my hand. "Just tell me if we have a deal or not?"

Inspector Abberline places his ghostly hand in mine, and we do as good a job of shaking as is possible when my fingers slip through his. He settles back in his chair, twirling his moustache around his finger.

"So..." he says. "You want to know about Jack the Ripper."

"Yes. I want to know how and why a long-dead murderer attacked me and my..." The word *boyfriends* dances over my tongue, but I swallow it back, "...friends."

"Let me guess, he had red vapours curling out of his eyes, and was controlled by some kind of deranged clergyman?"

I make finger guns at him. "Got it in one. We know he's a revenant."

Abberline's face clouds over. "The Order of the Noble Death have seen occasion to bring my nemesis back to the Living realm no less than three times since he was first banished to hell."

"Wait." I take a long sip of my G&T. I can tell I'm going to need it. "You know about the Order? You're saying that Jack the Ripper has come back before?"

"Aye. The Order does not like to do their own grunt work. What use is the power to raise the dead if you can't make yourself masters over them? They raise philosophers to analyse their scriptures, Pythagoras to balance their books, some fellow named Steve Jobs is doing their IT helpdesk, and murderers to act as their personal army. But the Ripper is their prized weapon. You must have really got under their skin for them to send him after you."

Or Vera did.

I could certainly imagine that. Vera got up everyone's goat.

As quickly as I can, I explain exactly what happened to Vera, and what we experienced in the graveyard. Edward even describes in excessively poetic detail how he went inside the Ripper and used his memories to help us track down Abberline. The ghost detective actually looks impressed, and Edward preens.

"The first thing you should know is that you didn't kill him," Abberline says. "Not for good, anyway. You merely slowed him down."

I groan. "I was afraid you'd say that."

Abberline nods. "The Order will call the Ripper back to them as soon as they realise he and the priest are gone. Or he might come back on his own, if he's angry enough. He will not stop until he has recreated each of his five grisly murders at the whims of the Order. He will take his victims, and then disappear until he is needed again."

"What do we do?"

"You don't understand. There is nothing you can do. The Ripper is impossible to catch, even more impossible to kill."

"So what do you suggest I do?"

"From what you're saying, the Ripper has been employed to kill people with your gift. So I suggest you find three more women who can do this resurrection magic, and make certain he gets to them first."

What. The. Actual. Fuck?

"My father would approve of this plan," Edward says.

"That's exactly why it's not an option," I growl. "I'm not going to throw anyone to this monster, and I'm not going to sit around and wait for the Ripper to tear me to pieces. So if you want me alive to resurrect you, you'd better come up with something better than this."

Abberline shrugs. "There's a priest at All Souls Church. It's just around the corner. I catch up with him for a chat sometimes. He's the one who told me about the Order. He hosts a weekly ghost circle where all the local spirits go to talk about things that bother us."

"Tell me more about this ghost circle." Edward raises his hand. "I have many grievances that I wish to air—"

"You think we should talk to a priest?" I shake my head. "No, thank you. I've had enough of the clergy trying to murder me."

"This priest is different. He hates the Order. And he's...well, he's a bit odd. Always quoting poetry." Abberline shrugs again. "You just have to meet him."

"Why didn't you say so?" Edward tries to shove me out of my seat. "A man after my own heart. Let us go and see this troublesome poet-priest."

22

BREE

I want to run over to that church right now, but it's already late and we need to return to our hotel. We have another appointment to keep.

We wave goodbye to Abberline, who goes back to yelling about historical inaccuracies as more people crowd the street in front of Aldgate Tower to join the Ripper tours.

Midway through cursing out a jovial American tourist who unintentionally walked through him, Edward disappears. The moldavite in my pocket must have finally stopped working. I look at Pax, squeeze Ambrose's hand, and breathe a sigh of relief. "Okay, he's gone. Let's get this show over with."

"I was beginning to think he'd never leave." Ambrose's eyes sparkle with joy. "I really hope this works, Bree. I want to do this for him. I want to give him the incredible gift of being able to touch you."

That's because you're impossibly kind, and none of us deserve you.

Pax has become distracted by a display of souvenir Ripper knives, but I pull him away and we get back on the tube.

A couple of stops later, we alight and – after a brief detour to a fish and chip shop to pick up some dinner – walk a block to our hotel, a crumbling old Tudor building that had once been a grand estate. It was now a cheap hotel – cheap by London standards, which meant that I had to empty my savings account to afford the Imperial King Suite. But it's vital we stay in that particular suite.

I duck under the low sign that proclaims the building 'The Most Haunted Hotel In London,' and fumble in my purse for the old-fashioned key to the door. The lady behind the front desk frowns at me as she watches me and my burly warrior and chatty gentleman carrying our greasy takeaways up to the room, but who is she to judge?

Gilded portraits of the building's most famous resident line the staircase, between framed newspaper clippings describing hauntings in the building, including sightings of a woman in a white gown peering into guests' bathtubs and tipping them out of the very bed I'm sleeping in.

I turn the second heavy key in the door, and the three of us crowd into the King Suite, which isn't exactly what I'd call fit for a king. Edward would certainly turn up his spectral nose at it. But that's what you get when you're on a budget in London.

The three of us crowd around the tiny TV table to eat our dinner. Ambrose is too excited to sit still. With every drip of the pipes or creak of the old building, he practically leaps out of his chair. "Is that her? Has she arrived yet?"

"Calm down and eat your chip butty. I'll tell you when I see her."

Once we are satiated, Pax picks up his sword and paces the room, checking under the bed and in the closet. Ambrose sits beside me as I dump out the contents of Dani's 'ghost attraction' bag on the lumpy bed.

A slow smile plays across my face as I finger the carefully chosen objects. An elegant lace handkerchief. A little silver hair comb. A vial of floral perfume. A small bottle of absinthe I sent Dani as a joke present from my trip to Prague. I grab my phone and whip off a quick text to Dani.

> Bree: You're amazing. You thought of everything.

> Dani: Years of you retelling Edward's stories of his time with the countess have imprinted in me an indelible image of her.

> Bree: You're still amazing.

> Dani: Hey, I'm almost as excited as you are to meet the poet prince in the flesh. Go get your man, girl!

I toss my phone aside and arrange the objects on the bed. I take the perfume and spritz it around the place, then light the candles, and wait.

And wait.

And wait.

"I'm bored now." Pax twirls his sword around on his finger. "Can I go to the park and feed the squirrels?"

"No. I need you here, just in case the countess isn't exactly thrilled to meet Edward's new paramour."

"Maybe if you recite one of Edward's poems?" Ambrose suggests hopefully.

"Oh, that's not a bad idea." I rack my brain, but if I'm honest, I kind of tune out a lot of Edward's poetry. It is really, *really* bad. The only poem of his that comes to mind is the one about my ass:

> *"Ah, fair creature, thy posterior doth entrance,*
> *A vision that captivates, by fate's own chance,*
> *In the realm of desire, where passions reside,*

Thine alluring curves, no secrets to hide..."

"Edward, is that you?"

The temperature drops.

The curtains flap, even though the windows are shut up tight.

The candles flicker.

I swallow hard. Pax raises his sword. Beside me, Ambrose jiggles his leg in excitement.

"Hello?" I call out.

A grey shape walks through the bathroom wall and stands at the foot of the bed. She wears a diaphanous white gown, her golden hair in loose ringlets that fly about her porcelain face. The front of her dress is stained pink from where her husband stabbed her after she discovered him in bed with his mistress.

And through her spectral body, I can see the outline of the bathroom door and my socks strewn across the floor.

The ghost of the Countess Marie de Rothschild glares down her perfect nose at me. "Who are you, and what have you done with my Edward?"

23

BREE

I've seen pictures of the Countess de Rothschild in many of Edward's biographies, but even as a spectre, I'm unprepared for her beauty. I try to speak, but I find I can't summon my voice, not when the only thing I can see is Edward's dark eyes worshipping this perfect creature. How am I ever supposed to compare to her?

But then I remember Edward's rapturous expression the other night, when I let him float inside me, and I feel bolstered.

She may be exquisite, but Edward and I have something special.

"Edward, my darling? Have you come to visit me? Have you crossed the oceans of the underworld to find me again?" She sweeps the room before pausing on me. "You there! Who are you? Where is my Edward? What are you doing in my house?" She flies at Pax. "Uncouth scoundrels! This is *my* home and I'm waiting for my lover, Edward—"

"We're friends of Edward," I say quickly.

"Friends of my Prince Eddie?" Her hand flies to her mouth. "I don't believe you. You certainly don't look the sorts to be his friends. Your bosom isn't nearly comely enough to please him."

"He likes my bosom just fine." I fold my arms. "But if you

mean the *Prince Eddie* who loves rhyming couplets and getting his jollies with the circuit breakers, then yes, we're his friends and we need to speak to you."

"That sounds like my Eddie," she purrs, draping herself over the corner of the bed. "Tell me about this electrical socket. Why, I haven't had a decent orgasm since...since the night Eddie died, in fact. Why, the things that man can do with his tongue—"

Her Eddie? I can't help the flare of possessiveness engulfing my heart as she speaks. I don't want to think of his tongue being anywhere near her, even though their affair was literally *centuries* ago.

This is why you should never look up the ghosts of your lover's exes.

"You were with Edward when he died?" Ambrose leans forward excitedly. "Did you see him fall out the window?"

"Alas, no. We had finished our liaisons and Edward had fallen into an opium-laced stupor. I tucked him into bed and went to rejoin the revelry downstairs. Edward and I had shared the last bottle of wine, you see, and I wanted to see what other delectable treats awaited me downstairs..." Her dreamy eyes rolled back in her head as she went to someplace in her memories.

"Who else was present during these...revels?" We have the list of names Mina dug out of the history books, but several of the guests may have already fallen into opium stupors of their own at that stage. My heart races at the realisation that this woman might have been Edward's murderer, or that she might have seen something that could help.

The countess ticks them off on her fingers. "The naughty Earl of Bainbridge. Caroline of Bexley, some French tart whose name I can't recall, the artist Cavendish, the occultist Thronsden – and Hugh – Eddie's best friend, of course. He brought a case of French absinthe, which was just as well because we drank all the wine."

"Did anyone leave the party after you joined?"

"But of course! Caroline and the Earl of Bainbridge went out into the back garden to serenade the moon. Hugh went out to chop more firewood, Cavendish, Bainbridge and Thronsden fornicated in the downstairs bathtub—"

I'm never using that tub again.

"So any one of them could have snuck upstairs and pushed Edward out the window?"

"I suppose so." The countess shrugs. "But they all loved Eddie dearly. He put on the most delightful parties, and he threw money at them all so they could concentrate on their artwork. You can't possibly think one of them could have done it."

"Actually," Ambrose cuts in. "We think you might have done it."

"What?" she recoils, horrified. "You think I could have hurt my Eddie?"

"Yes, that's precisely what we think," I growl. I'm sick of her referring to *my* Edward as *her Eddie*. "You could be lying to us about leaving the room and rejoining the party. After all, from what you've described, everyone was far too inebriated to know if you were there or not. You could easily have pushed him out the window."

"What possible reason would I have to murder him?"

"Because he refused to marry you." I remember Edward's memory, her clinging to him and begging him. "I believe that you told him that if you can't have him, no one could."

She pales. "I didn't mean that I wished to kill him. Why, and deprive the world of that man's extraordinary tongue? No, I was hysterical, drunk, I only wanted him to be mine...and besides, how would I have killed him? I am but a delicate flower and Edward is a strong oak."

"Hmph," Pax glowers. "I disagree with this description, although I suppose Edward does have arms like little twigs."

"You could have waited for him to fall into his opium stupor and then dragged him to the window," I say. "He has a little bruise on his neck from where someone held him. There's always a way available to a determined murderess."

"But I didn't murder him!" the countess sobs. "I won't tolerate this slander in my own house, upon the scene of my own murder!"

I wince, because it is cruel to confront her here. But if she killed Edward...

"I don't have to stand for this!" The countess hurls herself at the wall, but the moldavite I'm still carrying means that instead of falling through it into the room beyond, she crashes into it and drops to a heap on the floor.

"H-h-how did you do that?" She glares up at me, rubbing her side.

"I have powers you cannot fathom," I growl. "I am a human who can reach you beyond death, which means that I can fuck with you. I can even make you cross over, so you won't be able to haunt this place any longer."

It's a bluff, but I'm hoping she won't call me on it.

"No, I don't want to cross over," she moans, throwing herself dramatically to the floor. "I like it here. This is my home. I like meeting all the people and seeing their eyes bug out when I surprise them in the bathtub."

"You'll never again tickle a guest in the bathtub." I rub my hands together. "Unless you tell us the truth about that night."

"I—I—I—am, I swear it on my Eddie's virile member!" she trembles, wrapping her arms around herself. "I couldn't hurt him. I love him. I was going to leave my husband for him. I would become his permanent muse. We would run off to France together after the party was over. Why would I want to kill him?"

Edward was going to run away with this woman?

That hits me harder than I expect. Edward has always talked about the Countess de Rothschild in the same way he speaks of all his other exploits – as a knock between the sheets and nothing more. But was there something deeper between them? Why has he never mentioned it?

I slump back on the bed. The countess could still be lying, but she certainly sounded distressed. I believed her, which meant that if she wasn't the murderer, she might be able to help us figure out who it is.

But then I recall the rest of the foggy, opium-laced memory I fell into when Edward was inside me, when he told her that he wouldn't go away with them. What she's saying doesn't mesh with that memory. "Edward was going to run away *with* you?"

"Well, he hadn't exactly agreed yet," she says primly. "But I was working on it. I *can* be very persuasive."

"You will regret this. You will regret giving up your life for me. I am not worthy of your devotion, and I do not love you as you deserve to be loved. You must stay, and endure, and let your pain fuel your art. But know that wherever I am, you will always be a muse to me."

Those were Edward's words to her. I understood what they meant now. I sat back on the bed and regarded the countess' tear-streaked face, and the bloodstains on her dress after her husband killed her. She tried to endure, and look what it got her. Women have never had it fair.

I warm to her, just a little bit. "Okay, so let us say for argument's sake that you didn't kill him. Do you have any idea who might wish him harm?"

"Apart from his father, you mean?" The countess brightens. "Yes, it wouldn't surprise me to learn that his father sent an assassin to scale the building, climb in through the window, and push Edward to his death."

Pax snorts.

I glance over at him in surprise, and he shakes his head. "This did not happen. I was guarding the grounds that night, as I did every night before I became mortal and must succumb to infernal sleep. If an assassin snuck into Grimwood, I would have seen him."

"You never said that you saw Edward fall."

"You never asked. And Edward would not like to know."

That's true.

I reel from this news. But if Pax didn't see who pushed Edward, or even that he was pushed, he can't give us any further information. I turn back to the countess. "It has to have been one of his friends at the party that night. Did Edward give any of them a reason to bear a grudge?"

"I do recall one thing," the countess frowns. "I left Eddie sleeping and went downstairs to see what all the splashing was about. Some time later, I don't remember when, I heard voices from upstairs. It was Edward and Hugh, and they were arguing. At least, they might have been arguing. I had had an awful lot of absinthe..."

"Either they were arguing or they weren't. Which is it?"

"Their voices were raised with passion," she snaps. "This is not an uncommon occurrence. Poets, you see, are naturally all aflutter with emotions. I shant expect you'd know anything about that. But Edward could be quite passionate, especially with his lovemaking—"

I don't want to hear it. "Can you recall what they were arguing about?"

After all, Hugh was the one who stole Edward's poem, 'Thou Comest a Thief.'

She shoves her hands on her hips and glares at me. "You're

asking me to remember something that happened four centuries ago, while I was dancing with the green fairy?"

"It's very, very important to Edward," Ambrose says. He's much better at this than I am. "If he could be here, I know he'd want to thank you for telling me all of this."

"Oh, dear Eddie." She clutches her heart and falls back onto the sofa. She must've expected to drop through the sofa, only because I'm still carrying my moldavite, her body slams into it. She yelps and jerks upright. "I don't like this. What have you done to me?"

"Never you mind about that," Ambrose says. "Bree will reverse it later. If you tell us everything you remember, then I can show you Edward's trick with the light fixtures."

She perks up at that. "Okay, yes, it's strange that you say this, and it's all rushing back to me. I passed Hugh on the staircase and he informed me that he needed to talk to Eddie. Something smashed downstairs. 'That's the last of it,' Hugh was yelling, and Edward said, *'I'll* say when we're done.' And then... and then Hugh says something like, 'I won't take it,' and Edward responds with, 'I'm a better poet than you will ever be.'"

"I remember nothing more after that, just more raised voices and at some point, glass smashed, but Eddie was always getting merry and breaking things. The next time I saw Hugh, it was after he found Eddie's body. He was lying in the bathtub, with a new bottle of wine in his hands, and he was murmuring Edward's name over and over again."

So Hugh and Edward were alone in his bedchamber, arguing about poetry, right before Edward fell to his death. And in my vision, I saw a dark shadow looming from the corner of the room...

That doesn't seem suspicious at all.

"You don't happen to know what became of Hugh?"

Did he become a ghost? Can we confront him?

The countess waves a hand. "Oh, he went the way of all great poets – he smoked too much opium and went for a midnight swim in the Thames. They found him floating face up the next day, naked as the day he was born, the words of his final poem scrawled across his chest."

"That sounds like the kind of violent death that might turn a poet into a ghost," Ambrose says hopefully.

"How should I know? I can't leave this blasted house. Now." She stares pointedly at the light switch. "Tell me about naughty Edward's latest trick."

24

BREE

After a wretched night's sleep punctuated by the Countess de Rothschild wailing about Edward and the disgruntled stompings of other guests when they discovered the fuses had blown out, Ambrose has to shake me awake so we can get downstairs in time for breakfast.

I *had* hoped that the two of us could finally have our first night together since Ambrose became a Living, but between Pax stealing all the blankets and the countess's shenanigans, it didn't live up to the romantic ideal that Ambrose aspired to, and so he kissed my hand like a gentleman and offered to sleep on the sofa.

So I lay awake all night with Pax's arm thrown protectively over me, my skin flushed with heat at the thought of what we *could* be doing if we didn't have our ghostly visitor... and now I look and feel like shit.

"It's continental and cold drinks only," the landlady snaps as she drops a bowl of yoghurt on the table in front of me. "The blasted power is on the fritz."

"Sounds delicious." Ambrose reaches for a slice of untoasted bread. How can that man be so chipper? Isn't he desperate to tear all my clothes off, the way I am his?

I wish I could see Edward. He'd talk to Ambrose, tell him to stop being so much of a gentleman waiting for the right time and just fuck me already. I grip the moldavite in my fist and think of him, but it doesn't conjure him in front of me. I guess once the ghost mojo pulls you back, I need to be nearby to bring him with me again.

But we can't go home yet. We're staying in London for one more day.

We have to attend church.

I *need* to meet this mysterious priest Abberline told us about.

Outside, the weather is your typical British summer – overcast and cool, with takeout packaging skittering across the footpath. Ambrose slips his arm in mine and we stroll through a small, oak-lined park on our way to All Souls. Pax walks a few steps in front of us, his sword swinging off his belt. No one comments on it. This is London, after all.

We reach the church. It's a spooky, gothic affair with a towering spire piercing the grey sky. A couple of people walk around the churchyard, squinting at names on the ancient graves, but there don't appear to be any services today. The church door is closed.

We go up to the door and knock, but no one answers. I hunt around for a listing of services, but find nothing except a little sign that says, 'Thursday Spirit Circle: All Welcome' and a picture of a smiling ghost. We're *definitely* in the right place, but it's not open. Can a church be *closed?* Is that allowed?

"Your puny Christian god is no match for my Roman strength." Pax cracks his knuckles. "I shall find our priest if I have to break every door in this temple."

But as he rams his shoulder into the door, it flies open, sending him flying across the marble floor.

"It's unlocked," I call out to him.

"It would appear so," Ambrose says brightly.

"So I don't get to smash the door?" Pax makes a face as he picks himself up off the floor.

"Not this time."

The door bangs on its hinges, and I step through into a dark, empty church. A narrow aisle leads past the rows of wooden pews to a small altar within a gothic stone archway. Dappled light reflects from the stained glass windows.

I take a step inside, peering into the gloomy corners, searching for a priest. *Why is this place so—*

"Halt, in the name of Odin. Who goes there?"

Pax draws his sword and leaps in front of me as a large, bearded man hurls himself from behind the altar and thunders down the aisle toward us. The figure raises his own sword and charges at Pax.

Is he carrying a sword?

I squint at this man who rushes toward us. He isn't a man so much as a beast, with a wild, scraggly beard strung with colourful glass beads, long, braided strawberry-blond hair swinging halfway down his back, and wearing a tunic, woollen pants, leather boots, and a fur-lined cloak.

He looks a bit...like a Viking, but that's crazy. Why would a guy in a Viking costume be in a church?

The beast of a man stops halfway down the aisle, his sword tip pointing directly at Pax's throat. "My Thain will not be disturbed. Turn around, or by Odin's name, you shall regret your impertinence."

My heart hammers, but Pax peers at the man with interest. "You...you carry your sword as if you know how to use it."

"Would you like to find out, friend?" the beast growls. "Gaze upon thy destiny, for with this sword I will cleave your lying maggot mouth from your swine head!"

"By Jupiter's bendy beanstalk, I'd like to see you try!"

Pax screams, the Viking screams, and I scramble away as they leap at each other.

Their swords clash. Pax leaps onto a pew and attempts to stave the Viking's head in with the pommel of his sword, but the Viking simply swipes Pax's knees out from beneath him, sending Pax crashing to the floor. Both of their swords slide away across the marble floor. The Viking climbs on top of Pax, wrapping his huge hands around my Roman's throat.

"No, stop!" I cry out.

Beside me, Ambrose squeezes my hand, dragging me back to the safety of the doorway.

"In Odin's name, surrender!" the Viking yells, bearing his weight down on Pax's throat.

"Never!" Pax manages to choke out.

He reaches up and pinches the Viking's nose.

The Viking drops his hands from Pax's throat and lets out a high-pitched yelp as he grips his face. Pax rolls away and dives for his sword, but the Viking kicks it away.

"You...you bug on Thor's mighty hammer!" he cries as he goes after his own sword. He raises it above his head as he stalks toward Pax. "You foetid carbuncle on Loki's wrinkled arse! I'll...I'll..."

"Stop!"

A black-clad figure rushes from the sacristy.

"No, no, this won't do. Please, Björn, lay down your weapon. These are our guests."

To my utter surprise, the beast immediately lowers his sword and slinks back, looking sullen.

"Pax!" Never letting go of Ambrose, I rush to Pax and help him to his feet. Pax coughs and rubs his throat, but he seems unhurt. He looks in confusion at the newcomer. "Am I fighting you instead? Do you think this a wise battle to choose? You are puny and will snap like a twig."

"I will indeed, friend." The man places his hand on Pax's shoulder. "Which is why there will be no blood spilt in this church. Come with me, all of you. I was just brewing a cup of tea."

"So no battle?" Pax looks disappointed.

"No battle, but I do have a chocolate log, and some Jammy Dodgers, if that's any consolation. And I can even converse in your native Latin if you prefer." The man looks over at me and winks. It's only then that I realise that his outfit is a priest's black robe.

This must be the priest that Abberline was talking about, but...

"You...you know that Pax is..."

"A Roman warrior?" The priest smiles. "Yes. I recognise the design of his sword and the timbre of his insults. Funnily enough, he's not the first Roman warrior I've encountered."

"And your friend isn't a Dungeonmaster, but..."

"Bjorn is a Viking from the 9th century AD, yes." The priest taps the beast's leather armour. "He was killed by the monks defending this monastery from sacking, and he haunted the churchground for several centuries. But now he is flesh and blood, like your two friends here. Come into the sacristy with me. I see that we have much to discuss."

25

BREE

The priest leads us through the small, gothic arch to the left of the altar and through a small room housing the robes and other implements for Holy Mass. At the rear of the room is another arched door, which he pushes open.

Inside is a small sitting room, containing mismatched wooden chairs, a desk shoved under the window, and piles of books cluttering every surface. Mina and Quoth would feel right at home here. A cup of tea and a half-eaten slice of chocolate log sit beside the torn leather armchair. Another armchair with stuffing coming loose sits facing his desk.

The priest gestures to the chairs. "Please, make yourselves at home. I'll cut you some chocolate log. The kettle will take a few minutes to boil."

I help Ambrose find the edge of the first armchair, and he settles in. I shuffle some books off the chair opposite his and sink down. The priest heads into a small kitchenette, sets a kettle on the gas hob, and pulls out three mismatched cups. He lifts the lid off a biscuit tin to reveal a perfectly baked chocolate log. Björn offers him a dagger, but the priest waves him off and pulls a cake slicer and some saucers from the cupboard and starts serving generous slices.

"That's my slice." Pax grabs the tin from the priest's hands and swipes his finger in the cream.

"No, it's mine." Björn grabs for the tin, but Pax holds it out of reach.

"I'll duel you for it."

The Viking's eyes widen with delight. "Can we?"

The priest waves his hand at a small door in the back of the room. "Go down into the woods where no one can see you. And you will only fight until first blood. Cake is not a 'to-the-death' battle."

"That's only if it was for the last Lindt ball." Björn nods vigorously as he pushes the door open, revealing an overgrown path down through the cemetery toward a small copse of trees. Calling it a wood is rather generous.

"Correct. Lindt balls are better than sex." The priest sighs. "And I should know."

I watch in a kind of stupor as Pax trots off across the church-yard after his new friend, both of them swinging their swords and talking about how they're going to best each other.

My life is surreal.

The priest shuts the door behind him and hands me and Ambrose each a plate with our own slice of chocolate log. I notice the way he helps Ambrose curl his fingers around the edge and locate the fork. The kettle boils and he pours us each a cup of tea.

He's young, maybe early thirties, with sandy blonde hair and kind eyes. But I've been fooled by kind eyes and a priest collar before.

Now that his guests are served, the priest sinks into his own chair and cuts off a piece of cake. He brings it to his lips and sighs happily.

"I suppose," he says as he cuts off another large piece, dwindling Pax or Björn's slice down to less than half, "that you came here to see me. Which ghost put you up to it?"

"Detective Abberline."

"Ah, yes. Sometimes, to catch a scoundrel like the Ripper, you need to employ an equal or greater scoundrel. Abberline wasn't scoundrel enough, although heaven knows he tried." The priest finishes chewing and rounds on me with those haunted blue eyes. "Now, shall we get down to business?"

The cake turns to dust in my mouth. It hits me that this is the first time I've ever been in the room with someone like me before. Well, I met Vera in her shop, but I didn't know that she was like me at the time. "I don't really know where to begin."

"Your name would be a good start."

"Oh, yes. I'm Bree. Bree Mortimer."

"Ambrose Hulme, at your service." Ambrose bows his head. "And the fellow with the sword is Pax Drusus Maximus."

"Well, Bree Mortimer and Ambrose Hulme, welcome to All Souls Church. You can see that I run a very different kind of congregation around here. I'm Father Maxwell. It's a pleasure to meet you both."

"If it's a pleasure, why did your Viking almost kill us back there?"

"You have to forgive Björn. He's very protective." Father Maxwell steeples his fingers. "I've had a lot of trouble over the years. Now, Bree, I gather that you are a Lazarus."

I start at the term. It's only the second time someone has called me that, and the first one tried to kill me. He was *also* a priest.

"I suppose I am." I huff out a breath. Ambrose reaches over and brushes his fingers over my arm, steadying me.

"Admitting it is the first step." Father Maxwell says with a kind smile.

I grip my teacup in my hand and take a sip. The tea is a little calming. "The last priest who I spoke to raised Jack the Ripper from his grave to come after me."

"Ah, so I see the Order of the Noble Death has found you."

"You know about them? How come they haven't come for you?"

In response, the priest pulls open a tiny drawer in his desk and removes an object. A wooden box. He opens it and holds it up so I can see the contents.

It's a collection of spiky metal crosses – identical to the one I pulled from Father Bryne's chest.

"What is it?" Ambrose asks excitedly. "Gold? Candy? Some sort of treasure map?"

"It's a box filled with crosses like the one Father Bryne wore," I say, fishing my own out of my pocket and pressing it into his fingers. "But there must be at least twenty in there."

"Having one's own personal resurrected berserker comes in handy," the priest says mildly as he replaces the box in the drawer.

"Why, Father, that doesn't seem very 'love thy neighbour' of you," I smile.

Despite my fear, I think I like this guy.

"The Order darkens the doorstep of everyone with our powers, eventually." Father Maxwell's voice darkens. "They know not to come too close to this church now. Between Björn's sword and the charms I've worked on the boundary, they never stick around long. But The Order keep a careful eye on me from afar. I've no doubt that they already know you visited me. You're not the first rogue Lazarus who has found me." He steeples his fingers.

"How do they know? Do they sense Bree's magic?" Ambrose asks.

"No. You can chat to ghosts all you like and the Order

won't trouble you. It's only once you figure out how to raise the dead that they get all biblical on your ass." He says this with a pointed look at Ambrose that he, of course, totally misses.

"I don't know how I do that," I say, which isn't entirely true. Now isn't the time to tell him I've been training my powers with a group of ghost witches. "It's just sort of happened by accident."

"You've done it twice, I see. I think you have a fair idea of how our resurrection magic works." There's no fooling this priest. "My question for you, Bree Mortimer, is what do you want from me?"

"According to my research, I killed Jack the Ripper, but where 'the Veil is weak', he could potentially come back. That's not going to work for me. I want Jack the Ripper to be gone forever. I don't want him to hurt anyone else. I don't want the Order to send any more revenants after us."

"Unfortunately, that's not a wish I'm capable of granting. The Order will never stop hunting you. And I'm going to assume also that you don't wish your newly Living friends to be ashes and dust once more?"

"No." I reach across and place my hand protectively on Ambrose's chest. "These guys have been my friends since I was a kid. I love...I love having them in my life for real now. I don't want to lose them."

"Then you need to learn how to protect yourself from the Order and the monsters they will send after you. You may have banished Jack the Ripper, and it's very unlikely that he's powerful enough to sneak back through the Veil, but he is only the first."

I shudder. Father Maxwell leans forward. "I can help you protect yourself. But first, tell me what you know about your resurrection powers."

I swallow. "Okay, so, ever since I had an accident when I was five and hit my head, I've been able to see ghosts—"

"That's not entirely true." Father Maxwell sips his coffee. "Our power is innate within us. We've always been able to see spirits, from the day we were born."

Excuse me, *what?*

I let out a breath in a long wheeze. I've always been able to see ghosts? That doesn't make any sense. Why don't I remember?

But then I *do* remember something. I remember Edward telling me that he was certain I could see him as a toddler. That I would sometimes point to him or offer him my toys. A shiver runs down my spine.

Ambrose squeezes my hand. "I always told you that you were special."

"It takes years for all the facets of our ability to manifest," Father Maxwell explains. "Bumping your head probably sped up the process. Jiggled something loose, as it were. We don't usually gain the power to converse with ghosts until later in life. And all Lazarii carry within us the ability to restore ghosts to life. A ghost is simply a soul that has yet to cross over. When we die, our souls enter the Veil, and from there they are judged and sent on to the Lands Beyond, where not even men of god like me know what becomes of them. We are one end of a string that reaches through the Veil – we can pull a soul back out again and give that soul a body. After all, a body is simply stardust and energy."

I never wanted to be special. I wished and wished that I could be normal. I often thought that if I just hadn't gone out on my bike that day, I never would have been Bree the village freak. I stare down at Ambrose's fingers wrapped around me, so warm and reassuring and real, and I realise that it's not true anymore.

I've stopped wishing I was normal. I am who I am – I am Bree, and I'm a Lazarus. I always thought my power came because of a stupid accident, but it's part of me. It *is* me.

I don't want to be normal, not if it means I never met Ambrose, Edward, and Pax. And I will fight until my dying breath to keep them at my side.

I look over at Father Maxwell, and he gives me another one of his shy smiles. "It's okay, Bree Mortimer. You're among friends here."

"Okay." I nod slowly. "Okay. So I was born with these powers to reach into the Veil. And since I was five I've been able to see and talk to ghosts. I live in this old manor house in Grimdale, so I see a lot of them around. Pax and Ambrose and Edward – he's still a ghost, so we couldn't bring him along today – they were my friends. Sometimes that was difficult, especially as a teenager. They wouldn't shut up. Sometimes I forgot that no one could see them but me, and it made me look weird in front of the other kids. I was a target for bullies, and I guess I didn't deal with that very well. When I turned eighteen, I went away travelling, and when I returned to Grimdale a couple of months ago and met my three ghost friends again, things were different."

The priest raises a knowing eyebrow. "Different how?"

"Sometimes, I can touch them – actually feel the edges of them. And when they're close to me, they can interact with the human world. They bump into furniture or hold things. Another Lazarus named Vera gave me a moldavite stone, and when I have that in my pocket, they can leave the house and travel with me for a time."

"Hmmm, this moldavite stone is news to me," Father Maxwell says. "This is why the Order tries to snuff us out. They want to prevent us from finding each other and sharing information about what we can do. But everything you've described is part of coming into your power. Your abilities have been developing all these years, but because you actively sought to stay away from ghosts, you didn't notice until you returned."

I've been wondering what's changed since I returned, and it turns out that what's changed...is me. "That's not all. I've started seeing things."

"Let me guess – silver cords stretching from ghosts?"

I tell him about the silver cords that wind from every person and ghost, how I brought Pax and Edward to life, and also how I was able to heal Pax after the Ripper stabbed him.

"This is interesting." Father Maxwell stands on his long legs and crosses his cramped library, pulling a few books off the shelves seemingly at random. "It takes many Lazarii decades to discover the secrets of their resurrection powers – the use of the cords that tether us to the Veil, and the need to find the spark, the catalyst of the ghost's unfinished business. You have figured things out early. And you have done something few of us have been able to do – you have sent the Ripper back into the Veil. Can you tell me how you did that?"

"I don't really know." I describe how I stabbed him with his own knife, and what we found out from our books, that with his master dead, the Ripper was temporarily mortal.

Father Maxwell sips his tea, his eyes never leaving my face. Out the window behind his head, Pax and Björn wrestle on the edge of the wooded parkland behind the church.

Father Maxwell flips the book in his lap around, showing me a horrific image of a shadowy serpent beast. I gasp as I realise that I've seen this same image once before. A cruder version was drawn in the occult book Dani was studying at Nevermore Bookshop. The creature is called a Soul-Eater.

Only in this image, a woman holds onto one of the Soul-Eater's horns and twists a blade into its gut.

"This is Saint Ekaterina slaying a demon. She was a Lazarus, and she travelled the world as a healer and exorcist during the Middle Ages. She sent many a demonic being back through the Veil before she was hanged as a witch, only for her miracles to be recognised many centuries later. Very little is known about her, but I was lucky enough to inherit this book of her writings. Hers is the only written account I've ever read of how a Lazarus might bring a ghost back to life again. The Order has worked hard to expunge all other traces in the historical record. They don't want Lazarii they don't control to get their hands on this magic."

He turns to another page, and I find myself recognising this drawing as well. A cruder version was drawn on one of the pages Vera left me.

"That's a picture of a revenant." I stare down at the page as a shudder wracks my body.

"Correct, and I'm impressed that you've uncovered this. Revenants are the soulless bodies of people who were once alive. We can think about them a bit like the golems of Jewish myths – they are capable only of base urges, and they exist only to fulfil their purpose. That's why the Order raises killers as their soldiers, because their revenants retain their base urges to maim, to kill. But Saint Ekaterina knew how to stop them; first, by poisoning their master so that their hold slipped, and then, when the revenant was mortal, slaying it with its own weapon to bind its evil. This is exactly what you did to Jack the Ripper."

I shudder at the memory of the Ripper's smile as he plunged his knife into Pax's chest.

"But we're not like that, are we?" Ambrose asks, a tremor of fear creeping into his bright voice. "Pax and I aren't revenants? We're as full of soul as we've ever been."

I glance across to my adventurer, his eyes round with fear, his fingers entwined with mine, squeezing tight. And I don't need Father Maxwell to give me an answer. Ambrose is nothing like the Ripper.

"Only God can see the truth of your soul, but yes, as far as I know, you are whole once more," Father Maxwell taps the book. "It's true that if the Veil were weak, the Ripper would be able to come back, but trust me, the Veil is well-guarded. It is safe. But it will only be a matter of time before the Order raises the Ripper again, or something worse. But I think I might be able to find something in this book to protect you. I need to study the text more carefully. The Latin is very tricky, but perhaps your Roman can help me—"

CLANG.

The sound makes all of us leap from our chairs. I glance out the window and realise I can no longer see Pax or Björn. The door flies open, crashing against the wall and sending several books cascading down on Ambrose. Björn and Pax make two attempts to crowd their bulk through the tiny door before Pax relents and allows the Viking ahead of him.

"You must come quickly, Father," Björn says, his voice grave. "We have another one."

26

PAX

The priest is already on his feet when we enter the room. "Excuse me," he says to Bree. He hurries after my new friend Björn. Bree's eyes meet mine, wide and curious.

"Pax, what's going on?"

"I do not know. Björn and I were locked in a fierce battle of wits when..." I grab her arm and pull her toward the door. "You must see for yourself."

"And me, too." Ambrose smooths down his coat. "I want to know, too."

There's no time to argue, to force them both to remain behind in the temple where they are out of danger. Bree has that look in her eyes, that one that says she's more stubborn than a Carthaginian in the middle of a good siege. I grab Ambrose's hand and drag them both through the church and out into the cemetery where Björn and I had been fighting.

I don't like this place, either, with its rows of crooked grave markers like the teeth of a Gorgon. These are bodies buried within the walls of a city, which is not okay. But Björn is so comfortable here, I didn't want to show him my weakness.

And now...

I lead Bree over to a tall grave with a stone cross, where a girl of barely fifteen summers sits with tears streaming down her cheeks. She burst through the woods and interrupted our battle right as Björn was showing me his legendary Thor's Hammer Shuffle, causing him to lose his balance and nearly slice off his own toe.

She had a child in her arms. A boy barely five summers old, with the same fiery red hair and deep freckles across his nose. She lay his limp body at Björn's feet and implored him, "Get Father Maxwell. He can save my brother."

Now, the priest is bent over the boy, who is lying on the grass, the shadow of that stone cross passing over his deadly pale face. His chest does not rise. Whatever the priest hopes to do, it is too late, for the boy has travelled to Hades.

Björn gathers the girl in his arms, holding her against his chest, soothing her hair. He meets my eyes, warrior to warrior. Understanding passes between us. We have seen too much death on the battlefield, but we feel each fallen comrade as if it were our first.

This boy has died before his time.

The priest has his eyes closed. He holds his hand over a circular wound on the boy's chest, twisting his fingers in the air. I've seen enough moving pictures to recognise a bullet hole. From a miniature siege weapon, which I believe is called a gun. These are appalling weapons, coward's weapons. If you want to kill a man, you should do it face to face, with a sword, where you can see as you turn his guts into tagliatelle.

"What's he doing?" Bree asks Björn, but the Viking shakes his head, his long, beaded beard slapping against his jaw. The red circle on the boy's chest spreads further, and both of us are lost in visceral memories of battle.

The girl sobs as the priest holds the boy. "Please, Father. I know you can perform miracles. Please..."

Bree must see on my face that I'm stricken. She and Ambrose wrap their arms around me, but her eyes don't leave the priest as he passes his hands over the boy and mutters his useless prayers to his sadomasochistic god.

"I can see them," she whispers. "The cords. He's...holding the boy's cord. He's trying to bring him back..."

Above our heads, the dark clouds roll over. Thunder cracks in the distance. The air grows thin, full of malice. I make the sign against evil. Jupiter is displeased. The dead are supposed to stay dead.

The boy opens his eyes and coughs.

The priest removes his hand from the boy's chest. I can see that beneath the blood, the wound has closed over. The priest drops a small metal object from his hand onto the grass. The bullet.

The boy has healed. He clings to Father Maxwell and coughs and hacks and splutters. A cold chill slithers down my spine.

This feels wrong. The air is stretched too thin, as if the church steeple has torn a hole in the heavens.

The girl sags in Björn's arms. "Thank you, Father."

Father Maxwell stands, dusting dirt and leaves from his black clothing. "You must be careful, Kiera. You know you shouldn't be hanging around those people."

"I know." She wraps her arms around the boy and glares at all of us in turn. I recognise that fire in her eyes – it burns inside me whenever I think about someone taking Bree away from me. "But they're the only family we have. Brayden and I don't have anywhere else to go."

"Björn will go around and see your father again, see if that calms things down. If we want to keep Brayden safe, we need a new plan." Father Maxwell places a hand on his shoulder. "Take Brayden and wait for me in my office. I will see what I can do."

Björn walks the two of them in the direction of the church. He nods at me over his shoulder. I nod back. I am proud of my new friend Björn and the work he does here. Bree has been worried that I would not fit in her modern world, but Björn has shown me that there is always work for men like us. I must continue to protect Bree, the way he protects Father Maxwell and his parishioners like Brayden.

Bree steps up to Father Maxwell, an unreadable look in her eyes. "What happened here?"

"Brayden was caught in the middle of his older brother's turf war, another unfortunate victim of the rising gang violence in London. There are a lot of gangs in this area, and these kids... they get caught in the crossfire. I do what I can. I make sure they know that there is always a sanctuary for them here at All Souls, but..." he crosses himself fervently. "Often, when they come to me, it is too late."

"But not too late for Brayden. How did you resurrect him without his unfinished business?"

"The same way you resurrected Pax after he bled out from the Ripper's blade. Unfinished business is required for ghosts who are separated from their earthly body. But Brayden still had his body. I can tie together the severed pieces of his cord and restore him."

"How many people have you resurrected, Father?" Bree asks.

At her question, the air trembles.

"I have lost count."

"Are there...consequences to this?"

"There are always consequences." The priest closes his eyes. "But how can I refuse a soul that is crying for help? How could I let Brayden die?"

Above our heads, the thunder cracks again.

Whatever power Bree and Father Maxwell wield, the gods are not amused.

27

AMBROSE

It's a week after our trip to London. Bree's spirits have improved after our conversation with Father Maxwell. After he found Brayden a new shirt to wear from the church's charity bins and took some details from Kiera so he could help her get a job and a place to live, he taught Bree how to create wards using Saint Ekaterina's spells. He anointed several of the crosses he took from Order Knights with scented oils and spoke words of magic over them. Bree and I spent the week hammering these warding crosses into the dirt in all the corners of Grimwood Manor and Nevermore Bookshop. That should keep Bree – and all of us – safe from the Ripper when he returns, as long as we're inside either of those two buildings.

All of this should be terrifying, but Bree is handling it better than I expected. She's singing in the shower, helping her dad paint the guest bedrooms and her mum haul furniture into the outbuilding, and even letting Edward recite some of his poetry for her.

She has answers. She knows what she is.

She's not running from her powers any longer.

She's even practising her magic. Today, she finds me as I arrive at the cemetery for my morning shift.

"Ambrose, hold these flowers." Bree presses several stalks into my hand.

"I'm the one who's supposed to give *you* flowers. And these don't seem very bright." I touch the petals and find that they're shrivelled and brittle.

"Just hold them steady, will you?" she says with a smile in her voice. I can't see what she's doing, but I sense her hands moving in the air around me. The stalks grow warm between my fingers, and the brittleness in them disappears as the stalks swell with fresh moisture. *Life.*

A soft fragrance wafts through the air.

"Touch them now," Bree says.

I run my fingers over the petals, which are now plump and full. The flowers have gone from shrivelled dead stalks to beautiful blooms. I shove my nose right inside and breathe deeply. They smell positively *divine.*

Of course, I think everything Bree does is divine.

"Bree, you made the flowers grow again! That's amazing."

"I know, right? I've been practising on plants. It makes sense to have control over my magic." She lowers her voice. "I've been trying to give Dad's giant cucumber a little magic, too, to make up for not watering it. It's now so large that he might have to cut the door off the greenhouse to get it to the fair."

"I love that."

"I'm getting pretty good with flowers and fruit, but their unfinished business is simple. Flowers want to bloom and fruit wants to be eaten. But I can't bring myself to practise on people. The witches are all well and good, but they know nothing about resurrection magic. I just wish that someone like Vera or Father Maxwell could teach me instead," she says. "I'm still terrified that I'll do something wrong and end up hurting one of you. I guess we could look up the other witches buying moldavite from Vera's list, but with the Order of the Noble Death watching me, I don't want to lead them to more Lazarii."

"I think you're doing pretty well on your own," I tell her. "Are you ready for our date this afternoon?"

"Of course." She kisses me on the cheek, leaving a burning fire in my skin that will take hours to fade. "I wish it was a proper date where we could finally, you know, *shag*. Waiting for the perfect time is driving me crazy."

Just hearing her be so crass about the fact makes my gentleman's staff jerk to attention. He couldn't agree more.

"Me too," I assure her honestly, because I have been quite flustered that we haven't been able to be alone together yet. "But I have my whole life ahead of me to enjoy your company. We should not disrespect your parents by doing such things in their home, and Mina's place is rather crowded. But Edward's happiness is more important than our...frustrations. I'll meet you right here by the gates at the end of your shift. I really hope we've found the answer."

"Me too."

I have made some small progress on my own personal project – Operation Make Edward a Living.

After hearing from Countess de Rothschild that the poet Hugh died by drowning in the Thames, I've looked up all the ghosts associated with the river on Mina's computer, but haven't come across one yet who resembles him. I will keep searching, but in the meantime, I have another avenue to chase.

Hugh Bancroft's poetry.

As one of Britain's foremost Romantic poets, Hugh's work has been immortalised in many books and even transcribed into Braille volumes that Mina was able to procure for me. And his final poem, the one that he had scribbled in a note in his pocket when his body was found, makes for interesting reading. It is a terrible, grief-soaked apology to someone he has hurt.

It also turns out that there is a museum dedicated to Hugh Bancroft in the village of Crookshollow, where they hold many of his personal papers and letters. And Bree has agreed to accompany me there today.

We're going to find the answer to Edward's unfinished business today. I can *feel* it.

BREE IS WAITING for me at the gates, as promised. I'm pleased to learn that she's alone.

"I lied to Edward and told him that we're visiting a museum of French Art, which he declared 'thoroughly boring and unrefined' and refused to join us," Bree explains as we walk to the train station. Pax also opted not to join us because he and Mike have already planned a bike ride out to the old mill for a picnic, but he *does* insist that Bree bring along her sword. Luckily, it fits crosswise into her backpack.

We take the train to Crookshollow. Mina has been teaching me about some of the accessible features of public transport, and I'm delighted to find a tactile map of the station, tactile markings on the ground to help guide me to the edge of the platform without falling off (a constant fear of mine when I was last Living), and Braille on the train telling me which button to press to open the doors. This beautiful, imperfect world is starting to feel like it wants me to be part of it, and I must confess that my feet once again itch to explore.

But I don't want to be a solo traveller, ever again. Not when I can have Bree by my side.

Forty-five minutes later, we alight and walk to the museum, which is actually a small stone manor house on the edge of the village where the poet Hugh Bancroft lived when he wasn't in London. It is not nearly as grand as Grimwood Manor, but I note the evenness of the cobbles beneath my feet as we ascend the front path, and determine that it has been well cared for.

We pay an entrance fee and Bree hands me a contraption that I fit over my ears. It barks information at me as we walk around the museum. How marvellous! I learn all about Hugh Bancroft's life and poetry as we wander through the house and grounds. I'm even allowed to touch some of the displays. Museums have come a long way from my day, when they were just rooms in grand houses filled with looted objects and brains in jars.

The tour finishes in a large sitting room at the front of the house. I can tell from the way the light fades as we enter that the curtains are drawn. Bree leans close and whispers to me, "The windows are draped with the most amazing gold damask curtains. Everything is in shades of emerald green and gold. It looks...it looks like just the kind of room Edward would love."

The commentary from my contraption informs me that this was Hugh's 'absinthe parlour' where he entertained fellow writers, musicians, artists, and other bohemian folk. Famous occultists conducted seances in this room, and the trendiest folk of London clamoured for an invitation.

I pick up one of the faux crystal absinthe glasses, but nearly drop it when the voice mentions Edward.

I squeeze Bree's fingers.

"I heard." She squeezes back as we move deeper into the room. "Edward was a frequent visitor to Hugh's home. I can't believe he's never mentioned that Hugh lived so close by before. There's a display of letters in the corner. Let's have a look."

I pause the recording to listen as Bree reads out Hugh's

letters. One rails against his London editor for rewriting one of his essays without permission, while numerous others detail wild tales of debaucherous parties. I admit that my chest tightens with a little envy. The Van Wimples had such lovely gatherings at Grimwood, but they were nothing like what Hugh describes.

No wonder Edward finds me so dreadfully boring.

Perhaps, if we ever do manage to solve his case and bring him back, I will allow him to show me more of his ways...

"Ambrose..." Bree whispers. "Did you hear what I just read?"

"Please repeat," I say, ashamed of myself for drifting away when Bree needs me.

"It's a letter addressed simply 'To my friend,' and it's written by Hugh." Bree clears her throat. "It's dated from just before the party and Edward's death. Listen."

"To my friend. I have read the poem you enclosed in your last missive, and I must admit that it is a fair attempt, although it brings to mind something that I have wished to say for some time. I pen these lines with the utmost respect and reverence to our friendship, hoping that my words may yet find a place in the chambers of your dark and licentious heart. I have long put off this letter out of respect for your position, but it is my duty as a poet to speak truths that may resonate beyond the verses of mere frivolity.

As always, I stand in awe of your grandeur, and your most splendid revelries in the countryside where true artists such as myself are free to pursue our every intellectual purpose. Truly, the world sings praises of your prowess as the sovereign of revels. However, as I contemplate the grandeur of your festivities, I cannot help but notice that the realm of substance remains untrodden in your path.

While those in our circle applaud your ability to amuse and delight, there lies an overshadowing concern for the truly talented and earnest artists who surround you. Your name carries weight and influence, but the world will not take our artistic endeavours seriously when your libertine ways are at the centrepiece of the narrative. As you revel in increasingly debased pleasures, the efforts of your genuine and passionate friends may be dismissed as mere dalliances with indulgence.

I entreat you, my dear prince, to reflect on the greater purpose of your position and the impact you can make beyond the ephemeral pleasures of the present. Your father's court awaits your return with open arms. Embrace the mantle of advocacy for your most beloved friends, who are the true artists of repute, for within the royal heart lies the power to foster a renaissance of creativity and intellectual advancement. Imagine the profound influence you could wield, not just as the Prince of Revelry, but as a patron of culture, literature, and art! Support those of us who strive to leave an enduring legacy of beauty and meaning, for our work enriches not only your kingdom but also the very essence of humanity. If you cannot do this, then I fear that there is nothing left for us, that's the last of it, and I shall have to consider—

"And...what? What?" I'm bouncing on my heels with excitement. "What must he consider?"

"That's it. The letter is torn. The rest of it has not survived." Bree shudders. "Ambrose, those words...'that's the last of it' – they are the *exact* words that Countess de Rothschild said she heard Hugh speak to Edward the night he died."

"Hugh wanted Edward to return to his father's court." I think back to all the nights when Edward had stuck his head in the liquor cabinet, and his usual guarded nature had let slip certain details of his unhappy family. His father beating him when Edward expressed an interest in art school, his father doling out much worse punishments when Edward refused to participate in a royal hunt. Any true friend of Edward would never suggest such a thing.

And he insulted Edward's poetry, claiming that Edward's work lacks substance. For the most part, that's true. But Edward's final poem, the one Hugh stole, is a work of deep and harrowing emotion that still makes me tear up a little.

This letter would have wounded Edward deeply. But clearly, Hugh felt ardently about it, and so, this must have been what they quarrelled about on the night Edward died.

"That's exactly the words that he was saying to Edward the night he died," Bree says again quietly, as if she can't quite believe it. "And then, he took Edward's poem for his own..."

"But still," I say, trying to stamp down the churning in my gut. "We must not jump to a hasty conclusion. This means only that two friends were quarrelling, not that Hugh murdered Edward."

This is exactly what I suspected, but hearing the evidence with my own ears suddenly makes me wish more than anything that it wasn't true. I wish Edward hadn't been murdered by his dearest friend. I wish he'd been loved and respected the way he deserved. The way Pax, Bree, and I love and respect him.

Although we are both reluctant to move on from the letter, there is one final room on the tour. Bree leads me through a narrow passage at the rear of the room. The recording explains that we are now entering a room that was hidden from the public, and only discovered recently when workers were rewiring the museum.

"We have named this The Room of Repentance. This room represents the later years of Hugh's career, where he became a virtual recluse, and his poems became dark, twisted tales of guilt and despair. Hugh wrote often of some desperate act he committed in his youth, an act that all but ensured his fame and fortune but that also doomed his soul—"

"Ambrose," Bree says suddenly. "I need to get out of this room."

"Of course. Let's go."

She grips my arm tightly, and we retreat out the door and back into the museum's gift shop. Bree's trembling all over.

"Whatever is the matter?" I wrap my arms around her, almost knocking over a display of keyrings. Bree manages to catch it before it falls over.

"I'm sorry, I don't know what's wrong with me. That room…" she shudders again. "Be thankful you couldn't see it. It was filled with the most grotesque images. Hugh had scribbled all kinds of things on the walls. The words, 'my prince,' and 'I'm sorry,' and 'I stole it,' over and over and over."

"Hugh did it." The cold reality settles in my chest. "That's the only explanation. Hugh is Edward's murderer."

"This is terrible." Bree rests her head on my shoulder. I squeeze her, hating that she is sad but liking the way she fits against me and the swell in my chest that I can comfort and protect her. "I don't want to tell Edward that his friend murdered him. I don't want to think of it, that someone could have pushed him out that window simply for being who he is. All this because Hugh didn't want him around anymore. Why can no one see what I see in him? Why must his life be so tragic? It's not *fair*."

"But it is also wonderful. Now that we have found Edward's murderer, we can set him free."

"But Edward is always rejected, always left behind." Bree's voice grows small. "Even the people Edward thought were friends would push him out a window and let him rot outside for three days—"

"I'm sure that's not true—"

"It *is*, Ambrose. I know you don't like to think of it, but that's what Edward will see as soon as we tell him. Edward cannot see Hugh's secret room. It will break him. But you're right, we need to show Edward that letter, explain that we know it's Hugh who killed him. Edward deserves a second chance at life, to be the man he was never allowed to be in his first. But we're never going to get him to set foot in the door of this museum. And I can't say that I blame him."

"Then we must bring the letter to him," I declare.

"How will we do that? I don't think the museum lends out artefacts to wayward Lazarii."

"Then we must steal it."

"I CAN'T BELIEVE we're breaking into a *museum*," Bree says as Quoth unlatches the lock on an upper window with his beak. "Being alive has corrupted you, Ambrose Hulme."

After I'd convinced Bree to return to the museum after dark, she fired off a quick text to Mina. Half an hour later, a very pooped raven dropped onto Bree's shoulder and offered his services as an expert lock pick.

"It's a pity I'm not a ghost anymore," I muse as we wait for Quoth to poke around inside. "I could simply walk through the wall."

"Yes, but then how would you pick up the map?" Bree asks. I hear the smile in her voice.

"Easy. You'd be outside with a moldavite in your pocket. You would be on guard for anyone who might try to thwart our illegal shenanigans."

"And suppose someone did try and, how do you say, thwart our shenanigans?"

"Why, I would leap out of the wall and frighten them away," I say proudly. "I can be quite terrifying, you know. Ask Kelly Kingston."

"Oh, I know." Bree is struggling to hold back her laughter.

"I would frighten them into a stupor, giving us ample time to escape, in the spirit of a fat cock."

Bree's laughing so hard that she struggles to speak. "Do you mean, with big dick energy?"

"Precisely."

"It seems you thought of everything. Too bad you're not a ghost anymore."

"While I admit that I miss some aspects of the spirit life..." I lean forward and touch my lips to hers, "I much prefer being a man."

"I much prefer you as a man, too," Bree murmurs against my lips. Her fingers tangle in my hair, and she pulls me closer. "Ambrose, I can't stand it anymore. I need you. *All* of you."

I swallow. I can't deny that my mind has been much occupied with thoughts of our first night together as woman and ex-ghost. And my gentleman's staff has been rather insistent about his desires. He's so stiff around her that it's becoming difficult to walk. Right now, he's standing to attention, and I shift my weight so he doesn't jab into Bree's leg. A gentleman must retain some respectability.

Although, right now, I'm not thinking about respectability. I'm thinking about how amazing Bree's tongue feels against mine, and how much I'd like to undress her and run my hands all over her beautiful curves, and kneel between her legs and taste her.

"The timing has not been right. I'm certain when we're finally able to..." I search frantically for a descriptor that hasn't come from Pax or Edward's vocabulary, "...make love, it will be beautiful and special and—"

"Screw that. I just want you inside me. It *has* to be tonight. I think I'll die of desperation if I have to wait another day—"

"Ow." I rub my head. "What was that?"

"Croak!" A pair of talons dig into my shoulder.

Thanks, bird. I needed a distraction. I think I might have been about to do something very ungentlemanly...

"Quoth says that he's sorry, but he'd been trying to get our attention for a good five minutes. He has the letter." Bree pats the bird's head. Her voice sounds all strained and husky, and it makes my staff tighten. "I guess we were distracted. Thanks for getting this for us, Quoth."

"We appreciate you, bird." I dig out the package of dried berries in my pocket and tip a few onto my hand for him.

"He says that he's too tired to fly all the way back to Argleton, so we must carry him ourselves. And stop on the way to buy him a bag of nuts." Bree pauses as Quoth croaks some more instructions. "And maybe a mouse."

I grip the rolled-up letter in my hand. "Then let us make haste, for we have a final ghost to re-Alive."

28

BREE

By the time we get back to Grimdale on the train, it's nearly midnight. My eyes are aching to close, but I'm wide awake. The letter sits on the table between us – Edward's unfinished business that we found together – and while Quoth makes little wheezing noises with his head tucked into his wing on the chair beside me, Ambrose and I drive each other crazy with need.

Foreplay with a prim and proper Victorian gentleman is something quite extraordinary. Ambrose won't do anything bold on a train where other passengers might see, but that makes everything we do somehow more wicked and delicious. A brush of his foot against mine, his fingers trailing down my arm or wiping a loose strand of hair from off my cheek. Me dropping my teabag on the floor so I can bend over and stroke his crotch until he gasps and begs me to stop...

Okay, that one was a little cruel.

Every touch burns a torch inside me that only he can quench. By the time the train pulls in at Grimdale, I think I'm going to spontaneously combust.

I don't care if we have to drug my parents or send them away on false pretenses. I need him *tonight*.

With a final huff in my ear about turning him into a criminal, Quoth flutters off toward Argleton, his bag of nuts clamped between his beak. Ambrose and I trudge up the hill to Grimwood Manor, the letter burning a hole in my purse and the warm hand resting on my elbow making me imagine all sorts of filthy scenarios for how the rest of this night will go.

Maybe we turn Edward tonight, and then the two of them could...

But before I can even reach for the door handle, the door flies open. A stormy-faced Pax glares at us both, his sword raised. "Where have you been?" he demands. "You were supposed to be home *hours* ago. I was just about to start feeding people to lions."

"How would that help find us?" I ask.

"I suppose it wouldn't." Pax scratches his head. "But it would make me feel better. When I'm worried about you, I need to maim."

"Fair enough." I yawn. I'm too tired to explain to Pax about anger management. "Where's Edward?"

"Where do you think? In the study, driving me crazy with his poetry."

"And my parents?" I didn't exactly want them home when Edward came back to life. I needed some time alone with him before I figured out how to explain him to them.

"With Maggie at the Cackling Goat, reclaiming their crown as the king and queen of Pub Quiz Night."

"Excellent." That means they'll be out until last call, and they'll come home so utterly pissed that the house could be burning down and they wouldn't notice.

This is good news, because I have plans for my Victorian gentleman and my dark prince and their corporeal bodies...

With Ambrose gripping my arm and making me weak at the knees, I take the stairs two at a time. We enter the guest lounge just as Edward drops to one knee on the rug, his face a picture of misery as he intones, "Oh, Death! Thy presence casts a pallid gloom, A spectre haunting life's ephemeral bloom, In yonder vale, where graves their secrets hold, The fickle breath of life, by thee, grows cold...Brianna, you have returned."

He straightens, pulling himself together, but I saw the misery on his face. Edward, who always tried to make us believe he was above everything and everyone. He feels loss and betrayal deeper than I ever knew.

And I'm about to break his heart all over again. Will the gift of his new life be worth it? I hope so.

"Edward, can you...um, sit down," I say. "Ambrose and I have something to tell you."

"Only if you sit beside me." Edward flops dramatically into the chaise, wincing as his thigh goes a little too deep into the cushion. "I'd like to feel the ghost of your body against mine, since it's all I'll ever have of you."

I sit down beside him, letting my leg brush his, feeling the strange, unearthly warmth that emanates from him. This could be the last time I feel that kind of ghostly touch...but soon I'll have Edward, flesh and bone, and that will be so much better.

I glance into those pitch-black, fathomless eyes, and my heart does a little skip. What's he going to do to me tonight?

A delicious shiver runs down my spine. I can't wait to find out. And with Ambrose learning from the dark prince...

All those perverse things he's whispered in my ear, which of them will he want to try first?

What will I let him do?

As Edward leans in close, his full lips resting in a pout, I know the answer is...anything.

"Edward, I..." I try to come up with the words, but they've

disappeared beneath the intensity of his gaze and the molten lava coursing through my body. "Ambrose has something to tell you—"

"You were murdered!" Ambrose blurts out.

Edward's eyes narrow. "Don't toy with me, adventurer. I have ways of wringing truths from you that are more vicious than the Roman could even imagine."

"I resent that," Pax calls gleefully from the doorway. "I have an excellent imagination. Once I invented this drinking game where you have a turnip and a trident and—"

"I'm telling the truth!" Ambrose cries before we are subjected to an in-depth recitation of the rules for Pax's turnip game. "We figured it all out. You didn't merely fall out the window. You were *pushed*."

"That's why you have that bruise on your neck," I explain. "It's from someone's hand."

Edward rubs the spot on his neck, his dark eyes unfathomable.

"Your unfinished business was to find your murderer," Ambrose waves the letter around. "Well, we've uncovered the truth for you."

In a hurried breath, Ambrose excitedly explains his deductions into Edward's unfinished business and how we found our way from the Countess de Rothschild to the Hugh Bancroft museum. He leaves off some of the more disturbing stuff I told him about Hugh's secret room, which I think is wise.

"Hugh has a room in his house dedicated to me?" Edward's eyes flash.

Of course, that *would* be the one feature Edward focuses on in this whole sordid tale.

"The guilt of what he did to you ate him up inside. I know it's no consolation, but..." I place the letter on the table in front of him. "This is our proof. This is a letter where Hugh explains that he wanted you to give up your life in Grimwood and return to your father's court to make him value the arts. This was what the two of you fought about before you fell. The countess heard you arguing right before glass smashed. It all makes sense."

I unfurl the letter in front of Edward. His eyes scan the first couple of lines, but then he falters. "I...I don't recall this letter at all."

"Perhaps you blocked it out. It was dated only a few days before your death. According to the countess, you and Hugh quarrelled in your room mere minutes before you fell to your death."

"I cannot believe *this*..." Edward's eyes return to the letter. "That scoundrel pretended to be my friend. He thinks all my artistic works were mere pageantry? And then he had the audacity to *steal* my work. How *dare* he? I'll cut out his tongue. I'll flay him with my own hands...no, that will be messy. I'll...I'll send Pax to deal with him!"

"Just say the word, prince." Pax cracks his knuckles. "I'll make ravioli out of his spleen."

"Edward, Hugh's already dead. He drowned in the Thames, haunted by the guilt of what he did to you. But I think you're missing the point here. We've solved your unfinished business."

"You...does this mean..." Edward's eyes blow out. "You'll bring me back to life again? I can be Living?"

"Yes."

"Then I don't wish to waste another moment without you in my arms." Edward inclines his head. "You may begin my transformation."

"Yes, I will. Right now. I just..." I grasp for the silver cord that twines from his chest, but it slips through my fingers. I try again, but the cord slides through my grip again, like a piece of spaghetti sliding off the edge of a plate. "Hmmm."

"Hmmm? That's not the noise my woman should make

before I strip her and fill her belly button with sweet wine and sup—"

"No, hang on," I place my hand on his chest, over the silver cord, closing my fingers around it. But it's no use. Edward's body isn't glowing with light, either. Nothing feels right. "Something's wrong."

"Bree?" Ambrose's voice rises with concern.

"Nothing's wrong!" Edward puffs out his chest so that my hand sinks inside it, even as his face screws up in pain. "Who cares that what you're doing is excruciating when I'm going to be a human again. It bothers me not that it feels as if you're pulling my soul out through my nostrils when I'm going to be able to sweep you into my arms and finally, *finally*, I will show you what some princely cock will do and—oof."

As he's reaching for me, Edward's hands slip right through my arm, and he falls through the table and ends up on his hands and knees. "Owwww. It hurts so bad." He rolls on his side, clutching his shoulder where it took the brunt of his table fall. "Why did I just fall through that table?"

"Because you're still a ghost." I drop his silver cord. Tears spring in my eyes. "I'm sorry, Edward. It's not working. You're not being surrounded by light the way Pax and Ambrose were. Uncovering your murderer wasn't your unfinished business after all."

"But...but it must be!" Ambrose's voice squeaks. "We puzzled it all out. We solved the mystery. What could be more important to Edward than figuring out who killed him?"

"Well, it certainly wasn't discovering my oldest friend betrayed me," Edward says drily as he gets to his feet and swipes invisible dust off his ghost flouncy shirt.

"Edward..." I step toward him, but the grim look in his eyes stops me in his tracks. All we've given him is the cruel words in

Hugh's letter, and he will internalise them, turn them over and over until they are part of who he believes himself to be.

We were trying to help, but we've made things so much worse.

"It's okay. We'll keep looking." Ambrose thumps his fist on the sofa arm. "There must be something we missed. We'll talk to the other ghosts, maybe there are other spirits around who knew Edward in real life, and they can help us—"

"Don't concern yourself." Edward snaps to his feet. "I am perfectly happy to remain a spectre."

He's not happy, though. He's miserable, and he's hopeless at hiding it.

"Edward—" Tears prick in my eyes. "Don't be like that."

"I'm being only myself, Brianna." Edward steps away, his voice remote, devoid of the emotion that I know is welling inside him. "If you'll excuse me, it's late, and I should turn in for the night. While I still have a boudoir to myself, I intend to enjoy it."

With that, he sweeps off. I look over at Ambrose. He pretends to be immersed with a loose thread in his greatcoat, but I can see from his wobbling lip that he's completely crushed.

"Forgive me," he says without raising his head. "I have made things worse."

"It's not your fault."

"I was so *certain*..." he whimpers. "We solved the mystery. We found Edward's murderer. That *must* be his unfinished business."

"Maybe we were wrong about Hugh?"

Ambrose screws his face up. "But...it doesn't feel wrong, does it? The letter, Hugh's final words to Edward, Hugh's guilt... they must all be connected."

"Or maybe there's something Edward's soul seeks more than the truth about his murder?"

"Perhaps…" Ambrose strokes his chin. "Yes, maybe that's it! We must look deeper. Maybe there's a clue in one of Edward's poems. Although it is a great trial to immerse myself in such self-aggrandizing drivel, I shall get to work immediately on my analysis."

"But, Ambrose—"

Our night together?

But Ambrose is muttering ideas to himself as he gathers his cane. He's already too wrapped up in saving Edward to remember our plans. I try to stamp down my disappointment. He's doing this because he is kind, and good, and wonderful. But it stings.

With a quick kiss on the cheek, Ambrose saunters off to ride on the trolley on the back of Pax's bike to Mina's, leaving me with an aching pussy and a delicate heart.

I place my head in my hands. "I don't know what to do about Edward."

"We could throw him into a sack with a monkey, a snake, and a chicken, and then throw the sack into the duck pond?" Pax says helpfully.

"*What?*"

"What?" Pax shrugs. "It is called *poena cullei*, the penalty of the sack, and it is a popular Roman punishment. It's quite funny to watch. We all take bets on which animal deals the killing blow. Although I guess it wouldn't work on a ghost."

"That's very helpful, Pax, thank you. But I'd like to keep Edward around."

Pax tilts his head to the side. "As…a boyfriend?"

Not you, too. I can't deal with any more trouble from ghosts or ex-ghosts tonight.

"As…" I screw up my face. "As our *friend* who we care about, even when he is a dick."

Pax shoots me a funny expression. He turns on his heel and slowly stomps down the stairs. A moment later, the door slams shut behind him.

Great. All my men are ignoring me, and I am so horny even the suit of armour in the corner is starting to look good. Could things around here get any crazier?

Don't answer that.

29

BREE

I'm sitting on a rug in the foyer of Grimwood, and I'm cosy, warm, and happy. I'm playing with some blocks, and it's the most exciting thing in the world to stack them together into a great tower and then knock it over. I'm a monster! I'm Godzilla flattening a city!

But I'm not alone anymore. A woman kneels down next to me. She's wearing a bright pink suit with a matching pink suitcase and umbrella leaning up against the sofa. She's even wearing pink lipstick. How interesting!

I reach for her, because I want to play with the Pink Woman who has a nice smile. Maybe she'd like to bust over block towers, too. But my arms are much smaller than I remember, and I'm not very good at balancing, so I fall over.

"Oops, there you go." She holds me under the arms and sets me upright. Her smile is so pretty. She reminds me of my mother, except that Mum never wears pink.

"Hello, Bree," she says. "I've come a long way to find you. I wanted to see if you have the gift I gave you, and it seems that you do. It's a beautiful gift, but it's also a curse. That's why I couldn't stay here, but maybe you're stronger than me. They

263

have never stopped hunting me, and I think they're getting closer. I don't believe I'll be around to see you grow up, but I have left you everything you need in my rose garden. Sylvie has done so well for herself. I am so proud—"

THWACK THWACK THWACK.

The noise reverberates through the whole house. I glance all around, but I can't see what's making the noise. My stomach twists with fear. Tears spring in my eyes, and a loud wail bubbles up inside me.

I don't like the noise. I want it to stop!

"I think someone needs you, dear," the Pink Woman says. She starts to disappear in a cloud of pink mist.

"Nooooo," I cry. I grab for her, but my fists grasp only air.

I know she was about to tell me something important, but—

THWACK.

I'm jolted from bed. It takes me a moment to realise that I'm not sitting on the rug with the Pink Woman, but in my room, the sheets tangled in a ball at my feet, my arms outstretched as if I might somehow be able to pull the Pink Woman from my dream.

What an odd thing to dream about. And what was it that woke me up?

THWACK. THWACK.

That's right. The noise. It sounds like a small object hitting glass or something. And it's definitely in my bedroom.

Ice runs down my spine.

The Ripper has come back.

But how did he get past the wards?

Shit, shit, shit.

And Pax and Ambrose aren't here. What do I do?

I pull the covers up to my chin, listening hard as something hits the window outside. What I wouldn't give to find Pax at the end of my bed, watching over me. But he's had to give that up now—

THWACK. THWACK.

There it is again.

It's coming from the window.

My heart hammering, I slide out of the edge of the bed, grab the sword that Pax insists I keep beside the bed (he does have some great ideas), and approach the window. I press my back against the wall and listen. Yes, I can hear something outside, rustling in the bushes.

Slowly, I insert the tip of the sword behind the curtains and lift it a little so I can see. But as soon as I see who's responsible for the noise, my heart does a little patter and I throw the curtains open and push up the sash.

"Ambrose?"

He stands in the middle of the garden beneath the window, next to a family of concrete badgers, and grins up at me. "Bree, you did hear me? I thought you must be sound asleep."

"I *was* sound asleep. It's three in the morning! What are you *doing* here?"

Ambrose swallows, his Adam's apple bobbing. "I realised that I was so engrossed with Edward's unfinished business that I left here without saying goodnight."

"You came all this way and woke me up to say goodnight? It's actually morning now. How did you even get here?"

"I called an Uber. Mina showed me how." Ambrose looks sheepish. "She said that I needed to get over here and—" he raises his hands to make air quotes, "—'shag your brains out.'"

Mina is a good friend.

But there's only one problem with this little plan...

"You could come in, but my parents are home," I say apologetically. "They probably won't wake up, but I know you feel strange about that."

"Perhaps..." Ambrose holds out a hand. "You could come down here?"

"I don't think that will be much better. Between the nosy neighbours and the ghosts everywhere, nowhere in this town is private, and I don't have enough money to get a hotel room. That trip to London wiped me out—"

"I can think of one place."

Yes.

My heart races. I know exactly where he's thinking.

"Give me a second." I step back from the window and hunt for my boots. I sleep naked, so I pick up my black trench coat and shrug it over my shoulders, doing up two of the buttons. I don't need a condom, because I'm on the injection and I've made them all get tested and it turns out that being a ghost for a century or ten *does* cancel out any nasty ancient STIs you may have picked up. Both Pax and Ambrose are clean.

As a teen, I snuck out of the house more times than I'd like to admit, usually to hang out in the cemetery with Dani. It's actually easy to sneak out of a B&B because my parents expect guests to come and go at all hours, so they don't worry about an unlocked door. But I'm not even going to go to the front door, not with Ambrose standing there, looking incredible in the moonlight. Not when I have a ground-floor bedroom now.

I shove the sash window as high as it will go. "I'm coming down."

"Is that safe?"

I swing my legs out and pull the tails of my trench coat through. "Sure. There's not much of a drop, and no prickly rose bushes or anything in the flower bed." Something about the word *rose* gives me a little chill, but I don't have time to wonder why.

I push off and drop ungracefully to the ground, managing to leap over the border garden without crushing any of Dad's flowers or decapitating a badger statue. I run to Ambrose and throw my arms around him.

My lips find his and the kiss we share...it makes my body come *alive*. Ambrose can always do this to me – with just the touch of his lips he can make me feel like the world is new and exciting and wonderful. His hand cups my cheek, angling me just right so that he can go deeper, so that he can take his fill of me.

When he pulls away, his lips are slightly bruised, and his whole face is bright and smiling. "You know," he says. "I once climbed out that same window."

"No way?"

"Oh, yes, Cuthbert had just acquired a new mummy for his museum, and I was dying to have a look at it, but Penelope was annoyed with him for some reason, so she said that no one was going anywhere near that dusty old museum of his until he had completed whatever task she had set him. So we waited until she was asleep and snuck out together."

I can't help but laugh. "Trust you to sneak out of the house so you could go to a *museum*."

Ambrose's long eyelashes flutter as he loses himself in his memory. "Cuthbert and I unwrapped the first layer of bandages that night. We found many amulets of gold and precious stones nestled between the ancient linen. I know that it's wrong to take things from other cultures, to use wealth to buy and sell pieces of history like trinkets, but being able to touch that mummy, to see it with my fingers, to smell the ancient dust and the resin and the honey wax seals on the canopic jars, it was one of the happiest memories of my life."

"I know." I rest my head on his shoulder as we walk. "But maybe no talk about mummies tonight, okay?"

"I agree. We have so many other things we can talk about,

like how soft your hair feels in my fingers, and how happy I am that you came out with me tonight."

I let him lead me where he wants to go. The only sound is the rap of Ambrose's stick on the ground and the hoot of a distant owl. We descend the path that winds around the back of the house, duck through the hole in the fence and find ourselves in Grimdale Cemetery.

My heart pounds as a soft smile plays on Ambrose's lips. Our feet crunch over the fallen leaves that we never seem to be able to clear away.

Of course he would bring me to the graveyard. We both love this place, in our own way. And it's blissfully free of ghosts. Ambrose was the only ghost who could ever get over his fear of death enough to walk in Grimdale Cemetery with me.

So it seems fitting that we walk here together now, under the pale moonlight, while our need for each other courses in our veins.

The tension coils between us like a spring. I can see Ambrose's silver cord swirling through the air around us, the blue streaks inside it twitching with anticipation. Pure need dances down my spine and gathers into an insistent ache between my thighs.

We've waited so long.

I don't want to wait any longer.

Ambrose must be thinking the same thing. He tugs me forward eagerly until we're standing in front of the Witches' Monument – that smooth, modern edifice of stone. We circle it, so that the monument's height will hide us from anyone who happens to walk past the gate.

Perfect.

"Is this pleasing to you?" He gestures to the moonlit night, to the deserted cemetery, to the graves that tower around us like protective megaliths, as if it could be anything other than perfect. "I had wanted to take you somewhere comfortable, somewhere adventurous, somewhere that reflected the beauty in your soul. But I'm without means, and I am desperate, and I can think only to be impetuous—"

"Ambrose," I laugh as I turn to him. "Stop talking and kiss me."

"I only want you to be happy—"

"*Ambrose—*"

He pulls me to him and captures my lips in his.

The kiss is soft and slow, but under the moonlight, his lips take on a new power. As our bodies move together and our lips open with invitation, we conjure some kind of ancient fae magic that winds itself around us, cocooning us in this moment that is only for us to enjoy.

I loop my arms around him, standing on tiptoe so I can deepen the kiss. Ambrose's hands hold my cheeks, his fingers stroking over my skin, threading through my hair, like he is weaving the spell with his touch.

Part of me could kiss him like this forever, suspended in this perfect moment. But my body is humming with need, and the dark magic we've conjured demands the ritual be complete. My hands roam over the planes of his body, tugging at the buttons on his shirt, skimming over his fly. Ambrose tenses when my fingers caress his length through his trousers, and the groan he lets slip is so exquisite that it hurts.

That moan of his frees all the fireflies trapped in the dark corners of my soul. Although I know, academically, that this thing between us is fragile and built of glass that can so easily shatter, I don't feel that in my heart. I am safe with Ambrose. I don't know if I've ever felt truly safe before.

"May I?" His hands tremble a little as he undoes the first button of my trench coat, but it's not nerves. It's *excitement.*

"Please." The need in my voice stuns me. And it makes

Ambrose's whole face break out into a gentle smile that makes me warm all over, inside and out.

He gets both buttons undone and shoves my trench coat down. I shrug it off, the moonlight kissing my naked skin as his hands roam over my body.

"You are so beautiful," Ambrose whispers as his fingers graze my nipples until I moan his name. "I have been all over the world, but nothing I have experienced can compare to how you feel in my arms."

I gulp down a swell of emotion that squeezes my heart.

I wish I could tell him that he's the same for me, that I fled to every corner of the world to hide from this exact moment, because I've been so afraid to open myself up to him, to Edward, to Pax. I've been terrified that they would care for me as much as I care for them, and then I would lose them.

Because no one understands loss and loneliness like a Lazarus.

But I can't push the words past the lump in my throat. And the way Ambrose is looking at me, his eyes heavy-lidded and glittering with magic, even though I know he can't see me, it feels as though he sees something deeper, something beyond normal human vision. There are no words left for how beautiful he is.

Instead, I go for his clothes, because if Ambrose can strip me bare with just a few words, then I can do the same to him. I fiddle with his buttons. He hasn't changed from earlier, so he's wearing the new clothing I brought him. A pair of nice brogues, slim-fitting trousers with nice tailoring that he likes, and a black shirt with a textured weave that delights his sense of touch. Beneath the moonlight, his hair glimmers like spun gold, and I run my hands through it as he shrugs out of his shirt.

I toss his shirt into the rose bushes and run my hands over

the hard dips and grooves of his stomach. He's like a Greek statue, all perfect proportions and elegant panes.

I can't believe that he's mine.

"Bree." Ambrose clasps my cheek and he angles my face back, kissing me deep and hard. And that's not the only thing that's hard. His cock presses against my leg, and my heart leaps when I feel how desperate he is for me.

We waited so long, but now is our time.

The perfect night.

I whimper as Ambrose's lips leave mine, but he kisses down my neck, his tongue laving over a spot that makes my knees weak.

"You've been learning too many tricks from Edward," I breathe, clinging to him as he rolls my nipples between his fingers.

He laughs, his voice a low rumble. "I think you enjoy it."

"I do. Please, don't stop."

My fingers curl against Ambrose's bare back as he holds me close and explores every inch of me with his hands and mouth. I don't want to make assumptions that all blind men make good lovers, or if it's just Ambrose, but he paints me with kisses in a way that makes me feel like a work of art.

I finally manage to pull down his fly and unbutton his trousers. I push them down his hips, along with his boxers, and draw him out.

Ambrose groans against me as I pump his shaft between my hands. "Please, Bree, if you keep doing that, I don't know how long I'm going to last. However much you want me, trust me, I need you more."

His voice cracks. The sound is like a lightning rod straight through my heart. I slow my strokes, and he takes that moment to grip my hips and spin us both around.

My back braces against the cool stone of the monument.

Honestly, I need that right now, something to hold me upright, to anchor me to the earth, because it feels like he might just whisk me away to some enchanted realm.

Ambrose kneels in front of me, his hands reverent as he strokes my thighs.

"You'll wear out the knees of your trousers," I tell him, even as I angle my hips toward him.

"It's worth it to feel you come apart on my tongue."

And then I can't say any more, because his mouth is on me and oh, *oh*, but Edward has taught him some tricks. My sweet Ambrose has such a wicked tongue. He plunges it inside me, teasing my entrance, before returning to swirl and lathe over my clit.

My breath comes out in ragged gasps. The silent cemetery shrouds me in friendly shadow as Ambrose's tongue builds the aching pressure with fast, hungry strokes.

His finger teases my entrance, then slides inside me. Part of Ambrose is inside me. It's the joy of it, the sheer wonderfulness of it, that sends me gasping over the edge of a knee-liquifying orgasm.

He grips my legs as I come apart on his tongue, just like he promised. But he doesn't get up.

"Please," I whimper. "I need you inside me."

"But I wanted to—"

"Ambrose, I will literally *die* if you make me wait for your cock any longer."

"Then I suppose it's a good thing we're in a cemetery."

He stands up, and the corner of his mouth turns up into a crooked little smile that reminds me a little of Edward. Ambrose wraps one arm behind my back, around my waist, his fingers splayed across my skin. I no longer feel the odd ghostly tingle from him, but this is even better.

His lips find mine again, and I taste my own pleasure as his tongue works its magic. His kisses turn soft, tender, as he kicks off his trousers and boxers.

Ambrose lines himself up. I'm so wet that he slides in easily. His shoulders tense, and the guttural, ungentlemanly groan that he lets out as he enters me hits straight in my core.

"I've waited several lifetimes to touch you like this," he whispers. "The woman I love. You are so beautiful."

His hips retreat, but before I can take a breath, he thrusts, driving himself so deep that he tears a moan from my lips.

"What does it feel like?" I ask him, because Ambrose sees the world through sensation, and he describes even the most mundane things like they are poetry.

"You feel...amazing," he breathes. "You feel like coming home, like a warm fire after a weary day's travel. You feel like... like...like a gift."

I wrap my legs around his back, driving him deeper. He takes my weight in his hands, and doesn't stop. With each thrust, he shoves me against the wall. His golden hair flops over one eye, but he doesn't stop, doesn't care how dishevelled he's becoming. I'm not the only one falling apart.

Ambrose feels amazing. I am so full of him. Heat surges against my skin as his strokes build the aching pressure in my belly once more.

"You are all I've ever wanted. This moment, right here. I never want it to end."

"It doesn't have to." I grip him tighter, my body moving with his as he slams into me.

The fire between us flares even hotter than before, and our two silver cords twist and swirl together as they wrap around us.

He's all I see and hear and smell and feel. His eyes are wide open, and even though I know he can't see me, I am sinking in their azure depths, swimming in the secret, hidden parts of his soul.

Ambrose's lips find mine, and his kisses swallow my moans as he takes me deeper until I'm nothing but wild, enchanted sensation.

We come apart at the same time. His teeth scrape my shoulder as he leans against me, and my body slackens under him, my legs dropping to the ground.

It takes us several moments for us to catch our breath.

Ambrose's arms circle me and he pulls me down. We both lean our backs against the Witches' Monument, our legs and arms tangled together, our sweat-slick bodies still hot to touch.

"I just earned my goth credentials," I say. "Sex in a cemetery is right up there with driving a hearse, sleeping in a coffin, and panicking at a disco. Dani will be *so* proud."

"What does sex in a cemetery have to do with an architectural period?" Ambrose sounds confused. His cheek rests against mine, and my heart stutters.

"Never mind." I turn my face toward the owl, who has moved to a tree on the edge of the cemetery to serenade us with hoots. "Hey, that owl is watching us. Get lost, you pervert. You'd better not be hooting about my breasts."

I shake my fist at the owl, and Ambrose laughs, his whole body trembling.

"Bree, I love you."

Shit.

Those words turn my blood to ice.

Ambrose turns to me, his lips parted in a slight, hopeful smile, his eyes sparkling like the ocean.

I scramble for something to say. "The sex was amazing, Ambrose. You don't have to tell me you love me to get me to sleep with you again. I'm yours any time. Seriously."

"I'm not saying this to manipulate you," he says earnestly, his finger stroking along my cheek. "It's truly how I feel."

I know.

Me t—

I swallow.

Several frayed heartbeats pass.

"I can't...I can't say those words back," I manage to choke out.

"I know. It's okay. Really, it is. To be here with you, under the moonlight, it's more than I could have ever dreamed. You are enough for me, Bree, and whatever you feel for me, it *is* enough. But one thing that being a ghost has taught me, it's that tomorrow could be too late for the important things. The things that truly matter. I want you to know what I feel for you, because this love is like a song inside me that's bursting through my skin. I have fallen, so hard and so fast that I have toppled over a cliff, and you are my parachute."

I can't be your parachute, I think, as I hold him, as the moon streaks cold and lonely across a starless sky. *I'm the one who's falling.*

30

BREE

"Bree, your boyfriends are here," Mum calls from downstairs.

"They're not my boyfriends," I say through gritted teeth as I drop the roller I was using to paint the third-storey guest room. I reach the stairs as Mum lets Pax and Ambrose into the house. Ambrose smiles sweetly at her, as if he didn't sneak me out of the house last night so we could fuck in the cemetery.

My thighs have the most delicious ache, and every time I move I remember the way his hands roamed over my body. But then I remember what he said to me, and I get all cold and jittery. I don't want Mum to give Ambrose or Pax any false ideas.

"You three spend an awful lot of time together to not be dating," Mum frowns at me. "Your father and I aren't prudes, you know. We had an open relationship in college. Mike was particularly fond of this sweet philosophy major—"

"Ew, didn't need to know that."

"All I'm saying is, if you need to tell us something, we will understand." Mum pats my shoulder. Pax looks at me expectantly, but when I don't say anything, his shoulders slump and Mum fills in the silence. "What are you three doing today?"

The three witches are giving me another magic lesson before my shift at the cemetery, and Ambrose and Pax are going to hunt for more of Edward's old friends and check the wards around Grimwood and Nevermore Bookshop. But I can't exactly say that to my mother. "We're just going to hang out, go for a walk in the woods." I remember that I left my moldavite stone in my room. "I'll be back in a second, I've just got to grab something from my room."

As I head down the hall, I hear Pax say to my mother, "So if I want to be Bree's boyfriend, what do I need to do? Is there a secret ritual to perform, or must I slay her last boyfriend in battle? Because I'm willing to do whatever it takes."

I hurry to my room before I have to hear my mother's answer. Pax will not let up with this commitment thing, and it's so damn hard because I don't want to hurt him, and I *do* care about them. They are more to me than just scorchingly good sex. But...we have Jack the Ripper, and Edward being Edward, and I just...I don't have time to think about feelings, or why it is that even the idea of those three little words makes my mouth feel like it's full of sand.

I just need things to stay as they are, for now. But how can I get him to understand that?

I grab the moldavite off the bed, plus the bag of herbs from Vera's box, on the off-chance the witches can tell me what it's supposed to do. I also grab an extra jumper, because an English summer is no promise of decent weather. As I head back into the foyer, my eyes dart over the wall of family portraits we have hanging over the stairs. There's several of me with my parents, one of five-year-old me grinning next to my brand new red bicycle, and several of Mum and Dad's parents and our relatives

– including an old portrait of a stern-looking lady wearing a pink blazer.

"Hey, Bree-bug," Dad calls from the door at the end of the hall that leads out into the garden. He kicks off his Wellingtons and joins me in front of the portrait wall. "I was just checking on my prize-winning cucumber. The festival is only a few days away and she has never looked better! It's like magic. What are you looking at?"

"Oh, just our life." I lean against his shoulder as my eyes dart from frame to frame. My favourite is the big family Christmas we host every year. All Dad's brothers and their wives and my cousins invade Grimwood for a week, and Mum and Dad cook up a huge Christmas feast and we each buy a silly Secret Santa present that costs less than five quid. My stomach twists when I think that I haven't been back for Christmas in five years...and now I'd never get another Christmas like that. "We've had some fun times."

Even though they don't show up in the pictures, Edward, Ambrose, and Pax are part of every memory of this house. I was looking forward to making memories with them that could hang on this wall, but I guess not...

"We certainly have," Dad's voice catches.

My eyes fall back on the painting of the woman in the pink blazer. Something about her face stirs a memory, but I can't grasp it. It's not so much a vision of her, as a *feeling*. I've met her before. Except I haven't, because she's a great-something-or-other and I'm pretty sure she died before I was born.

It's strange, because I've passed this portrait a thousand times and never got this sense before, but now...

She's the lady in my dream.

The dream I had the other night, when Ambrose woke me up. She was *in* my dream. And she said...

I gaze at the portrait, my heart hammering against my

chest. The rational part of my brain tells me that I've passed this wall of photographs and portraits thousands of times, so of course my subconscious mind would incorporate her into my dream. She probably represents Grimwood in my mind, a symbol for all the secrets of this house that are being painted over…

…but I'm too attuned to magic now to assume anything is a coincidence.

"Who is she?" I point to the portrait. "I remember you telling me once, but I've forgotten."

"Oh, that's your great-grandmother, Elsie. Your mother's grandmother. She owned the house before we did. I think you would have liked her. She always sang to her own tune, as your mother would say."

"Did I…" I frown at the image. "Did I ever meet her?"

Dad gives me an odd look. "She died about five years before you were born. Even your mother didn't have much to do with her, which is why it was such a shock when we inherited the house. Elise never married, which was a bit of a scandal in her day, and she raised your grandfather Bert all alone. He got out of Grimdale as soon as he came of age, a bit like you; he had itchy feet, I think. Or perhaps he just wanted to escape all the gossip about his mother. Anyway, Bert moved up north, met your grandmother, and raised his family. He never came back to Grimdale, not even for a visit. I don't think Elise was in the house much, either. She was a bit of a vagabond, liked to travel all over. Your mother had only been to Grimwood once, for Elsie's funeral, before we got the news that we inherited it."

"Wow. I didn't know any of this."

"I've probably told you a hundred times, but when you were a kid you only wanted stories about dashing princes, fierce warriors, or gentleman adventurers. Nothing else would hold your attention."

Or perhaps some rowdy ghosts were distracting me. "I'm not sure I've changed much."

"And that's why I love you." Dad leans over and kisses the top of my head. "Listen, Bree-bug, your mother asked me to tell you. We're having the first open home on Sunday. Gwen says the ad campaign has been going well and she has some interested buyers. She wants to get them in to look at the house."

A hard lump forms in my throat. "An open home? But the paint will barely be dry!"

"We've got time to air the place out a little, and they'll hardly be rolling around on the walls. I know it's hard for you to think about selling Grimwood." Dad kicks the baseboard affectionately. "Believe me, it's breaking our hearts, too. But sometimes we have to make hard decisions. Your Mum's right, I've been kidding myself for a long time that I could still look after this place. It's too much for your old man and his shaky hands. Grimwood deserves someone who will give it the love it deserves."

"Yes, it does." I try not to get choked up at the idea of that someone not being my parents.

I fail.

Just when I finally feel like I've got a hold of myself, the rug is being pulled out from under me.

Dad opens his arms. I fall into him, just like when I was a little kid. I breathe in deep, savouring that sawdust and pine scent that's uniquely Dad.

I let a tear fall onto his collar.

"Oh, Bree-bug." Dad pats my hair. "It's totally okay to be sad when our time with the house comes to an end, but this is a new chapter in our lives. Grimwood will go on without us, and we will go on without her, and everything will work out for the best, I promise."

"Okay."

I don't want to lose Grimwood. But Dad's right – barring some kind of lottery win, we don't have the money to keep this place running, and I've seen him struggle to do things with his hands, like hold nails. Jobs that used to take him five minutes now take half an hour, and Mum's already run off her feet – she can't pick up any slack. There will come a time when it's just too much for them, and they need to move on before then, or they will end up hating this place, and that would be worse.

I'm not a kid anymore. I can handle hard truths.

I hold my father and squeeze him hard, as if my hugs have the same healing powers that his once did when I was a kid. As if I can hold him tight enough and love him hard enough that I can cure his Parkinson's.

Over his shoulder, I see Pax at the end of the hallway, watching us. His jaw tightens, and he peers from me to my father and back again. His blue eyes widen with a look of utter delight, and my stomach sinks into my toes.

Why does Pax have a look on his face like he's planning something?

Should I be worried?

31
EDWARD

*B*ANG BANG BANG

"Edward, wake up, or by the gods, I will sculpt your eyeballs into delicious truffles, like the ones on Bake-Off last night."

I bolt upright. I've heard all manner of threats over my many centuries of maudlin existence, but the Roman has a certain poetic elegance that cannot be denied. "You may enter."

Pax thumps the door again, before realising it's not locked and stumbling through. (I don't have the dexterity to lock my own boudoir, oh the humanity of it.) His cheeks are ruddy and one of his Roman sandals has slid off his foot, hanging on to his ankle by a thin leather strap. Pax skids to the edge of my bed and glares down at me, hands on his hips.

"Pax, what are you doing in my boudoir?"

He starts at my appearance. "You are still a ghost."

"My, we are intelligent."

"From the way Bree and Ambrose were jumping around last night, I felt certain you would be human by now."

I felt certain too, for a moment there. But my hope is forlorn. I should know that by now. The only thing that got me through the night is immersing myself in the memories I saw when I was inside Brianna. The secret thoughts she let me see are enough to keep my from losing myself utterly to desolation.

And now there is a Roman disgracing my boudoir. How has my afterlife come to this?

"It's a good thing I'm not, because if you were I would have run you through the moment you burst into my private chambers. What do you *want*, Pax?"

I want Pax to go away. I want to wallow in my own misery and reread Hugh's letter over and over until the words are etched into my soul. I want to stamp down the wretched hope that surged through me when Brianna first handed it over and said that it could turn me Living.

Not only am I still a ghost, but I'm a *murdered* ghost.

I'm a walking cliche.

And I still have no clue what unfinished business I could have.

But the best way to get Pax to go away is to distract him with something shiny or give him what he wants (which is easy enough, since what he wants is usually someone to watch his cooking show with him). So I rest my head on my hands and listen with half an ear as Pax paces across the rug, flapping his hands in agitation.

"I saw Bree talking to her father. He told her that the real estate agent will return on Sunday. And this time she is bringing people who want to buy the house!"

"And?"

"And I think that we should make sure they know *exactly* what kind of house they're buying."

A slow smile spreads over my lips. "Sometimes, Roman, you and I speak the same language."

"We do. You taught me modern English because you said

that Latin was too difficult and your schoolmaster used to punish you when you got your declensions wrong—"

"Yes, yes, fine. Whatever devious plan you have in mind, consider me at your disposal."

Pax rubs his hands together with glee. But he doesn't stop pacing. And he doesn't leave.

"Is there something else?"

The Roman's eye twitches. I glare at him. He shifts his weight from foot to foot.

Is Pax...*nervous?*

"Out with it," I snap. "Or I will be forced to draw the truth from you with a particularly vicious sonnet."

"I need you to show me how to make love."

Of all the words I expected to come out of Pax's mouth, those were somewhere near the bottom of the list, alongside, "Only silly people enjoy fish sauce with every meal" and "I've decided to employ the use of a fragrant oil so the rest of you don't have to enjoy my natural manly musk."

Which is *rather* manly...but still.

Pax wants me to show him how to...make love?

Me.

"No offence, Roman, but you're not my type."

"By Jupiter's dangly dongle, I do not wish to make love to you!" Pax looks so horrified at the thought that I can't help but feel a little offended. "I wish to make love to Bree."

"From what I've seen, you've done perfectly well on your own. Not as well as I might, of course, given the same corporeal appendages, but I guess she'll never know what she's missing—"

"Bree still will not call me her boyfriend." Pax sets his jaw into a firm line. "She won't call any of us her boyfriends. She says it's because her parents won't understand, but they told her just now that they do. She says that she's too worried about the Ripper's return to think about it, but I believe she thinks about it all the time. I told her that I would wait as long as it takes her to feel comfortable, but I'm not good at waiting! I need action! Ambrose says that your beanstalk could make women declare their love to you. You will show me how to use mine to do the same to Bree."

"If Brianna is not in love with you, then not even my carnal tricks will convince her otherwise."

I go to turn away from him, so he can't see the lie in my eyes. I know my Brianna. She *is* in love with Pax. I see it on her face every time he's in the room.

She merely won't say the words because she's afraid.

She does not know she is afraid, but I'm a man who has lived with fear and regret long enough to recognise its shadow.

Brianna has already lost Pax twice. Three times, if you count when she told us to leave and we lived in the dreadful attic. She believes that if she holds her whole heart back from him, it won't be broken if she loses him again.

She is wrong, of course, but women must be allowed their indulgences even when they are wrong.

My Brianna is not so different from me. I am holding my heart back from her because it is tearing me apart that I cannot be with her as the others can.

"Please, Edward?" Pax wheedles. "If you help me, I'll let you win our next duel in front of Bree."

"Not good enough."

"Fine. I'll let you win the next duel against me and you can choose the moving picture channel for the next week—"

"A-*hem.*"

"—the next *month,*" he roars. "Will you help me?"

"Very well." I turn around, throw my hair over my shoulder, and snap my fingers. "Come here. On the bed."

Pax remains glued to the doorway, looking like he's second-guessing this whole thing.

"Do you want to learn how to make love or not?" I pat the satin pillow. "On the bed. Now."

Pax glowers at me, but he steps closer. I grab the buckle of his belt and attempt to jerk him closer, but all I manage to do is put my hand through his torso. He huffs at me and moves closer until our chests nearly touch and I must look up into that smug Roman face of his. Gods, he really is a monster of a man.

If he weren't so wretchedly annoying...this might be exciting. It's been a long time since I had a man in my bed, and I was always a sucker for the strong, machismo types.

"Here beginneth your lesson in making love to a woman. First, you must get close. Skin on skin is vital."

Pax shuffles closer, until his huge chest presses against mine, and his thighs are practically inside me. His sword is shoved down the leg of his trousers, and I instruct him with a nod to remove it and place it beside the bed.

"No swords in the boudoir. You're liable to cut your own member off in your enthusiasm."

"Should I be taking notes?"

My lip curls. "You can't remember not to cut your own dick off?"

Pax yanks the sword out and tosses it away. The tip buries itself into the wall, leaving the blade and pommel wobbling. Pax glares at me and folds his arms. "What next?"

"Now, you must stare deeply into her eyes." I run my finger along his chin, forcing him to move his head so that he stares at me. His icy blue eyes narrow, and I slap his cheek, which hurts me more than it hurts him. "Not like that. Look at me like you can't believe how lucky you are to be in my presence. And no matter what you see reflected back at you, you cannot flinch or move away. Do you understand?"

"Yes."

Pax's eyes widen.

"Next, you must hold her softly. None of your rough Roman hands wandering everywhere. Make her feel safe." I lift my arms to the sides. "Go on, hold me."

Pax frowns as he shoots an arm out and it goes straight through my wrist. I wince.

"Well, obviously you can't *actually* hold me, but pretend I'm Brianna. Show me you can be soft and caring."

Pax leans in and tries to wrap his huge tree trunk arms around me. I hold up a hand and he backs off.

"Too hard, too much. I'm not a Druid you're about to crush to death. I'm the woman you love. Try for a little tenderness. Like this."

I lean in, slowly. I move one hand over his chest, my fingers trailing lightly across his skin until I feel the warm tingle in the tips. Pax's eyes flutter shut, but I slap his cheek and he opens them again.

I lean in even closer and wrap my hand slowly behind his neck. The other hand I move behind him, placing it with fingers splayed upon the small of his back, cradling him against me while touching as little of him as I can get away with.

"When you're like this, she feels safe," I say. "Your hand behind her neck ensures that she remains looking at you. This is vital. The eyes are the windows to the soul. Now, you try."

I drop my hands and Pax leans in, copying me exactly. His thick fingers trail across my collarbone, over the exposed skin at the nape of my neck where my shirt remains open. His hand dips to the small of my back, nudging me until I close the thin sliver of space between us. Now our faces are only an inch apart, and if I move a single ghost muscle, I'll end up with Roman limbs inside me, which is not a thing I desire.

This feels...

Okay, so, it doesn't feel horrible. In fact, if I'm being completely honest, my cock is doing a little jig. There's something intensely exciting about being this close to someone so large and dangerous, and knowing I can't escape him but that he'll never, ever hurt me. I am safe, and I am terrified, especially when he gazes at me with such focused intensity. He's taking this whole 'don't blink' thing to heart.

I've been with men before, of course. I've been with several men at once, in a single bathtub. (It *was* the seventeenth century. Who didn't have bathtub orgies?) But I've never been so intimate with someone who can snap my neck without even breaking a sweat.

My pulse speeds up, and I don't even *have* a pulse.

I like this.

That is...*fascinating*.

"Now what?" Pax rasps, his voice husky and strange.

Now what, indeed?

I have lived with this Roman for four long centuries, and never ever have I stopped to study the hard set of his jaw, or how that feral bloodlust in his eyes makes my heart gallop...

"Edward," Pax snaps. "I require more instructions. Don't make me chop off your testicles and use them as hacky sacks."

"Yes," I squeak, not daring to ask what a 'hacky sack' might be. It's probably something he learned from Mike. "Right. Now, you must say the things that are in your heart."

"My heart wants to chop off your testicles and use them as hacky—"

"Not to *me*. To Brianna."

"Oh. I can do that." Pax's whole face breaks out into a smile. "I will tell her that Venus would be jealous of her glorious buttocks, and that I would love nothing more than to slather her in fish sauce and—"

"Not exactly what I meant, but it's a start." I sigh, trying not to get distracted by the line of stubble on his jaw. "I meant more along the lines of, 'Brianna, in all the world's great wonders, there is no heart that beats in tune with mine as yours does.'"

"Okay, I will try." Pax screws up his face. "Bree, when I'm with you, you make me feel as happy as when I am gutting an enemy and swinging his intestines like a skipping rope—"

"No!"

"Give me some words, then, poet."

"Very well, since I must do everything myself. Repeat after me. Brianna, I fell in love with your courage, and your kindness..."

"Brianna, I fell in love with your courage, and your kindness."

I have to close my eyes because my cock is so hard. "And even when the world has told you that you are wrong, or strange, or odd, you have never been those things to me. To me, you are perfect. You are the reason I don't want to fall asleep at night, because the waking world is finally better than my wildest dreams—"

"And even when the world has told you that you are wrong, or strange, or odd, you have never been those things to me, and I'll stab anyone who says them. To me, you are perfect. You are the reason I don't want to fall asleep at night, because the waking world is finally better than my wildest dreams."

Pax beams proudly.

"Very good," I whisper. "You may also add, 'I love you to the point of madness, and even if you were to never feel for me as I do for you, I would not be a slave to my love, because my love for you has freed me from the weight and the pain of life. You have freed me, and I am always yours.'"

"I can't remember all that."

"Fine, fine." I shake my head, struggling to find my voice. "The first bit is enough."

"Now what?" Pax's breath brushes my lips.

"Now, you must kiss her."

He blinks.

"And *when* you kiss her," I continue, wrestling back some control over my emotions, "you cannot attack her mouth with your tongue like it is some Druid army that needs conquering." I grip my hand behind his neck. "You must be soft. You must write the poetry of your feelings with your tongue. Like this."

With that, I draw Pax to me, and press my lips to his.

My tongue slides over his, caressing, calming, stopping him when he gets too excited and jumps around. He is an excellent kisser, but he is so forceful that it's impossible not to be swept along with him. But if he is to get Brianna to declare her love for him, it must be on her terms.

I try to redirect Pax, but that Roman is so impossibly stubborn, and as his tongue snakes over mine, and his hand behind my neck presses against my ghostly skin enough to *edge* me with pain, I find myself faltering. It doesn't help that the man kisses the way he does everything else – with a wild Roman power coursing through him, conquering everything he touches.

Conquering *me*.

Something in this kiss has rattled loose the laces around my heart. I don't merely want this Roman to keep doing *exactly* what he's doing, but I want to loosen my tongue and spill my own confessions to Brianna.

I keep my eyes fixed on his, and do my best to imagine that he is my beloved Brianna and that I am telling her all the dark and secret thoughts in my heart through this kiss, and that perhaps if I can get Pax to feel something of what I feel, he will be able to get through to her.

It's difficult, because of the stubble and the annoying way

Pax glares back at me with those intense icicle eyes of his. And I have to keep shifting so he can't feel how hard I am for him.

No, not for him.

Never for him.

I don't think.

Just as I cannot take the tension any longer, as I imagine taking his hand and directing it to stroke my throbbing, aching cock, he jerks away. His lips are raw, his eyes glazed over.

"Pax?" I snap my fingers in front of him, but his eyes remain unfocused. "Do you understand the things I've taught you?"

"Yes," he says. His face breaks out into a wide, beautiful grin. "I understand perfectly."

And then he turns around and leaves.

I flop back down to float over my bed, wiping my eyes, where ghostly tears have gathered unexpectedly.

"Pox-ridden Roman," I mutter. "He'll be the death of me."

32

PAX

It is the day of the open home. Bree and her mother have been in the kitchen all morning, baking apple pie. According the Gwen the Real Estate Agent, if the house smells like apple pie, it's a homely scent that's more enticing to buyers. Personally, I don't know how you can have a 'homely' smell without wine and blood and leather armour, but I noticed that no one asks the Roman these things.

The doorbell rings. "That will be Gwen with the first potential buyers!" Sylvie drops the pie on top of the oven, removes her apron, and rushes to the door. "Mike, they're here!"

"Coming!" Bree's father calls from my bedroom, also known as the 'junk room,' which he has been trying to 'square away.' I gather this means that Sylvie wants him to get rid of his stuff, but instead he's shoved it all into the closet and is trying in vain to lock the door.

Bree hangs back in the kitchen, sweeping up the icing sugar from the floor. She looks miserable, but we're going to change that.

Edward and I are in place, ready to enact my brilliant idea. Edward peers at me from around the corner, and flashes me his

293

smile that Bree describes as 'devilish.' We haven't spoken about the lovemaking lesson he gave me. It was all very odd. I was following his instructions perfectly, imagining I was kissing Bree and pouring all Edward's poetic words into her so that she would love me, and then I realised that I *wasn't* kissing Bree, but I was kissing Edward, and that it was rather pleasant, like slaying Druids on a lovely summer's day. I'd like to do it again, but after the way I ran out of there, he must think me a mighty coward, so it's best if I don't mention it.

Besides, we have more important things to worry about. Like a certain real estate agent and her plan to make Bree sad.

"—this large, elegantly-appointed entrance hall," Gwen says, waving her arms as she leads a man and woman into the house. "Freshly painted to bring out the historic features like these oak beams and that beautiful seventeenth-century wainscotting, this room will wow your guests from the moment they set foot in the door, and the sellers are willing to include any of the furniture and chattels you like."

"What's this stain on the floor?" The man frowns as he scuffs the spot where Ambrose shot Father Bryne.

"Oh, it's nothing to worry about." Sylvie stands on top of the stain. "Our daughter Bree had some friends over and they spilt a little strawberry daiquiri. Who knew that alcohol could get into the porous stone and stain it like that? We sure didn't. But don't you worry, we're working on getting it out. And you can put a rug over it, see?" She kicks out her leg, but then remembers there's no rug anymore, so instead she lays down the teatowel she's carrying. "There!"

"Now, if you follow me," Gwen urges the man into the eastern wing before he can look closer, which is probably for the best. I've learned that modern people don't consider bloodstains to be tasteful decor. "I'll show you the guest rooms. The house has been used as a B&B, but of course you could have a wing for guests, or fill it with children. These rooms are ready for your own personal stamp. Just look at these chandeliers!"

As they step into the first room and Gwen hits the light switch, Edward plunges his arm into the wall. The chandelier flickers. The man frowns.

"Is something wrong with the wiring?"

"Nothing's wrong with it!" Sylvie says, her voice as shrill as a gorgon. "We've had it certified. It's just an old house—"

Edward winks at me as he twists his hand. The chandelier flickers for longer this time. Something goes POP and there's a smell of smoke.

"That doesn't seem safe," the man says.

"If *you'll follow me*," Gwen says loudly. "We'll look at the bathrooms. They include some beautiful period features with modern conveniences..."

We traipse after the couple as they inspect the guest bedrooms and ensuite bathrooms. As they climb the stairs to the second floor, the woman stops to admire all the gilded portraits in the hallway.

"This house comes with a fascinating history," Sylvie says. "We have some books in our library that detail some of the more interesting owners, like the Van Wimple family, who left behind a lot of their fine Victorian furniture and curios."

"Oooh, I love history!" says the woman. "Are there any friendly ghosts?"

"Not that I've seen," says Mike, "but there *are* stories about the infamous Poet Prince Edward, a notorious rake who fell out of the upstairs window. Some people say that they can still hear his poetry whispered on the breeze—"

I wave at Edward. He drops to his knees on the top of the stairs and recites, "To the mortals dwelling within my haunted domain, Unaware they trespass, causing me great pain. My abode, once hallowed, now echoes with dismay. My great displeasure I seek to convey."

"Did you hear that?" the wife gasps.

"What?" her husband snaps.

"It was just the wind," Gwen says, although she glares at me as if I'm somehow responsible. I shrug, but I can't keep my eyes off Edward, who is descending the stairs with that princely smirk on his face.

"Someone said that they are greatly displeased by our presence. It almost sounded...like a ghost."

"Don't be absurd, woman. There's no such thing as ghosts."

"I swear I heard it! He sounds really angry, and he is a terrible poet."

"I heard it too," Sylvie says to Mike. "How odd."

"Ye who linger in this dwelling of mine. Take heed, depart, lest dark fates entwine," Edward waves his hands through the man, who rubs his arms as goosebumps appear on his skin. "By the moon's pale glow, I bid you leave. Or face the wrath that this pissed-off spectre shall conceive."

I glance at Bree. She stares at Edward as he gets right up in the woman's face. She covers her mouth with her hand. I hope she's enjoying this as much as we are. We'll get rid of these people, and Sylvie and Mike won't be able to sell Grimwood.

The man starts trembling. "D-d-does anyone else hear that?"

Mike's reached the top of the stairs. "I'm sure it's nothing. I must have left my laptop open, and Moon has jumped on the keyboard and opened my podcast app."

"Yes, that's it!" Gwen says brightly. "Just a silly podcast of terrible poetry. Not a spectre at all."

"The intruders, shaken, finally concede," Edward intones, jabbing his finger in the direction of the front door. "Heeding the ghost's warning, they take heed. Through moonlit shadows, they hasten away, Leaving the haunted dwelling, afore the break of day."

He flings his arms at a side table, and has enough ghost mojo to fling the objects on top down the stairs.

"Argh!" the husband cries as a picture frame sails past his face.

"That was no podcast!" the woman shrieks.

The man grabs his wife's arm and they tear off down the stairs.

"B-b-but you haven't even seen the master bedroom!" Gwen cries out.

"I don't think we're interested. Thank you."

The door slams shut behind them, echoing through the house.

Gwen leans against the wall, fanning her face with her hand.

"They didn't even collect their coats," Sylvie says forlornly.

"What *was* that voice?" Mike peers all around the landing. Edward moves aside before he can step through him. "It really *did* sound like it was coming from up here, but there's no one here."

"Maybe it *was* a ghost," I say. "He sounded pretty angry. I don't think he wants you to sell the house."

"I don't care if it's Jason Voorhees here for a murderous rampage," Sylvie says with a hint of savagery that I admire. "We've got to do this. Mike, Bree – roll up the rug in the office and bring it into the foyer. We need to cover this stain!"

Bree shoots me a look as she follows her father. Edward folds his arms and grins triumphantly from the top of the stairs. I give him a nod. Edward and I make a great team.

He bites his bottom lip, and I try not to think about the other day, when I came to him for advice on lovemaking. I was supposed to pretend that he was Bree while I kissed him, but it was difficult because Edward doesn't kiss like Bree. He kisses exactly the way you expect.

What I didn't expect was that I liked it.

But I don't have time to think about kissing when we are in the heart of battle. The doorbell rings. Gwen bustles the next couple inside – two women wearing flouncy dresses – and she decides this time to begin in the kitchen. This is good news, because that is my room.

Edward makes all the lights flicker as they enter the large kitchen, but the couple don't seem deterred when Gwen explains that away as old wiring. But we have a surprise waiting for them.

I hid my old Roman uniform behind the radiator. I haven't been able to wear it since I because Living again. Bree said that I wouldn't be able to blend in with it, and also that it smelled like the blood and sweat and filth of war.

I thought that our guests might like a whiff.

As our group moves to the centre of the kitchen to admire the Aga, the smell slams into us. Ooof. Even I must admit that it's not pleasant. I can even smell the garum I spilt on there from my pre-battle breakfast.

Edward stands behind me, holding his nose with one hand while fanning the smell in our direction with the other.

The two women recoil. "What's that smell?"

"Well, you see," I explain, using a speech Ambrose prepared for me. "The house was built over the site of an ancient battleground. This room was right where the Roman soldiers set up their camp. It's said that you can still smell the burning bodies of the Celtic warriors they slayed, as well as the acrid tang of their fishy garum sauce."

(This isn't entirely true; the camp was near the back of the garden, with easy access to the water supply and a more defensible perimeter, but Ambrose said that didn't matter.)

"It reeks." The taller of the two women pinches her nose.

"Do you mean that there are Roman soldier ghosts marauding about the place?" The shorter woman clutches a crystal necklace in her long fingers.

"Oh, yes, a whole legion of them," I say brightly. "They're great company. They will teach you drinking games."

"Bree, please tell your boyfriend to stop telling such ridiculous stories," snaps Gwen.

"He's not my boyfriend."

The two women exchange a look that implies they're not accepting of sharing their new home with Roman ghosts.

Heathens! May Mars curse them all.

When Bree doesn't do anything, Gwen turns to Sylvie. "Get rid of that smell!"

"I don't know where it's coming from?" Sylvie wails. She grabs her pie off the counter. "Here, sniff this beautiful home-made pie. *This* is what the house usually smells like—woah!"

As Sylvie leans toward the women, Edward sticks out his foot and, because Bree is nearby with moldavite in her pocket, Sylvie trips over it. She goes flying. The pie sails from her hands and hits the tall woman in the face.

"Argh!" The woman staggers backwards. Apple and pie crust drip down her cheeks.

The women leave soon afterwards. Next, Gwen lets in two brothers from a hotel chain, but they're turned away when Edward pulls books off the shelves in the nook and pages through them.

Then there is the London lawyer, who runs out after opening the linen cupboard to discover my sword resting on the towels, with the dried blood still staining the blade. I wave at him as he scrambles into his four-wheeled horseless carriage. His feet are still sticking out the window as he races away.

While Gwen is having a meltdown in the kitchen, I take a

tin of tuna from the cat food cupboard and move through the empty guest rooms, smearing it into the vents so that the smell moves through the whole house. It's quite clever, actually. Ambrose was the one who thought of it. He has a rather devious streak when—

"Pax, what are you doing?"

I whirl around. The tuna can clatters on the floor.

Bree is standing in the doorway, hands on her hips, looking delicious enough to eat even though her honey eyes are flashing.

"What does it look like I'm doing?" I whisper innocently. "I'm putting fish in the vents."

"But *why?*" Bree wails. "And why is Edward out there whispering terrible sonnets and tripping my mother and...and...omg, you're sabotaging the viewing!"

"We are making you happy," I say. "You do not want anyone to buy Grimwood. Well, we will make certain that no one does."

"Oh, Pax..." Bree frowns, and for a moment I think that she's going to yell at me, that I've done everything wrong and messed up again. But then she throws her arms around me. "Thank you."

"Excuse *me.*" A dark shape moves through the wall. "If anyone should be thanked, it's me. I'm the one out there, doing all the hard work, waving my hands through people and composing some of my finest sonnets and lifting books as if I'm the servant..."

Bree rushes over and hugs him. "Edward, you're amazing. Keep up the good work."

"My pleasure," Edward says as he plunges his hand into the wall. The lights flicker, and in the next room, Gwen shrieks as another lightbulb bursts.

33

BREE

"Well, that was a complete bust." Mum slumps down in her favourite armchair, a glass of sherry clutched protectively to her chest. "I felt certain that we'd have at least one offer today, but it's as if the universe is against us. How did *twelve* lightbulbs manage to blow in a single day? On today of all days?"

"I know, it's so *strange*." I glance over at Edward, and can't help the grin spreading over my face. "Who knew we really had ghosts?"

"There are no bloody ghosts!" Mum snaps. "We have a house that's falling down around us and no one to take it off our hands."

"We have to be patient, Sylvie." Dad doesn't look up from the puzzle he's doing. He keeps dropping the pieces on the floor, but he doesn't seem bothered by it.

"Maybe if no one wants this place, you'll have to hire someone else to run the B&B instead?" I suggest. "Pax is strong, maybe he could help with the DIY jobs around the place. I know he'd appreciate the extra money."

And then he might learn some skills that could help him find a job. Skills that don't involve stabbing people.

"We've already considered it, but we can't afford to pay anyone else. The guesthouse has only worked because your father and I don't pay ourselves a wage." Mum punches a pillow. "If you can find someone willing to work for free, I'm all ears."

"You could get an investor? Someone to give this place an infusion of cash to fix the roof, maybe redecorate the rooms and attract higher-paying clients. If we could charge what they do at the Queen Elizabeth Hotel, then you could afford to keep Grimwood—"

"We've already thought of that, love," Dad says. "But honestly, we wouldn't know the first thing about finding an investor. And reinventing this place and getting it up to scratch for high-end clients is not a project I want to take on right now."

As if on cue, he fumbles his puzzle piece, and it drops into his tea.

"You didn't happen to meet any cute billionaires on your Kerouac journeys?" Mum pipes up. "We could do with a knight in shining armour right about now, ideally one who will also give us lots of grandchildren."

"I volunteer," Edward calls from his position beside the fireplace. "I cut a striking figure upon a steed, and I *am* rather virile—"

"Nope, sorry." I kick out my feet, showing off my tracksuit pants, knotted hair, and pie-stained Blood Lust t-shirt. "Would you believe that no billionaires are interested in this? I know, I can't understand it, either."

"I can't bear to sit in this house another minute." Mum stands up and smooths down her dress. "Mike, how about going to the pub to drown our sorrows? Bree, do you and your not-boyfriends want to come, too?"

"Actually, no." I pretend to stifle a yawn. "I'm pretty beat. Today really took it out of me. I think I'll stay in and go to bed early."

As I leave the room, I grab Pax's hand and yank him down the hallway, beckoning Edward to follow.

I drag him into my room and slam the door behind me, checking that it's bolted. Ambrose looks up from the desk at the window with a start, where he's been working on his Braille. "Bree?"

Edward floats through the wall, a stern expression on his face.

"The three of you..." I glare at them. "I can't believe you did that."

"I didn't do anything," Ambrose says. "I was at the cemetery all day, and you cannot prove otherwise."

"Please," I roll my eyes, which is silly because he can't see that. "I know who came up with the idea to give Pax that speech about the ghosts of the Roman legion. That has Ambrose Hulme written all over it."

"Guilty," Ambrose's face breaks into a grin.

"It was all Pax's scheme," Edward says. "Will you castrate him? I'd like to watch."

"Are you kidding?" I gesture to Pax's crotch. "Castrating such a fine beanstalk is a crime against Jupiter. You are all amazing. You...I can't believe you care about this house as much as I do."

"We don't care about the house," Pax growls.

"Speak for yourself," Ambrose pipes up. "I quite like this place."

"After four centuries in this dump, I'd happily see it burn to the ground," Edward drawls. "We didn't do it for Grimwood. We did it for you, Brianna."

A warm feeling starts in my heart and spreads through my whole body, right down to my toes. No matter what happens, these three are always looking out for me.

I'm so incredibly lucky to have them.

"You…" A lump forms in my throat. I have to swallow twice to get the words out. "Thank you."

"You don't have to thank us," Pax says. "We're here to look after you. Always."

Pax moves forward with lightning speed, capturing me in his arms. His hand circles my neck, tilting my head up, and his lips capture mine.

Something about this kiss is different.

It might be the way that he's looking down at me, his pale eyes so open and sincere. Or it might be the way he holds me, as if I am something precious that might shatter beneath his touch, never to be put right again.

No. It's the way his kiss has become soft, tender, as if he is speaking to me in some ancient, dead language that can only communicate with shared breath. And the words he is saying seem like desperate foolish words of love.

Pax breaks away and throws a look over his shoulder at Edward. "Am I doing it right?"

"You are a perfect student." Edward bows his head.

"What's going on?"

But my curiosity is cut off when Pax pulls me in again. He walks me back until my knees hit the edge of the bed. I sit down, pulling him down with me.

Our bodies move together as he undresses me, all the while kissing me in this slow and painfully beautiful way, his eyes never leaving mine. The silver cords shimmer around us, reminding me that he is here, and real, and mine.

And yet somehow, I'm not sure I have truly known Pax until this moment. In his eyes, I see myself as he sees me, and it frightens me how much he cares for me and the things he would do to keep me safe. He's trying to tell me with the sweet brush of his lips that he will fight for me, but I don't think I'm worth a warrior's final stand.

What he's doing to me now...this isn't his usual frenzied fucking. This is something else. Something...intimate.

"Remember when I told you I would wait for you?" he whispers against my lips. "I meant it. I will wait until the gods destroy the earth for you to love me the way I love you."

"Pax..."

"I want to be your boyfriend. I want to take you to moving pictures and be on your pub quiz team and grow old and grey together. I want to teach you how to use your sword and carve up our enemies together. Most of all, I want to hear the beautiful words, 'I love you,' fall from your lips. But I will wait."

"Please..." I whisper, although I don't know what I'm asking.

Please stop.

Please don't stop.

Please don't love me.

Please love me until your dying breath.

"Pax came to me for a lesson," Edward says as he lies down beside me. "He wanted to learn how to make love to a woman like a poet, instead of simply fucking them into oblivion like a warrior. That is what he's doing."

"Edward gave me a speech to remember," Pax says as his finger strokes my breast. "But I forgot it. Besides, it was his words, not mine."

"You..." I can't believe this is happening. "You gave Pax a speech."

"It went something like this." Edwards dark orbs bore into

mine. "Brianna, I fell in love with your courage, and your kindness. And even when the world has told you that you are wrong, or strange, or odd, you have never been those things to me. To me, you are perfect. You are the reason I don't want to fall asleep at night, because the waking world is finally better than my wildest, most debauched dreams. I love you to the point of madness, and if even if you were to never feel for me as I do for you, I would not be a slave to my love, because my love for you has freed me from the weight and the pain of life. You have freed me, and I am always yours."

"I have some things to say, too," Ambrose declares as he climbs on the bed on the other side of me. "I had the most amazing day today, at a real job, talking to people about history. And it's all because of you, Bree. You taught me that I can be happy anywhere, and you made the afterlife a joy. I can't wait to spend my days as a Living man with you. Loving you is the greatest adventure."

Gods. The three of them...

Pax, who did something so utterly out of character as to go to Edward for help just to show me the depth of his feelings. Edward, who is here even though he's still a ghost and we have no clue if we can ever make him real again. And Ambrose, who has been through hell and back but never ever has anything but a smile and a kind word for everyone.

My heart hammers against my chest.

"I..." I flick my gaze between Pax and Edward. I touch Ambrose's cheek. "I love you. I love *all* of you."

The words rush out of me. As soon as I say them, the fear creeps in...a crawling sensation in my veins that this love of ours is doomed, that one day I'm going to lose them.

In New Zealand, I went bungy jumping with a group of backpackers. I remember standing on the edge of the platform, staring down at a canyon. The guy gave my bungy cord a final tug and told me I was safe to jump...

No one is safe when they leap over the side of a cliff, not when every atom in my body screamed at me to turn back, that bodies aren't supposed to go over cliffs, that girls like me, girls with powers I cannot explain, aren't supposed to fall in love.

But I'm tired of holding myself back. It's terrifying out here on the ledge, but I can't go back now, not when I've waited so long for them.

So I jump...

And I land in their arms, and on their cocks. I close my eyes and lose myself in the sensations. Their hands slide all over me, rolling my nipples in their fingers, dragging their nails down my back, teasing and tickling me. Everywhere Edward touches, he leaves a trail of heat across my skin, like ghost dust.

And as Ambrose enters me with a happy little sigh and Edward takes a nipple in his mouth and Pax cups my cheeks with his huge hands and kisses me like I am his goddess, I know that I never have to worry about falling again.

I have my parachute.

34

BREE

"Wake up!" My dad's voice calls through the halls, followed by a familiar *CLANG CLANG CLANG* that rattles my teeth.

Both Mum and I are not morning people, so whenever Dad had to get us up for an early appointment, he'd roam through the echoey halls of Grimwood, banging a wooden spoon on the bottom of his cast iron skillet.

CLANG CLANG CLANG.

"Time to go, Sylvie, Bree!"

"Rot in hell!" I yell back, slamming a pillow over my head.

"Consider yourself divorced!" my mum screeches from the other end of the wing.

The day of the Grimdale Giant Vegetable Festival has arrived.

Annoyingly, this means that we must get up at the asscrack of dawn to harvest Dad's cucumber and bring it to the judging tent before the festival begins.

"I am ready!" Pax booms as he slides his feet into his sandals. He always gets up at sunrise. "May the gods smile upon your vegetables."

"I too am ready for an exciting day at the festival." Ambrose tucks in his shirt.

Why is everyone so bloody *cheerful?*

Oh, right. It probably has something to do with the incredible sex we had last night. All four of us, together. And the fact that Mum and Dad didn't bat an eye that Pax and Ambrose didn't go back to Nevermore Bookshop.

Pax grabs my ankles and drags me out from under the sheets. "You must arise! We have a festival to win. This is even more exciting than the gladiator games! I've been practising my lewd hand signals for the other contestant's vegetables."

"I hate everything," I grumble as I cling to the edge of the bed.

"You sound just like a poet," Edward murmurs in his insouciant voice as he slouches over the chaise lounge. "Come back to bed and let's write words on each other's skin with our tongues for the rest of the day."

"Sounds like a bloody good idea to me."

"No." Pax grabs me around the waist and deposits me on the ground before shoving me in the direction of the bathroom. "Now go."

Bloody bossy Romans.

I emerge from the bathroom a few minutes later to discover Ambrose holding up an outfit for me. "You chose my clothes?"

"We look after you, remember? You didn't look like you were going to do it yourself. I love the texture of this shirt," he says, fingering the edge of a bell-sleeve blouse. He's chosen to pair it with a set of tiny black shorts. It's actually a pretty good combo.

"I chose those," Pax says proudly as I pull on the shorts. "Lots of ass."

"Thank you, Queer Eye for the Roman Guy. Are you coming out to the garden with us?" I ask Edward.

"To roll around in the vegetable patch?" He wrinkles his nose. "I think not. I shall perform my toilette so I look my best for the festival. All the ghosts in the village will be present, and they must see their prince in his finery."

It's on the tip of my tongue to remind him that the only outfit he *can* wear is the one he died in – a billowing silk shirt open to expose his chest, oversized codpiece, and breeches, with a shard of glass sticking permanently out of his backside. But that would be cruel.

And after what Edward did to me last night, I'm not going to be cruel.

I stumble downstairs to find Dad waiting in the kitchen, dressed in a pair of bright green overalls and red Wellingtons, his trusty spade in hand. "Your mother needs a few more minutes to get ready, so you can help me do the honours."

"I am most honoured to slay the mighty cucumber," Pax booms.

"Did you know that Pax has a real green thumb?" Dad says with a smile. "He's been helping me do a little weeding in the garden."

"I am good at pulling up the useless plants." Pax thrusts his fist in the air. "Take that, weeds! I tear you from the earth so the pretty flowers may thrive."

Dad leads us all out to the greenhouse, like a pied piper piping the children to their doom. "Here she is!" He throws open the door to reveal his freakishly large cucumber. "My pride and joy. What do you think about this beauty, Bree-bug? I call her the Lady-Killer, because the new organic spray I invented is working wonders on the ladybugs."

"Wow..." My hand flies to my mouth. "That's...it's...um..."

Somehow, possibly as a result of my doses of resurrection magic, Dad's large and slightly curved cucumber has grown a couple of knobbly bits on the end...so it looks like an enormous cock and balls.

I mean, I'm no prude, but this is *ridiculous.*

"Isn't she beautiful?"

"It is impressive in girth!" Pax booms.

Ambrose runs his fingers along the surface. "This is the largest cucumber I've ever known to exist!" he declares. "But why does it have these two knobbly bits on the end?"

"Oh, don't mind those. I think they're a side effect of the fertiliser I use. The judges say it doesn't matter if a fruit is misshaped, as long as it's impressive."

Oops, it looks as if my magic has been a little lopsided.

The cucumber is indeed impressive. It's impressive that my father has managed to grow a ridiculously large cucumber that looks *exactly* like a dick and balls, and he seems to be completely oblivious.

I cannot believe we're going into the village with that thing. Everyone is going to see it.

I flash to an image of Kelly and Leanne, and what they're going to say.

But then I look across at Pax, who is beaming with pride as if he were the one who grew the cucumber, and Ambrose, who looks as if he's doing everything in his power not to laugh, and I realise that I don't give a shit about what Kelly and Leanne think. Dad is having a blast, and I'm going to enjoy today with him, because who knows how many days like this we have left?

Lovingly, Dad shows Pax how to cut the cucumber from the plant. Pax helps Dad manoeuvre the cucumber onto his bike trailer. I pick several smaller cucumbers from the other plants in the greenhouse, which I place in the bike's basket to offer at the vegetable exchange Dani's mum is running.

Pax hops on his bike and declares himself the bodyguard of

the cucumber. Dad takes Pax's pink bike and the pair of them head off in the direction of the village. I haven't ridden a bike since the day I fell off and started seeing ghosts, and Ambrose can't ride, so he and Mum and I walk together into the village, carrying cases of Mum's homemade jam and Dad's entry form for the judges.

When we arrive, Mum and I make a beeline for the coffee cart. I get drinks and cupcakes for the guys – Pax has a cappuccino and Ambrose happily sips away at his hot tea.

Dad has already set up his cucumber in the display tent. It has a table all to itself, with a light shining on it so that everyone can see its er...girth. We only get a quick glimpse at it before we're ushered out of the tent again, but I glance around and I can't see another vegetable that's quite as large or as lurid as ours.

"They're doing the judging now," Dad explains as we walk away from the tent and get coffee from the cart. "So none of us are allowed inside for another half hour. I didn't get a good look at all the entries, but I saw Tom Clarkson whip out his cucumber and his isn't nearly as big as mine."

I choke on my coffee. Beside me, Edward laughs heartily.

"You're happy today," I whisper as we wander around the craft stalls.

"Today, I have the love of a beautiful woman, and the world feels bright." Edward places his fingers in mine, sending that delicious tingle up my arm. I hope the ghost mojo will keep him with us for most of the day.

We make our way through the festival stalls and games. Pax immediately spies the high striker game where you hit the button with the hammer to win prizes. He rushes over.

"But of course," Edward sighs. "The Roman can't resist an opportunity to show off his strength. Where is the poetry competition? Does this village have no culture?"

I gasp in mock horror. "How can you say we have no culture? You're forgetting about the Morris dancing."

"Forgive me, I didn't realise that such rich intellectual pursuits were awaiting me."

"Two quid for a go," the vendor calls, thrusting the hammer at us. "Test your strength! Swing the hammer against the block and try to ring the bell at the top. You sir," he waves to Pax. "You look like a strong fellow. Do you want to win a cuddly toy for your lady?"

Pax gives me his puppy dog face and I cough up a coin. He grabs the hammer and swings all his weight down with his swing. The vendor winces as the pin hits the bell with such force that the bell shatters into a million pieces.

"I win!" Pax pumps his fist in triumph as the gathered crowd claps and cheers for him.

"That's the sexy man who was swimming in the duck pond," an old lady whispers to her friend. Her friend nods in appreciation.

The red-faced vendor grudgingly offers Pax a choice of over-sized cuddly toys. Pax chooses a lion and hands it to me with a flourish.

"You Romans and your lions," I grin as I lean in and kiss him.

The lion is quite heavy, but he's so soft and snuggly. I wrap both my arms around him and bury my face in his fur and kind of waddle around after the guys, who are darting from one booth to another. Edward is doing a great job of describing things to Ambrose.

"...and here you have a game where you toss coloured balls into the mouths of hideous clowns. My father used to play something similar at court, except instead of the clowns he used the heads of peasants on pikes. There's another where you toss balls to knock over milk bottles...Oh, and here's one where you shoot tiny ducklings with some kind of miniature siege weapon. It seems a bit unsporting. You should at least have some foxes…"

"That's a gun, and I want to play a game," Ambrose says.

"Then it will cost you one quid," a familiar, bored voice says.

My blood chills as I recognise Leanne behind the counter, managing the milk bottle toss and the duck shooting games. She starts when she sees me. "Bree? I—I didn't notice you there behind that lion."

"Pax won it for me," I say.

Pax leans across the counter, and Leanne backs away, no doubt remembering when he pulled her into the duck pond. He thumps the counter. "Yes, this looks fun. I will play with the siege weapons and Ambrose will toss balls at bottles. But I don't wish to shoot innocent baby ducks. Do you have any Druids?"

"H-h-he can't play." Leanne backs away from the counter, staring at Ambrose. "He's blind. It's against health and safety."

"That's okay," Ambrose says brightly. "We'll find another game."

"No, we won't. Ambrose is as competent as that six-year-old kid you've just given a gun, and he's a hell of a lot safer. We're playing."

Leanne's lip trembles. I don't blame her. She's been through a lot lately. Wordlessly, she accepts my money, dropping it into the till as if it's poison, and then tosses Pax a gun. "Take the range on the far end," she hisses. "I'll get the balls."

We move down to the range and I help Pax to set up his tiny siege weapon (gun. It's a gun that fires little rubber caps at the ducks). I'm just showing Pax how to fire it and explaining that he has to shoot the ducks and can't shoot the people who are shooting the ducks when I notice Edward sneaking up behind Leanne with a suspiciously sinister smile on his face.

"Edward," I hiss. "What are you doing?"

He winks at me as he leans close to Leanne's ear and whispers, "You let my friend Ambrose win the game, or I will visit you in your sleep tonight, and it will not be pleasant."

Leanne stiffens. She recognises Edward's voice from Kelly's house. She digs a handful of tiny plastic balls from a container in front of her. "Um...s-s-sure. Here are your balls. You toss them at the bottles and try to knock them over, and then you get a p-p-prize."

"Fun! Like this?" Ambrose lobs a ball directly at Leanne. She's too slow to duck, and it hits her right in the nose.

Pax falls over laughing. I can't help it – I snort.

Leanne grabs her nose, tears streaming down her face, but Edward leans in and whispers something to her, and she staggers to her feet and plasters a smile on her face.

"That was..." Leanne tries to speak through the pain. "That was a great shot, but this time try to aim at the actual bottles."

"Oops," Ambrose says. "Sorry."

"No need to be sorry. Try a little to the left and about a foot higher."

Pax grabs Ambrose's shoulder and turns him to face the rows of milk bottles set up on the shelves. Ambrose lobs his balls one after the other, whooping each time. Every single one of them misses.

"Did I hit anything?" he asks.

"No...but that's actually part of the game!" Leanne's face is pale, and she gingerly touches her swelling nose. "You won our grand prize. This giant stuffed duck."

She practically throws it at Ambrose. Pax reaches over and tucks it under his arm.

"We accept this duck." He tosses his gun on the counter. I notice he has bent the barrel so no one else can use it. "I've decided that this game is cruel to ducks. No one else is to play it until you put some Druids up, instead. Obey me or I shall return and bend all your tiny siege weapons into lovely shapes."

"S-s-sure." Leanne practically throws an out-of-order sign at the shooting range.

"You're safe…" Edward whispers in her ear. "For now. But remember my warning next time you think about being cruel to Brianna. Or anyone else, for that matter."

"Leanne, what are you doing?"

I stiffen. That's Kelly's voice. I look up and see her striding over to the booth in her designer boots and a Zimmermann dress.

"Why have you shut the duck booth down? That's raising money for Riley's football club. And why are you talking to Cheddar Cheese? You're as bad as Alice, hanging out with the freaks."

"K-K-Kelly, he's back. Th-th-the ghost!"

Edward takes the opportunity to shove his hands into the cotton candy machine on the stall next door.

"Hey," the owner cries as the candy spins wildly off the spool and dances through the air, seemingly of its own accord. "What's going on? The machine's never done that before!"

Edward whirls the ball of cotton candy through the air.

He dumps it on Kelly's head.

Kelly screams as her perfect hair is subsumed in sticky candy. She runs in frantic circles with this giant pink bird's nest on her head, tearing at the candy and trying to get it off her. It sticks to her fingers and clothing, covering her in pink tufts.

I can't hold in my laughter any longer. Pax nudges me, and I take my phone from the basket of cucumbers on my arm and snap a couple of pictures.

"I've got a new screensaver," I grin at Pax.

"That's a great look for you, Kelly," another familiar voice says behind me. I turn around to see Alice and Dani, arm in arm.

Kelly glares at all of us and stomps off, yelling that she's going to sic her lawyer on the cotton candy cart.

"I don't know what happened," Dani says with a conspiratorial look at the space she thinks Edward is occupying. "But I think Kelly is starting to get the idea that she's not as cool as she used to be."

"I got photos." I pull my phone out of the basket. Alice and Dani crowd around. I notice that Alice isn't defending or running after her old friend. Instead, she snuggles deeper into Dani's arm. I guess their friendship is over now. I can't say I'm sad to have Alice in our corner.

Dani shoots me a look. I know what she's asking. She wants Alice to know the truth. I shake my head. Today isn't the day for it. I'm here to support my dad and have a break from worrying about the supernatural. Besides, the Ripper hasn't come back. Maybe...maybe we're safe...for the moment.

"Nice lion," Alice says with a smile.

"Pax won it for me. And Ambrose won me the duck. Ambrose, this is Alice. And this is Ambrose, my...er, boyfriend."

Ambrose beams at the word, and the way he lights up almost makes it easier to say.

Almost.

"Ambrose Hulme, pleased to make your acquaintance." Ambrose thrusts his hand out in front of him, his elbow remaining at his side, as Mina had taught him.

"Alice." Alice shakes it, eyeing him up approvingly as he turns back to wait for Pax to get back with some cotton candy for him.

"It's a pleasure to finally meet you," Ambrose beams. "I've heard so much about the famous Alice and Dani."

"All good things, I hope?" Alice smiles.

Dani steps forward and wraps Ambrose in a hug. "I'm so happy that you finally got her to admit her feelings," she whispers. "Don't tell the others, but you were always my favourite ghost."

"And you were my favourite Living," Ambrose beams. "After Bree, of course."

"Of course." Dani pulls back with a smile. "Ambrose is doing tours at the cemetery, too. He's made the place quite famous thanks to some viral videos about a little-known Victorian blind adventurer."

"That sounds fascinating. We shall have to come along to one of your tours. So you're Bree's boyfriend?" Alice gives me an appreciative nod. "What happened to the tall, loud one with the impressive muscles?"

"Pax, oh…he's over there, at the fruit stalls." I point to where Pax is holding up a pair of melons to his chest and doing a dance that has my father practically on the ground in hysterics. "He's also my boyfriend. I guess…I guess I have two now."

"Hmmph," Edward pouts, but the twinkle in his eye tells me he doesn't need me to answer.

I wish I didn't have to leave him out. I wish we'd been able to figure out his unfinished business. But we're not giving up. Ambrose is deep in research, and I'll help just as soon as I know that Jack the Ripper is gone for good.

"I want you to meet someone, too." Alice turns around and tugs a man who was enraptured by Pax's dance. "Dad, this is Bree, Ambrose, and Pax. This is my father, Richard."

"Hello!" the man says brightly. "How are you today?"

"We're good, Mr. Agincourt. We're enjoying the festival. How are you? You're an archaeologist, aren't you?" I remember what Alice told me the first time I visited her at the museum. "We really enjoyed visiting the Roman exhibit the other week."

"I'm so happy you liked it." He beams. He looks a lot like Alice with his severe features, but his whole face lights up when he smiles. "It's decades of work cataloguing those finds and building a picture of the Roman settlement at Grimdale, but I'm proud of what we accomplished. It's lovely to see young people take an interest in history."

"Your daughter is a big part of that. She's done amazing things – she's introduced a whole new generation to the history of the area."

"How do you know my daughter?" His face crumples in confusion. "You're a bit old to be her friend – she's thirteen. She just started at Grimdale Comprehensive and she wants to be an archaeologist like her old man. I think you'd really like her, but she's fallen in with these bad girls lately. I don't know what I'm going to do, but I suppose she'll figure it out for herself—"

Behind his head, I see Alice's smile wobble. My heart opens for her. I know all too well what it's like to see your parents getting older and know that your relationship to them is changing.

But while my dad's body might be betraying him, he still has his mind. I can't imagine the kind of cruelty the dementia has wrought on Alice and her family.

Dani sees Alice's face and comes running over, two small cotton candy cones in her hands. She throws them at me and takes Mr. Agincourt's hand.

"Oh, there you are, Mr. Agincourt." Dani beams. "I'm Dani. A friend of your daughter. Do you want me to take you to get a cup of tea and a scone?"

"Yes, please. That would be lovely." He lets Dani lead him away.

Alice's shoulders sag. "I'm sorry about Dad."

"Don't be."

"He has good days and bad days. Today is actually a good day." Alice's eyes mist over as she watches Dani and her dad exclaim over a display of knitted tea cosies. She plasters a smile on her face. "He may think I'm thirteen, but at least he still remembers me. How's your dad?"

I point to the competition tent. Dad is now standing outside in a circle of amateur gardeners waving their arms about as they compare the girth of their vegetables. He's got cotton candy stuck to his cheek. "He's hoping to win the vegetable festival with his enormous phallic cucumber."

"Phallic cucumber?"

"It's a little deformed on one end," I say. "It looks exactly like a cock and balls."

"Please, that's nothing. I saw Maggie wheeling in a basketball-sized sweet potato that's totally shaped like a vulva. if this village didn't want rude vegetables, it shouldn't have created the Giant Vegetable Festival."

"True that. But when you go in there, try not to laugh out loud, okay?"

Alice smiles. "I make no promises."

We stand there, not saying a word, watching as Dani and Mr. Agincourt are pulled into Dad's group. Soon they're all laughing together.

Something brushes my arm. I look down and see Alice's hand.

Instinctively, I take it, and squeeze.

She blinks, and I think I see a rogue tear in the corner of her eye, but then she rubs her eye and it's gone.

"Your dad knows how much you love him," I say to her. "Maybe not every day, but inside him is still a person who knows, and nothing that happens to him now will erase the wonderful man he is."

"Right back at you," she says with a sniff.

"Yeah." I swallow hard. "I guess we both have to remember that this might be the hardest thing we'll have to endure in our lives. Much harder than, say, being able to see ghosts or hiding the body of a dead priest or worrying that you haven't sent an infamous Victorian serial killer fully back to hell."

Alice furrows her brow at me. "What are you talking about?"

"Nothing. I'm rambling. But look at our dads – all they need is a cup of tea and a silly village festival and they're right as rain. Hey, do you want a cucumber? They're from Dad's garden and they're not as pornographic—"

"Bree!" a gruff Scandinavian voice calls behind me. "I must speak with you!"

It's too much to hope that I might have a few moments of peace.

"Looks like you're needed," Alice says with a smile as she turns to see who's calling me. "You do keep some strange company, Bree Mortimer."

I whirl around to see a large, familiar Viking shoving his way through the crowd, an axe strapped to his back and his blond beard wild about his face. Behind Björn, Father Maxwell is practically tripping over his robes to keep up. They're both panting as if they've run straight from All Souls.

Bjorn's ice-blue eyes betray concern, but it's Father Maxwell who really has my blood racing. He looks like shit. His eyes are bloodshot and there are cuts all over his skin and his clothing is rumpled and filthy, the collar stained with what looks suspiciously like blood.

As they near me, I notice that Father Maxwell's eyes aren't just bloodshot, they're *haunted*. He looks as if he's witnessed something so horrifying that he will never be okay again.

This is not good.

"What are you doing here?" I grab the priest's arm and drag him away from the festival, across the town green to the edge of the duck pond. Pax, Ambrose, and Edward fall away from Dad's circle of friends and gather around me. "I thought that you'd be in danger from the Order of the Noble Death if you leave the church."

"I am," he mutters. "But I had to warn you. And I need your help."

"What's this about?"

"Remember when you asked me if there are consequences to bringing the dead back to life?" Father Maxwell closes his eyes. "Well, I'm dealing with one of those consequences right now. The Veil...it's..."

I study the lines on his face, his wild, haunted eyes. He appears hollow, all the goodness scraped out of him. I think if I tapped him on the shoulder, he'd topple over.

"Tsk, tsk, it looks like someone has been wielding a little too much resurrection magic."

The three witches emerge from the baking tent. Mary rubs her belly and mutters something about the scones, but Lottie and Agnes circle Father Maxwell, frowning as they inspect his dishevelled form.

"Get back, harridans," Father Maxwell mutters, but there's no bite to his words.

"I wouldn't call us names if you want our help, Father," Agnes says. "And judging by the look of you, you need more than prayer to cure this ill."

"You know what's wrong with him?" I ask.

"I've seen that look before," Lottie frowns. "It was a couple of years back, some young lads were playing with a spirit board in the woods, and one of them accidentally summoned a—"

Lottie's words are cut off by a scream. I whirl around. The vegetable tent shakes as a black mist envelops it. People scatter in all directions. One of the festival judges staggers out the door of the tent, bleeding from his nose and eyes.

"Help!" he yells. "It's horrible. It's—"

But his words cut off into a piercing shriek as he's dragged back into the tent by an invisible force. A moment later, a spray of crimson decorates the side of the tent.

"What is this?" I yell, shaking Father Maxwell's collar.

"Look what you've done, priest," Agnes huffs. "You've gone and led it straight to Grimdale."

"Led what? What is that?"

"*That*," the priest says as he crosses himself frantically, "is a demon."

35

BREE

I don't have time to contemplate the absurd notion of a demon crashing the Grimdale Giant Vegetable Festival, because the village is panicking. People scatter in all directions, knocking over stalls and shoving each other out of the way. I see Alice and Dani grab hold of my dad and Mr. Agincourt and drag them away from the tent.

A cacophony of screams and shrieks rises from the tent, and the whole thing shakes. More crimson splatters the walls. It looks like a terrible horror film, but it's real.

Blood. That's blood.

My heart leaps in my throat as the screams abruptly cut off.

The tent flap opens.

Something slithers out.

Has Jack the Ripper returned?

No, something worse.

My stomach lurches.

A Soul-Eater.

The creature is made of shadow and smoke. It moves along the ground like a snake crossed with a sinister wind-up toy. Its edges blur, so it's impossible to focus on it for more than a moment without your eyes going wonky. Scraps of tent fabric and other...bodily stuff...hang from the tips of its curved horns, and a whip of fire flicks from its ghastly maw of a mouth to set the tombola booth alight.

It moves through the festival with a tremendous wave of wrongness, a sense that it is completely out of time and space. It is not supposed to be here.

And it knows only one thing – it knows only horror.

Stunned, many Grimdale residents freeze, unable to believe what they're seeing. I wave my arms, urging them to flee. But I'm too far away. All I can do is watch in horror as the creature slithers and skitters through the crowd, slashing with its claws of shadow and burning with its fire whip. The fruit and vegetables on display wither and rot in its presence, and where its body slithers, it leaves behind scorched earth.

Blood stains the green grass and paints the Whack-a-Mole booth with rivers of crimson.

"What do we do?" I cry, dropping my lion.

"We must stop it before it hurts more people," Björn says sternly.

"You have my sword, brother." Pax sets down the giant duck.

"Pax, no!"

But before I can stop him, Pax whips his sword from the leg of his trousers (how the fuck was he hiding it in there?) and he and the Viking stride toward the Soul-Eater. Pax slashes at it with his blade, but all he manages to do is slice the air.

The Soul-Eater whirls around, and that great whip of fire lashes out and wraps around Björn's ankle.

The Viking hollers with pain. He slashes his blade through the fire, freeing his leg. But as he staggers back, he can no longer bear his own weight.

He collapses to his knees. Pax leaps in front of him as the creature rears up again.

"Run!" Pax booms as he raises his sword. "Leave this place. Run back to your homes and hide."

You don't have to tell the village of Grimdale twice. They don't even stop to form a queue, but scamper away as the beast...creature...fucking *Soul-Eater* advances on Pax.

"What do we do?" I cry. "Pax?"

"Quickly, we don't have much time." The priest pulls something from his pocket. I recognise the wooden box he kept in his desk, filled with the spiky crosses he'd taken from members of the Order of the Noble Death. "Do you still have Father Bryne's cross?"

I pull it out of my pocket.

"And you're packing moldavite, I assume?"

I nod again, dipping my hand into my other pocket.

Father Maxwell's shoulders sag. "I think between the two of us, we will have enough power to banish it back through the Veil. But first, we need to trap it with a demon mark."

"What's that?"

"Demon is a Christian word for something far older – they are malevolent spirits, infinitely more powerful than your friend Jack the Ripper, who have been given a new name and a new purpose by whatever Lord can wield them. The Soul-Eater's name is the source of its power. Whoever controls the name, controls the beast. What we need to do is draw the image of its name into the earth and then lure him into it."

"But we don't know the its name."

"I do. It's..." Father Maxwell says a word that's halfway between a phlegmy cough and a power ballad. "This particular Soul-Eater has been chasing me for some time."

"What the fuck did you do to be *chased* by a Soul-Eater?"

"It's drawn to my resurrection magic. Björn has always been

able to help me hold it off, but it's never been able to fully penetrate the Veil before. I gave it too much power."

"What do you mean, it's drawn to your magic?"

"There's no time to explain!" The priest bends over and scratches at the dirt with his hands. The summer sun has baked the village green solid, and all he succeeds in doing is pulling out a few blades of grass. "It's no use. This earth is too hard. We'll never draw the symbol here."

"What about the fruit?" I ask, jiggling my basket of cucumbers on my arm.

"Yes," Ambrose cries. "We use the fruit to create the demon mark."

"That could work." The priest's eyes flutter shut. "It's worth a try. Bring me all the fruit you can."

I dump out my basket of cucumbers. The priest arranges them in a circle.

"We need more!"

I peer over my shoulder. Pax is now chasing the Soul-Eater through the farm animal petting zoo. He's discarded his sword in favour of the hammer from the hi-striker game. The Soul-Eater howls as Pax smashes its horn into the tea cosy booth.

Heart pounding, I rush to the nearest vegetable stall and grab handfuls of heirloom purple carrots. I run them back to Father Maxwell.

"I need something large and round," he yells at me as he begins to line up the carrots in an esoteric shape.

"Pax!" I yell as I sprint back. "I need melons!"

"Toooo Valhalla! Odin owns you all!" Björn hefts himself up and springs toward the Soul-Eater, his sword slashing through the air. Pax ducks as Björn swings his sword over his head, diverting the Soul-Eater's attention. Pax grabs two of the largest melons from a nearby display and bowls them underarm at me.

I throw my arms out to catch them but they sail right past me. Physical education was never my strong suit.

Father Maxwell hobbles across the grass and retrieves the now slightly squished melons. He places them inside his demon mark. He fumbles with his box, opening it and tipping out the crosses onto the ground. He starts to stab them into the hard earth around the circumference of his circle, the way we did when we set up the wards around Grimwood and Nevermore Bookshop.

"Lead him over here!" Father Maxwell calls to Pax and Björn once he's finished.

"Bree, I want to help," Ambrose cries as he crawls toward me.

"You *are* helping," I say as I drop to my knees. I find the cross in my pocket and stab it into the ground, closing the circle. Father Maxwell waves his hands over them, and the crosses light up briefly, then fade back again.

"What can I do?" Edward's face is even paler than usual.

"You can be silent, spirit." Father Maxwell frowns at the crosses. "We need something to entice it into the circle. It needs to taste our resurrection magic, but I'm too weak. I can't do it."

"You want me to pour magic into the fruit?" I stare down at the symbol. I may have been getting better at controlling my magic, but I'm too terrified to be able to do this now. I blink, but no matter how hard I squint, I can't see the silver cords.

"Bree, it's okay. It's all going to be okay," Ambrose says. "You don't have to use your magic. I have what he needs."

Ambrose steps into the circle.

36

BREE

"Ambrose," my voice wavers. "Get out of that circle. Now."

He folds his arms. "No. My veins are humming with your resurrection magic, and I have a fresh soul that's already been beyond the Veil once. If we need something to draw the creature into the circle, then I'm our best bet. Tell me that I'm wrong."

I can't.

Because he's right.

I don't know how I know this, but I know he's right.

But I don't want to lose him. I *can't.*

There has to be another way.

I grab Father Maxwell's sleeve. "You can't let him do this."

"It's too late now. They are coming."

No, no, no.

I fling a look over his shoulder. Pax and Björn are backing across the grass, leading the Soul-Eater toward our trap.

My breath stutters. Pax and Björn are a glory to behold. They dance around each other, tying up the Soul-Eater as it tries to outsmart them, always staying just out of reach of its

331

fire. Slowly, they force the Soul-Eater across the green, where it leaves a scorched trail in its wake.

"Ambrose, stand your ground," Father Maxwell commands.

"I won't move until you give the word," he assures. He flashes his bright grin, but it wobbles a little at the edges.

Fear wells inside me. "Ambrose, you don't have to do this."

"I won't let anything happen to you," he assures me.

The Soul-Eater bears down on us. It stops, its fire tail whipping across the grass, its shadow snout raised in the air, sniffing.

And then it rises up like a serpent ready to strike, and flings itself toward the circle.

37

AMBROSE

I swallow down my terror as I hear Father Maxwell say, "Here we go. The moment the beast is inside the walls, Ambrose must leap free. And then we have to slam the portal shut."

"I don't know how to do that," Bree cries.

"Yes, you do," he rasps. "Cut the black threads."

"Cut the black threads? Have you been into the communion wine? I don't see any—oh."

She sees them. I knew she would. I knew my Bree would find a way to stop this creature.

Which is just as well, because I feel certain that this rash decision might be my last.

I am honoured to die to save Bree and my friends. I will not let them down. No matter how desperately I want to flee, how my whole body trembles as it senses the heat and the wrongness of the Soul-Eater's approach, I will not leave this circle until I know they have the beast contained.

The Soul-Eater is close now. I can hear the crack of its fire tongue whipping through the air, the rolling wave of its bleak miasma that threatens to pull me in.

I *know* without seeing – as I know that the sky is blue and Bree is beautiful – that if I am pulled into its embrace, I will not die.

The horror that awaits me will be far worse than death.

My soul.

Everything that makes me who I am will be *devoured.*

I square my jaw and dig my boots into the hard earth. I have had every adventure a man could possibly dream of. I have seen the world. I have escaped death once before. I have loved and been loved by a remarkable woman.

My feet are glued in place. I don't believe I will be able to move. I'm so terrified that I am frozen...

I will meet my fate content, as long as I stand my ground. As long as I stay...right here...as the Soul-Eater comes closer, as its fire whip lances through the air around me, as it drags me into its ghastly darkness...

"Now!" Father Maxwell cries.

"Ambrose, move!" Bree screams.

Her voice jerks me from my terror. For Bree, I find the strength to move.

I leap backwards, not knowing if that is the right direction, for the creature's horror is pressing in on all sides of me. My foot catches on a melon and I slip. I land hard on my ass, but before I can scream, the Soul-Eater is upon me.

It screams at me in its unintelligible language. I feel it force my mouth open and slide inside me, its fingers that are not fingers reaching through me, fishing around in my organs, making a mockery of my earthly body. And in that moment, I *see* the beast.

Not with my eyes, but with some kind of deep, inner part of me. I stare into the eye of pure evil, and it plunges its darkness inside me, right into my heart, and claws from me the last vestiges of humanity.

I close my eyes as the world fades from knowledge, as I topple into the void...

38

BREE

I scream as I watch the Soul-Eater bound across the circle in his hunger to reach Ambrose.

Ambrose slumps, the light in his eyes flicking out as the soul-eater's dark mist plunges through his mouth down into his chest.

The creature holds Ambrose there and draws back his hand, claws unsheathed, ready to deal the final blow, to take his bright, beautiful soul from him.

"Keep the wards up!" Father Maxwell yells at me. "Don't let it escape."

"Clear your mind," Agnes snaps from where she and the other two witches watch from the bushes.

I snap back to the magic lessons. *Clear your mind.* I focus on the black cords winding from the Order's pins and spreading around the edges of the demon mark, reaching for the edges of the beast as it embraces my poor Ambrose. I try to let it all go, to wink away my fear, and to focus on being in the shed with my dad, painting the soap box racer and singing along with The Who.

Ambrose tries to scuttle backwards on his ass even as the

soul-eater's mist pours inside him. But not fast enough. The creature rears up—

I *push* with my mind.

The black tendrils circle the beast. Just as it raises its fire whip and its black hole of a mouth opens wide to swallow Ambrose, a black cord winds around the whip, tethering it in place.

The Soul-Eater lets out a noise so horrifying that it knocks me to my knees. The mist tears from Ambrose's throat. Beside me, Edward is weeping openly. Pax rushes the circle, but when he tries to swing his sword at the beast, he can't get through. The black cords rise higher, blocking him out.

"Ambrose!" I cry.

Ambrose turns to the sound of my voice, his face stricken. But when he tries to push through, he can't make it, either.

The Soul-Eater thrashes as more and more black cords wind around its body. The Veil is calling it home. It throws itself against the circle, but it's a firefly trapped in a jar. It can't go anywhere.

And neither can Ambrose.

"Cut the threads!" Father Maxwell cries out.

I don't hesitate. I reach out and grab the threads. They feel hot and sticky in my hands. I tug at them, all the time pushing the magic through my fingers, the way the witches taught me. The threads snap away in my hands, whipping around to wrap the Soul-Eater tighter, until the black cords become a large, dark hole in the centre of the circle that grows and grows, dragging the beast into it, reaching right out to the edge of the demon mark where Ambrose is desperately trying to cling on.

I know with bone-chilling certainty what I'm looking at – a portal to the other side of the Veil.

"Oh, drat and botherations," Ambrose exclaims as the

ground starts to fall out from beneath him. His feet swing in mid-air, directly above that hole of nothingness.

"Ambrose!" I grip the edge of the earth and surge forward. I manage to grab Ambrose under the armpit just as he slides into the hole after the creature, but his weight drags me right over the edge of the demon mark.

I scream as we both tumble into the darkness.

39

BREE

I cling to Ambrose as the Veil closes in around us.

We're falling. We're going to fall into the other side of the Veil and—

Something grips my ankle like a vise, making my body jerk. I almost let go of Ambrose but manage to hold on.

"I've got you," Pax growls, his grip firm around my ankles. "I'm pulling you up."

"Bree," Ambrose cries. "Hold on."

"I won't let go," I promise. It takes every ounce of strength I have, but I feed my right arm beneath Ambrose's shoulder, knitting my fingers together. My arm sockets scream from the pain of his dead weight. All around me, the shadows dance, their tendrils licking my skin.

*Let go, let go, join us...*the darkness whispers. And there's another sound, too, so loud that it makes my head pound.

Laughter.

Jack the Ripper's laughter.

No. I will not be like you.

You are like us, Brianna. You are a creature of shadow. You are an angel of death. Join us in the Veil...

The Ripper laughs and laughs and laughs.

With a grunt, Pax hauls us up. He goes slow, and my whole body shudders with the effort of holding onto Ambrose. The shadows press against my skin, and I can feel them tugging on me, trying to drag me back down into that hungry maw.

But Pax is stronger than all the nasty things waiting for me on the other side.

He tugs me and Ambrose over the edge, and rolls us out of the circle to safety. As soon as Ambrose is free of the void, the ground closes over with a sickening *THUD*.

The demon mark, the Ripper's laughter, the whispers – they're gone.

"Ambrose?" I roll over and touch his face. His cheek is badly scorched, but other than that, he seems unharmed from the mist. "Are you okay? Is your soul—"

"Did I do it?" Ambrose's cracked lips curl up into the sweetest smile. *There he is, soul and all.* "Did I get rid of the Soul-Eater?"

"You sure did." I hug him close. He winces as I wrap my arms around his chest, but he doesn't pull away. "You were so brave. You saved us all."

"Oh, great," Edward drawls. "Ambrose is the hero again. Why not give the rest of us a turn?"

"I couldn't have done it without you." Ambrose kisses my nose. "All those magic lessons with the witches have paid off."

"I can't believe I did that." I'm exhausted. I feel like a face-cloth wrung out. I turn to ask the priest what exactly it was that we just did, and scream again as Father Maxwell slumps to the ground.

"Priest!" Björn drops his sword and hobbles to his side. His leg looks really bad. The Viking lifts the limp priest and slaps his cheeks.

Father Maxwell's head lolls to the side. His eyes flutter open. "I'm sorry," he chokes out. "I'm so, so sorry..."

Pax shakes him. "You've got some explaining to do."

But the priest is out cold.

Something he said earlier plays on the back of my mind. I need him to explain what he meant about the Soul-Eater being drawn to his magic. He doesn't get to nope out of this conversation after bringing this nightmare down on our heads.

I grab Father Maxwell by the collar and shake him roughly, but his head flops about awkwardly and he doesn't wake up. "Damn you to hell, Father!"

"Bree, if you'd like me to turn his eyeballs into rum truffles for you, I am happy to oblige," Pax says from behind me, his voice tinged with sadness. "But right now, I need *your* sword."

I turn. Pax stands over Björn. The warrior has fallen to the ground, his body too weak to even clutch at his leg, which is surrounded by a thick black mist. His face is screwed up in silent agony.

"I've been touched by the Soul-Eater," Björn gasps out. "This wound cannot be healed."

"That's not true," Pax cradles his friend's head in his lap. "Bree?"

I glance down at Björn, at the mangled, blackened mess that is his leg, and the thick mist spreading up his thigh. Black smoke pours from the wound where the fire-tongue wrapped around him.

"You can do it, Bree," Lottie urges me. "It's the same as all those plants you healed."

"Only with a lot more bones and arteries," Mary adds.

"And mind you don't get it wrong, he'll grow a third hand or a beanstalk there instead," Agnes adds.

"Yes, thank you *so much* for your help and encouragement." I place my hands over the wound, and I go to the place where the witches taught me once more. I clear my mind. I'm weak, exhausted, but I find myself back with my dad and that pot of red paint.

The cords appear – the pieces of Björn's life unfurling from him as the wound takes his life from him. I collect the severed ends of his silver strings and twist my fingers, knitting them back into his flesh.

As I do, the wound closes over, and the black smoke disappears. Björn rolls over and gets shakily to his feet. He and Pax embrace.

I sit back on my heels, breathing hard. I did it. Mary and Lottie do a little victory dance.

Björn gathers me into a bone-crushing hug.

"May Thor smile upon you for saving me, Bree," he says as he drops me and scoops up Father Maxwell in his enormous arms. "You are a strong warrior. Father Maxwell was right to trust you. But I fear your trials are only just beginning."

40

BREE

"What will you do now?" I ask Björn as he carries Father Maxwell across the village green.

"I must return the priest to All Souls. It is dangerous for him now outside of the wards. The Order will hear of this, and they will come after him with force, and there may be others, too, from beyond the Veil. When the priest is well again, he will tell you everything you need to know."

"Can't *you* tell me? That was Jack the Ripper laughing on the other side of that hole. Things are *somewhat* urgent."

"I do not understand the world of the dead," he replies simply as he hefts the priest's limp body over his shoulder. "I know only that Father Maxwell is sorry to bring all of this trouble down on your head."

I shrug, because as pissed as I am at the priest, I don't want Björn to feel worse. "Things were getting too quiet around Grimdale."

With a final fist-bump for Pax, Björn trudges off toward the train station.

The rest of us trudge back to the festival.

Everything is a mess. Stalls are overturned, flags and

banners burned and torn to shreds. As we wander around, surveying the damage, people crawl out of their hiding places, clutching wounds.

Pax picks up the giant yellow duck and the lion from where we dropped them and inspects every surface. "You are strong, little friends. You survived. You are worthy of coming home with us." He tucks the plushies under his arms.

I look for signs of the Soul Eater's poison – the black mist that attacked Björn. But I don't see any, except for the bodies of those killed in the Giant Vegetable tent.

I want to heal them all, but I don't dare. I can still feel the Soul-Eater licking my skin. True horror is closer than I could have imagined.

"Bree, is that you?" It's Maggie. She's clinging to Pax's neck as he carries her toward the green. She's bleeding from a head wound, but I don't see any black mist near her.

"Maggie, are you okay?"

"Nothing a little bandage and a kiss won't fix. Besides, it's long been my dream to be manhandled by such a fine specimen," she says as Pax carries her off to where the village doctor is performing triage. People lie on the green, moaning and talking softly as they tend to their injuries and discuss what ghastly being attacked the festival.

"I'm telling you, it was aliens," says Dani's mother. "They were attracted by our giant vegetables, which they require for their mating rituals. I think we just narrowly avoided being probed."

"It was some kind of freak weather pattern," says Frank, the village mechanic. "That's all it is. My granddaughter has been warning me that climate change will be the end of us. I just didn't know the climate was quite so...malevolent."

"Maybe it's a gas leak?" suggests Maggie. "I saw it on the

telly once – a town in America had a gas leak and everyone started hallucinating strange monsters—"

"No, I'm telling you that there's something dark and sinister going on in this village," Maggie's friend Debra shoots back. "I bet it's witches. Black magic. Why else would that nice Father Bryne have ran out without even saying goodbye…"

"Something strange is definitely going on in this village. Why, just the other day I found one of Ralph Sommersby's old golfing trophies floating in the duck pond…"

I don't know how we're going to explain this, or even whether anyone in the village saw Pax and Björn battling the Soul-Eater, and me and Father Maxwell and Ambrose banishing it with our vegetable demon mark. Can we pass this off as a gas leak?

But that's a problem for another day. Right now, I need to make sure…

"I see your parents," Edward says quietly. "They're over by the Giant Vegetable tent. They're unharmed. Your dad is helping Alice's father out from beneath a large avocado."

"Thank you." With Ambrose's arm resting firmly in my elbow, we head toward the Giant Vegetable tent, when someone tackles me from behind.

"Argh!" I whirl around, my fists raised, my heart leaping in my throat. But then I smell Dani's signature perfume, and she wraps her arms around me and squeezes the life out of me.

"Bree?" Dani's breathless voice croaks. "You're okay?"

"I'm okay."

"I was so worried," she whispers. "I saw Pax and that Viking guy attacking that *thing,* and you and a priest on the hill with all those cucumbers. And Ambrose, you were so *brave.*"

"Thank you." Ambrose takes a bow, although I notice that his legs are still trembling. "It is a pleasure to serve."

"So what was that, anyway?" Dani narrows her eyes. "And if you tell me it's a gas leak, I *will* kill you."

"It's..." the words dry on my tongue. "I'll explain, but away from everyone."

Dani's grip tightens on my arm and she drags me over to the duck pond.

"What is *that?*" Dani jabs a finger at the singed circle in the grass. "Apart from the village beautification committee's collective heart attack?"

I swallow. "That was caused by a Soul-Eater."

"Excuse me?"

It pours out of me, everything Father Maxwell said about demons being attracted to our magic, and how we opened that black hole and sent it back to hell, and how Ambrose and I almost fell in after it.

"I'm so scared, Dani. The revenant and the Order of the Noble Death are one thing, but how are we supposed to fight actual demons? I don't want this power anymore. I don't want the responsibility of—"

"Excuse me?" Alice's voice cuts in. "Did you say demon?"

41

BREE

Shit.

I whirl around, but I know exactly what I'm going to see.

Alice glares at me and Dani with a strange expression on her face, one that jolts me back to a memory of primary school.

The school playing field backed onto Grimdale Wood, and Dani and I were having a picnic and holding up our Tupperware containers of leftovers for the three witches to sniff, when Kelly, Leanne, and Alice stumbled upon us. Kelly and Leanne immediately started laughing and calling us names, but Alice just glared at us with the same expression she's wearing now, as if she was *disappointed* in us.

"Alice, it's not what it sounds like..." Dani reaches for her, but Alice jerks away.

"That's good. Because it sounds like you're implying that the fire that just broke out in the festival is a *demon,* which is of course ridiculous."

"What did you see?" I ask.

"What did I see? What did I *see?*" Alice snorts. Her voice goes all high and strange. "I saw a fire. A simple fire with black smoke that might have been put out quickly if *her* boyfriend and that insane guy dressed as a Viking hadn't fanned it by leaping around with swords, and now people are dead and the festival is ruined and..."

Alice wobbles on her feet, screwing her eyes shut. I feel a pang of something – another memory that belongs only to me. I remember cowering all on my own in Grimdale Cemetery, fervently wishing that I didn't have to see and hear these strange supernatural things. That's exactly what Alice is feeling now. She wants everything to go back to normal, but it won't. Because a demon attacked the village today, and some part of her knows it.

"I *think* that's what I saw," Alice sobs. "Because if I close my eyes, I remember that the fire had horns, and that it didn't move the way a fire would, and that it spoke in this terrible, rasping voice...but that's what I saw. A fire. Isn't it? *Isn't it?*"

Dani looks up at me, pleading. And I make a split-second decision. I'm tired of hiding. What's the point? I am who I am, and this problem is not going to go away because I keep it a secret. I nod to Dani.

"Come and sit down," Dani says softly. "Bree will explain."

Alice allows Dani to wrap her arms around her, pulling her down onto the nearest bench...which just so happens to be right where Mary is hovering, sniffing at a cream bun that someone left behind when they fled.

"Mmmmm," Mary purrs. "I like it when they add a little dollop of jam. It really elevates the flavours, don't you agree, Lottie? And this one is still warm from the ovennnnnnnnarrrgh! *Who sat on me?*"

Alice slumps on the bench, wrapping her arms around herself. "It's chilly," she mutters.

"Watch where you park that ass of yours, dear." Lottie waggles a finger at Alice.

"You should really educate your friends about proper ghost manners," Mary huffs, slinking down to the other end of the bench, as far from Alice as she can get while still being within sniffing distance of the cream bun. "Although…if she were to share those caramels she's hiding in her pocket with the rest of us, I might see my way to forgiving her."

"Mary would like you to open the bag of caramels in your pocket," I say.

"What?" Alice's head snaps up. "What are you talking about?"

"Mary is the ghost of a lady about our age who was hanged as a witch on the village green in 1523. You just sat on her, which is why you felt cold all of a sudden. When people walk through ghosts, it hurts them, so I try not to do it if I can help it. But Mary says she'll forgive you if you let her sniff your caramels." I wince as Alice's mouth drops open. "Ghosts can't taste things, but they can smell food. It's one of the few pleasures they have, and Mary especially likes food."

Alice shoots me a look like she's not sure whether to burst out laughing or have me committed. But she reaches into her pocket and opens up the white paper bag. The scent of salted caramel fills the air, and Lottie, Mary, and Agnes all bend in to have a sniff. I take the moldavite in my hand, and when Mary reaches into the bag, she pulls out a caramel.

Alice's eyes widen as the caramel moves through the air in front of her. "I…I can't believe this. It's just like…"

"…at Kelly's house?" I ask. "That was ghosts, too. They were getting revenge for me. I'm sorry if they scared you."

Pax, the cheeky bugger, leans in and nabs a handful of caramels from the bag. "They taste even better than they smell," he says to the witches as he pops one in his mouth.

"I curse you that both sides of your pillow should always be warm," Agnes snaps. "And that every time you experience a hangover, a small child next door will decide to practice the French horn!"

"Can I have one?" Ambrose asks. Pax hands him a caramel and he chews happily. "Oh my, they really are lovely."

"I curse you that the butter for your toast be forever cold and unspreadable, and the chocolate chips in your biscuits be always raisins!"

"That's harsh," Ambrose chews happily. "But also fair. May I have another caramel?"

"Who's he talking to? And did the air just get warmer?" Alice glances all around.

"That's the ghosts. They can alter the temperature. Sometimes they make things cold, sometimes warm. It depends on their mood."

Edward steps forward, taking up his poetic pose. "The living maiden, her eyes wide with awe. Listens to my verses from centuries raw. Invisible fingers pluck a spectral lyre. As this ghostly poet stokes her artistic fire."

"Who said that?" Alice whirls around. "Some nonsense about a lyre."

"That's Edward," I say. "He's my third boyfriend. He's a ghost."

"Your boyfriend is a—"

"Ghost. And Pax and Ambrose were, too. They were also at Kelly's house. Now they're ex-ghosts. It turns out that as well as having the power to see and talk to spirits, I can also resurrect them if conditions are ideal. But other things can come into the Living world, too. Namely, revenants and creatures that some call demons, like our friend the Soul-Eater who attacked the village today."

"A demon...came after you?"

"Technically no. It was after Father Maxwell. But let's not split hairs."

I sit down on the bench, making sure to move the cream bun to the end for the ghosts to sniff, and explain everything to Alice about being a Lazarus and seeing spirits and ghost rules. Well, almost everything. I leave out the bit about Father Bryne coming after me and killing him and hiding his body. I trust Alice...but not that much.

"You knew about this?" Alice shoots a look at Dani, who nods. "You might have told me we were hanging out with a real-life ghost whisperer."

"It's not my secret to tell. Besides, it's not as if Bree talking to ghosts is a secret. You've known about it since primary school."

"Yes, but I didn't think it was real. I just thought she was odd or faking it for attention, so that you'd stay her friend."

"I *am* odd." I grin. "And it's all real. Including the Soul-Eater. Which is a big problem. Because while we managed to send that particular one back to hell, more might be coming. I heard Jack the Ripper laughing. I think he's trying to get back."

"Jack the Ripper..." Alice's voice trails off. "And Vera's death? Was that supernatural, too?"

I nod sadly. "I've got a lot of work to do. I can't let this happen again. But we're going to need to figure out what to tell the village, because I won't do much good if I'm locked away in an insane asylum."

"I can help with that," Alice says. "I write articles some-times for the *Grimdale Gazette*. I can write a piece explaining that it was a weather phenomenon. Or a gas leak – people seem particularly fond of that one. The villagers believe everything they read in the paper, so that should at least stop everyone in the village from panicking that it's the second coming."

I nod. "That would help. Thank you. Thank you for everything."

"Just let me make sure my dad gets home okay, and then we

should brainstorm." Alice stands up. "Me and Dani and you, and all your ghosts and ex-ghosts and ghouls and other super-natural goolies, okay?"

"Okay." I place my hand in hers and give it a squeeze. "Pub?"

42

AMBROSE

The six of us (plus a lion and a duck) spend the afternoon jammed into a booth in the corner of the Cackling Goat. Bree shows Alice a bunch of images from Vera's books on her mobile phone and they identify the Soul-Eater in one. I nurse something called a Tequila Sunrise that *does* succeed in making me feel a little sunnier. Dani makes Bree swear that she won't use her powers any longer and Bree agrees, but I know that she's not being truthful.

Because Edward is still a ghost.

Because if Jack the Ripper is trying to come back, the Bree needs all of us at her side.

And I know we're close to figuring out his unfinished business.

I try to stir up my old excitement for Edward's resurrection, but I can't shake the feeling of unease that settles in my stomach.

It doesn't help that all around us, the villagers are in an uproar over the festival. Alice has already started spreading the word that it was a faulty gas main, but of course some people don't believe it. After all, gas leaks don't tend to tear people apart with horns or whisper demonic words on the breeze.

A few tables away from us, I can hear Bree's parents chatting to Maggie and a bunch of their friends. Thankfully, apart from the unfortunate judges in the Vegetable Tent, no one else was seriously hurt – except for Björn, and Bree fixed him up. The burn on my cheek has been bandaged by the village doctor, and it's already feeling a little better.

As for the rest of me...I touch my arm to my chest, to the spot where the Soul-Eater plunged itself inside me. I carry no mark nor wound from his attack, and yet, I do not feel quite myself. I'm all strange and stretchy, like my soul has been flattened into a pancake.

After a time, Bree, Dani, and Alice have nothing more to say about Soul-Eaters, and Bree's parents get up from their table. Bree stands too. "I'll go home now, I think. Thank you for listening," she says to Alice.

"Thank you for kicking that Soul-Eater's arse," Alice replies. A warm hand lands on my shoulder. "You too, Pax, And you, Ambrose."

"What about me?" Edward yells. "I would have helped, I swear, if I had a body."

"Fat chance," Bree says with a thin smile as she slides her hand beneath mine, and we follow her parents out of the pub. Pouty Edward floats ahead of us, and Pax brings up the rear. Bree says he looks a sight with a giant plushie under each arm. We don't say much on the walk home.

"Well, that was an eventful day," Mike says with a little smile in his voice as he holds the door open for us. "We should celebrate."

"What on earth are we celebrating?" Sylvie snaps as we pile into the lounge in the east wing. "The festival was ruined and people are dead and something *attacked* our town. It attacked our *daughter*."

"Don't be ridiculous, Sylv. You heard them at the pub, it was nothing but a gas leak causing a strange phenomenon. We're celebrating the fact that we're all alive and that, technically, I won the festival."

"Oh, Mike," Sylvie scolds. "As if anyone still cares about that after this senseless violence."

"That's precisely why we *should* care." Mike snaps his fingers. "I have just the thing."

He rummages in the liquor cabinet and returns with a bottle. "I brought this from that chateau we visited in the South of France, remember, honey?"

"That place was terrible, and the wine tasted like vinegar."

"Psssh, that's not what you said after you drank three glasses. Look, it's even got a little dust on it, as if it's an authentic old bottle, worthy of celebration." Dad fumbles around in the cabinet for glasses. "Ambrose, Pax, care for a tipple?"

Beside me, Bree's gone all stiff and silent. I nudge her. "Are you okay?"

"That's it," she whispers. "That's *it.*"

"What's it?"

"He was looking out the *window.*"

"Who? What window?"

"Ambrose, I've figured it out. I've figured out Edward's unfinished business." Bree stands up. "Sorry, Mum, Dad, I'd love to stay and celebrate with you but I have to...see a ghost about a thing."

I can't see what happens next, but Edward yelps. "What are you doing? Unhand me, woman. I won't be made to leave when French wine is being offered, even if it is inferior as smells like feet—"

"Go with her," I whisper. "You won't regret it."

I'm excited. I truly hope that she has figured it out.

"I'll be right back," Bree tells her parents. "I've just...er, got a text from another friend. He's arriving in the village soon. Can I bring him here to meet you?"

"Of course, dear," Mike says. "As long as he enjoys mediocre French wine and picking up my puzzle pieces for me."

"Okay, great. Dad, the pry bar is still hanging in the garden shed, right?"

"Yes. What do you need—"

"I'll be right back." Bree hurries Edward out of the room, leaving the two of us with Mike and Sylvie. I hear a cork pop, and Mike starts going on about the bouquet.

"She's acting very odd tonight," Sylvie says.

"She's always odd. That's our Bree. Did you want a glass, Pax? Ambrose?"

"Only if I can water it down, as a true Roman would," Pax declares.

"Sure, we can put some water in it for you. And here, for you, Ambrose. I hope you enjoy it."

I hold the glass in my hands and breathe deep. But just as I go to take a drink, something slams into me. A feeling of *wrongness.*

It reminds me of the feeling of the Soul-Eater's tongue of shadow in my throat, but it can't be. The beast is gone. The portal into the Veil is gone.

Yet it feels like he is right here in this room, his mist crawling about inside me.

I search around for some reason for this feeling. "Pax, can you see something odd about this room?"

"No," Pax says. "Unless you mean people drinking wine without watering it down...wait, yes, there is something outside the window. It is the night. It looks...*wrong.*"

"The night looks wrong?" I stand up. Pax loops his arm in mine and drags me over to the window.

"I see Bree and Edward walking toward the cemetery. There are many stars in the sky tonight," Pax says. "But not over the cemetery. It is as if a black cloud hovers there, but I see no cloud."

Pax falls silent. For a moment, I swear I can hear the faintest snatch of cruel laughter, but then it's gone.

A shiver rockets down my spine. "I don't like this. I feel... cold. But not a normal kind of cold."

"There's only cold. No different types."

"No, there are different types. When I was travelling across Russia during the winter, I experienced a kind of cold that lives in your bones. That's a different type of cold to getting into a bath after others have finished, and the water has cooled. And it's vastly different to what I'm feeling now, which is a kind of creeping, unsettling coldness and...that's *it*."

"What's it?"

"It feels like I'm touching the Soul Eater," I whisper. "Remember how Dani's research said that Jack the Ripper could come back where the Veil is weak? Well, I think that the Veil is weakening over Grimdale."

"Maybe the Soul-Eater weakened it."

"I believe so. Oh, this could be a bit of a pickle." I dust off the front of my frock coat. "Father Maxwell said that the Soul-Eater was attracted to his magic, and Bree says that she's figured out how to bring Edward back. What if using her resurrection magic allows evil to cross the Veil and come for her? We need to stop her. *Now.*"

43

BREE

"Are you carrying that pry bar because we're going to fuck up Kelly Kingston's horseless carriage?" Edward's lips curl back into a smirk. "Because your prince is amenable to that. But I must insist that you first allow me to whisper a poetical curse in her ear. I have one written for just such an occasion."

"We're not going to haunt Kelly."

"Then I must confess to being confused as to the nature of our outing."

We near the end of the path and step in front of his mausoleum. "Do you trust me?"

Edward's lip wobbles as he peers up at the leering cupids that guard the door to his eternal resting place. "I trust you with my afterlife."

"Then come with me." I hold out my hand.

After a few moments, he takes it. His ghostly fingers slip into mine.

In my other hand, I hold the ancient key to the mausoleum that I swiped from the ticket office.

We have keys to all the mausoleums in the cemetery. We go

361

in sometimes to check on things, make sure there's been no vandalism, and to do a bit of cleaning. But I've never been inside Edward's tomb. It felt wrong somehow to disturb his rest, even though Edward's afterlife hasn't exactly been restful.

Tonight, that changes.

We walk over the threshold together. I lift my mobile up and shine my torch around the dim interior. The walls are elaborately carved with dancing skeletons – memento mori revelling in their danse macabre. In the centre of the room is a long stone sarcophagus, the lid carved with a line by John Dunne.

'Go and catch a falling star.'

"I always loved that poem," Edward says with a sigh.

I move around the sarcophagus, peering into every shadowy corner, not certain what I'm looking for.

But then I see it.

"Brianna, what are we doing here?" Edward's voice rises. "I thought you'd solved my unfinished business, but we're not going to bring me back to life by hanging out in this sepulchre."

"Ambrose thinks you were murdered. He was certain because of what Ozzy said that someone pushed you out the window, and so he's had us running around the country, chasing up centuries old leads and talking to the ghosts of all your friends."

Edward pales. "You spoke to my friends?"

"Some of them. Most passed away peacefully, as the rich tend to do. But the Countess de Rothschild says hello."

"Just hello?" His mouth lifts into a smirk. "She usually has so many uses for that tongue of hers."

She says a lot more, but I'm not going to tell you that.

"Anyway, that's not the point. The point is that today, I figured something out. You weren't murdered. Ozzy was mistaken, as we all were. But you and Hugh *did* argue right before you died. You argued about the wine."

"That seems likely. Hugh was always trying to drink me under the table." Edward's smirk grows wider. "He never succeeded."

"What the countess overheard wasn't you and Hugh arguing about his letter. I don't even know if he sent that letter to you, because otherwise, surely you wouldn't have invited him to Grimwood? No, from the way it was all scrunched up and torn, I think Hugh wrote it and threw it away or hid it amongst his papers. I don't think he believed those things he said at all, but I think he was feeling jealous and insecure because you were his brilliant friend, the Poet Prince, and you had just written the greatest poem of you life, and he was feeling a little insecure.

Edward frowns. "But what he said on the night I died—"

"Hugh was telling you that you were out of wine. He said, 'that's the last of it,' as he heard a bottle smash downstairs. He was trying to tell you that the party was over, that you were all too trashed. But you said, 'I'll say when we're done.' You wanted to keep going. He said, 'I won't take it,' meaning that he won't deal with you in your current state. You had just told the countess that you wouldn't run away with her. I think you were in one of your moods, and Hugh was trying to calm you. I think that Hugh was trying to get you back to bed, and you were insisting that you were the greatest poet and drinking from the bottle you had with you, and when Hugh left you there, you got up to get some more wine for the party. You moved toward your secret wine cellar, which you saw out the window, completely forgetting that you were on the second-storey."

"I don't understand. Why would it matter if I were on the second-storey? I would simply stumble to the cellar. I'd be more likely to fall down the stairs than out the window."

"Look."

I point at my feet, to where the stones on the floor don't quite meet. Edward bends down and inspects the flagstones. "I still don't see what some loose stones in a tomb have to do with me. Surely this is a matter for the groundskeeper."

I take the pry bar and insert it between the stones. It takes a few goes since I don't exactly have a lot of time between wrangling ghosts to get to the gym. I manage to lift the stone enough that I can slide it across, revealing a hole in the floor just large enough for a small person to fit through. A steep stone staircase curves down into the gloom, the passage bedecked with spiderwebs.

I hold my hand out to Edward. "Come on, then."

"I won't be going down there." Edward shudders. "That's no place for a prince. There might be spiders."

"Toughen up." I grin as I hold up the crowbar. "Whatever monster lurks down there, we can take it."

But I swallow down my own fear as I take a step down. My boots kick up layers of dust. I glance back over my shoulder.

Edward takes a tentative step, then another. He screws up his face. "It smells strange." He screws up his nose. "Very sweet. You don't think it's poison, do you? My cousin died from breathing bad air."

"This room hasn't been opened in nearly five hundred years, and if it was a cellar, it's probably close to airtight. It's going to be a bit musty. But look, I'm okay." I grin at him. "Come on."

I continue carefully down the staircase until my feet land on a cobbled floor. The stone is worn smooth from use. Edward must have had reason to come down here a lot. There's a wooden door in front of me. It's locked, but the door has rotted that one swift hit with the pry bar and the whole lock falls out of the door. I push the door open and step into the room beyond, and beckon Edward to follow.

Edward lands beside me. "Are you satisfied, Brianna? I have debased myself by crawling into this rat hole beneath my tomb, and I don't see—"

"Can you see now?" I can't help the grin spreading across my face as I shine my phone's flashlight around the space.

The light's beam illuminates a series of stone niches, each one containing rows upon rows of glass bottles. The light catches and shimmers, creating rainbow prisms that dance along the curved roof of the building. The room stretches back toward Grimwood, a long tunnel that appears to have no end.

And every inch of it is stacked to the brim with wine.

"My secret wine cellar." Edward's eyes widen as he takes in the rows and rows of dusty bottles. "I can't believe you found it. I thought for certain I had drunk it dry, and that's why I couldn't remember it."

He moves through the rows, his eyes widening. I hold up the light so he can read the labels on the bottles.

"This is a Bordeaux I got for the countess because the colour of it perfectly matched her favourite dress," he says, and pulls out another. "And this...I had to hunt for ages for this. Hugh and I travelled to France and we rented this tiny castle in the south with a cellar full of this stuff. We wrote poetry and danced on the lawn and started a riot in the village. It was a hoot. I paid a king's ransom for this but I managed to track down the exact wine for Hugh's birthday."

"According to the countess, you delighted your friends by teasing them about the location of this cellar. Only Hugh knew your secret. That's why he was found drinking in the bathtub after you died. He went to the cellar and got wine to drown his sorrows. He truly *was* your friend. He may have stolen your poem, but he punished himself for the theft for the rest of his life. He *did* want to honour you. He thought you deserved to take this secret with you into death, like an Egyptian Pharaoh, so he built your mausoleum over the entrance."

"All this time..." Edward breathes. "I thought they didn't care for me. I thought they only used me for my wealth and notoriety."

"I can't speak for all of them, of course. But Hugh and the countess, their love for you was genuine. You're quite a remarkable person, Edward. I cannot imagine spending any time with you and not succumbing to your charm. I mean, just *look* at this place."

"What is this except for a useless prince's folly?" Edward says sourly.

"Why did you collect all these bottles and put them together down here?" I ask. "It wasn't because you particularly like wine. You chose these for your friends. You chose them because you wanted to share them with people. You know the true pleasure of life is to spend it with people who understand you, who challenge you, who light you up."

I pull out a bottle and study the label. It's handwritten in French, but the date is unmistakable: 1623.

"An excellent year," Edward nods sagely.

My heart stutters over a thought that hasn't crossed my mind before. I'd been so excited about what this room might mean that I hadn't even considered its contents. "Edward, these bottles must be worth a fortune now."

"They were worth a fortune, then," he says haughtily. "I may have been a rake and a wastrel, but you cannot accuse me of being cheap."

"No, you don't understand. There's expensive wine, and then there's wine that's five hundred years old. This...this is *millions of dollars* right here in this room." I roll my eyes at him.

"Trust you to be a rich bastard in the afterlife, too. You could do all kinds of things with this money."

But when I look over at him, Edward isn't listening. Which is odd, because Edward is always interested in wine. Instead, he's frowning at his chest.

"Brianna. I feel...strange."

"Not strange," I say as I grip his cord in my hands, pulling him closer. "You feel *alive.*"

The cord shimmers in my fingers, growing warm against my skin as a bright white light surrounds both of us. I'm familiar enough with the sensation now from bringing back Ambrose and Pax that I don't shy away from it, but I hold my grip and wind that cord between my hands.

"Brianna..." Edward's voice croaks.

I lean in.

I kiss him.

He tastes like wine. Wine and debauchery.

He tastes *solid*, his tongue firm and determined as he seeks the warmth of my mouth. His hand wraps around the back of my neck, tangling in my hair as he tugs me closer, giving his whole body and his broken, princely heart over to the kiss.

It's the first time Edward has properly kissed someone since he's last been alive, but golly, he's still *damn* good at it. He's so good that I forget to breathe, and end up gasping against him, clinging to him as his lips and tongue heat my body in this cold, damp, airless cellar.

Eventually, Edward pulls back, his dark eyes shimmering. "You brought me back."

I grin. "It figures that your unfinished business would be locating your secret wine cellar. What's the first thing you want to do now that you're a Living human again?"

Edward grabs a bottle from the stack. "I want to celebrate."

"You can't open that. It's probably worth thousands of

pounds. You could buy a thousand bottles of Dom Perignon if we want to celebrate."

"Look around, my Brianna." Edward gestures to the vast tunnel. "We have enough wine here for a lifetime. For *two* lifetimes. Actually, maybe only one. I do *quite* enjoy wine. Although not as much as I enjoy you."

He leans forward and captures my lips in his. And I forget about the dusty tunnel and the stale air. All that matters is him.

Edward breaks the kiss to peel off the wax seal on the bottle. He does this expertly, as if it was only yesterday when he last opened a bottle of fancy old plonk. I guess some things are muscle memory. I'm amazed that the cork slides out easily. Edward holds the bottle up to his nose and sniffs.

"It smells like you, Brianna. It smells of pear, and almonds, and sweet, beautiful *life*. And look at this colour – it reminds me of your hair. It's as if, when I chose this bottle, I knew I was waiting for you."

He holds the bottle out to me.

"Ladies first."

I take the proffered bottle and sniff. It doesn't smell poisonous. It smells...like wine. Kind of sweet, expensive wine. Almost more like plum or...yes, *pears. Do I really smell like this?*

I take a tentative sip.

Oh.

Oh.

Wow.

"I could get used to this." I hand him back the bottle. "You're going to ruin me for eight quid plonk."

"Bah, it should be illegal for that donkey piss you and Dani used to drink in the cemetery to be called wine. Why, I imagine even Roman wines have something more to offer." Edward sighs with happiness as he takes a swig. "This is the dream. I am alive, and I have expensive wine and a beautiful woman."

"Should we be necking it from the bottle like this?" I ask, still nervous about consuming something so old and expensive. "Doesn't that ruin the flavour? Isn't it supposed to breathe in the glass or something?"

"Now that you mention it," Edward's eyes glitter. "I do believe there is a better way to taste this vintage."

He tosses his head back and takes a swig. Before I know what's happened, he grabs me, yanking me against his body with one solid, protective arm. His other hand grips behind my neck, tilting my head back.

As he kisses me, he passes the wine between, the liquid cooling my tongue. It tastes like nothing else I've ever tasted before. Like summer and pears, with this sweet, nutty nose. It's astounding, but not as astounding as Edward's kisses, or the way he feels now that he is a living, breathing *man*.

My hands roam over his body, taking in the hard planes of his chest, the narrowness of his waist, and the curve of...

"Ow," Edward winces.

...the glass shard sticking out of his ass.

Edward leans around and pulls it free. His face collapses with relief. "To think that's the last time I'll ever have to pull it out. Now, come here."

"You're bleeding. Doesn't that hurt?"

"With a beautiful woman in my arms?" Edward sweeps me into his arms. "No, I barely feel it at all."

Edward's fingers tug at the fabric of my t-shirt. I shrug out of it, moaning with pleasure as he lays kisses over my collarbone, as his hands greedily palm my breasts. His eyes darken as he returns to plunge his tongue between my lips. "I have dreamed of this day for far too long. When I touched you, I saw all kinds of things. Your memories. Your dreams. I saw the things you longed for me to do to you. And now I can enjoy you, and I fully intend to do just that."

He backs me up until my feet hit the edge of a narrow stone bench. Edward's eyes darken even more, becoming as black as the starless sky above the graveyard. His hands press on my shoulders, forcing me down onto the bench, laying me before him. He gazes down at me as if I am a painting at the Royal Gallery that he is studying, as if I am something somehow remote, somehow far from him.

"I'm here," I say, to bring him back to me. "I'm yours."

His lips curl into that heart-melting smile. "I know. And finally, I get to taste you."

In one swift motion, he is rid of my jeans and panties. His hands push my legs wide and he buries his face between my legs.

My back arches and my fingers curl as Edward tastes me like he is sampling some fine wine. How is he doing that with his tongue? I mean, this is some lost knowledge, right here. Indiana Jones should be hunting this shit out because modern men can't lick pussy like this and omggggg...

The orgasm slams into me, hard and fast and unexpected, leaving me a quivering mess. While I'm still a bundle of jelly, Edward yanks my legs closer, unbuttons his pantaloons, and positions himself between my legs.

He sheaths himself inside me in one stroke.

I gasp, gripping the edge of the bench as I take him, all of him. And there is a *lot* of him to take. Edward's not quite as big as Pax, but he didn't have a reputation written about in the history books for nothing.

And the way he looks down at me now, his sharp, too-pretty cheekbones illuminated by the faint beam of my discarded mobile, he is every bit the wicked prince.

I'm so wet that despite his size, he slides in easily. And damn, does it feel good. He hits every spot, every part of me that's been calling to him across the Veil.

My heart stutters. He's here, inside me. *Finally.*

Our bodies move together as if we were made for this moment. He leans over me, bracing himself against the bench as he bends to kiss me, consuming my thoughts with that wicked tongue of his until all that exists is him, only him.

His hips thrust wildly as he drives deeper, demanding everything that I can give. He fucks like a wild animal, but his kisses...those are the kisses of a man consumed by love, and they are for me...

Edward cradles me in his arms and picks me up off the bench. He strides across the cellar, his cock still nestled inside me, and presses my back against the wall. Bottles jangle in the niches on either side of me, but I don't care. I am drunk already on his kisses and his caresses.

"My Brianna," he whispers as he pushes inside me.

I lock my ankles together behind his back, pulling him deeper. My hands roam over the corded muscles on his back, as if I must map every inch of him with my fingers to make certain that he's real. With one hand, Edward cups my breast, stroking it lovingly before pinching the nipple hard enough to make me moan.

"I know exactly what you like, my Brianna," he whispers. "For we were made for this. For fucking. For pleasure. For beauty. For love."

His hips buck against mine. My prince's beautiful face twists into an expression of utter rapture. His eyes fix on mine, and those black orbs never waver from me as we fall apart together.

Fuck.

That was...

SCRAAAPE.

"What was that?" Edward asks sleepily, pulling his face from where it rested on my shoulder.

I drop my feet to the ground and stand up on shaky legs, one ear listening for the sound. There it is again, a harsh scraping sound from somewhere above our heads.

Is it rats? I didn't even contemplate that there might be rats down here.

"Spiders?" Edward asks in a small voice.

I shudder and pull my shirt over my head, hating the idea of a rodent scampering over my naked skin. I pick up my mobile and swing the beam around the room, searching for rodents.

SCRAAAPE.

My blood runs cold.

SCRAAAPE.

No, it's not rats or spiders.

"It's someone moving the flagstones back into place!" I cry.

Edward and I bolt for the stairs at the same time. We crash into each other in the narrow tunnel entrance, our limbs tangling together. In the moments it takes us to untangle ourselves, another muffled scraping noise can be heard, this one much louder and heavier.

I reach the top of the staircase first. Sure enough, it's been closed up. I lay my back against the stone and push with all my might, but it won't budge. Above us, the heavy scraping noise has stopped. "I think he's moved your sarcophagus on top of the entrance."

Edward slumps against the wall. "It's that poxy Roman playing a prank on us. It has to be. When I get out of here, I'm going to feed *him* to a lion."

In the pale beam of my mobile phone flashlight, I can see how huge his eyes are. He doesn't believe this is Pax.

Especially not when I train the light on the stone, and notice a tendril of red smoke curling from between the seams.

Red smoke.

The Ripper.

As if on cue, the narrow passage erupts with the familiar, chilling notes of Jack the Ripper's laughter.

Why is it so loud? It shouldn't be this loud when we're hearing it through the stones.

We swap places. Edward makes a face as he braces his shoulders against the stone. He grunts and struggles and swears, but he can't make the stone move, either.

As I watch him, I become aware of the musty taste in the back of my throat, and the exquisite preservation of all the bottles down here.

"Edward? When you had this cellar constructed, did you by chance include a handy window or ventilation shaft or secret tunnel leading to the house?"

"Of course not," he replies. "Wine will remain in much better condition if the room is sealed tight. I would have instructed my men to make this room as airtight as...oh."

Yes, *oh.*

"There's no air down here," I say. "And no one knows where we are. If we don't get some help soon, we're going to suffocate."

TO BE CONTINUED

Will Bree and Edward escape in time? What will escape through the Veil next? Will Ambrose ever get an ice cream? Find out in the final Grimdale book, *Not A Mourning Person.*

http://books2read.com/grimdale4

What do you get when you cross a cursed bookshop, three hot fictional men, and a punk rock heroine nursing a broken heart? Read book one of the Nevermore Bookshop Mysteries — A Dead and Stormy Night — to get the story of Mina and her book boyfriends.
http://books2read.com/adeadandstormynight

(Turn the page for a sizzling excerpt).

Can't get enough of Bree and her boys? Read a free bonus scene from before Bree left on her travels, as well as her playlist, along with other bonus scenes and extra stories when you sign up for the Steffanie Holmes newsletter.

http://www.steffanieholmes.com/newsletter

There are some books that absolutely fly from your fingers, as if the story itself is already written inside your heart, and you just have to get it out before it spontaneously combusts.

Ghoul As A Cucumber was not one of those books.

It may not seem like it, given all the cucumber jokes, but this one I had to wrench from some dark places. I had to confront some shit, in the same way that Bree has to confront her demons (both literal and metaphorical). And I had to do it all on deadline. But here we are! I hope you enjoy the third story as much as I have (mostly) enjoyed writing it.

Our three ghosts are all fictional – they don't exist historically, although the details about their costumes and memories are as real as I can make them.

Pax's name means 'peace' in Latin. It's not a traditional Roman name, but I thought it was too fun not to use. He uses the word 'verpa', which is a vulgar Latin word for penis. And his insult – vappa! – means scum! (It refers to wine that's gone sour). His views on Druids are his own.

Ambrose is based on one of my own personal heroes – the Victorian adventurer, James Holman. Holman became mysteriously blind in his early 20s, and when this curtailed his naval career he first put himself through medical school and then set off on a series of adventures across the world. He was known as the 'Blind Traveller'.

Using a cane to rap on the ground, Holman was able to learn about the spaces around him through echolocation. He would walk holding a rope, which was then tethered to a carriage, so that he remained on the road. He wrote books about his travels using the frame with strings that Ambrose describes.

Holman's books were at first well-received, but he then became a bit of a novelty and wasn't taken seriously as an adventurer. People even said that he couldn't really be blind. He rode elephants in Ceylon, fought the slave trade in Fernando Po Island, helped chart the Australian outback, and was captured in Siberia by the Tsar's men on suspicion of being a spy. He was not killed, though, but ejected to the frontier of Poland.

His final manuscript – an autobiography encompassing all his travels – was never published and likely did not survive. He died in obscurity and is buried in London's Highgate Cemetery – the very place for which Grimdale Cemetery is based. Jason Roberts wrote a wonderful biography of Holman called *A Sense of the World* and I highly recommend it.

You might not know this, but I'm legally blind. Unlike Ambrose, Mina, and Holman, my eyesight didn't disappear one day or fade over time. I was born with the genetic condition *achromatopsia*, which means my eyes lack the millions of cone cells required to recognise colours and perceive depth. I'm completely colour blind, light sensitive with poor depth percep-tion, I squint and blink all the time, and struggle to make eye contact. I'm so short-sighted I'm considered legally blind.

I love being able to write stories where people like me get to have adventures, save the world, and discover that they can be sexy and have their happily ever after.

There are so many people who've supported me and believed in me, even when I struggled to believe in myself. My family – my Mum and Dad and sister Belinda.

A special shoutout to my writer fam – Angel Lawson, Bea Paige, Daniela Romero, Eden O'Neill, Rachel Jonas, AK Rose, and EM Moore. You have been one of the greatest joys in my life over the last two years.

To my found family, the bogans – my brothers and sisters of metal. I apologise for the volume of our shenanigans that end up in my books.

Always, to my cantankerous drummer husband, who is everything. Every hero I write is a piece of you and what you mean to me.

And lastly, to you, my readers, for going on this journey with me. I love you more than words can say.

A portion of the royalties from the sale of this book are donated to Parkinson's New Zealand. Thank you for the work you do!

Every week I send out a newsletter to fans – it features a spooky story about a real-life haunting or strange criminal case that has inspired one of my books, as well as news about upcoming releases and a free book of bonus scenes called *Cabinet of Curiosities*. To get on the mailing list all you gotta do is head to my website: http://www.steffanieholmes.com/newsletter

I'm so happy you enjoyed this story! I'd love it if you wanted to leave a review on Amazon or Goodreads. It will help other readers to find their next read.

Thank you, thank you! I love you heaps! Until next time, may the absinthe flow freely and may all your most scandalous dreams come true!

Steff

EXCERPT
A DEAD AND STORMY NIGHT

Uncover the secrets of Nevermore Bookshop in book 1, *A Dead and Stormy Night*

http://books2read.com/adeadandstormynight

Wanted: Assistant/shelf stacker/general dogsbody to work in secondhand bookshop. Must be fluent in classical literature, detest electronic books and all who indulge them, and have experience answering inane customer questions for eight hours straight. Cannot be allergic to dust or cats – if I had to choose between you and the cat, you will lose. Hard work, terrible pay. Apply within at Nevermore Bookshop.

Yikes. I closed the Argleton community app and shoved my phone into my pocket. *The person who wrote that ad really doesn't want to hire an assistant.*

Unfortunately, he or she hadn't counted on me, Wilhelmina Wilde, recently-failed fashion designer, owner of two wonky eyes, and pathetic excuse for a human. I was landing this assistant job, whether Grumpy-Cat-Obsessed-Underpaying-Ad-Writer wanted me or not.

I had no options left.

I peered up at the towering Victorian brick facade of Nevermore Bookshop – number 221 Butcher Street, Argleton, in Barsetshire – with a mixture of nostalgia and dread. I'd spent most of my childhood in a darkened corner of this shop, and now if I played my cards right I'd get to see it from the other side of the counter. It was the one shining beacon in my dark world of shite.

I don't remember it looking so... foreboding.

Apart from the faded *Nevermore Bookshop* written in gothic type over the entrance, the facade bore no clue that I stood in front of one of the largest secondhand bookshops in England. A ramshackle Georgian house facade with Victorian additions rose four stories from the street, looking more like a creepy orphanage from a gothic novel than a repository of fine literature. Trees bent their bare branches across the darkened windows and wisteria crept over grimy brickwork, shrouding the building in a thick skin of foliage. Cobwebs entwined in the lattice and draped over the windowsills. There didn't appear to be a single light on inside.

Weeds choked the two flower pots flanking the door, which had once been glazed a bright blue but were since stained in brown and white streaks from overzealous birds. A pigeon cooed ominously from the gutter above the door, threatening me with an unwelcome deposit. Twin dormer windows in the attic glared over the narrow cobbled street like evil eyes, and a narrow balcony of black wrought iron on the second story the teeth. A hexagonal turret jutted from the south-western corner, where it might once have caught sun before Butcher Street had built up around it.

When I used to hang out as a kid, the first two floors were

given over to the shop – a rabbit warren of narrow corridors and pokey rooms, every wall and table covered in books. The previous owner – a kindly blind old man named Mr. Simson – lived on the remaining two floors, but for all I knew, the new owner used that space as an opium den or a meat smoker.

At least the flaccid British sun peeked through the grey clouds, which meant I could make out these finer details of the facade. The buildings on either side of it were cloaked in the creeping black shadow that now followed me everywhere. I squinted at the chalkboard sign on the street, hoping for some clue as to the new owner's personality, but all it had on it were some wonky lines that looked like chickens' feet.

This place is even more drab than I remember. It could use a little TLC.

That makes two of us. I squinted at my reflection in the darkened shop window, but I could barely make out the basic shape of my body. At least I knew I looked fierce when I left the house, in my Vivienne Westwood pleated skirt (scored on eBay for twenty-five quid), vintage ruffled shirt, men's cravat from a weird goth shop at Camden market, and my old school blazer with an enamel pin on the collar that read, 'Jane Austen is my Homegirl.' Combined with my favorite Docs and a pair of thick-framed glasses, I'd nailed the 'boss-bitch librarian' look.

That is, if you ignored the fact that I pushed my nose up against the glass to see my reflection, and twisted my head in order to see all the details of my outfit because of the creeping darkness in the corners of my eyes.

Please, Isis and Astarte and any other goddess listening, let me get this job. I can't deal with any more rejection.

I smoothed my hair, sucked in a breath, pushed open the creaking shop door, and stepped back in time.

As the shop bell tinkled and the smell of musty paper filled my nostrils, I became nine years old again – the weird outcast kid whose mother was banned from school events after swindling the chair of the PTA with a Forex trading mastermind program that was really just a CD-rom of my mother comparing currency trading to doing the laundry. (It was his own fault for getting swindled. Who even uses CDs anymore?)

As soon as the school bell rang I'd sprint into town, duck through this same door and escape into another world. I'd curl up in the cracking leather armchair in the World History room with a huge stack of books and read until my mother finished her shift and came to collect me. Books became my friends – characters like Jane Eyre and Dorian Grey the perfect substitutes for the kids who were horrible to me. When I was older and the guys at school sneered at me and fawned over my best friend, I fell into books again – this time to fall in love with the bad boys, the intelligent boys, the boys filled with anger and lust and pain. Dark horses and anti heroes like Heathcliff and Sherlock Holmes, and melancholy authors like Edgar Allan Poe spoke directly to my soul.

Mr. Simson barely said a word to me, but he never seemed to mind the fact that I read every book in the shop but couldn't afford to buy any. Sometimes he'd even let me riffle through the boxes of rejects before he sent them away for recycling. People would come into the store and try to sell Mr. Simson stacks of airport books – James Patterson and John Grisham paperbacks that no one buys secondhand. When he refused their generous bounty, they'd creep back at night and shove the volumes one by one through the mail slot, so Mr. Simson always had stacks of them lying around. I would smuggle the books home to our housing estate – If Mum caught me reading she'd lecture about how men didn't like smart girls and we'd have a big row – and read them under the covers at night or hidden in my textbooks during class.

It was in Nevermore Bookshop where I first discovered punk

music. I found a box of battered 1970 zines in the Popular Music section, and I lost myself in faded photographs of bored teenagers with bleached mohawks. None of them fit in, and they didn't give a shit. I was in love.

The memories flooded back as I stepped into the gloomy interior. My boot landed on a thick carpet in the wide entrance hall, flanked on either side by tall shelves crammed with books. A small line of taxidermy rodents peered down at me from tiny wooden shields nailed along the moldings. *I don't remember those.* The new owner sure had strange taste in interior decor. But then, he had written that acerbic job ad...

I ran my fingers along the spines of the books, moving carefully to avoid tripping over the stacks of paperbacks littering the floor. Must and mothballs and leather and old paper caressed my nostrils. The air practically *sweated* books.

"Hello?" I called, coughing as dust tickled the back of my throat. *Was the bookshop always this dusty?*

Hello, beautiful. A voice croaked from behind me. I whirled around, a retort poised on my lips. But no one was in the doorway. I twisted my head to peer into the corners of the room, but I couldn't penetrate the shadows.

Where did that voice come from?

"Hello?" I called out. *The first thing I'm going to do if I get the job is brighten this place up a bit.*

Something rustled in the dark corner above the door. I glanced up. My eyes resolved the shape of an enormous black bird perched on the top of the bookshelf. At first I assumed it was stuffed, but it unfurled a long wing and flapped it in my face.

"Argh!" I flung my arm up, slamming my elbow into a stack of books, which toppled to the ground. The raven croaked with satisfaction and folded its wing away.

What in Astarte's name is a raven doing in here? It'll poop over the books. I wonder if it's roosting in the roof somewhere? We'll have to find that if we want to chase it out...

"Croak," said the raven with an accusatory tone, as though it had heard my thoughts.

"I guess you kind of suit the place." I glared at the bird as I bent down and fumbled for the books. "A raven in Nevermore Bookshop. Once upon a midnight dreary—"

"*Croak.*" The raven's yellow eyes glowed. Something in that croak sounded like a warning.

"Fine. Fine. I didn't come here to quote poetry to a bird." I stood up and rubbed my throbbing elbow. "I want to talk to the boss. Do you know where I might find him?"

As if it understood the question, the raven dropped off the shelf, swooped past me, and flew around the corner, disappearing through an archway on the left. I followed it into what would have once been a drawing room and was now a jumble of mismatched shelves and junkstore furniture. In the middle of the room were two heavy oak tables – one holding a large globe, the other a taxidermy armadillo. Books stacked so high it looked as though the armadillo was building itself a border wall. Old cinema chairs and beanbags under the window formed a reading area, and the large lawyer's desk that had served as Mr. Simson's counter still took pride of place beside the grand fireplace, although the brass plaque on the front now read "Mr. Earnshaw."

The raven swooped around me and perched on the desk lamp, its talons clicking against the metal. It took me a few moments to register the man hunched over the desk – the dark, wavy hair that spilled over his shoulders obscured his face, and his black clothes faded into the wood behind him.

"We're closed." A gruff voice boomed from inside the hair.

"Your sign still says open."

"Well, flip it over for me on the way out," the voice managed to sound both exasperated and uninterested.

"Um, sure. Mr. Earnshaw, was it?" I waved. He didn't even look up from his paper. "I saw the job ad you posted on the Argleton app, and I wanted to—"

"App?" The head snapped up. Eyes of black fire regarded me with suspicion from beneath a pair of thick eyebrows, deep set in a dark-skinned face of such remarkable beauty I sucked in a breath.

The new proprietor was younger than I expected him to be – Mr. Simson had been an old man even when I was a girl – and far too handsome to be working in a bookshop. His exotic features and sharp cheekbones belonged on the cover of a fashion magazine. The defiant tilt of his chin and twitch of his haughty lips concealed a storm raging inside him.

Danger rolled off him in waves. Danger... and desire.

Thick muscles bulged at the seams of his shirt. He'd rolled the sleeves up to his elbows, one thick forearm graced with the tattoo of a barren, gnarled tree and some words in cursive script below.

Even though he was an Adonis, this Mr. Earnshaw also looked like a complete wanker. He scrunched up that perfectly-sculpted nose, his lips curling back into a sneer. "What the devil is an app?"

What kind of weird question is that? "Um... you know, an application for your phone, so you can get the bus timetable or talk to your mates or—"

"Don't talk to me about *phones*," Earnshaw snapped. "People spend too much time on their phones."

Right. I'd forgotten the part in the job ad about hating ebooks. *This guy must be one of those weirdos who eschews technology.* "Oh, I agree. I mean, phones should only be used for calling people. And checking social media. That's it. I would never read on mine," I blubbered, shoving my phone behind my back. "I mean, studies have shown it can cause long-term eye damage and—"

"No matter how long you keep talking, it's not going to change the fact that we're closed. What do you *want?*"

"I'm applying for the assistant's job." I fumbled in my purse for the envelope I'd carefully sealed, trying to avoid accidentally showing him the ereader tucked behind my makeup case. "I've got my resume in here for you with all my qualifications and—"

"I don't need that. If you want the job, tell me why I should hire you."

"Right, well…" This was the weirdest interview I've ever been to. Earnshaw's eyes stabbed right through me, turning my insides to mush. I opened my mouth, but then he blinked, long black lashes tangling together over those eyes – they were like black holes, gobbling whole universes for lunch. A shiver started at the base of my neck and rocketed down my spine, not stopping until it caressed me between my legs.

Now I wanted the job more than ever, just so I could stare at this specimen all day. Bloody hell, I always did have a thing for surly bad boys. I blamed Emily Brontë. The brutish and untamable Heathcliff ruined me for nice guys.

"If your answer is to gape at me like a bespawling lubber-wort," he growled, "then you can take the job and shove it where the sun don't shine—"

"That's *not* my answer." My cheeks flared with heat. *Who even is this guy? Adonis or not, how'd he get off talking to customers and potential employees like that? No wonder the place is deserted.* "I was just collecting my thoughts. You should hire me because I'm a hard worker. I'm punctual. I have some retail experience, as well as design expertise so I can do graphics and window displays—"

"I don't care. Why do you want to work *here?* No one wants to work here. That was the whole *point* of the ad."

I racked my brain for an answer to that question. *What does he want from me?* "Um... I guess because I used to hang out in the bookshop all the time as a kid. I know where all the books go and I've personally helped Mr. Simson fix that till on at least two occasions." I pointed to the ancient contraption the raven was pecking.

Earnshaw glared at me, his eyes flicking over my face as though searching for something. He didn't say a thing. The silence stretched between us until even the raven got bored of hunting for worms in the credit card machine and stared at me, too.

Is he waiting for more?

"And... um, I have all sorts of useful skills." I scrambled for anything that might endear me to this strong-chinned man. "I have a fashion degree, so that's probably not useful. But I am a Millennial, so I can do the store's social media. I could build a website—"

You can see it, can't you? That strange voice said. *It's obvious. She's the one he told you about.*

Earnshaw grunted. I narrowed my eyes at him. *Does he hear it, too?*

Just hire her already, that voice said again. *She's pretty.*

"Hey!" I glanced over my shoulder, looking for the owner of the voice so I could kick them in the nuts. But there was no one else in the room.

Was it Earnshaw? But the voice didn't sound like him, and judging by the way he was still staring at me, he already thought I was nuts. *Maybe he didn't hear the voice after all?*

Besides, the voice sounded like it came from *inside* my head.

Please, don't tell me that on top of everything else, I'm now hallucinating voices—

I like her, the voice interrupted. *I bet she'll bring me treats. Berries, smoked salmon, maybe even a hard-boiled egg.*

I peered over my shoulder again. *Are they hiding in the hallway? Behind the beanbag stack?* "Who's there?"

Earnshaw's head whipped up. "Who are you talking to?"

"You didn't hear that? Someone prattling on about salmon and eggs."

Earnshaw's eyes narrowed. He reached out and clamped an enormous hand around the raven's beak. "You didn't leave the door open, did you? We're supposed to be *closed.*"

"No. I..." My shoulders sagged. *Who am I kidding? This is hopeless.* "I guess I'll just be going now. Thank you for your time and—"

"You start tomorrow," Earnshaw glowered. "We open at nine. Be here at eight-thirty, but don't let anyone else in. If you're late, the bird gets your paycheck. Welcome to Nevermore Bookshop."

TO BE CONTINUED

Uncover the secrets of Nevermore Bookshop in book 1, *A Dead and Stormy Night*

http://books2read.com/adeadandstormynight

BOOK BOYFRIENDS MAY DO IT BETTER...
...BUT THEY'RE MORE TROUBLE THAN THEY'RE WORTH.

After being fired from my dream fashion job, I return home to my village under a cloud of failure and take a job at the quaint Nevermore Bookshop. I'm hoping for an easy few months while I get my life together.

But this is no ordinary bookshop.

A mysterious curse on Nevermore brings infamous fictional villains from classic literature to life in the real world.

My "easy" job involves rescuing customers from a 6foot4, grumpy, tattooed Heathcliff, drinking tea and evading the authorities with suave villain Moriarty, and making art with Edgar Allen Poe's shy, cheeky, raven shifter, Quoth.

As if that isn't crazy enough, my ex-best friend shows up dead with a knife in her back, and I'm the chief suspect.

I'm going to have to Agatha Christie this shiz if I want to clear my name.

OTHER BOOKS BY STEFFANIE HOLMES

Nevermore Bookshop Mysteries

A Dead and Stormy Night

Of Mice and Murder

Pride and Premeditation

How Heathcliff Stole Christmas

Memoirs of a Garroter

Prose and Cons

A Novel Way to Die

Much Ado About Murder

Crime and Publishing

Plot and Bothered

Grimdale Graveyard Mysteries

What do you do when three hot AF, possessive ghosts want to jump your bones? Find out in this spooky, kooky paranormal romance series set in the same world as Nevermore Bookshop.

You're So Dead To Me

If You've Got It, Haunt It

Ghoul as a Cucumber

Not a Mourning Person

Kings of Miskatonic Prep

Shunned

Initiated

Possessed

Ignited

Stonehurst Prep

My Stolen Life

My Secret Heart

My Broken Crown

My Savage Kingdom

Stonehurst Prep Elite

Poison Ivy

Poison Flower

Poison Kiss

DARK ACADEMIA

Pretty Girls Make Graves

Brutal Boys Cry Blood

Manderley Academy

Ghosted

Haunted

Spirited

Briarwood Witches

Earth and Embers

Fire and Fable

Water and Woe

Wind and Whispers

Spirit and Sorrow

Crookshollow Gothic Romance

Art of Cunning (Alex & Ryan)

Art of the Hunt (Alex & Ryan)

Art of Temptation (Alex & Ryan)

The Man in Black (Elinor & Eric)

Watcher (Belinda & Cole)

Reaper (Belinda & Cole)

Wolves of Crookshollow

Digging the Wolf (Anna & Luke)

Writing the Wolf (Rosa & Caleb)

Inking the Wolf (Bianca & Robbie)

Wedding the Wolf (Willow & Irvine)

Want to be informed when the next Steffanie Holmes paranormal romance story goes live? Sign up for the newsletter at www.steffanieholmes.com/ newsletter to get the scoop, and score a free collection of bonus scenes and stories to enjoy!

About the Author

Steffanie Holmes is the *USA Today* bestselling author of the paranormal, gothic, dark, and fantastical. Her books feature clever, witty heroines, secret societies, creepy old mansions and alpha males who *always* get what they want.

Legally-blind since birth, Steffanie received the 2017 Attitude Award for Artistic Achievement. She was also a finalist for a 2018 Women of Influence award.

Steff is the creator of *Rage Against the Manuscript* — a resource of free content, books, and courses to help writers tell their story, find their readers, and build a badass writing career.

Steffanie lives in New Zealand with her husband, a horde of cantankerous cats, and their medieval sword collection.

STEFFANIE HOLMES NEWSLETTER

Grab a free copy of *Cabinet of Curiosities* — a Steffanie Holmes compendium of short stories and bonus scenes — when you sign up for updates with the Steffanie Holmes newsletter.

http://www.steffanieholmes.com/newsletter

Come hang with Steffanie
www.steffanieholmes.com
hello@steffanieholmes.com